William Schwenck Gilbert

Foggerty's Fairy

And other Tales

William Schwenck Gilbert

Foggerty's Fairy
And other Tales

ISBN/EAN: 9783337082024

Printed in Europe, USA, Canada, Australia, Japan

Cover: Foto ©Andreas Hilbeck / pixelio.de

More available books at **www.hansebooks.com**

AND OTHER TALES

BY

W. S. GILBERT

LONDON

GEORGE ROUTLEDGE AND SONS

BROADWAY, LUDGATE HILL

GLASGOW MANCHESTER, AND NEW YORK

1890

LONDON :
BRADBURY, AGNEW, & CO., PRINTERS, WHITEFRIARS.

NOTE.

———◆———

THIS Book contains several Tales upon which the Author subsequently founded plays, which achieved more or less success. "Foggerty's Fairy" is the groundwork of a play of that name, which was produced six years since at the Criterion Theatre. "An Elixir of Love" is the basis of "The Sorcerer." "Creatures of Impulse," "The Wicked World," and "Comedy and Tragedy," in their original forms, will also be found in this book. None of the Tales, except "Comedy and Tragedy," were written with a view to subsequent dramatization.

W. S. GILBERT.

CONTENTS.

Contents.

FOGGERTY'S FAIRY.

CHAPTER I.

"On, dash it all!" said Freddy Foggerty, "he knows me, and I shall be tried for desertion!"

Freddy Foggerty was a confectioner on a small scale in the Borough Road. He did not begin by being a confectioner, for his career had been a chequered one, and his ups and downs had been many. He began life as a Gentleman's Baby, a situation which he filled for about three years with much credit, when he found himself promoted to the rank and standing of a Gentleman's Little Boy—a position which carried with it an improved scale of dietary, and an emolument of twopence per week, on a Judge's tenure, that is to say, *dum se bene gesserit*. He passed through the various grades of boyhood and adolescence without having distinguished himself, except as a remarkable and exceptionally ordinary kind of boy, with this one distinguishing feature—that he had developed no prominent characteristic of any kind whatever. At nineteen, he became a Government clerk in the Bitter Beer branch of the Malt and Hops Department of the Inland Revenue Office. In this capacity he distinguished himself by the invention of a new system of cooking accounts, but the Heads of his

Department looked coldly and indeed suspiciously on his discovery, and, treating him with the jealous brutality that usually characterises Government officials in dealing with humble inventors, required him to send in his papers without further delay. Too proud to discuss the question with his blinded superiors, he retired at once, and, finding himself penniless, enlisted in a regiment of Highlanders. He served with some distinction as a soldier for nearly three days, but the brutality of the regimental barber, who cut his hair so short as to be absolutely unbecoming (and this in spite of his earnest remonstrance), disgusted him with the service, which he quitted abruptly, to the surprise and consternation of his Colonel, and the bitter disappointment of the Field-Marshal Commanding-in-Chief. Feeling that a life of comparative seclusion in some distant region would best harmonise with his then state of mind, he shipped himself as a stowaway on board the *Rattan* (A 1), 800 tons, Captain Gilgal P. Bonesetter, then loading in the London Docks, and to sail for New York forthwith. After a dignified seclusion of eleven days behind a pork cask, he was discovered by the boatswain, who introduced him to Captain Bonesetter, who received him with open arms and closed fists. The Captain's big dog Jupiter, had just been washed overboard, and Captain Bonesetter, with the unaffected hospitality of a true sailor, immediately placed the animal's kennel at Mr. Foggerty's disposal. The dog's spare collar was found to fit him admirably, and the dog's daily rations were quite as much as Mr. Foggerty's stomach could digest. It was the Captain's whim to treat him as if he had really been a dog, and Mr. Foggerty, entering fully into the spirit of the joke, barked, ran about on all fours, sat up on his haunches, and caught a biscuit off his nose, for all the world as if he had been trained to do so. The joke lasted nine weeks and five days, by which time the ship had sighted the American continent, and Mr. Foggerty, having been comfortably provided at the Captain's expense with an entirely new and perfectly well-fitting suit of tar and feathers, was placed ashore at Sandy Hook, with a roving commission to go just wherever he pleased, and do just whatever he liked.

Delighted with his newly-acquired liberty (for a long sea voyage, even under the most agreeable circumstances, is a cramping thing), Mr. Foggerty set off in the direction of New York, the singularity of his appearance in the Captain's suit evoking some amusement, and not a few comments, from the ladies and gentlemen of Port Monmouth. But Mr. Foggerty set all conjecture at rest by explaining that he was the Duke of Northumberland doing it for a wager—adding that the feat he had undertaken was accomplished, and he would feel much obliged if somebody would kindly scrape him down and " loan " him a suit or two of clothes, a gold watch, and an eye-glass, until he could communicate with his solicitor in London. He further stated that the wager was made with a certain Royal Personage of the *very highest possible* rank, and that he was prepared to settle the amount won (£37,000 and Balmoral) on trustees in trust to build a cathedral and found a bishopric for Port Monmouth. Upon hearing of this pious resolve the clergyman of the parish, the Rev.

Hicks K. Plappy (who liked the idea of the bishopric), scraped him down and provided him with everything he could possibly require, including a marble bust of himself, and a cow with five legs, for many years the surprise and glory of the state of New Jersey. To these gifts he superadded his daughter Louisa, a beautiful young lady of twenty—marrying them himself that His Grace might not have a chance of changing his mind. The wedding was magnificent, and His Grace (who had stipulated, as the only condition upon which he could consent to marry Miss Plappy, that his *incognito* should be strictly preserved for ever) started with his blushing bride from New York, per *Cuba*, for England the same evening. On his arrival at Liverpool, his wife, who was anxious to assume her real station, urged upon her husband the propriety of immediately throwing off his *incognito*, a course which appeared particularly advisable as she had read of another Duke of Northumberland, then in England, and she was anxious to know which of the two was the right one. But Foggerty explained that the other Duke was an impostor who had taken advantage of his absence to assume his name and rank, and that he proposed to remain in obscurity for the present, just in order to see how far the sham Duke would carry his pretentions. His wife objected, naturally enough, to this course; but Foggerty was firm, and there was nothing more to be said. He proposed that while they were watching the movements of the sham Duke, they should amuse themselves by purchasing the goodwill of a confectioner's shop in the Borough Road, and play at being tradespeople. To this course Her Grace was obliged to consent. The game had lasted about twelve years, and was still going on, when our story commenced, for Foggerty (as he preferred to be called) had not yet done watching the movements of the sham Duke, who was now dealing with Northumberland House as if it really belonged to him. These are Freddy Foggerty's antecedents, which we have set out at some length because it is essential to a proper appreciation of his astonishing adventures that these details should be clearly understood.

Freddy Foggerty was seated on his counter in a very uncomfortable frame of mind. A sergeant of Highlanders had that morning entered his shop to purchase some acidulated drops. On seeing Mr. Foggerty it was observed that the sergeant stared at him in a very remarkable manner—so much so that Mr. Foggerty had said to him, "It's lucky for you, sergeant, that it's me, and not my wife, you are staring at so rudely, for she is strong and stands no nonsense." Upon which the sergeant remarked that it was a fine day (which it was not, for it was snowing heavily), and went out of the shop, leaving the acidulated drops behind him in his nervous agitation. This little incident served to set Freddy in a roar, until he suddenly recollected that this very sergeant was very like the very sergeant who had enlisted him some thirteen years before, and it was this sudden recollection that caused him to use the exclamation with which this story opens—"Oh, dash it all, he knows me, and I shall be tried for desertion!"

He was terribly agitated, for he was really prosperous as a confectioner; moreover, he was extremely fond of his wife, and he had two children. The thought of his being torn away from his business and from them, with the shop going to rack and ruin while he served his time in the ranks, was too much for him, and he burst into tears.

"Cheer up, Mr. Foggerty," said a pipy little voice.

He looked up, but could see no one. At last his eye rested on a small twelfth-cake in the window, and he was surprised to see the little plaster-of-Paris fairy which had crowned the top of it hop off her box of sugar-plums, and pick her way carefully through the tracery that decorated the surface of the cake. She travelled on slowly, tumbling over a harlequin, and getting her skirt entangled in the fringe of a gelatine "cracker," until she reached the edge of the cake. She looked over the edge of the little parapet that ran round it, and said:

"I'm afraid, Mr. Foggerty, it's too high to jump, and I shall tear my clothes if I try to scramble down. Will you kindly let me step on to your hand?"

Freddy, who had never seen anything of the kind before, was much interested in her movements, and helped her down at once with the utmost propriety, like a man of gallantry as he was.

"What is troubling you, Mr. Foggerty?"

"Why, miss, thirteen years ago I enlisted, and three days afterwards I deserted, and I have just been discovered, and now I shall be taken up, tried, and imprisoned, and then, perhaps, have to serve out my time as a soldier."

"Indeed," said the young lady, "that will be a pity, for from what I have seen of Mrs. Foggerty I don't think she will do the shop justice. She's a respectable young woman, but with no taste for business."

"Louisa is quite the lady, though," said Freddy.

"Oh, a perfect lady, but I see things from my position in the shop that you don't see. Take my word for it, Mrs. Foggerty is no business woman. Only the other day a little girl came in for three-pen'north of chocolate cream. Well, Mrs. Foggerty not only gave her the chocolate for nothing, but added a Bath bun and a penny ice, and told her to come in again whenever she liked, and bring all her young friends. Now that's all very nice, but it's not business," said the fairy, with decision.

"Mrs. Foggerty is all heart," said Freddy; "besides, she is a born lady, and can't bear the idea of selling anything."

"I wish you would tell me your history," said the fairy.

"Oh, with great pleasure," said Freddy. And he told her his history, just as I have been telling it to you.

"It seems to me, Mr. Foggerty, that your career has been a very discreditable one," said the fairy, when Mr. Foggerty had finished.

"I'm not proud of it, miss. I've done many things in my time that I've had reason to regret. There are many incidents in my career that I'd give anything to blot out."

"Oh, indeed," said the fairy. "Now I think I can help you to do that. First of all, how many ornaments are there on that twelfth-cake?"

"Three large ones," said Freddy: "a Ship, a Harlequin, and a Policeman, besides crackers and other unimportant trifles."

"Very good," said the fairy; "take these ornaments off the cake, and whenever you wish to obliterate any one deed of your life and all its consequences, eat one of those ornaments."

"And the deed will be obliterated from my history?"

"Entirely," said the fairy; "you will be as though it had never been committed."

"I am very much obliged to you," said Freddy.

"Not at all," said the fairy, "I'm very glad to have had it in my power to assist you."

And so saying she made her way back to the bon-bon box on the top of the cake, and became plaster-of-Paris once more.

Freddy scarcely knew what to make of his adventure. He was not so foolish as to believe in fairies, but still, without committing himself to a belief, *there she was.* As to his being able to obliterate an event of his life by eating one of the ornaments on the cake, why that was preposterous. He could understand that he might obliterate his life altogether by so doing, for they were coloured, for the most part, with arsenite of copper and chromate of lead, but *any one event*—it was out of the question.

As these ideas floated through his head he looked down the street, and saw a corporal's guard in the distance. It was marching straight towards his shop. A crisis was about to take place. It was too awful. To

be torn away from his beloved wife and adored children
—no, no! Drowning men catch at straws, and Freddy
crunched the Ship, ejaculating at the same time a
sincere wish that his return to England from NEW YORK,
AND ALL ITS CONSEQUENCES MIGHT BE OBLITERATED FROM
HIS HISTORY FOR EVER!

CHAPTER II.

THE fairy was as good as her word. A remarkable
change took place in Mr. Freddy Foggerty's condition. The confectioner's shop, the twelfth-cake, the
house, the street, the corporal's guard, all vanished in a
moment, and Freddy found himself lying in a comfortable cot in a ship's stern-cabin.

Freddy was wondering where he was, and how he got
there, when the cabin-door opened, and a black man put
his head in.

"Seven bells, Massa Foggerty."

"Oh!" said Freddy; "how's her head?"

"S.S.W. and by S.—light breeze freshenin', Massa
Foggerty."

"Oh! then I'll tumble up."

Freddy felt it incumbent upon him to appear to know
exactly where he was, and to be surprised at nothing.
He determined to make no inquiries, but to leave it to
time and accident to enlighten him as to the circumstances in which he found himself, and proceeded to
dress himself in a pair of blue serge trousers (in the

pockets of which were the Policeman and the Harlequin), a pea-jacket with gilt buttons, and a cap with a gold band. He completed his toilet and went on deck. He then saw that the ship was a fine bark, with raking masts, and perhaps a tonnage of 800. She carried two long carronades.

"Mornin', cap'en," said a tall wiry Yankee mate. "With a breeze like this I reckon we shall take tarnation snakes out of yon Britisher."

"No doubt of it," said Freddy. "Where is the Britisher?"

"About three miles off the starboard quarter," said the mate, pointing in the named direction with a telescope.

"I see him—that is *her*," said Freddy.

"If this breeze lasts she'll never overhaul the *Flying Clam.*"

"And if she should," said Freddy, "who cares?"

He looked anxiously at the mate, to see if *he* cared.

"Wal, *I* du for one. The crew du for another. *And* the cargo du for a third."

"The cargo? I don't see how it can concern the cargo?"

"Wal," said the mate; Ho! ho! ho! that *is* a good'un. Don't see how it can consarn the cargo! No, no—you'll never beat that if you tries a year, cap'en! Bully for you, old man! Ho! ho! ho!"

"Ho! ho! ho!" laughed Freddy, mechanically; "Bully for me, as you say."

"You du make me larf, you bet!" said the mate. "Can't consarn the cargo! No, not at all. Ho! ho! ho!"

"I think," said Freddy, "I should like to have another look at the cargo." For he began to wonder what it consisted of.

"Whelps!" shouted the mate to the boatswain, who was serving out grog to five-and-twenty skulking-looking ruffians, "the cap'en wants another look at the cargo. Take the cap'en into the hold."

"Ay, ay," cried the boatswain. He handed the pannikin to his mate, and went down the main hatch. Freddy followed him. On the main deck he lighted a lantern, and then descended a second "companion," and so reached the lower deck. He then raised a bolted and barred trap-door, and prepared to descend a third ladder. At this point Freddy perceived that the atmosphere in the neighbourhood of the cargo had a distinct and recognisable flavour of its own.

He descended the third ladder. The boatswain held up the lantern, and Freddy formed his first impression of the cargo, and his first impression was that it was cocoa-nuts. But a closer inspection showed that each cocoa-nut had two white glaring eyeballs, and he then formed his second (and right) impression, which was "niggers." As his eyes became accustomed to the darkness he saw that the hold contained from forty to fifty black people, of both sexes, huddled together in a dreadfully uncomfortable manner.

They were chained two and two, the chain of communication running through a staple in the deck. It flashed upon Freddy that he must be the captain of a slaver, at that moment hotly pursued by one of Her Britannic Majesty's ships of war.

It now becomes necessary to explain the circumstances under which Mr. Foggerty came to fill such a position. They are shortly as follows:

If Mr. Foggerty had not returned from New York to England, his career would have taken an entirely different course. He would have lived for some months on the speculative bounty of the Rev. Hicks K. Plappy, who would have secured himself from ultimate loss by taking bills at twelve months for his son-in-law's keep. Eventually, however, the reverend pastor's suspicions would have been aroused, and Freddy's pretentions to the dukedom would have undergone a thorough investigation before a magistrate. He would then have been tried, and convicted of obtaining money and goods under false pretences, and sentenced to twelve months' imprisonment, with hard labour, in the "Tombs." In this retreat he would have formed a bowing acquaintance with a seafaring man of evil countenance, and their sentences expiring on the same day. Freddy and the seafaring man would have set forth "on the tramp," to take whatever good or ill luck might turn up for them. At length the sailor would have found work on board a blockade-runner, and Freddy, who would have known very well that there was no chance of his being engaged as one of the crew, would have shipped himself once more in his old and favourite character as a "stowaway." A certain smartness and activity which characterised all of Freddy's movements would have recommended him to the skipper, and he would eventually have formed one of the ship's crew. In this capacity he would have distinguished himself so remarkably that he would in a couple of years, have been promoted to the rank of boatswain's mate. On the cessation of the American War his ship would have traded to the east coast of Africa in ivory and gold dust, and Freddy, who by this time would have saved about two thousand dollars, would have purchased a sixteenth share in her. From this point his promotion would have been rapid, and in six years he would have saved money enough to purchase her out and out, and trade with her on his own account. He would have discovered that the slave trade was still more profitable than that in gold and ivory, and (keeping it secret from Louisa, who would be living luxuriously somewhere in Florida, under the impression that her husband was a blameless merchant) he would have devoted himself to its prosecution with an energy which might with equal profit, and less risk, have been expended upon a more legitimate speculation.

However, Freddy knew nothing of what *would have happened*, if his return to England and all its consequences had been blotted out of his career, and felt himself somewhat at a loss to account for his position.

" Great heavens," said Freddy, on realising the exact character of the cargo, " these must be slaves ! "

" The cap'en will be the death o' me one day ! " roared the boatswain in the middle of an uncontrollable fit of laughter.

" How horrible ! how awful ! " said Freddy. " Torn from the bosom of their families—cramped and crippled in a filthy hold, and in an atmosphere in which a candle will hardly burn—it's horrible, it's appalling ! "

" The cap'en's joke agin all others, I allers say ! "

screamed the boatswain, who in the excess of his merriment had to hold on by the ladder to save himself from falling. "He acts it all to the life, that's sartin!"

Freddy recollected himself and forced a grim smile. "Shut the devils up again," said he.

"This yere's the slow match," said the boatswain, pointing to the end of a piece of yarn which lay on the lower deck. "It's in beautiful order, and burns two minutes."

"Oh, to be sure," said Freddy, "that is the slow match. Quite right. Of course the other end communicates with—"

"With an open barrel of powder in the magazine, 'cordin' to your own orders, cap'en."

"Quite correct. And now let me see whether you fully understand my instructions. When are you to set light to it?"

"As soon as the Britisher's first shot strikes our hull. Then up we goes, and there's an end of the *Flying Clam*, crew, cargo, cap'en and all."

"Admirable!" said Freddy, white with terror, "only —I've been thinking that—perhaps on the whole there is something rather contemptible, not to say downright cowardly, in this summary and comparatively painless way of evading the punishment our captors may have in store for us."

"Wot!" yelled the boatswain.

"Why, reflect," said Freddy. "If we blow ourselves up they may say that we do so because we are afraid of them! The thought is unendurable! No, no—let us evince a truer and a nobler courage than that of the mere suicide. Let us rather express our indifference to penal servitude by submitting with sullen contempt to whatever punishment these bloodhounds may think proper to inflict upon us!"

And Freddy's nostrils dilated with a noble scorn that would have fitted a Protestant martyr in the reign of Queen Mary.

"Wal!" roared the boatswain, as he clutched at Freddy's collar. "Of all the yelping cocktails—but stop a bit—stop a bit!"

He put his pipe to his mouth and blew shrilly upon it —"Tweet! tweet! tweet! twilly, twilly, twilly,— twee-e-e—twip, twip, twip—twee-e-e-e! All hands on upper deck!" He ran fore and aft along the main deck, piping and shouting down each hatchway.

The crew tumbled up in all haste—men of all nations —many black and brown—all scowling and tigerish. They stood on both sides of the upper deck according to their watches.

"Mr. Slip!" shouted the boatswain, foaming at the mouth. "Mr. Slip, and men all. Lookee yere. This yere cap'en of ourn—this yere lanky cocktail—this white-livered devil's chicken—he's showing the white feather—he's a cur—a slinkin' coward—a shiverin' cocktail! He won't fight, and he won't sink—he's going to give in—if you'll let him, mates, if you'll let him!"

The boatswain's fury had almost exhausted him, and he lolloped on to a carronade from sheer weakness.

"Shame! shame!" yelled the men, who seemed to contemplate a general rush at Freddy.

"Wot's this?" said Slip, taking Freddy by the

collar and presenting a six-shooter at his head. "Now, lookee yere, cap'en. Wot's your program*me?* What do you pur*pose* to du?" Freddy recollected himself, for he felt that a crisis was at hand, and that his only chance lay in carrying it off with a high hand.

"To fight till the last drop of my blood shall trickle on these snowy decks, and then, mingling with the blue ocean beneath our feet, proclaim to all who may chance to see it that Rule Columbia, Columbia rules the waves, Yankee traders never, never, *never* will be done out of their slaves!"

A yell of joy rang through the air as the confused metaphors of their beloved captain sank into the souls of the crew. He perceived his advantage, and lost no time in following it up.

"Now, my men," said he, "what shall we do with these lying mutineers, who for ends of their own have endeavoured to stir you up against your captain?"

"Overboard!" was the universal verdict, and a hundred hands clutched at the mate and the boatswain. In another moment they were hurled, gurgling, into the deep.

In the meanwhile, the wind had freshened considerably, and the British frigate (to whom no one paid any attention during the excitement of this scene) came up, hand over hand.

"Here you," said Freddy to a middle-aged person, who had been foremost in throwing over the first mate —and whom he concluded on that account to be the second mate—"take charge of the slow match on the lower deck, and when I give the word 'go,' set light to it."

"Ay, ay, sir!" said the second mate. And he slowly

and reluctantly disappeared (with a very pale face) down
the main-hatch. "Bang!" from the Britisher. The
shot, a thirty-two, flew high over their heads, carrying
away one of the main topsail lifts.

"Carpenter!" shouted Freddy.

"Ay, ay, sir!"

"Stave in the boats."

"But—"

"Not a word, or I'll blow your head off."

The carpenter took an axe and sullenly obeyed orders.

"Boatswain's mate!"

"Sir!"

"Can she carry any more sail?"

"Not an inch, sir."

The chase lasted half-an-hour, in the course of which
the Britisher rapidly overhauled the slaver, for the breeze
had increased to half a gale. At length a round shot
carried away the mizzen about two feet below the
necklace, and with a fearful crash the mast and its
cumbrous gear fell over the ship's quarter. Two men
were carried overboard with it.

"Go!" shouted Foggerty down the hatch. He took
out his watch; the crew held their breath, and each
man nervously clutched at something.

"Go it is!" replied the muffled voice of the pale
mate, as he obeyed the order from the lower deck. In
another moment he rushed up the companion.

"The match is fired!" screamed he, "and in two
minutes we shall be blown to feathers!" And so
saying he flung himself overboard—an example which
was followed by the greater part of the crew.

Freddy looked at his watch for a minute and a half.

"I NOW WISH," said he, very deliberately and distinctly as he masticated the Policeman, "I NOW WISH THAT MY TARRING AND FEATHERING AND ALL ITS CONSEQUENCES MAY BE BLOTTED OUT OF MY HISTORY FOR EVER!"

CHAPTER III.

WITH the muffled sound of a distant explosion ringing in his head, Freddy found himself sitting in a comfortable room fitted up partly as an office, and partly as a luxurious study. He was seated at a handsome mahogany writing-table, furnished with every little luxury that can reduce the toil and enhance the pleasures of pen-work. Above a handsome statuary marble mantelpiece hung a portrait of himself in the act of addressing society at large on the subject of a scroll of parchment with a pendent seal, and regardless of the threatening appearance of a raging thunderstorm, from which a pillar and a crimson curtain afforded an inadequate protection. Beneath his feet was an Axminster carpet of astonishing pile, and two or three easy-chairs, with a comfortable welcoming " come along, old man " sort of expression, stood about the room.

"It is quite clear," said Freddy, "that I'm a banker's clerk of some kind. I wonder what Bank I belong to. Rather a prosperous concern apparently—or, what is still more likely, a flashy and unsubstantial one."

He took some paper from a stand in front of him, and

found it headed "Royal Indelible Bank, 142, Threadneedle Street, E.C." He then noticed that all the books on his desk were stamped "Royal Indelible Bank," and the official seal, which stood ready to his hand, bore a similar inscription.

He walked to the door and opened it. He found that it communicated with a very large room, in which forty or fifty clerks were at work.

"By Jove!" thought he, as he contrasted their apartment with his own luxurious private room, "banker's clerk be hanged! I'm a banker, or something very like it, and on a large scale too!"

At this moment the clock struck five, and all the clerks rose simultaneously, and began to wash their hands at little stands provided for the purpose. When they had completed their toilettes they went out in twos and threes, passing his door as they did so, and saying, "Good evening, sir," very respectfully, as they went by.

"I suppose," thought Freddy, "I ought to go too. I wonder where I live." So he took down his hat from a peg and followed the last clerk out. He saw the porter (a stout responsible-looking person in a quiet business-like livery), at the end of a passage, holding the door open for him.

"Now," thought Freddy, "how the deuce am I to find out where I live? I can't ask the porter, he'll think I've been drinking." He felt in his pockets for some cards, but he could not find any. "I'll go back," thought he, "and look in the Directory. I'm sure to be a householder."

But just as he was turning back the porter said to him, " Your carriage is here, sir," and as he spoke a quiet brougham, drawn by a pair of handsome greys, pulled up at the door. This relieved him of all anxiety. He stepped in, saying " Home !" to the groom, just as if he knew where Home was.

He leant back on the soft cushions as the brougham drove off.

" Come," thought he, " this is better—this is something like. A good berth—secretary or manager perhaps —in a substantial Bank—at least we'll hope it's substantial—and a brougham and pair to drive me home to some snug little villa in the Regent's Park ; or perhaps a good house in Bedford Square, and Louisa and the children waiting for me at home. I wonder how Louisa's looking. Dear Louisa ! I'm glad she wasn't on board the slaver !"

The brougham drove down Oxford Street.

" Ha !" thought he, " it isn't Bedford Square. Well, I am glad it isn't Bedford Square. I prefer the Regent's Park. By-the-bye, I wonder what my income is ?"

He felt in his pocket, and found a pocket-book containing business appointments and important memoranda —all in his own writing, and many of them incomprehensible to him owing to their being written in a kind of cypher or shorthand with which he was not familiar.

" I hope," thought he, " I shall find the key to these, or I shall get into a mess."

He read through several legible memoranda, and eventually lit on the following :—

" Sept. 29th. Qr's. Sal. £375,

"Fifteen hundred a year, eh? Well, that's pretty good—but this pair of horses can't be done on that. I hope I'm not exceeding my income; perhaps Louisa's come into money."

He settled in his own mind that old Plappy was gathered to his fathers, leaving everything to his child.

The carriage drove past the Marble Arch, and along the road towards Bayswater. Tommy watched the progress of the carriage with much anxiety.

"I won't live in Bayswater," said he. "If it's Bayswater I'll move to-morrow. I do wonder where I live. I suppose if I asked the groom he'd think it odd." However, it wasn't Bayswater, for as this thought passed through his mind the carriage drove into Lancaster Gate, and stopped at No. 352.

"Whew!" said he. "Lancaster Gate, eh? Freddy, Freddy, this can't be done on £1500 a year, or anything like it. Something wrong, Freddy, I'm afraid." And he shook his head at himself, and held up his finger in a very reproving manner.

The door was opened by a grave man in a very handsome livery, and Tommy entered the house with much misgiving.

"Anybody in?"

"Only my lady, sir," said the man.

"Only your lady?"

"Yes, Sir Frederick. Her ladyship is up stairs."

"Oho!" thought Freddy. "*Sir* Frederick, and her ladyship, eh? So I've been, knighted I suppose. Perhaps I'm a baronet. I hope I'm a baronet for Theodore's sake."

"Any letters?"

"Only one, Sir Frederick."   It was directed to

"SIR FREDERICK FOGGERTY,
  "&c.,   &c.,   &c.,
      "352, Lancaster Gate, W."

"Only a knight, eh?   Well, it might be worse—I suppose I've been a sheriff.   Now to surprise Louisa!"

He ran upstairs without stopping to examine the pictures in the hall, or the handsome bust of himself on the first landing.   He entered the drawing-room, a spacious apartment tastefully furnished in French grey satin and ebony, but it was empty.   As he turned from the room he met a nursemaid coming downstairs with two children, a girl of three and a boy of two, whom he had not had the pleasure of seeing before.

"Papa tum 'ome!" cried the little boy.   And the two children, released by their nurse, ran and possessed themselves of his two legs.

"Papa tiss Tiny!" said the little girl, making vigorous efforts to swarm up his right leg.

"My dear child," said Freddy, who had a pleasant way with children, "I'm not your papa."

The nurse smiled a weak smile, as who should say, "Master's joke is always so amusingly chosen."

"Yes, yes—you papa!" chorused the two children, with an emphasis which carried conviction with it.

"Whose children are these, nurse?" said Freddy.

"I'm sure I can't say, sir," replied the woman with an agreeable simper, as humouring her master's whim.

"Don't be a dashed fool, girl," said Freddy, losing his temper.   "Whose are they—tell me directly?"

"Dear me, Sir Frederick, yours of course!" said the woman, in great terror. "Yours and my lady's, Sir Frederick. What a question, Sir Frederick, and on this day of all others!"

"Oh. Go!"

The nurse lost no time in hurrying herself and the children out of the presence of a master in whom she detected signs of incipient insanity.

"Mine, eh?" thought Freddy. "I've no recollection of— I've made up my mind not to be surprised at anything, but really this discovery makes a greater demand upon my powers of self-control than I bargained for."

However, he regained his equanimity, and went up stairs. He opened the door quietly. A lady was seated at the glass, and a maid was doing her hair.

"Boo!" exclaimed Sir Frederick, playfully.

The maid started, and the lady turned round—it was *not* Louisa!

"I—beg your pardon—I thought—that is, I was told—"

"Come in, darling," said the lady, and a very stout, jolly-looking lady she was. "Come in. I'm so glad you've come home early." And so saying she ran to him and gave him a sounding kiss in the very heart of his right cheek.

It was quite clear that it was not Louisa, and it was equally clear that it was someone in whose room he had a perfect right to be. Who was she? He had a delicacy in asking the question—indeed he felt that his position was altogether a most delicate and difficult one.

"There's nothing wrong in the city, dear?" said she, noticing his embarrassment, and misinterpreting it.

"Nothing whatever—dear."

"That's right. It wouldn't have a secret from its little wifey, would it, on this day, too, of all others?"

The truth flashed upon him. If he had never been tarred and feathered he would never have made the acquaintance of the Rev. Hicks K. Plappy, and so would never have married his daughter Louisa, but would probably have married someone else, to wit, the buxom jolly red-faced lady who was at that moment plumping kisses into the very heart of his right cheek. The delicacy of his position was not all diminished by the discovery.

"Poor Louisa!" exclaimed Freddy, with unaffected grief, for he was very fond of her. "Poor darling Louisa!"

"Frederick!" exclaimed the stout lady.

"And the dear, dear children! I shall never see them again!"

"Frederick! on this day, too, of all others!" screamed the stout lady. "Explain yourself this moment, I insist!"

Freddy pulled himself together in a moment.

"It's a sad story," said he. "I had a dear, dea. sister—whose existence I have hitherto kept a secret from you, for, many years ago, she disgraced her family by marrying a villain—a pickle-merchant, who had extensive works in Lambeth. His business has gradually declined, owing to the rapid rise in the price of copper, and he and Louisa and her innocent babes have emigrated to New Zealand."

It *was* a sad story, and he knew it, but there was no other way out of it.

"Dear Frederick," said the lady, "you always had a feeling heart. I knew there was something wrong, directly I saw you."

Freddy felt dreadfully hypocritical, but what was he to do? If he had explained to Lady Foggerty that an hour ago he was a Yankee slave captain, with a dear wife Louisa and two beloved children in Florida, and that a few hours before that he was a confectioner in the Borough Road, and that Louisa assisted him in his business, Lady Foggerty would have declined to accept his explanation, militating, as it would have done, with her own experience of him during the last four years. On the whole, I think it was one of those exceptional occasions on which a story is allowable, and having to tell a story, I don't know that he could have pitched upon a better one.

He retired to his dressing-room to prepare for dinner. He found the room luxuriously furnished, with two large easy chairs of the most inviting description, and a comfortable sofa, on which his dress clothes were laid out. He threw himself into one of the chairs, and as he sank in it, he thought to himself as follows :—

"As a speculation, this change has not turned out so badly. I have exchanged a lawless life of continual peril for one of assured prosperity and perfect lawfulness. There are only two drawbacks to it. I am afraid I must be living considerably beyond my income, and I have exchanged a pretty and ladylike wife for a stout and vulgar one. I wonder how I came to marry so gross a person; for I was always a bit of an epicure in such matters. There must have been some reason for it," said he, musingly. "I wonder what it was?"—then with a sudden start, "I have it! I must have married her for her money? That's it—she was a wealthy widow, no doubt, and I married her for her money."

Having settled this point, much to his own satisfaction (for it quite accounted for his extravagant style of living), he proceeded, with the assistance of a quiet valet, to dress for dinner.

"Which studs will you wear to-night, Sir Frederick?" said the man.

"Oh, well, let me see, which did I wear last night?"

"The plain pearls, Sir Frederick."

"Then I'll wear the plain pearls to-night."

"Beg pardon, Sir Frederick, but if you remember one of the pearls came off, and you told me to take it to the jeweller's."

"True, how stupid of me! Well, I'll wear the others."

"Which others, Sir Frederick?"

"Which others?" said Freddy angrily. "Why, *the* others to be sure! Which others *should* I mean, you donkey?"

The valet shrugged his shoulders, and Freddy finished his toilet. As he was putting the final touch to his tie, the lady's maid rapped at the door.

"Please, sir, my lady says will you hurry please, as some of 'em have arrived."

"Who has arrived?"

"Mr. and Mrs. Bortle, and Lord Portico, Sir Frederick."

"Oh, I'm coming. Dinner party, eh?" said he to himself as he went downstairs. "Rather awkward."

He entered the drawing-room and shook hands very heartily with Lord Portico, telling him it seemed an age since they met (which it must have done, as this was the first time they had seen each other), and asking very cordially after Lady Portico, who had been dead about six months. Lord Portico's indignant stare proved to him that he had made some mistake, so he was more careful in his demeanour towards Mr. and Mrs. Bortle, bowing coldly but respectfully to them, which was not right either, as Bortle was his wife's father and had procured him his appointment, and Mr. and Mrs. Bortle had just returned from India after an absence of six years, and the meeting ought to have been a very effusive one. Several other guests arrived, including Mr. and Mrs. Crabthorne (Mrs. Crabthorne was Lady Foggerty's sister) and Sir John Carboy, the eminent accoucheur, who had presided at the birth of Freddy's two little children. In short, it was quite a family party, as Freddy took occasion to observe in an under-breath to Lady Foggerty, who replied, "Well, I should think so, and on this day, too, of all others!"

"I wonder what day of all others this is! I don't like to ask," thought he.

"By-the-bye, dear," said Lady Foggerty, "I forgot to give you this." And she slipped into his hand a piece of paper containing the list of guests told off into couples. He was rather taken aback, because he only knew the Bortles and Lord Portico by sight, but by dint of listening to the conversation, he contrived to hit on the right people, and when dinner was announced down they went.

He managed to get through his dinner pretty comfortably. He had Lady Carboy on his right, and Mrs. Bortle on his left, and as he contrived to confine the conversation to general topics, he did not " put his foot into it " more than twenty or five-and-twenty times during the course of the meal. He was much puzzled, however, by Lady Carboy's and Mrs. Bortle's continual reference to " this day of all others," and he determined to find out what day of all others it really was. He could scarcely ask them without seeming absurd, so he called the butler to him and whispered—" Here, what's your name? In the name of mischief, tell me, *what day is* this ? " to which the butler, thus solemnly adjured, replied " Tuesday, Sir Frederick," which afforded him no clue whatever to the mystery.

After dinner, Sir John Carboy rose and said—

" Ladies and gentlemen, it is not usual to drink healths at modern dinner parties, but there are occasions when the strict forms of etiquette may be relaxed, and I think you will agree with me that this day of all others is one of them. I need not detain you by dilating on the auspicious character of the event we are here to celebrate—the circumstances are known to you all. I will content myself with proposing that we drink the health of my dear old friend, Sir Frederick Foggerty, and my still older, and (may I add ?) my still dearer friend, his admirable wife."

This short and (to Freddy) unsatisfactory speech was received with much applause, and Freddy observed, with some apprehension, that two fat tears stood in Lady Foggerty's little eyes. At last a bright thought occurred to him—"It must be the anniversary of our wedding!" Primed with this fortunate suggestion, he rose and spoke—

"Ha—hum—sir—!" (*he had forgotten Sir John's name*). "My dear, my very, very dear old friend, in rising to reply to the toast with which you have been good enough to couple my name, and that of my dear, my dear (*he had never heard his wife's name*), my dear wife, I feel no little embarrassment. On this day, never mind how many years ago (*with a deep sigh*), Heaven blessed our union—I say—Heaven blessed our union"—

"Hear, hear, my dear boy, my very dear boy," from old Bortle, who was boo-hooing in his handkerchief.

"It's all right," thought Freddy, "it *is* the wedding day." Then he continued—"Yes, on this day, never mind how many years ago—more than I care to look back upon—"

"Four years, only four, my dear boy," sobbed old Bortle from behind his handkerchief.

"On this day four years ago, my wife and I were married."

"Frederick!" exclaimed Lady Foggerty, springing to her feet, "pray recollect yourself."

"I said, my dear, that on this day four years ago, on this day of all others, you and I were happily married—"

Lady Foggerty screamed and fainted. Mr. Bortle, her father, rose, purple with rage, and thus delivered himself:

"Fred! Fred Foggerty! you're drunk—drunk at your own table! He *must* be drunk—to insult his wife in this manner—on this day of all others! Look, sir! Look at your work, scoundrel! She's fainted! Confound you, sir, she's fainted!"

"Be composed, Mr. Bortle," said Lord Portico.

"Be composed! No, sir, I shall *not* be composed. I am not here to be dictated to by anybody, whatever his rank, Lord Portico—be he baron, viscount, earl, marquis, duke, or king. We are invited here on the pretence of celebrating the fourth anniversary of the birth of my daughter's son and heir, and this insolent joker, whose fortune I and my daughter have made, rises and publicly states at his own table—*at his own table, mind*—that on this day four years ago, and on this day of all others, and not until this day, he and she were happily married—were happily married—happily married!"

At this point the purple old gentleman fell back gasping in his chair, and was carried out of the room on the very verge of apoplexy, followed by all the ladies in tears.

"I am sorry, my friends," said Foggerty, when the door was closed, "that my poor little joke should have been so unfortunately misconstrued by Mr.——by my very dear father-in-law. Pray let us forget that it happened, and be as jolly as though I had replied in terms that had melted you to tears."

Sir Frederick was readily excused, and after a short interval of rather forced conversation, the gentlemen rose to join the ladies. At this moment the butler put a telegram into Sir Frederick's hand. It was as follows:—

"Gone Coox,   *to*   Sir Frederick Foggerty,
   "Cripplegate,   352, Lancaster Gate.
  "*Crumph jagger pantiboom rubbleburby cowk.*"

Sir Frederick stood in the hall, puzzling himself with this document, when the street bell rang and a servant opened the door to two tall stout persons, who inquired for Sir Frederick Foggerty.

"I am he," said Freddy.

"Sorry to trouble you at this time of night, sir," said one of the men, "but business is business, as you very well knows."

"My maxim through life," said Sir Frederick.

"I suppose you can guess our errand?"

"I conclude it has something to do with this," said Sir Frederick at a guess, handing them the mystic telegram.

"Exactly. So the Gone Coon is in it?"

"The Gone Coon is in it. Indeed, he has been in it some time."

"Much obliged for the information. It seems from this telegram that we were just in time."

"Just in time."

"I suppose in another ten minutes you'd have been off?"

"Five. Five minutes. But I'm very glad you managed to catch me at home."

"So are we, Sir Frederick," said the man with a chuckle. "I suppose you'll come quietly?"

"As a mouse. Shall I go with you, or follow you in an hour's time?"

"Well, I think it would be more satisfactory if you were to go with us," said the man, grinning to his companion. "Well, you *are* a game one, I will say that. 'Taint every man in your position as could cut jokes on the brink of penal servitude."

" What ? "

"I'm afraid it'll be that, Sir Frederick. There's the bonds and the two bills on Pogson and Blythe—you know."

" Forgery ! " said Sir Frederick, throwing himself back into an arm-chair. " It's monstrous ! Come here, all of you," shouted he up the stairs,—" come at once, will you ? "

" I say, Sir Frederick, none of this, you know," said the men, drawing their truncheons; " you said you'd come quietly, and if anything of a rescue is attempted——"

" Nonsense, I'm coming quite quietly." By this time the guests had lined the staircase, listening in great astonishment to the excited proceedings in the hall.

" Look here," said Freddy to his friends. " It's several degrees too bad. Five hours ago I commanded a slaver, and at four this afternoon I was a confectioner in the Borough with a wife and a fine boy. I have during the last few hours been apparently a prosperous banker, with another wife whose acquaintance I had much pleasure in making, and a couple of children for whom I can't account in any way whatever. No matter, I have a fine house in Lancaster Gate, and a circle of agreeable friends—more or less titled, some of them— and all of them agreeable in many respects. Now, it seems I'm to forfeit all these advantages, because in some bygone time while I was not me but somebody else, Sir Frederick Foggerty and an unknown person called the ' Gone Coon ' (probably an *alias*) forged certain bills and securities. Not I, mind you, but me, before I was I ! "

The guests received this lucid statement of facts in

mute surprise. "Gettin' up the scaffolding for a plea of lunacy!" whispered one of the detectives to the other.

"Frederick!" screamed Lady Foggerty from the top of the stairs (she had gone upstairs to bathe her eyes, and only rushed down in time to hear the latter part of Sir Frederick's speech). "Frederick—my darling, my beloved husband—don't take him, gentlemen—he loves me so dearly—it's not true—he never did a dishonest act in his life—don't, don't take him—and on this day of all others!" and so saying, the poor soul fell fainting at his feet.

"Lead on," said Sir Frederick.

And so they handcuffed him, and drove him off to Marlborough Street Police Station.

He had no substantial defence, but threw himself upon the mercy of the Court, in a speech which has been preserved in the annals of the Old Bailey, as the type of what such a speech should be.

He said, "My Lord, and gentlemen of the jury, I cannot deny that I, before I was me, may have been guilty of the charge imputed to me by the learned counsel for the prosecution, to whose very able and very lucid recital of the varied incidents of my career I have listened with much curiosity. That I have rendered myself amenable to the law I admit. But reflect. I have been for some hours past the toy and sport of a Twelfth Cake fairy, who has tempted me to change my original condition—that of a confectioner in the Borough—for, firstly, that of a slave captain; and secondly, that of a fraudulent banker. Was I a banker or only a manager to a bank? A manager—thank you. Don't you see the difficulty of my position? That fairy, gentlemen, has been the curse of my life. Let it be a warning to you all in that box, and above all to you my Lord on the bench, to beware of supernatural assistance. Trust to your own exertions, gentlemen, and you'll all do very well. I am very much obliged to you all for the attentive consideration you have devoted to my case, and as I know you are about to return a verdict of guilty (*here the jury bowed*), which will probably be followed by a sentence of penal servitude for life from my lord up there (*here the learned Judge bowed*), why, the best thing I can do is to make another change in my condition with all possible haste."

So saying, he drew the Harlequin from his pocket, and put it into his mouth, uttering at the same time these remarkable words, "I WISH THAT THE FAIRY ON THE TWELFTH CAKE, AND ALL THE CONSEQUENCES THAT SPRUNG FROM MY ACQUAINTANCE WITH HER, MAY BE BLOTTED OUT OF MY CAREER FOR EVER."

*　　*　　*　　*　　*　　*

And, behold, Mr. Frederick Foggerty found himself once more in his little confectionery shop in the Borough Road in the act of selling the Twelfth Cake, with the Policeman, the Ship, and the Harlequin and the Fairy on the top of it, to a very bilious old lady with whom it was sure to disagree.

And Louisa was in the back shop with Theodore, and whenever Mr. Foggerty related the history of his adventure with the Twelfth Cake, she indignantly stopped him, telling him that he was a donkey, and had been dreaming.

Which I think was very likely the case.

AN ELIXIR OF LOVE.

CHAPTER I.

PLOVERLEIGH was a picturesque little village in Dorsetshire, ten miles from anywhere. It lay in a pretty valley nestling amid clumps of elm trees, and a pleasant little trout stream ran right through it from end to end. The vicar of Ploverleigh was the Hon. and Rev. Mortimer De Becheville, third son of the forty-eighth Earl of Caramel. He was an excellent gentleman, and his living was worth £1,200 a-year. He was a graduate of Cambridge, and held a College Fellowship, besides which his father allowed him £500 a-year. So he was very comfortably " off."

Mr. De Becheville had a very easy time of it, for he spent eleven-twelfths of the year away from the parish, delegating his duties to the Rev. Stanley Gay, an admirable young curate to whom he paid a stipend of £120 a-year, pocketing by this means a clear annual profit of £1,080. It was said by unkind and ungenerous people, that, as Mr. De Becheville had (presumably) been selected for his sacred duties at a high salary on account of his special and exceptional qualifications for their discharge, it was hardly fair to delegate them to a wholly inexperienced young gentleman of two-and-twenty. It was argued that if a colonel, or a stipendiary magistrate, or a superintendent of a county lunatic asylum, or any other person holding a responsible office (outside the Church of England), for which he was handsomely paid, were to do his work by cheap deputy, such a responsible official would be looked upon as a swindler. But this line of reasoning is only applied to the cure of souls by uncharitable and narrow-minded people who never go to church, and consequently can't know anything about it. Besides, who cares what people who never go to church think? If it comes to that, Mr. De Becheville was *not* selected (as it happens) on account of his special and exceptional fitness for the cure of souls, inasmuch as the living was a family one, and went to De Becheville because his two elder brothers preferred the Guards. So that argument falls to the ground.

The Rev. Stanley Gay was a Leveller. I don't mean to say that he was a mere I'm-as-good-as-you Radical spouter, who advocated a redistribution of property from mere sordid motives. Mr. Gay was an æsthetic Leveller. He held that as Love is the great bond of union between man and woman, no arbitrary obstacle should be allowed to interfere with its progress. He did not desire to abolish Rank, but he *did* desire that a mere difference in rank should not be an obstacle in the way of making two young people happy. He could prove to you by figures (for he was a famous mathematician) that, rank notwithstanding, all men are equal, and this is how he did it.

He began, as a matter of course, with x, because, as he said, x, whether it represents one or one hundred thousand, is always x, and do what you will, you cannot make w or y of it by any known process.

Having made this quite clear to you, he carried on his argument by means of algebra, until he got right through algebra to the "cases" at the end of the book, and then he slid by gentle and imperceptible degrees into conic sections, where x, although you found it masquerading as the equation to the parabola, was still as much x as ever. Then if you were not too tired to follow him, you found yourself up to the eyes in plane and spherical trigonometry, where x again turned up in a variety of assumed characters, sometimes as "$\cos a$" sometimes as "$\sin \beta$," but generally with a $\sqrt{}$ over it, and none the less x on that account. This singular character then made its appearance in a quaint binomial disguise, and was eventually run to earth in the very heart of differential and integral calculus, looking less like x, but being, in point of fact, more like x than ever. The force of his argument went to show that, do what you would, you could not stamp x out, and therefore it was better and wiser and more straightforward to call him x at once than to invest him with complicated sham dignities which meant nothing, and only served to bother and perplex people who met him for the first time. It's a very easy problem—anybody can do it.

Mr. Gay was, as a matter of course, engaged to be married. He loved a pretty little girl of eighteen, with soft brown eyes, and bright silky brown hair. Her name was Jessie Lightly, and she was the only daughter of Sir Caractacus Lightly, a wealthy baronet who had a large place in the neighbourhood of Ploverleigh. Sir Caractacus was a very dignified old gentleman, whose wife had died two years after Jessie's birth. A well-bred, courtly old gentleman, too, with a keen sense of honour. He was very fond of Mr. Gay, though he had no sympathy with his levelling views.

One beautiful moonlit evening Mr. Gay and Jessie were sitting together on Sir Caractacus's lawn. Everything around them was pure and calm and still, so they grew sentimental.

"Stanley," said Jessie, "we are very, very happy, are we not?"

"Unspeakably happy," said Gay. "So happy that when I look around me, and see how many there are whose lives are embittered by disappointment—by envy, by hatred, and by malice" (when he grew oratorical he generally lapsed into the Litany) "I turn to the tranquil and unruffled calm of my own pure and happy love for you with gratitude unspeakable."

He really meant all this, though he expressed himself in rather flatulent periods.

"I wish with all my heart," said Jessie, "that every soul on earth were as happy as we two."

"And why are they not?" asked Gay, who hopped on to his hobby whenever it was, so to speak, brought round to the front door. "And why are they not, Jessie? I will tell you why they are not. Because—"

"Yes, darling," said Jessie, who had often heard his argument before. "I know why. It's dreadful."

"It's as simple as possible," said Gay. "Take x to represent the abstract human being—"

"Certainly, dear," said Jessie, who agreed with his argument heart and soul, but didn't want to hear it again. "We took it last night."

"Then," said Gay, not heeding the interruption, "let $x+1$, $x+2$, $x+3$, represent three grades of high rank."

"Exactly, it's contemptible," said Jessie. "How softly the wind sighs among the trees."

"What is a duke?" asked Gay—not for information, but oratorically, with a view to making a point.

"A mere $x + 3$," said Jessie. "Could anything be more hollow. What a lovely evening!"

"The Duke of Buckingham and Chandos—it sounds well, I grant you," continued Gay, "but call him the $x + 3$ of Buckingham and Chandos, and you reduce him at once to—"

"I know," said Jessie, "to his lowest common denominator," and her little upper lip curled with contempt.

"Nothing of the kind," said Gay, turning red. "Either hear me out, or let me drop the subject. At all events don't make ridiculous suggestions."

"I'm very sorry, dear," said Jessie, humbly. "Go on, I'm listening, and I won't interrupt any more."

But Gay was annoyed and wouldn't go on. So they returned to the house together. It was their first tiff.

CHAPTER II.

In St. Martin's Lane lived Baylis and Culpepper, magicians, astrologers, and professors of the Black Art. Baylis had sold himself to the Devil at a very early age, and had become remarkably proficient in all kinds of enchantment. Culpepper had been his apprentice, and having also acquired considerable skill as a necromancer, was taken into partnership by the genial old magician, who from the first had taken a liking to the frank and fair-haired boy. Ten years ago (the date of my story) the firm of Baylis and Culpepper stood at the very head of the London family magicians. They did what is known as a pushing trade, but although they advertised largely, and never neglected a chance, it was admitted even by their rivals, that the goods they supplied could be relied on as sound useful articles. They had a special reputation for a class of serviceable family nativity, and they did a very large and increasing business in love philtres, "The Patent Oxy-Hydrogen Love-at-First-Sight Draught" in bottles at 1*s.* 1½*d.* and 2*s.* 3*d.* ("our leading article," as Baylis called it) was strong enough in itself to keep the firm going, had all its other resources failed them. But the establishment in St. Martin's Lane was also a "Noted House for Amulets," and if you wanted a neat, well-finished divining-rod, I don't know any place to which I would sooner recommend you. Their Curses at a shilling per dozen were the cheapest things in the trade, and they sold thousands of them in the course of the year. Their Blessings—also very cheap indeed, and quite effective— were not much asked for. "We always keep a few on hand as curiosities and for completeness, but we don't sell two in the twelvemonth," said Mr. Baylis. "A gentleman bought one last week to send to his mother-in-law, but it turned out that he was afflicted in the head, and the persons who had charge of him declined to pay for it, and it's been returned to us. But the sale of penny curses, especially on Saturday nights, is tremendous. We can't turn 'em out fast enough."

As Baylis and Culpepper were making up their books one evening, just at closing time, a gentle young clergyman with large violet eyes, and a beautiful girl of eighteen, with soft brown hair, and a Madonna-like purity of expression, entered the warehouse. These were Stanley Gay and Jessie Lightly. And this is how it came to pass that they found themselves in London, and in the warehouse of the worthy magicians.

As the reader knows, Stanley Gay and Jessie had for many months given themselves up to the conviction that it was their duty to do all in their power to bring their fellow men and women together in holy matrimony, without regard to distinctions of age or rank. Stanley gave lectures on the subject at mechanics' institutes, and the mechanics were unanimous in their approval of his views. He preached his doctrine in workhouses, in beer-shops, and in lunatic asylums, and his listeners supported him with enthusiasm. He addressed navvies at the roadside on the humanising advantages that would accrue to them if they married refined and wealthy ladies of rank, and not a navvy dissented. In short, he felt more and more convinced every day that he had at last discovered the secret of human happiness. Still he had a formidable battle to fight with class prejudice, and he and Jessie pondered gravely on the difficulties that were before them, and on the best means of overcoming them.

"It's no use disguising the fact, Jessie," said Mr.

Gay, " that the Countesses won't like it." And little
Jessie gave a sigh, and owned that she expected some
difficulty with the Countesses. " We must look these
things in the face, Jessie, it won't do to ignore them.
We have convinced the humble mechanics and artisans,
but the aristocracy hold aloof."

" The working-man is the true Intelligence after all,"
said Jessie.

" He is a noble creature when he is quite sober," said
Gay. " God bless him."

Stanley Gay and Jessie were in this frame of mind
when they came across Baylis and Culpepper's advertisement in the *Connubial Chronicle.*

" My dear Jessie," said Gay, " I see a way out of our
difficulty."

And dear little Jessie's face beamed with hope.

" These Love Philtres that Baylis and Culpepper
advertise—they are very cheap indeed, and if we may
judge by the testimonials, they are very effective.
Listen, darling."

And Stanley Gay read as follows :—

" From the Earl of Market Harborough. ' I am a
hideous old man of eighty, and everyone avoided me.
I took a family bottle of your philtre, immediately on
my accession to the title and estates a fortnight ago,
and I can't keep the young women off. Please send me
a pipe of it to lay down.' "

" From Amelia Orange Blossom.—' I am a very pretty
girl of fifteen. For upwards of fourteen years past I
have been without a definitely declared admirer. I took
a large bottle of your philtre yesterday, and within

fourteen hours a young nobleman winked at me in church.   Send me a couple of dozen.'"

"What can the girl want with a couple of dozen young noblemen, darling?" asked Jessie.

"I don't know—perhaps she took it too strong. Now these men," said Gay, laying down the paper, "are benefactors indeed, if they can accomplish all they undertake. I would ennoble these men. They should have statues. I would enthrone them in high places. They would be $x + 3$."

"My generous darling," said Jessie, gazing into his eyes in a fervid ecstasy.

"Not at all," replied Gay. "They deserve it. We confer peerages on generals who plunge half a nation into mourning—shall we deny them to men who bring a life's happiness home to every door? Always supposing," added the cautious clergyman, "that they can really do what they profess."

The upshot of this conversation was that Gay determined to lay in a stock of philtres for general use among his parishioners. If the effect upon them was satisfactory he would extend the sphere of their operations. So when Sir Caractacus and his daughter went to town for the season, Stanley Gay spent a fortnight with them, and thus it came to pass that he and Jessie went together to Baylis and Culpepper's.

"Have you any fresh Love Philtres to day?" said Gay.

"Plenty, sir," said Mr. Culpepper. "How many would you like?"

"Well—let me see," said Gay.   "There are a

hundred and forty souls in my parish,—say twelve dozen."

" I think, dear," said little Jessie, " you are better to take a few more than you really want, in case of accidents."

" In purchasing a large quantity, sir," said Mr. Culpepper, " we would strongly advise you taking it in the wood, and drawing it off as you happen to want it. We have it in four-and-a-half and nine-gallon casks, and we deduct ten per cent. for cash payments."

" Then, Mr. Culpepper, be good enough to let me have a nine-gallon cask of Love Philtre as soon as possible. Send it to the Rev. Stanley Gay, Ploverleigh."

He wrote a cheque for the amount, and so the transaction ended.

" Is there any other article ? " said Mr. Culpepper.

" Nothing to-day. Good afternoon."

" Have you seen our new wishing-caps ? They are lined with silk and very chastely quilted, sir. We sold one to the Archbishop of Canterbury not an hour ago. Allow me to put you up a wishing-cap."

" I tell you that I want nothing more," said Gay, going.

" Our Flying Carpets are quite the talk of the town, sir," said Culpepper, producing a very handsome piece of Persian tapestry. " You spread it on the ground and sit on it, and then you think of a place and you find yourself there before you can count ten. Our Abudah chests, sir, each chest containing a patent Hag, who comes out and prophecies disasters whenever you touch this spring, are highly spoken of. We can sell the Abudah chest complete for fifteen guineas."

"I think you tradespeople make a great mistake in worrying people to buy things they don't want," said Gay.

"You'd be surprised if you knew the quantity of things we get rid of by this means, sir."

"No doubt, but I think you keep a great many people out of your shop. If x represents the amount you gain by it, and y the amount you lose by it, then if $\frac{x}{2} = y$ you are clearly out of pocket by it at the end of the year. Think this over. Good evening."

And Mr. Gay left the shop with Jessie.

"Stanley," said she, "what a blessing you are to mankind. You do good wherever you go."

"My dear Jessie," replied Gay, "I have had a magnificent education, and if I can show these worthy but half-educated tradesmen that their ignorance of the profounder mathematics is misleading them, I am only dealing as I should deal with the blessings that have been entrusted to my care."

As Messrs. Baylis & Culpepper have nothing more to do with this story, it may be stated at once that Stanley Gay's words had a marked effect upon them. They determined never to push an article again, and within two years of this resolve they retired on ample fortunes, Baylis to a beautiful detached house on Clapham Common, and Culpepper to a handsome chateau on the Mediterranean, about four miles from Nice.

CHAPTER III.

We are once more at Ploverleigh, but this time at
the Vicarage. The scene is Mr. Gay's handsome
library, and in this library three persons are assembled
—Mr. Gay, Jessie, and old Zorah Clarke. It should be
explained that Zorah is Mr. Gay's cook and housekeeper, and it is understood between him and Sir
Caractacus Lightly that Jessie may call on the curate
whenever she likes, on condition that Zorah is present
during the whole time of the visit. Zorah is stone deaf
and has to be communicated with through the medium
of pantomime, so that while she is really no impediment
whatever to the free flow of conversation, the chastening
influence of her presence would suffice of itself to silence
ill-natured comments, if such articles had an existence
among the primitive and innocent inhabitants of
Ploverleigh.

The nine-gallon cask of Love Philtre had arrived in
due course, and Mr. Gay had decided that it should be
locked up in a cupboard in his library, as he thought it
would scarcely be prudent to trust it to Zorah, whose
curiosity might get the better of her discretion. Zorah
(who believed that the cask contained sherry) was much
scandalised at her master's action in keeping it in his
library, and looked upon it as an evident and unmis-
takeable sign that he had deliberately made up his
mind to take to a steady course of drinking. However,
Mr. Gay partly reassured the good old lady by informing

her in pantomime (an art of expression in which long practice had made him singularly expert) that the liquid was not intoxicating in the ordinary sense of the word, but that it was a cunning and subtle essence, concocted from innocent herbs by learned gentlemen who had devoted a lifetime to the study of its properties. He added (still in pantomime) that he did not propose to drink a single drop of it himself, but that he intended to distribute it among his parishioners, whom it would benefit socially, mentally, and morally to a considerable extent. Master as he was of the art of expression by gesture, it took two days' hard work to make this clear to her, and even then she had acquired but a faint and feeble idea of its properties, for she always referred to it as sarsaparilla.

"Jessie," said Gay, " the question now arises,—How shall we most effectually dispense the great boon we have at our command? Shall we give a party to our friends, and put the Love Philtre on the table in decanters, and allow them to help themselves?"

"We must be very careful, dear," said Jessie, " not to allow any married people to taste it."

"True," said Gay, "quite true. I never thought of that. It wouldn't do at all. I am much obliged to you for the suggestion. It would be terrible—quite terrible."

And Stanley Gay turned quite pale and faint at the very thought of such a *contretemps.*

"Then," said Jessie, "there are the engaged couples. I don't think we ought to do anything to interfere with the prospects of those who have already plighted their troth."

"Quite true," said Gay, "we have no right, as you say, to interfere with the arrangements of engaged couples. That narrows our sphere of action very considerably."

"Then the widows and the widowers of less than one year's standing should be exempted from its influence."

"Certainly, most certainly. That reflection did not occur to me, I confess. It is clear that the dispensing of the philtre will be a very delicate operation : it will have to be conducted with the utmost tact. Can you think of any more exceptions ? "

"Let me see," said Jessie. "There's Tibbits, our gardener, who has fits ; and there's Williamson, papa's second groom, who drinks, oughtn't to be allowed to marry ; and Major Crump, who uses dreadful language before ladies; and Dame Parboy, who is bed-ridden; and the old ladies in the almshouses—and little Tommy, the idiot—and, indeed, all children under—under what age shall we say ? "

"All children who have not been confirmed," said Gay. "Yes, these exceptions never occurred to me."

"I don't think we shall ever use the nine gallons, dear," said Jessie. "One tablespoonful is a dose."

"I have just thought of another exception," said Gay. "Your papa."

"Oh ! papa *must* marry again ! Poor dear old papa ! Oh ! You *must* let *him* marry."

"My dear Jessie," said Gay, "Heaven has offered me the chance of entering into the married state unencumbered with a mother-in-law. And I am content to accept the blessing as I find it. Indeed, I prefer it so."

"Papa *does* so want to marry—he is always talking of it," replied the poor little woman, with a pretty pout. "O indeed, *indeed*, my new mamma, whoever she may be, shall never interfere with us. Why, how thankless you are! My papa is about to confer upon you the most inestimable treasure in the world, a young, beautiful and devoted wife, and you withhold from him a priceless blessing that you are ready to confer on the very meanest of your parishioners."

"Jessie," said Gay, "you have said enough. Sir Caractacus *shall* marry. I was wrong. If a certain burden to which I will not more particularly refer is to descend upon my shoulders, I will endeavour to bear it without repining."

It was finally determined that there was only one way in which the philtre could be safely and properly distributed. Mr. Gay was to give out that he was much interested in the sale of a very peculiar and curious old Amontillado, and small sample bottles of the wine were to be circulated among such of his parishioners as were decently eligible as brides and bridegrooms. The scheme was put into operation as soon as it was decided upon. Mr. Gay sent to the nearest market-town for a gross of two-ounce phials, and Jessie and he spent a long afternoon bottling the elixir into these convenient receptacles. They then rolled them up in papers, and addressed them to the persons who were destined to be operated upon. And when all this was done Jessie returned to her papa, and Mr. Gay sat up all night explaining in pantomime to Zorah that a widowed aunt of his, in somewhat straitened circumstances, who resided in a small but picturesque villa in the suburbs of Montilla, had been compelled to take a large quantity of the very finest sherry from a bankrupt wine-merchant, in satisfaction of a year's rent of her second floor, and that he had undertaken to push its sale in Ploverleigh in consideration of a commission of two-and-a-half per cent. on the sales effected—which commission was to be added to the fund for the restoration of the church steeple. He began his explanation at 9 p.m., and at 6 a.m. Zorah thought she began to understand him, and Stanley Gay, quite exhausted with his pantomimic exertions, retired, dead beat, to his chamber.

CHAPTER IV.

The next morning as Sir Caractacus Lightly sat at breakfast with Jessie, the footman informed him that Mr. Gay's housekeeper wished to speak to him on very particular business. The courtly old Baronet directed that she should be shown into the library, and at once proceeded to ask what she wanted.

"If you please Sir Caractacus, and beggin' your pardon," said Zorah as he entered, "I've come with a message from my master."

"Pray be seated," said Sir Caractacus. But the poor old lady could not hear him, so he explained his meaning to her in the best dumb show he could command. He pointed to a chair—walked to it—sat down in it—leant back, crossed his legs cosily, got up, and waved his hand to her in a manner that clearly conveyed to her that she was expected to do as he had done.

"My master's compliments and he's gone into the wine trade, and would you accept a sample?"

After all, Mr Gay's exertions had failed to convey his exact meaning to the deaf old lady.

"You astonish me," said Sir Caractacus; then, finding that she did not understand him, he rumpled his hair, opened his mouth, strained his eye-balls, and threw himself into an attitude of the most horror-struck amazement. Having made his state of mind quite clear to her, he smiled pleasantly, and nodded to her to proceed.

"If you'll kindly taste it, sir, I'll take back any orders with which you may favour me."

Sir Caractacus rang for a wineglass and proceeded to taste the sample.

"I don't know what it is, but it's not Amontillado," said he, smacking his lips; "still it is a pleasant cordial. Taste it."

The old lady seemed to gather his meaning at once. She nodded, bobbed a curtsey, and emptied the glass.

Baylis and Culpepper had not over-stated the singular effects of the "Patent Oxy-Hydrogen Love-at-First-Sight Draught." Sir Caractacus's hard and firmly-set features gradually relaxed as the old lady sipped the contents of her glass. Zorah set it down when she had quite emptied it, and as she did so her eyes met those of the good old Baronet. She blushed under the ardour of his gaze, and a tear trembled on her old eyelid.

"You're a remarkably fine woman," said Sir Caractacus, "and singularly well preserved for your age."

"Alas, kind sir," said Zorah, "I'm that hard of hearin' that cannons is whispers."

Sir Caractacus stood up, stroked his face significantly, smacked his hands together, slapped them both upon his heart, and sank on one knee at her feet. He then got up and nodded smilingly at her to imply that he really meant it.

Zorah turned aside and trembled.

"I ain't no scollard, Sir Caractacus, and I don't rightly know how a poor old 'ooman like me did ought to own her likings for a lordly barrownight—but a true 'art is more precious than diamonds they do say, and a lovin' wife is a crown of gold to her husband. I ain't fashionable, but I'm a respectable old party, and can make you comfortable if nothing else."

"Zorah, you are the very jewel of my hopes. My dear daughter will soon be taken from me. It lies with you to brighten my desolate old age. Will you be Lady Lightly ?"

And he pointed to a picture of his late wife, and went through the pantomime of putting a ring on Zorah's finger. He then indicated the despair that would possess him if she refused to accept his offer. Having achieved these feats of silent eloquence, he smiled and nodded at her reassuringly, and waited for a reply with an interrogative expression of countenance.

"Yes, dearie," murmured Zorah, as she sank into the Baronet's arms.

*　　*　　*　　*　　*　　*

After a happy half-hour Zorah felt it was her duty to return to her master, so the lovers took a fond farewell of each other, and Sir Caractacus returned to the breakfast-room.

"Jessie," said Sir Caractacus, "I think you really love your poor old father?"

"Indeed, papa, I do."

"Then you will, I trust, be pleased to hear that my declining years are not unlikely to be solaced by the companionship of a good, virtuous, and companionable woman."

"My dear papa," said Jessie, "do you really mean that—that you are likely to be married?"

"Indeed, Jessie, I think it is more than probable! You know you are going to leave me very soon, and my dear little nurse must be replaced, or what will become of me?"

Jessie's eyes filled with tears—but they were tears of joy.

"I cannot tell you papa—dear, dear, papa—how happy you have made me."

"And you will, I am sure, accept your new mamma with every feeling of respect and affection."

"Any wife of yours is a mamma of mine," said Jessie.

"My darling! Yes, Jessie, before very long I hope to lead to the altar a bride who will love and honour me as I deserve. She is no light and giddy girl, Jessie. She is a woman of sober age and staid demeanour, yet easy and comfortable in her ways. I am going to marry Mr. Gay's cook, Zorah."

" Zorah," cried Jessie, " dear, dear old Zorah ! Oh, indeed, I am very, very glad and happy ! "

" Bless you, my child," said the Baronet. " I knew my pet would not blame her poor old father for acting on the impulse of a heart that has never misled him. Yes, I think—nay, I am sure—that I have taken a wise and prudent step. Zorah is not what the world calls beautiful."

" Zorah is very good, and very clean and honest, and quite, quite sober in her habits," said Jessie warmly, " and that is worth more—far more than beauty, dear papa. Beauty will fade and perish, but personal cleanliness is practically undying, for it can be renewed whenever it discovers symptoms of decay. Oh, I am sure you will be happy ! " And Jessie hurried off to tell Stanley Gay how nobly the potion had done its work.

" Stanley, dear Stanley," said she, " I have such news—Papa and Zorah are engaged ! "

" I am very glad to hear it. She will make him an excellent wife ; it is a very auspicious beginning."

" And have *you* any news to tell me ? "

" None, except that all the bottles are distributed, and I am now waiting to see their effect. By the way, the Bishop has arrived unexpectedly, and is stopping at the Rectory, and I have sent him a bottle. I should like to find a nice little wife for the Bishop, for he has Crawleigh in his gift—the present incumbent is at the point of death, and the living is worth £1,800 a year. The duty is extremely light, and the county society unexceptional. I think I could be truly useful in such a sphere of action."

CHAPTER V.

THE action of the "Patent Oxy-Hydrogen Love-at-First-Sight Philtre" was rapid and powerful, and before evening there was scarcely a disengaged person (over thirteen years of age) in Ploverleigh. The Dowager Lady Fitz-Saracen, a fierce old lady of sixty, had betrothed herself to Alfred Creeper, of the "Three Fiddlers," a very worthy man, who had been engaged in the public trade all his life, and had never yet had a mark on his license. Colonel Pemberton, of The Grove, had fixed his affections on dear little Bessie Lane, the pupil teacher, and his son Willie (who had returned from Eton only the day before) had given out his engagement to kind old Mrs. Partlet, the widow of the late sexton. In point of fact there was only one disengaged person in the village—the good and grave old Bishop. He was in the position of the odd player who can't find a seat in the "Family Coach." But, on the whole, Stanley Gay was rather glad of this, as he venerated the good old prelate, and in his opinion there was no one in the village at that time who was really good enough to be a Bishop's wife, except, indeed, the dear little brown-haired, soft-eyed maiden to whom Stanley himself was betrothed.

So far everything had worked admirably, and the unions effected through the agency of the philtre, if they were occasionally ill-assorted as regards the stations in life of the contracting parties, were all that could be desired in every other respect. Good, virtuous straightforward, and temperate men were engaged to blameless women who were calculated to make admirable wives and mothers, and there was every prospect that Ploverleigh would become celebrated as the only Home of Perfect Happiness. There was but one sad soul in the village. The good old Bishop had drunk freely of the philtre, but there was no one left to love him. It was pitiable to see the poor love-lorn prelate as he wandered disconsolately through the smiling meadows of Ploverleigh, pouring out the accents of his love to an incorporeal abstraction.

"Something must be done for the Bishop," said Stanley, as he watched him sitting on a stile in the distance. "The poor old gentleman is wasting to a shadow."

The next morning as Stanley was carefully reading through the manuscript sermon which had been sent to him by a firm in Paternoster Row for delivery on the ensuing Sabbath, little Jessie entered his library (with Zorah) and threw herself on a sofa, sobbing as if her heart would break.

"Why, Jessie—my own little love," exclaimed Stanley. "What in the world is the matter?"

And he put his arms fondly round her waist, and endeavoured to raise her face to his.

"Oh, no—no—Stanley—don't—you musn't—indeed, indeed, you musn't."

"Why, my pet, what can you mean?"

"Oh, Stanley, Stanley—you will never, never forgive me."

"Nonsense, child," said he. "My dear little Jessie is incapable of an act which is beyond the pale of forgiveness." And he gently kissed her forehead.

"Stanley, you musn't do it—indeed you musn't."

"No, you musn't do it, Muster Gay," said Zorah.

"Why, confound you, what do you mean by interfering?" said Stanley in a rage.

"Ah, it's all very fine, I dare say, but I don't know what you're a-talking about."

And Stanley, recollecting her infirmity, explained in pantomime the process of confounding a person, and intimated that it would be put into operation upon her if she presumed to cut in with impertinent remarks.

"Stanley—Mr. Gay—" said Jessie.

"*Mr.* Gay!" ejaculated Stanley.

"I musn't call you Stanley any more."

"Great Heaven, why not?"

"I'll tell you all about it if you promise not to be violent."

And Gay, prepared for some terrible news, hid his head in his hands, and sobbed audibly.

"I loved you—oh so, so much—you were my life—my heart," said the poor little woman. "By day and by night my thoughts were with you, and the love came from my heart as the water from a well!"

Stanley groaned.

"When I rose in the morning it was to work for your happiness, and when I lay down in my bed at night it was to dream of the love that was to weave itself through my life.

He kept his head between his hands and moved not.

"My life was for your life—my soul for yours! I

drew breath but for one end—to love, to honour, to reverence you."

He lifted his head at last. His face was ashy pale.

" Come to the point," he gasped.

"Last night," said Jessie, " I was tempted to taste a bottle of the Elixir. It was but a drop I took on the tip of my finger. I went to bed thinking but of you. I rose to-day, still with you in my mind. Immediately after breakfast I left home to call upon you, and as I crossed Bullthorn's meadow I saw the Bishop of Chelsea seated on a stile. At once I became conscious that I had placed myself unwittingly under the influence of the fatal potion. Horrified at my involuntary faithlessness—loathing my miserable weakness—hating myself for the misery I was about to weave around the life of a saint I had so long adored—I could not but own to myself that the love of my heart was given over, for ever, to that solitary and love-lorn prelate. Mr. Gay (for by that name I must call you to the end), I have told you nearly all that you need care to know. It is enough to add that my love is, as a matter of course, reciprocated, and, but for the misery I have caused you, I am happy. But, full as my cup of joy may be, it will never be without a bitter after-taste, for I cannot forget that my folly—my wicked folly—has blighted the life of a man who, an hour ago, was dearer to me than the whole world ! "

And Jessie fell sobbing on Zorah's bosom.

Stanley Gay, pale and haggard, rose from his chair, and staggered to a side table. He tried to pour out a glass of water, but as he was in the act of doing so the venerable Bishop entered the room.

"Mr. Gay, I cannot but feel that I owe you some apology for having gained the affections of a young lady to whom you were attached—Jessie, my love, compose yourself."

And the Bishop gently removed Jessie's arms from Zorah's neck, and placed them about his own.

"My Lord," said Mr. Gay, "I am lost in amazement. When I have more fully realized the unparalleled misfortune that has overtaken me I shall perhaps be able to speak and act with calmness. At the present moment I am unable to trust myself to do either. I am stunned —quite, quite stunned."

"Do not suppose, my dear Mr. Gay," said the Bishop, "that I came here this morning to add to your reasonable misery by presenting myself before you in the capacity of a successful rival. No. I came to tell you that poor old Mr. Chudd, the vicar of Crawleigh has been mercifully removed. He is no more, and as the living is in my gift, I have come to tell you that, if it can compensate in any way for the terrible loss I have been the unintentional means of inflicting upon you, it is entirely at your disposal. It is worth £1,800 per annum—the duty is extremely light, and the local society is unexceptional."

Stanley Gay pressed the kind old Bishop's hand.

"Eighteen hundred a year will not entirely compensate me for Jessie."

"For Miss Lightly," murmured the Bishop, gently.

"For Miss Lightly—but it will go some way towards doing so. I accept your lordship's offer with gratitude."

"We shall always take an interest in you," said the Bishop.

"Always—always," said Jessie. "And we shall be so glad to see you at the Palace — shall we not Frederick ? "

"Well—ha—hum— yes—oh, yes, of course. Always," said the Bishop. "That is—oh, yes—always."

* * * * * *

The 14th of February was a great day for Ploverleigh, for on that date all the couples that had been brought together through the agency of the philtre were united in matrimony by the only bachelor in the place, the Rev. Stanley Gay. A week afterwards he took leave of his parishioners in an affecting sermon, and "read himself in" at Crawleigh. He is still unmarried, and likely to remain so. He has quite got over his early disappointment, and he and the Bishop and Jessie have many a hearty laugh together over the circumstances under which the good old prelate wooed and won the bright-eyed little lady. Sir Caractacus died within a year of his marriage, and Zorah lives with her daughter-in-law at the Palace. The Bishop works hard at the art of pantomimic expression, but as yet with qualified success. He has lately taken to conversing with her through the medium of diagrams, many of which are very spirited in effect, though crude in design. It is not unlikely that they may be published before long. The series of twelve consecutive sketches, by which the Bishop informed his mother-in-law that, if she didn't mind her own business, and refrain from interfering between his wife and himself, he should be under the necessity of requiring her to pack up and be off, is likely to have a very large sale.

JOHNNY POUNCE.

CHAPTER I.

HOW JOHNNY POUNCE WENT TO THE BAD.

OR rather, how the Bad came to Johnny Pounce; for Johnny Pounce was a brisk, energetic little man, with a strong sense of his own duty towards his neighbour, and a very hazy and indefinite notion of his neighbour's duty towards himself; and it has been generally observed that the folk who appear to go to the bad of their own volition are distinguished by precisely opposite characteristics, inasmuch as they are, as a rule, neither brisk nor energetic (except in the matter of language) and while they have formed the liveliest possible conception of what is due to themselves from others, appear to imagine that their obliging conduct in consenting to exist is an ample set off against any account which might otherwise have stood against them in their neighbour's books.

He had been Johnny Pounce for many years. There is in the lifetime of most Johnnies an epoch at which the last syllable is cut off from the affectionate diminutive as being a species of undignified fringe, which,

although proper and consistent when taken in con-
junction with embroidered collars, frilled trousers, and
caps of peculiar construction, resembling nothing so
much as a concertina with a tassel and a spinal affection,
is wholly inconsistent with the maturer dignity of
jackets and highlow boots, to say nothing whatever of
whiskers and the *toga virilis*. But it was otherwise
with Johnny Pounce. There existed a legend in his
family that for some years after his christening he was
addressed and referred to on all occasions, formal or
otherwise, as John, with a view to the propitiation of a
rich uncle, likewise so-called, who was then, and for
ever after until he died, Something in Demerara, and
who was known to have entertained great objections to
anything in the shape of a corruption of his own name,
and who would, it was supposed, be proportionately
gratified at his nephew's christian name being maintained
in its integrity.

But the rich uncle died insolvent of Sugar, when
Johnny Pounce was six years old, to the great indignation of the Pounce family generally, and of those
immediately interested in Johnny's welfare in particular.
They had only one way of taking it out of the rich
uncle's memory, and they availed themselves of it without delay. John became Jack upon the spot, and the
name, whenever it was used, was rapped out with an
emphatic asperity, which, although in no way referable
to any misconduct on the part of its small proprietor,
plunged that citizen into great consternation whenever
family necessities required that he should be addressed
by name. A sense of injury is seldom so deeply im-

planted, however, that time will not do much towards up-rooting it, and in the course of years a compromise was effected, and Jack became Johnny. This consummation was brought about by various causes, and among others, through the intercession of the small owner himself as he considered the emendation was not so susceptible of startling emphasis as the shorter corruption, and more-over would give him more time to collect and arrange under various heads, those senses which were generally widely scattered whenever it was necessary to address him. A stern sense of the impropriety of disturbing the average which declared that every John shall be both Johnny and Jack in the course of his existence, may have had some influence in inducing Johnny's papa (who was then in temporary employment as a census clerk) to make the alteration. As Johnny grew up, he continued so small (if one may so express oneself) and evinced a disposition so pleasantly timid and so easily imposed upon, and interpreted by such a cheery, piping little voice, that the propriety, not to say the necessity, of continuing to identify him as Johnny Pounce, was tacitly admitted as a matter of course on all sides. So as Johnny Pounce he grew up, as Johnny Pounce he fought the battle of life, in a timidly courageous sort of way, like the comic soldier in the Battle of Waterloo, who is such a terrible coward until the necessity arises of engaging six or eight cuirassiers at once.

Hitherto, that is to say up to the date of Johnny's going to the Bad, the Bad had left him pretty well to himself. Johnny was far from being a rich man, for he was an attorney's clerk, but he was almost as far

removed, or so he thought, from being a very poor one.
At the age of thirteen he entered the office of Messrs.
Pintle and Sim, gentlemen, attorneys of Her Majesty's
Courts at Westminster and solicitors of the High
Court of Chancery, at a commencing salary of seven
shillings a week. The salary was small, but then so
was Johnny, and it was understood that the two should
increase and grow up together—an arrangement which
was fortunately broken through, for at fifteen Johnny
became, physically, a constant quantity. The salary
was, however, increased by small degrees, as the un-
obtrusive virtues of the recipient became uninten-
tionally conspicuous, until at the age of fifty-five he
found himself in the possession of one hundred and
fifty pounds per annum, together with his employer's
full and undivided confidence.

Johnny had married, at the age of twenty-one, a
pleasant round-faced little body of about his own age.
She was the daughter of the housekeeper then attached
to Pintle and Sim's offices, in Carey Street, Lincoln's
Inn Fields, and by her he had a son. The son, Young
John for distinction, was a tall young fellow, who had
been decently educated by his father, and effectually
provided for by Messrs. Pintle and Sim, who had
managed to procure for him a Government appointment
—a junior assistant clerkship in the office of the Board
for the Dissemination of Pauper Philosophy. Young
Pounce was looked up to as the great Pounce Court
Card, being the representative of Majesty in the Pounce
councils, and in that capacity was played with great
effect by Mrs. Pounce, whenever it became necessary, in

contest with a fashionable lodging-letting neighbour, to assert the family respectability.

Not that the office of the Board for the Dissemination of Pauper Philosophy was an aristocratic Government office, or even an agreeable one, as far as the clerks were concerned. To be sure it was situated in White-hall, and the hours were from eleven to five, which sounded well, but any aristocratic inferences drawn from these facts would be decidedly erroneous. It was to the Pauper Philosophy Office that all those shabby, not to say dirty, young men in caps and pipes, contrasting strongly with the graceful crowd of other more fortunate Government clerks, were making their way down Parliament Street at a quarter to eleven every morning, and it was at the door of the Pauper Philosophy Office that many unceremonious arrests were made by showy Caucasians, who looked quite gentlemanly by contrast with their dispirited and shabby prisoners.

In fact the Pauper Philosophy Office, from the President of the Board and Secretary down to the assistant messengers, lived in chronic hot water, which appeared to have had the effect of boiling them hard, so particularly impracticable were all officials connected with the establishment to each other and to the world at large. The President of the Board was in hot water, because he was ostensibly responsible for the proceedings of the office; and as he was a ministerial officer who in his ministerial capacity was also responsible for the good behaviour of five-and-twenty other departments, with the intricate working of which he was supposed to become thoroughly intimate by a species of

Divine Right immediately on his taking office, he found his time fully occupied in cramming up "explanations," wherewith to satisfy the awkward demands of members with a natural taste for figures. The Secretary was in hot water because remorseless leader writers invariably spotted him as the actual author of every official bungle, and called (about three times a month) upon the country for his instant dismissal. The Under-Secretaries were in hot water because they found that the Secretary, upon Parliamentary emergencies, was so fully occupied in cramming the President, that every detail of official business was referred to them for decision—matters upon which, as one was appointed by a Liberal, and the other by a Conservative Government, they never entirely agreed; and the clerks were in hot water because they were deeply in debt, because they hated each other (looking, as they did, upon each other as the stepping-stones to a yearly increment of £10 instead of £5), and because their prospects in life were limited to the remote possibility of their attaining, one at a time, the princely salary of £300, after a forty years' apprenticeship. And finally, the messengers were in hot water because the clerks owed them money, because they owed each other money, and because hot arguments as to the comparative official superiority of clerks and messengers arose upon every occasion upon which these functionaries came into collision.

There was only one class of officials connected with the Pauper Philosophy Department, which appeared to enjoy a comparative immunity from the general feeling of unhappiness and discontent which pervaded the office. These were the Examiners; a dozen or so of gentlemen who were appointed (for no reason that clearly appeared) at a salary of £300, rising (for no obvious cause) by large yearly instalments to £800. It was required of these gentlemen that they should smoke pipes, drink beer, make bets, come when they liked, go when they liked, do what they liked, and be saddled with no responsibility whatever. These twelve gentlemen were the stock mystery of the Civil Service. More questions were asked in the House about these functionaries than about any other minor topic of Parliamentary discussion, and they were naturally proud of the interest they excited. Sometimes, to be sure, this interest grew to rather too unwieldly dimensions to be pleasant, and in such cases it would become the duty of one of them to manufacture a return calculated to show, beyond all dispute, that the whole work of the Pauper Philosophy Office was, in point of fact, discharged by them, whereupon they would be much complimented in an indirect sort of way, and the subject allowed to drop for a time.

On Christmas Eve, in the year of grace 1854, Johnny Pounce entertained a small circle of his more intimate friends. Johnny lived on a second floor in Great Queen Street, Lincoln's Inn Fields, and on the second floor in question were assembled besides Johnny Pounce, and his wife, and his son John, Mr. and Mrs. Jemmy Feather, and Mr. Jemmy Feather, junior. Mr. Feather made a good thing of it as a clerk to Bolter, Q.C. Jemmy Feather was a short, stoutish, middle-aged gentleman, with a highly respectable gold chain, a

responsible-looking shirt pin, and a gold ring which was
a reference in itself. Mrs. Feather was a weazen little
body, with over lady-like manners, and a tendency to
be ultra-genteel. Mr. Feather, junior, was fifteen,
and in collars and straps. He was also in Bolter,
Q.C.'s chambers as a sort of under-clerk and beer-
fetcher. This fact was carefully concealed from Mrs.
Feather, who had been deluded by her designing husband into the idea that Mr. Feather, junior, spent his
day in an arm-chair, settling pleas and declarations
all day long, and occasionally meeting in consultation
such attorneys as his employer could not conveniently
find time to see. This hypothetical and rosy view of
the case reconciled his mamma to his entering the
service of a Queen's Counsel in such large practice that
his clerk drew about £300 a year in fees alone. Then
there was Joe Round, Mrs. Joe Round, and Miss Joe
Round, and Miss Joe Round's young man, in a pink
fluffy face, and blue stock with gold flies. Joe Round
was Deputy Usher at the Central Criminal Court. He
was a big, full-voiced man, with a red face, black curly
hair, and a self-assertive manner. He had a way with
him which seemed to say, "I am Joe Round. Take
me as you find me, or let me go, but don't find fault."
Mrs. Joe Round was a beautiful specimen of faded
gentility. She was an Old Bailey attorney's daughter,
and a taste for exciting trials had led her in early youth
to the C.C.C., where she saw Joe Round, fell in love
with his big voice, and married him. Miss Round was
a rather pretty girl, with flirting, aggravating ways,
which threatened to drive Miss Round's young man

(who was a Toast-master) into a state of utter despera-
tion. John Pounce, the younger, was present, but sat
apart, in a moody, sulky way, that created considerable
astonishment; for John was a strapping, good-looking
young-fellow, with plenty to say for himself, and always,
on occasions of festivity, in good humour.

The evening had been spent as most conventional
Christmas Eves are. There is a fearful ordeal to be
gone through by all who wish to see Christmas-day in
according to rule, and this ordeal is called Forfeits. By
way of atonement for an imaginary crime you are
required to perform an enigmatical and apparently impossible task. As there exist only about six of these
supplicia, and as everybody has known them, and their
solution by heart from the age of four, and as the tasks,
when known, are of the simplest possible description, it
is difficult to see in what particular feature the amusement consists. In nearly all cases the penalty in-
volves kisses to be bestowed on young ladies present,
which is an insulting view to take of what is usually
looked upon as a favour, and places the recipients,
moreover, in an embarrassing position. As there was
only one young lady present, Miss Round, she became
as a matter of course the implement of torture, to the
aggravation of the pink young toast-master who
appeared to be doing the reverse of drinking everybody's
health, and making no exception in favour of young
John, between whom and Miss Round an excellent
understanding seemed to exist.

Supper had been laid, devoured, and removed, and a
fragrant liquor looking like clear soup, but being, in

point of fact, rum-punch, had taken its place. Cheery little Johnny Pounce was ladling it out of a very large bowl into very small glasses, with a skill which argued an extensive practice, extending over a large number of consecutive Christmas Eves.

Johnny Pounce was eminently loyal, and there were three toasts that invariably obtained at his meetings, the Queen, Church and State, and the Firm.

"Ladies and gentlemen," he said, in proposing the last toast, "I call it still the Firm, though it's a Firm no longer except in name. Mr. Sim, as you have heard me say, left the business three years since, and he's now in Melbourne doing his ten thousand a year, God bless him. It's my conviction, gentlemen, that if ever there was a better-hearted man than Pintle that gentleman is Sim, and if ever there existed a nobler old gentleman than Sim that old gentleman is Pintle. They were good to me when I was a boy no higher than—than I am now, gentlemen, and they've made a man of me, and they've given me my old wife there (hear, hear)—my old wife there, who's looking just the same in my old eyes as she did thirty years ago, gentlemen. ("Go along, Johnny, do," from Mrs. Pounce). She's stuck to me through thick and thin, for I've had a hardish time of it, take one thing with another, and here I am thrown high and dry beyond the reach, as I humbly believe, of poverty, with my boy here—look up, young John—with my boy here a-serving the Queen ; (John, my boy, fill up)—a-serving the Queen, God bless her, and doing more to make his old dad's heart happy, by doing that for ninety pound a year than if he was managing a bank with five hundred.

Gentlemen, this is all Pintle and Sim, and what I say is, Here's the health of Pintle and Sim, and God bless 'em. The Firm, gentlemen."

The toast was received with all enthusiasm.

"Why, young John," said Johnny. "Cheer up, lad, you're terribly down-hearted to-night!"

"What's it all about, John?" said Jemmy Feather. "Give it a name, young John."

"I think Mr. John must be in love," said Miss Round.

"Nonsense, I'm all right, father. Don't mind me. I'm a bit low to-night, but it's nothing to speak of."

"Now, Mr. John," said Miss Round, "I insist upon your cheering up. It's a very bad compliment you're paying me; I declare you haven't spoken a word to me all the evening." And Miss Round assumed a becoming pout which had worked great things in bringing the young toast-master to the point.

The effect of the usually successful pout was quite lost upon Mr. John, who fidgetted upon his chair in an unsatisfactory and discontented way. Not so, however, upon the toast-master, who, remembering the effect the pout in question had had upon him in happier days, regarded young John with feelings of the bitterest hate. He was, of course, unable to convey any verbal expression of his sentiments on this point, so he contented himself with silently drinking innumerable ironical toasts, all of which professed to invoke blessings without number on the head of the young man.

A knock was heard at the door, and a drabby maid-servant put her head in.

"Mr. Pounce, sir, you're wanted."

"Eh, what, Maria, me wanted? Why, who wants Johnny Pounce at half-past twelve on Christmas morning?"

"It's a gentleman, sir. It's from the Firm. He's in the back room."

"God bless me, at this time of night! Excuse me, old friends, for a moment; I'll be with you again directly. Here, young John, take my place, my boy, and give 'em a song: I'll be back directly." And Johnny Pounce left the room.

Young John could not in strictness be complimented upon his conduct in the chair. The song which his father had suggested on leaving the room was loudly called for.

"Now, young John," said Round. "The song. Silence in court."

"Oh, do, Mr. John," chorused the ladies.

"For my sake," added Miss Round.

"Yes, for *her* sake," muttered the toast-master ironically.

"Look here," said John, "I'm not in cue for singing, and that's the long and short of it. Hang it all. Can't you see that?"

It could be seen, and very plainly, too. The poor fellow presented a depressing specimen of a convivial chairman.

"I believe it's usual to sing when called on," said the toast-master. "At least, that's the rule."

"Hear, hear," from Feather. "Now, gents, what do you say? The prisoner at the bar stands on his deliverance."

"Ha! ha! Good that. 'Stands on his deliverance.' So he does." This from Round.

"Now, gents, you shall well and truly try; eh, Round, my boy?"

"Certainly," said the usher. "'Well and truly try! Well said Jemmy. Good. Well and truly try. And true deliverance make.'"

Whether the result of this combination of forces, backed up as it was by the majesty of the Law, would have had the desired effect is uncertain, for at that moment Johnny Pounce entered the room as pale as a ghost.

"We're very glad you've come, Mr. Pounce," said Mrs. Feather, "young John is quite refractory; he won't sing, do what we can. Why, dear me, Mr. Pounce, what on earth's the matter?"

"There must be no more singing to-night; an awful thing has happened. Mr. Pintle fell down dead half-an-hour ago."

And Johnny Pounce dropped into his chair, and covered his face with his hands.

"Good God, Johnny! Dead!" said Mrs. Pounce; "Mr. Pintle dead!"

"Yes, dead; and me drinking his health not ten minutes since. Old friends, you'll forgive me, I know; but I'm afraid we must break up; it's an awful thing."

"And you a-drinking of his health!" reflected the toast-master, with an air which suggested that he regretted the circumstance as having a tendency to lessen the general belief in the efficacy of toasts, and, indirectly, in his professional importance.

The company arose to go amid an awkward silence, which was broken by occasional and spasmodic efforts at commonplace consolation.

The having to go away gave a heartless effect to the behaviour of the company; it seemed so like deserting a friend in the hour of need; but there was no help for it, and one by one, almost silently, the visitors took their departure.

"It's a dreadful thing," said Johnny, when he and his wife and son were left alone. "Disease of the heart: sudden, quite sudden; dropped down in his chair, and me sent to, to give up his papers; I must be off to the office."

"Oh, Johnny, Johnny! What are we to do? Poor Mr. Pintle! Such a fine old gentleman, and ten years more life you could have declared to; the picture of health he always was. Poor Mr. Pintle!"

And Johnny Pounce wrapped himself in a great-coat and shawl, and hurried through the driving snow across Lincoln's Inn Fields to Carey Street.

The visitors (for they were two) who had so unceremoniously disturbed Johnny's party were waiting for him in a hansom at the office door. One of them was an errand-boy, whose faculties seemed to be quite dispersed by the frightful occurrence which had just taken place, and which, in fact, he had almost witnessed. The other was a tall, dark, gentlemanly man, with a heavy black moustache and military bearing. He was John Redfern, the late Mr. Pintle's nephew and heir-at-law, and he held a captain's commission in a cavalry regiment. The mission upon which he had come was to fetch the will which was known to be in the office, together with such other documents as might refer to the affairs of the dead man, and to seal all cupboards, doors, and safes.

"Oh! here you are," said Captain Redfern. "What a deuce of a time you've been! Now, we'll get the will and other papers, and then you must come down with them to Russell Square, and deliver them into Mrs. Pintle's custody."

Poor Johnny opened the office door with some difficulty, for his hand shook violently, and his eyes were blinded with big tears. Although he winked and blinked hard at them, they couldn't take the hint, but rolled down his face until their identity was lost in that of the melting snow on his woollen comforter.

"Mr. Pintle's will, sir, is in this box; shall I take it to Russell Square, sir, or unlock it here?"

"Better open it now," said Captain Redfern; "Mrs. Pintle is, of course, greatly distressed, and would be unable to attend to it at present. Open it; will you?"

The box was opened, but no will was there: and the papers it contained referred only to mortgages effected upon his real property. Poor Johnny stood utterly dismayed, as he had a perfect recollection of having seen Mr. Pintle place it there a few days before his death.

"There is no will here, sir, and, yet, he always told me to look here for it if ever he was carried off suddenly. What's more, I saw him put it in here not three days ago. It was the day before yesterday when he kindly added a codicil, which increased the sum he was good enough to leave to me, sir; I'm his confidential clerk, sir, and have been for fifteen years, and he'd have told me if——"

"Well, but isn't there any other receptacle into which he may have placed it? Think now. Don't stand staring there, but bustle about and find it."

"Captain Redfern, I'm doing my best to think, but my head's not strong, and I've been terribly shook, sir. There are the drawers of his private table; it's the only place I can think of."

The drawers of the desk were opened one by one, and their contents overhauled. Memoranda, important letters that required his personal attention, stationery, and other matters of a similar nature, were there, but no will.

"I'm quite lost, sir," said Johnny. "It's the most extraordinary thing! He would never have distroyed it without telling me."

"Come along, you boy," said Captain Redfern to the office lad. "You can go," he added to Pounce. "I keep you on at your salary another week, during which time you will be always here in case you're wanted. At the end of the week you go. Take this as notice to quit. Stop: seal up the inner room;" and sealed up the inner room was.

Captain Redfern and the boy got into the hansom, and drove off to Russell Square. Old Johnny Pounce, completely staggered by what had occurred, locked the outer door, and trudged back through the cold slush to Great Queen Street.

His wife and son were still sitting up, talking over the event of the evening, when Johnny entered. The mother had evidently been recapitulating the chances of Johnny Pounce having been comfortably provided for;

and young John listened sulkily, but with interest nevertheless.

"Well, Johnny, back again! Now you just drink this right off before you say another word;" and she handed him a big tumbler of punch, which she had kept hot for him during his absence.

"No, no, my dear, no punch. It's a most extraordinary thing, but there's no will to be found. He must have destroyed it since the day before yesterday, and I've notice to go this day week. Thus ends forty-five years' faithful service!"

"Oh! Johnny!" sobbed his wife.

"Young John, my boy," said his father, "there's no knowing how long I may be without employment; for I'm an old man, John, and it'll be poor work, whatever it is. You're the head of the family now, young John, and it's your turn to show yourself equal to the position. You're the Queen's servant, John, and a gentleman. John, my boy, we must look to you."

"Don't look to me, father, for much," said young John, "for I got the sack this morning."

CHAPTER II.

HOW JOHNNY POUNCE SPENT A CONSIDERABLE TIME AT THE BAD.

THIS was a terrible blow to Johnny Pounce and his wife, who had a restless time of it that night. He knew very well that Mr. Pintle had made a will, and further, that his, Johnny Pounce's, name, was down in it for a thousand pounds, which was a sum sufficient to render him independent for life. If the will turned up, which appeared unlikely, all would be well; if not, the family prospects were particularly unsatisfactory. He was thrown out of employment, with no immediate prospect of obtaining anything half so good (for he was getting on in years), and had saved but little money, for he knew, or felt sure that he knew, that Pintle and Sim would never let him starve. Moreover, his son, whom he looked upon as the only prop and stay of the family respectability, had that day been ignominiously discharged from his clerkship.

And the manner of his dismissal was this. He had a few days before, in resisting a piece of unnecessary petty tyranny on the part of a fellow clerk in temporary charge of his department, used stronger language than was absolutely necessary. This was reported to the secretary. Now, the secretary had a double-action, back-handed way of dealing with complaints between " hands " (as he delighted to call them) of nearly equal rank, and the usual remedy was adopted on this occasion. Fox (the complainant) was rebuked for having used unnecessary tyranny, but it was shown that young John was doubly culpable, for he not only resisted the order, which he should have obeyed and then complained of, but he had also sworn a bad oath, and otherwise misconducted himself (being a hot-headed young fellow) to the annihilation of all order and discipline. So it was ordered that young John should forthwith publicly apologize to the miscreant Fox, which young John resolutely declined to do. So My Lords deliberated on the state of the case, and the result of the deliberation was that young John was required to deliver over into My Lords' hands his resignation of the appointment he held under them.

A more miserable young man than young John was on the afternoon of Christmas Eve probably never stepped out of a government office. He was absolutely penniless and particularly deeply in debt—in a small vulgar way—besides. He had borrowed £5 from a loan office, and he was in debt to the amount of some pounds to the tavern-keeper who supplied his dinner. His tailor and boot-maker had for months been a source of anxiety to him, sleeping and waking; and a miserable bit of kite-flying (of which he expected to hear more on the 1st of February) exercised a depressing influence over him, which appeared to increase in geometrical proportion as the day approached.

As a set-off to these claims, he had his half-quarter's cheque on the Postmaster-General for about £12, and a letter from the secretary accepting his resignation in My Lords' name.

Young John had, however, quite made up his mind as to his future course. The Crimean War was then in full swing, the battles of the Alma and Inkerman had both been fought in the course of the last three or four months, and the demand for young and active fellows to fill up the lists of the dead was unprecedented.

There were recruiting sergeants at every street-corner in Westminster, who talked with robust eloquence of the glories of the war—which they had not seen—and of the rollicking character of the life in the trenches—of which they had formed but vague and imperfect notions. Liberal bounty and a free kit were offered as a temptation, should the war itself be an insufficient attraction. Of the starving (with plenty within grasp, only under lock and key); of the dying for want of medicines and bandages, with stores of drugs and bales of lint within pistol-shot (only stowed in ship-holds); of the freezing, with new overcoats and rugs in tens of thousands a mile away (only under seal) nothing was said. In point of fact, of these matters very little was known in England. Young John had made up his mind that morning that he would take the shilling of the first smart cavalry serjeant who hailed him, so he spent an hour or two in writing a letter to his father and mother (enclosing his cheque on the Postmaster-General duly signed) and in packing up a scanty wardrobe, the greater part of which he determined to sell. He left his home before daybreak on Christmas morning, and bore away straight for a public-house in Charles Street, Westminster, the headquarters of a party of cavalry recruiting sergeants.

He soon found what he wanted. A non-commissioned officer of the 13th Light Dragoons was down upon him in a hail-fellow-well-met sort of way, with an affectation of joviality intended to convey an idea of what a particularly rollicking thing a soldier's life must be. Young John soon entered into conversation with the sergeant, and the sergeant, who was a liberal-hearted dog, stood a pot of beer (because it was Christmas-day) which they drank together.

Young Johnny asked few questions of the sergeant, but those that he did ask had reference principally to the nature of the life in store for him.

"Well," said the sergeant, summarizing the whole thing, "look here; eight in the morning *revolly*—up you get. You can get up at eight, can't you?"

Johnny thought he could manage it at a pinch.

"That's lucky. Well, you have an hour to dress; then comes breakfast—coffee or chocolate, bread and butter, and eggs or what not. Then once a week mornin' stables; twice a week adjutants' parade, one hour; other days, nothing except when for guard or fatigue, which comes (say) once a month. One o'clock, dinner – soup or fish (seldom both), and jint; pudden very rare. Then nothin' till six; six, evenin' stables once a week; other days, reading out loud, half-an-hour. Then nothin' till tattoo, which in crack regiments is mostly half-past eleven. At tattoo, roll-call, and bed. That's the programme."

Young John made some allowance for the gallant fellow's enthusiasm; extreme love of a profession often invests it with an attractive colouring.

"I joined eighteen months ago," the sergeant continued. "I'm but a young soldier, as you see, but I rose. In six weeks I was made a corporal with 5*s*. 9*d*. a day; in six more I was troop sergeant, with 8*s*. 4*d*. That's what I'm getting now; 8*s*. 4*d*. ain't bad for eighteen months. You'd do it in half the time."

"Now look here," said John. "Don't tell unnecessary lies. If the service was the worst on the face of the earth, I'd join it, because I've what people call, gone wrong, and I want to get away from this. I'm a strongish chap, and about the sort of man you fellows want ; so hand over the shilling. My name's John Cole ; age twenty-two ; previous occupation, clerk."

The sergeant vowed he was the very man he wanted. He admired pluck, he said, and had cut himself away from a lucrative profession because he wanted to see what blood was like. Most of the men in crack cavalry regiments were young barristers of arts or medical doctors, with here and there a young nobleman or two, under an assumed name. These young men had cut from home because their relentless parents, having set their face against the army as a profession, had refused to buy them commissions. That was his case. He was a barrister of arts once ; now he was troop-sergeant in Her Majesty's 13th Light, and thank God, *he* said.

All this was satisfactory, as far as it went, and young John Pounce was duly enlisted, under the name of John Cole, by the friendly sergeant. The subsequent medical examination and attestation were properly and satisfactorily undergone, and Private John Cole, of Her Majesty's 13th Light Dragoons, was drafted off to the regimental *dépôt*, and thence in about six weeks to the Crimea.

A thoroughly sleepless night is a fearful thing to undergo. It is bad enough when that sleeplessness is the result of sharp pain or irritating fever, but when it comes of a distressed or a disheartened mind, it is absolutely terrible. Poor old Johnny Pounce had a bad time of it that Christmas night. He tossed and rolled about, and changed the side of his pillow, and then, when it turned out that that energetic step was barren of good result, he got out of bed, and walked up and down the room; then he got into bed again and counted five thousand. "Five thousand" found him rather more wakeful if possible than he was when he began, so he gave up counting to listen to the ticking of the old Dutch clock. But the old Dutch clock called so loudly for "Linkman Toddles! Linkman Toddles! Linkman Toddles!" that he began to wish that functionary would appear, and satisfy the clamorous old instrument. Toddles not turning up, the clock gave him up for a bad job, and in despair at Toddles' want of faith, ticked out plaintively, "Come, Dyspepsia! Come, Dyspepsia! Come, Dyspepsia!" This awful invocation was too much for poor Johnny, who got out of bed once more, and finally stopped the dreadful machine. As morning broke, he fell into a restless tossing sleep, which only had the effect of giving him a racking headache. When he finally awoke, it was with a dull heavy sense of some fearful misfortune which had just happened to him, and when the events of the preceding night broke suddenly upon him, he buried his old head in his pillow, and sobbed aloud.

Matters were not mended by the discovery of the letter which young John had placed on the sitting-room table. It hardly wanted this to complete the family misery, and old Johnny and his wife were absolutely thunder-struck by this fresh misfortune. The letter did not say where young John was going, nor did it give any clue to the step that he was about to take. It merely said that he was going away for a while; and that if he could save any money he would send it from time to time to a post-office in the neighbourhood; that they were not to fret for him, as he would be sure to turn up sooner or later; that the cheque for £12 was for their use; that his dismissal was not attended by any disgraceful circumstances, and that he was their ever-loving son, Johnny Pounce.

Old Johnny's indignation at this desertion was unbounded.

" So that's my son, is it? That's my fair-weather son, whom I've brought up, and educated, and clothed, and fed, and whom the firm made a gentleman of. What'll the firm think of this, after all their kindness? "

Mrs. Pounce mildly reminded her husband that the firm was in Heaven.

" True, true—I forgot. If he'd only given us a hint as to where he was going; if he'd shaken his old dad's hand and kissed his old mother before he left, I could have forgiven him. But to desert his old parents just as soon as he found out that they were penniless and could help him no longer, was that like a son of ours, Emma? "

" Well, Johnny, for the matter of that, it may be that he was fearful of being an encumbrance. He's left his half-quarter's salary for us, and I'm afraid the poor boy has gone forth into the world without a penny in his pocket. I'd make a better breakfast this morning for the knowledge beyond doubt that he'd had one too. Perhaps he's hungry, Johnny."

" Hungry, Emma? Young John hungry, and me a-pegging away into bread and meat, and his half-quarter's cheque a-staring me in the face, and him hungry! What a dreadful thing to think of, old girl. Poor young John!"

They were not long in coming to the conclusion that he had enlisted. Johnny's duties called him to Carey Street, although it was Christmas-day, but Mrs. Johnny made it her business to wander about recruiting *dépôts* all day. Young John, however, carefully kept himself inside the public-house, and gave the friendly recruiting sergeant, who was not quite so friendly now— that professional gentleman having cooled down amazingly since the morning—a hint that he might possibly be sought for. So Mrs. Pounce's efforts were utterly fruitless.

Johnny spent every day of that ensuing week at the office. It was difficult at first to persuade oneself that that chair would never be filled by Mr. Pintle again; that the ruler, paper-weight, gum-bottle, pens, ink, and scissors, left as he had left them day after day for fifty years, had been arranged in their methodical order by him for the last time. The conveyancing clerk and the common law clerk were paid their salaries and dismissed by Captain Redfern, the heir-at-law, who was closeted all day long with old Johnny, going over various deeds, and making himself intimate with all the affairs of the dead man. On the Saturday evening old Johnny was paid his last week's salary of three pounds, and was informed that his services would for the future be dispensed with.

Old Johnny spent many a weary day, and trudged many a weary mile through snow and slush, after fresh employment. He was known and respected by many of Pintle's clients, and also by solicitors who had been opposed to Pintle and Sim; but he could get little from them. The fact that no will had been found, although it was admitted by Johnny that one had been made and deposited in his custody two days before Pintle's death, argued either gross carelessness or gross felony on the part of the confidential clerk; and, added to this, he was a feeble old man, and quite past learning new duties. A few of his better friends subscribed small sums for the old man's maintenance, and others gave his wife needlework, so that for some weeks they were kept from absolute want. But these weekly subscriptions dwindled down, one by one, as the recollection of old Johnny and his distress became less vivid, until at last they had nothing to depend on but a weekly five shillings, the subscription of a stauncher friend than the rest.

In his extreme distress he made an appeal to Mrs. Pintle. He dressed himself as neatly as his reduced circumstances would allow, and presented himself at her house in Russell Square. He had been there once before since Mr. Pintle's death, to ask permission to follow his old employer to the grave, but he was curtly informed that Captain Redfern would require him in the office that day, and therefore he could not be present. This rebuff, conveyed to him by a weak-eyed flunkey, who called him " my man," had had the effect of preventing his applying to Mrs. Pintle for assistance hitherto; but emboldened by hunger, and more especially by the thinning face of his once chubby little wife, he determined to put his pride in his pocket, and encounter the weak-eyed one once more.

The weak-eyed one was just in the transition state between a very old page and a very young footman. His precise functions in Mrs. Pintle's household were as indefinite as his age, for his duties extended from cleaning the windows to driving (at a pinch) the brougham. He was engaged in the familiar but necessary duty of cleaning the knives when Johnny called, and as Johnny inadvertently pulled the visitor's bell, the weak-eyed one was under the necessity of exchanging the linen jacket of domestic life for the black coat and worsted epaulette of ceremony, and of making other radical improvements in his personal appearance, before he opened the door. This functionary had, from a great many years' apprenticeship at opening street doors, taught himself to look upon society as divided into two great heads or groups—visitors and servants; and he who was not a visitor, was, from the weak-eyed one's point of view, a servant. He considered that a man's social position was typified by the bell he rang, and as there existed no intermediate bell for the numerous classes of callers who certainly could not aspire to the dignity of being visitors in the ordinary acceptation of the term, and who were equally far from being in the position of domestic servants, he recognised no intermediate class between the honoured drawing-room caller and the boy who brought the servants' beer. Avowedly a servant himself, he was affable, and, in a weak-eyed way, even cheerful, to those who identified themselves with the humbler bell; but he who, without due excuse, rang a bell which implied that he was a drawing-room visitor, became on the spot the object of the weak-eyed one's unutterable loathing and foul scorn.

Wretched Johnny stood on the steps waiting for the opening of the door, and improving the opportunity by blowing his frozen nose, that he might not be compelled to the commission of that indecency before Mrs. Pintle. Eventually it opened, and the weak-eyed one stood before him in all the respectable magnificence of expensive mourning.

"Well, what is it?" said that retainer, as soon as he had taken Johnny's measure, and assured himself of Johnny's want of title to the dignity to which he had aspired.

Now "What is it?" is a peculiarly aggravating form of address, and one which is much affected by haughty menials, Bank of England clerks, ushers in courts of law, and other insolent and overbearing underlings. Providence, however, who seldom inflicts a bane without producing an antidote, has mercifully endowed the questioned one with the power of making the return enquiry, "What is what?" which, being unanswerable, has the effect of invariably shutting up, humbling, and morally squashing the miserable flunkey whose misconduct brings it down upon him.

Johnny, however, being depressed in mind, enfeebled in body, and entertaining altogether the poorest possible opinion of himself and his claims to an honourable reception, and, moreover, not being aware of the magnificent revenge which lay within his grasp, humbly replied that he should be glad to see Mrs. Pintle, if convenient.

"What might you wish with Mrs. Pintle?" asked the weak-eyed one.

"I am the late Mr. Pintle's confidential clerk; I wish to speak to her in that capacity."

"Oh! indeed, sir, walk in," said the weak-eyed one, not feeling altogether sure that Johnny had not succeeded notwithstanding the depressing seediness of his appearance, in establishing his title to the visitor's bell after all. He perhaps thought that this melancholy state of things was the natural result of the absorbing nature of the confidences which had been reposed in Johnny by Mr. Pintle. The Queen's Counsel, who dined now and then at the house, were seedy, so, after all, that was no rule. So he showed Johnny into the library, and shortly returned with the information that Mrs. Pintle was in the drawing-room and would see him there. So Johnny walked up the softly-carpeted staircase, with much internal flutter, and much external mopping, and moreover, with much internal clearing of his husky throat. He found Mrs. Pintle dressed in the deepest black, and reclining in a spineless way on a comfortable sofa.

Mrs. Pintle was a lady of fifty, or thereabouts. She was a lank, limp lady, with pale straw-coloured hair turning grey, in that slack-baked pie-crust looking way peculiar to straw-coloured hair in middle age. She was a perfect monument of bombazine, crape, bugles, and jet, and if the depth of her sorrow could be fathomed in any way by reference to the funereal character of her appearauce, she must have been a wife to be proud of. The memorial erected in Kensal Green to the late Mr. Pintle's memory, covered as it was with Scriptural references (which were, no doubt, anxiously overhauled by all visitors to that cheerful spot immediately on their reaching home), was an admirable conventional tombstone, as tombstones go, but it was entirely eclipsed in efficacy by Mrs. Pintle herself, who possessed peripatetic advantages which carried a mournful recollection of the deceased lawyer into the very bosom of her visiting acquaintance. The only question was as to the comparative duration of the two monuments. Every article of furniture which admitted of black drapery was smothered in it, and the envelopes and note-paper were black, with a small white parallelogram in the centre. As you gazed on this melancholy state of things, you were almost tempted to wonder how it came to pass the pie-crust hair had not been placed in mourning also.

Johnny was immensely impressed by this dismal spectacle, and was much pleased at the contradiction it gave to the popular rumour that Mr. and Mrs. Pintle had not spent a particularly happy life together. He bowed with much reverence, an act which Mrs. Pintle acknowledged with a movement of the head, which bore the same relation to an ordinary nod that the Old Hundredth does to an Irish jig.

" You were my dear husband's clerk, I believe," she remarked.

Johnny bowed.

" You can take a chair, if you have anything to say."

So Johnny sat down on the edge of a very low *pric-*

Dieu chair, which was the only available seat immediately at hand, and twitched nervously at his old hat ; an operation which seemed likely to result in the immediate dissolution of that article of apparel. It is always an awkward thing, that hat. There are only three classes of visitors who are permitted to know what to do with it when they take it into a house which is not their own. The friend of the family, who comes to spend the evening, leaves it with the man in the hall ; the ordinary visitor places it on an unoccupied chair, and the carpenter deposits it on the ground ; but all others are required to hold it in their hands during an interview, and yet, if possible, to keep it out of sight. Johnny's was a self-assertive hat, which did not admit of easy concealment ; so he fidgeted it about until it actually appeared to be taking a prominent part in the conversation.

"Now, then," said Mrs. Pintle, "what do you want ? I suppose it's nothing about the will ? "

"Nothing about the will, ma'am. I've not been in the way of hearing about it lately."

"Well, then, what in goodness's name do you want ? Speak out, man, and have done with it."

Mrs. Pintle was one of that numerous class of mourners whose grief takes the form of irritability. Besides, she had jumped to the conclusion that Johnny's visit referred to the missing document, and was disappointed.

"Ma'am, I've never done this before, but it's help I've come for. I've been Mr. Pintle's clerk, man and boy, for five-and-forty year ; and—and now I'm in want, ma'am. I'm in absolute want. I've not come," said Johnny, hurriedly, anxious that he should not be misunderstood, "I've not come, ma'am, to mention that in the hopes that your kindness will immediately —will immediately—" (and he paused for a way of expressing it, and then added triumphantly) "will immediately put me right. God forbid. But if you would kindly put me or my wife (she's a young woman still) in the way of earning a livelihood—we don't care how humble it is, or how hard the work—we shall be deeply grateful."

"Is that all?" said Mrs. Pintle, with a cold official air which did not promise well.

"I've no more to say, ma'am," added he, "except that I've been living in a sort of way, on charity mostly, for the last six weeks. I've tried to get work, and failed. I don't know how it is, but I've failed. I'm not young, ma'am, but I've got plenty of work left in me, if I could only find some one who wants it."

"*That* is all, I presume?"

"That is all, ma'am."

"Then listen to me. My husband made a will—you know that?"

Poor Johnny knew it perfectly well. It had been the leading fact in his thoughts for weeks past, and there was no chance of his forgetting it. So he bowed.

"Very good. You know that my husband made a will. He placed it under your care. He gave it to you on the 22nd December. He died at midnight on the 24th. No will was to be found on the night of the 24th, and you have been unable or unwilling to produce it since.

I don't know which, nor do I care. You can draw your own conclusions. Now, you can go."

It burst upon Johnny all at once; a sort of suspicion appeared to attach itself to him that he knew more about the missing document than he cared to say. This was the solution of the difficulty he had in getting employment from solicitors whom he had known, and with whom he had been friendly in brighter days.

"Mrs. Pintle," he exclaimed, "listen to me for one moment. Is it possible that I am suspected of having suppressed Mr. Pintle's will. It is a horrible thing to have to say in connection with one's self, but you seem to think that I know more than I have said. Good God! ma'am! why I am the greatest sufferer by its not being found. I am a legatee for £1,000. If it had turned up, my wife and I should have been independent by this time. As it is, my wife is dreadfully ill from want, and I have not a penny in my pocket—not a penny, not a penny!"

And old Johnny fairly gave way, and sobbed like a child on the crown of the self-assertive old hat.

"Will you oblige me by ringing that bell?" said Mrs. Pintle.

Johnny obeyed, and the weak-eyed one responded to the summons.

"Give this person some bread and cheese in the kitchen, and then show him out," said Mrs. Pintle.

Johnny got up, brushed the obtrusive hat the wrong way with a trembling hand, and silently turned about and followed the retainer down stairs. When he reached the foot, he made for the street door.

" Didn't you hear missus say you was to have some food ? " said the weak-eyed one.

But Johnny made no reply. He tugged at the street door with the view of getting into the open air as soon as possible. It was a complicated street door, with five or six small handles, and it was only to be opened by a combined tugging of two handles at once.

The weak-eyed one sauntered up to him, with his hands in his pockets, and watched Johnny's efforts with much complacency.

" Go on, old boy, try again. Never give it up, go in and win." These and other remarks of an encouraging description, intended to spur Johnny on to fresh exertion, had the effect of irritating the poor old gentleman beyond all bounds.

" Damn you; open it, you dog, will you ? " exclaimed Johnny with (for him) supernatural vehemence. And the weak-eyed one obeyed with an alacrity which one would have scarcely looked for in a man who a moment before was taking life in such a leisurely manner.

Johnny tottered down the steps, shaking and trembling, and the weak-eyed one contemplated him from the door.

" Poor devil ! " exclaimed he. " Mad as flints ; quite as mad ! "

And Johnny tottered on bravely, until he reached the corner of Guilford Street. He then began to feel that his strength was almost at an end ; so he made an effort to turn round the corner, in order to get out of sight of the insolent flunkey, and that accomplished, fell heavily to the ground.

CHAPTER III.

HOW JOHNNY POUNCE CAME BACK TO THE GOOD AGAIN.

" Cole, I shall want you at my quarters immediately after inspection."

" Very good, sir."

The scene of this remarkable dialogue was the Crimea before Sebastopol; the speakers were our old friend Captain Redfern of Her Majesty's 16th Lancers, and Private John Cole of the same regiment, and regimental servant to Captain Redfern aforesaid.

Young John had proved to be too tall a man, and too heavy for the friendly recruiting-sergeant's corps, so he had been posted to a crack Lancer regiment then serving in the Crimea. In this regiment Captain Redfern held a commission, and as he went out in command of recruits, of whom young John was one, he was under the necessity of selecting one of them to act as a regimental servant during the voyage. His choice fell upon young John, who being extremely lazy and, moreover, utterly indifferent as to the future in store for him, accepted the situation.

Redfern and John got on exceedingly well together. John's superior education made him extremely useful to his master in many ways, and as Redfern was a particularly open-handed man, he and John became, in a distant sort of way, attached to each other. Redfern spent much of his spare time in poring over deeds and other legal documents referring to the estate of which he had become possessed through Pintle's death ; and as

John was formerly in the habit of assisting his father in Mr. Pintle's office, he had picked up sufficient technical knowledge to make himself useful as an interpreter whenever Redfern (whose legal ideas were crude and elementary) found himself at a stand-still.

Captain Redfern's regiment was posted on the heights above Balaklava, but as he was attached temporarily to the staff of a general officer, his duties as aide-de-camp brought him continually on to the scene of action before Sebastopol. He had on this occasion been in attendance on his general at a division field-day in which his own regiment took part, and he availed himself of an opportunity of interchanging the few words already recorded with his regimental servant before the parade was dismissed.

At the termination of the parade in question, young John cleaned his horse and accoutrements, and then hurried off to Redfern's tent. He found his master in the act of sealing a goodly packet, which appeared to contain a bundle of papers.

"Beg pardon, sir," said young John, saluting, "I believe you wanted me."

"Yes," said Redfern, "I want you particularly. Come in, and sit down on that chest."

Young John obeyed.

"I believe," said Redfern, "you're a man to be trusted."

"I hope so, sir," said young John.

"I hope so, too. Well, I'm going to trust you. But in the first place I must enjoin you to utter secrecy as to what I am about to say to you, until the time arrives when you may speak."

"You may trust me, sir; you may, indeed. I'll never breathe a word of it until you give me leave."

"Very good. Now listen. The attack is to be made to-night by the Second and Light division. You will not be wanted, but I shall, for the general's brigade forms part of the attacking column. It will all be in orders in half-an-hour. I don't know whether or not you believe in pre-destination, nor do I care, but I do, and that is sufficient for my purpose. John Cole, I die to-night!"

"I sincerely hope not, sir."

"Don't interrupt me. I die to-night; that, at least, is my firm impression. Now this is what I want you to do. I want you to take charge of this packet, which I now address to you. When I am dead you will open it, and act according to the instructions therein contained. If it should happen that I survive, I shall require it of you again, until I feel disposed to give it into your possession once more. Now, may I trust you with this?"

"Indeed you may, sir; I'll take great care of it; but I sincerely trust it will not be in my keeping many hours."

"I hope not, my man, but we shall see. Now, if after the attack I do not return to quarters, get leave to look after me; bring me in if you find me, and, whatever you do, don't leave my body in the open air longer than you can help. Now you can go. I shall want Rocket at half-past ten."

Young John saluted, and left the tent with the packet.

That night as Captain Redfern was carrying a message from one of the attacking columns to the reserve, he was struck by a rifle-ball, which entered his back and came out above his left arm. He died on the field within an hour of receiving the wound; and so his prophecy was verified.

Young John carried out his master's instructions faithfully. Shortly after receiving the intelligence of Redfern's death, he opened the packet, after having first satisfied the committee of officers that sat upon the dead man's effects, that it was duly addressed to him in Captain Redfern's handwriting. To his intense astonishment, he found that it was directed to Mrs. Pintle. He was not aware of the relationship that existed between Mr. Pintle and his late master, for although Captain Redfern was well known by repute to old Johnny long before Pintle's death, young John had never heard of his existence until he joined the 16th Lancers.

A memorandum addressed to young John accompanied the enclosure. It was to the following effect :—

"JOHN COLE,—When I am dead, take the enclosed packet to Mrs. Pintle, 74, Russell Square, London, as soon as you reach England. If there is any chance of your being killed before you leave the Crimea, entrust it to a comrade upon whom you can rely. If you know no one else in whom you can place implicit confidence, give it to the Colonel.

"I hereby make you, Private John Cole, C troop of Her Majesty's 16th Lancers, the legatee of all my moveables in camp, with the exception of the gold watch

I usually wear, which I leave to poor Annie Blake.
Her address is High Street, Little Petherington. And
I hereby appoint you the executor of this my last will
and testament.

"HERBERT REDFERN,

"Capt., H.M. 16th Lancers."

The Crimean war was at an end, and the troops were
on their way home again. Thinned and shattered as
they were, they yet sufficed to afford evidence of the
noble stuff they had left behind them on Cathcart's
Hill, and in the Valley of the Shadow of Death. As
they marched through great towns in their tattered
uniform, with bearskins and shakoes half shot away,
their faces bronzed, and covered with ragged beard; and,
above all, their colours shot off almost to the pole,
carried by dirty ragged lads, who still somehow looked
like gentlemen—lads who had already seen more misery
and sickness in their young lives of twenty summers
than the oldest spectator in the enthusiastic throng of
spectators that gathered to welcome the old troops home
again—as these sturdy warriors tramped through the
English towns they had little expected to see again,
women went into hysterics, and strong men, after
shouting themselves hoarse with a kind of mad welcome
that let itself go free to take what form it would, threw
themselves down upon the grass, and there lay prone,
and wept like women. For each man who saw a
brother, or a friend, in those thinned and broken ranks,
saw one he had hardly reckoned on ever seeing again;
and he who counted no personal friends or relations

among those rows of shattered warriors, saw thousands who had endeared themselves to him by their undaunted pluck in battle, and above even that, by their heroic and unmurmuring endurance of pain, privation, cold, disease, and hunger. And it was no disgrace to the men of peace that they did so weep, for even the staunchest heroes in that battle-thinned band—men who had laughed at the Russian shell, and laid wagers as to where it would fall; men of the "thin red line," who had fought at Balaklava and lit their cigars on the parapet of the Redan, marched that summer into Hyde Park, and as the Queen pinned the Cross of Valour over their sturdy hearts, choked themselves into tears that no physical anguish could have wrung from them.

Young John had risen in the service since the death of Redfern. He was now troop-sergeant, and one of the smartest men in the squadron. His regiment was quartered at Hounslow on their return, and he was attached to the troop stationed at the old barracks at Kensington. His first care on reaching London was to find his father and mother. He had from time to time sent small sums of money to them, but he had never heard from them in reply, and it was with the apprehension of learning the details of some sad misfortune that he knocked at the old house in Great Queen Street.

The same drabby servant-girl opened the door, but she did not recognise young John in the strapping, set-up soldier, with the thick brown beard, who stood before her. She knew nothing of Johnny Pounce's whereabouts. He and Mrs. Pounce had left Great Queen Street eighteen months ago, owing much rent, and nobody in the house had heard of them since. She shouldn't wonder if they'd got into trouble. She had heard something about a will, and people said that they were no better than they ought to be. Oh, of course, he could leave a message if he liked, but he might as well leave one for the Lord Mayor.

Young John turned away with an aching heart, for the full sense of his ingratitude in leaving them at the critical moment, burst upon him.

He next called at Russell Square, with the object of placing Captain Redfern's packet into Mrs. Pintle's hands. But Mrs. Pintle had long since left the house in Russell Square, for it was a much larger establishment than she, in her reduced circumstances, could afford to keep up. The footman who opened the door told him that when Mrs. Pintle left she gave directions that all letters directed to her late address should be forwarded to an address in Michael's Place, Brompton, but that was ever so many months ago, and she might not be there now. However, he had better go there and ascertain her present address, if she had moved. So young John walked back to the Strand, and mounted a Brompton omnibus, which put him down at the address to which he had been directed.

He found Mrs. Pintle in drawing-room apartments in Michael's Place. He obtained admission to her without difficulty, for the weak-eyed flunkey had been dismissed with the rest of the household, as soon as Mrs. Pintle gave up all hope of finding her husband's will. She was reclining on a horsehair sofa of decidedly serious presence, and was still in mourning, but this time it was for her nephew.

She was surprised at seeing a brown-faced sturdy soldier enter the room, and her astonishment was not diminished when he announced himself as a soldier of the late Captain Redfern's regiment, for Captain Redfern and she had never been on particularly friendly terms, and since Mr. Pintle's death they had come to open war. The mourning that she wore was not by any means the result of emotion at that officer's death, but sprung from a species of natural taste for tombs, and everything that pertained thereunto.

"What is your business with me, soldier?" she asked.

"Beg pardon, ma'am; have I the honour of speaking to Mrs. Pintle?"

"You have."

"I'm the bearer of this parcel from the late Captain Redfern. He directed me to place it in your hands as soon as I returned to England. I only arrived four days ago, and I've availed myself of the first leave of absence I could get to bring it to you."

And young John touched his forehead, and wheeled about to depart.

"Stop," she said. "You must wait until I see what it is about."

And she attempted to open the parcel, but her hands trembled so that she could not unfasten the knots, so young John whipped out a pocket-knife, and solved the difficulty after the original Gordian receipt. The enclosure was contained in another wrapper, and upon this second wrapper being hastily torn asunder, there tumbled out of it a note addressed to Mrs. Pintle, together with the will of the late Josiah!

Mrs. Pintle was one of those hard-faced ladies who have schooled their countenances to obey them implicitly. Mrs. Pintle's face was in a state of perfect discipline, and expressed no astonishment whatever. Not so, however, her voice.

" My God ! my husband's will ! "

Young John could scarcely believe the ears that conveyed Mrs. Pintle's exclamation to his brain, and felt much more disposed to trust to the eyes that told him that, judging from Mrs. Pintle's countenance, nothing extraordinary had happened. However, the same eyes subsequently contradicted themselves, as he read the endorsement, " Will of Josiah Pintle, Esq."

" Mr. Pintle's will, ma'am," he exclaimed; " I had no idea of that ; he didn't tell me what it was. Why, my father is down in that for a thousand pounds ! "

" And who is your father ? "

" Pounce, ma'am ; Johnny—I mean John Pounce, ma'am—the late Mr. Pintle's confidential clerk."

" Then your name is Pounce ? "

" My real name is, ma'am : I enlisted, shortly after Mr. Pintle's death, as John Cole ; but my real name is Pounce."

Mrs. Pintle, after satisfying herself that the will was genuine, proceeded to open the accompanying note. It was to the following effect :—

" Before Sebastopol, 1855.

" Amelia Pintle,—Long before this reaches you I shall be a dead man. We were never on friendly terms, and the words that I am about to write to you will not mend matters. Whether they do, or whether they do not, is a question that will not in any way disturb the skeleton that by that time will be bleaching in this infernal country.

" You always considered me an extravagant and unconscientious scoundrel, and I give you credit for your discernment. I don't attempt to exculpate myself, because I do not care enough for you or anybody in the world to make it worth my while to do so. As I have already stated, by the time this is opened I shall be dead beyond all possibility of doubt. I live only for life, and posthumous honour or dishonour is a matter upon which I am most completely indifferent. As evidence of my sincerity, I not only enclose Josiah Pintle's will, but I also give an account of the manner in which it came into my possession.

" On the 24th December, 1854, I dined with Mr. Pintle. On that occasion you were, you may remember, confined to your room by some sort of indisposition. After dinner, as Pintle and I sat over our wine, we talked over family matters, and, among others, of the disposition of his property after death. He told me that he had that evening brought his will to Russell Square with the express view of reading it over to me, in whom, you may remember, he reposed (contrary I am bound to say, to your advice) much more confidence than I either desired or deserved.

"He opened the document and began to read it to me, as I sat with my back towards him, for he had turned round to get the full benefit of the light of the chandelier. He read for perhaps a couple of minutes, and then stopped. I concluded that he was considering the advisability of not reading to me the ensuing paragraph, which might perhaps refer to a trifling legacy which he intended to bestow on me. After a pause, I asked him why he did not go on, and, as he made no answer, I turned round to repeat my question. He was dead.

"I alarmed the household; but, before they answered my summons, it occurred to me that, as I was his heir-at-law, and moreover deeply in debt—and further, as nobody but myself was aware of the fact that the will had been taken from the office, I might as well take possession of it and destroy it altogether. Accordingly, I took possession of it, and, in due course, of the bulk of Mr. Pintle's property. On second thoughts I did not destroy the will, for, as I was under orders for the Crimea, I thought it possible that I might be killed, and, in the event of that melancholy occurrence, neither the will nor the property would be of any further use to me, whereas they might prove of considerable value to yourself and the other legatees. So they are quite at your service.

"Herbert Redfern,
"Capt., H.M. 16th Lancers."

Mrs. Pintle folded the letter deliberately, restored it to its envelope, and placed the envelope in her pocket.

i

“I shall not want you, Pounce,” she said. “If, as you say, and I see no reason to disbelieve it, your father is a legatee for a thousand pounds, he will, of course, receive it, when the will is proved; that, however, will probably be, under the circumstances, a work of time. In the interim, as I have done your father the injustice of believing that he—that he did not act with perfect openness in the matter, I shall be happy to make him a small allowance. You had better send him to me.”

“If I can discover him, ma’am, I will; but he’s left his old lodgings, and no one knows where he has gone to!”

“Then, find him. You had better advertise. Now, you can go.”

Young John left Mrs. Pintle’s house with a heart as heavy as when he entered it, for there appeared but little chance of his finding old Johnny and his wife; and, moreover, he had made the discovery that his late master, for whose memory he entertained a sincere regard, was, in point of fact, an unmitigated scoundrel.

He had the rest of the afternoon before him, and he spent the early part of it in sending advertisements to the principal daily papers. It was four o’clock before this was satisfactorily accomplished; and then he took a steamboat from Blackfriars, intending to go to Chelsea, and thence to Kensington. But the boat did not go higher than Westminster Bridge; so he landed there, and determined to take the omnibus at Charing Cross.

As he walked down Parliament Street, he had to pass the scene of his former labours, the Pauper Philosophy

Office; which appeared, as far as he could see, to be getting on uncommonly well without him. There was the same old over-fed office-keeper at the door, there were the same two Caucasians waiting on the steps, and there were all the twelve Examiners looking out of the twelve windows as of yore. There was the Lord President's carriage at the door, and there, no doubt was the Lord President in the Secretary's room, learning a practical reply to the eminently practical question which would be asked in the House that night, "Whether there was any truth in the statement that it was the practice of the Board for the Dissemination of Pauper-Philosophy to educate and train young paupers to an extraordinary pitch of pauper perfection, at an enormous public expense, with the express view of qualifying such paupers to impart instructions in the rudiments of Pauper-Philosophy, and that accomplished, to take away from their sphere of duty such Pauper-Philosophers as may seem to the Board to be peculiarly well qualified to train and educate other young paupers, and reward them with Assistant-Clerkships in the Office for the Dissemination of Pauper-Philosophy?"

As young John speculated on this possibility, it occurred to him that he would turn into the office, and look up some of his old friends. He passed the Caucasians and the office-keeper unrecognized, and made his way up to the garret in which he had worked for the five years that preceded his dismissal.

It was just as he had left it, for promotion in the Pauper-Philosophy Office was a work of many years. As he entered the room he was greeted with a stare of surprise, which was directed not so much at him (for he was unrecognized) as at the uniform he wore.

"Don't you know me, lads?" he said, "Pounce—John Pounce!"

"John Pounce!" exclaimed the five clerks. "Lord! you don't say so?"

And sufficiently hearty greetings ensued, for John had been a sort of favourite in his way.

Inquiries as to what events had occurred since he left the office followed; and one, more hearty than the rest, saw in young John's return a reason for standing much beer.

"Where's Shab?" asked the hearty clerk. "Send him here, somebody!"

And somebody went for Shab.

"Who's Shab?" said John.

"Shab? Oh! You know——no, he's since your time. Oh! he's a rum 'un is Shab. He runs errands, and fetches beer, and posts letters, and does odd jobs. Shab ain't his name—its affectionate for shabby genteel—so called because he looks like a Member of Parliament down on his luck."

And the door opened, and Shab introduced his head.

"Want me, gentlemen? Anything I can do?"

"Here, Shab, old boy, a gallon of beer, and you so much as look at it and I'll knock your empty old head off. D'ye hear?"

This was a coarse speech, but it was not said unkindly. Shab was a general favourite, for he was always at hand when wanted, and never grumbled at his *honorarium*. He had seen better days, as the saying is, having originally been employed on odd jobs in the Pauper-Philosophy Office as a law-stationer's clerk: but old age came upon him, and his hand trembled so that he became unfit for his work. So he became a hanger-on to the office in which he had temporarily served, and picked up occasional coppers as a kind of out-door message carrier.

"Why you look out of sorts; had your dinner, Shab?" asked the clerk.

"No, sir, no—not yet."

"Thought not; you look hungry. Here's sixpence for you—no I haven't got it."

"Looks hungry," thought young John, "by Jove, he is hungry too. Here, my man," added he aloud, "here's a shilling for you, and in God's name get something to eat."

A clerk from another room burst into the office.

"What's this I hear about Jack Pounce come back again?" said the new comer. "Jack, old chap, doosid glad to see you. Why, what are you doing in a uniform?"

The answer was interrupted by an extraordinary proceeding on the part of poor old Shab.

"Jack! Young John! O God!"

And poor old Johnny Pounce fell into his son's arms.

.   .   .   .   .

So old, so feeble, so broken, had cheery little Johnny Pounce become since he went to the bad. His rusty old suit of clothes was the cast-off of a waiter, just as he himself was the cast-off of society. He was living in a miserable attic in Tothill Fields, and his once buxom little wife was in the fever ward of the Westminster Hospital.

There cannot be much need to tell how it all ended. How his son told him of the discovery of the missing will; how old Johnny and he went to Mrs. Pounce's bedside, and broke the news to her, gently at first, and then all at once with a sort of spasmodic rush; how Mrs. Pintle did her best (in a faded kind of way) to atone for the unjust suspicions which she had cast upon the old man; how the sick woman recovered her strength by slow degrees, until she was able to leave the Hospital for the old rooms in Great Queen Street; how the Will was proved beyond dispute, after a lapse of six months or so; how one thousand pounds were paid to old Johnny, without deduction, by Mrs. Pintle, and how a handsome annuity was purchased for him with the money; how young John was bought out of the service, and enshrined in a high desk in the office of Pintle & Sims' successors, having been articled to the new firm by Mrs. Pintle herself, who further undertook to make him an allowance until he was admitted—are matters that would take many pages to tell in detail, and matters, moreover, which the reader will probably feel inclined to take for granted.

And so it was that Johnny Pounce, having gone to the Bad, and having spent a considerable time at the Bad when he got there, eventually, came back to the Good again.

LITTLE MIM.

THE only point on which Joe Paulby and I could ever bring ourselves to agree was that his cousin Mim was the only young lady in the world who was worth falling in love with. Joe Paulby was eight, I was seven, and his cousin Mim was six. Joe was a strong, rough, troublesome boy, and I was small and weak and delicate; and if it had not been that we were both deeply in love with the same young lady I believe I should have hated him. That solitary bond of sympathy served to bind us more or less firmly to each other, and I seldom quarrelled with him except when his regard for her showed signs of cooling down.

She was a pretty, fragile little lady, with quaint ways of her own, and a gentle frightened manner of dealing with her boisterous playmate which seldom failed to bring him to a sense of order. She loved us both very dearly, but I think Joe was her favourite. Although a rude, unpleasant boy to others, to her he was quiet and gentle enough; but perhaps this palpable submission appealed more directly to the little lady than my undemonstrative and colourless affection. But she was very fond of me for all that.

Neither Mim nor I had any parents, and we lived with Joe's papa in a great gaunt, draughty house in Bloomsbury Square. Captain Paulby was our guardian—a tall, bony, unsympathetic widower—who governed his house as though it had been a regiment of soldiers. A scale of dietary was hung up in the nursery, and from it one learnt how many quarter-ounces of cocoa, how many half pounds of bread, and how many tablespoonfuls of arrowroot we consumed in the week. An order-book was brought into the nursery every morning, in which the detail of the day's duties was carefully set out, and to the instructions it contained implicit and unmurmuring obedience was exacted. It regulated the hours of rising and going to bed, the school hours and the hours of relaxation, when and where we were to walk, and what we were to wear.

We were placed in charge of a nurse—Nurse Starke—a tall, muscular, hardened woman of forty. She had a stern unrelenting face, close lips, hard grey eyes, and a certain smooth roundness of figure, which on looking back, suggests the idea of her having been turned in a lathe. I never see the masculine old woman who lets lodgings in a pantomime without thinking of Nurse Starke. I am bound to say, however, that she was scrupulously, indeed aggravatingly, clean and neat, and in that respect of course, the analogy falls to the ground.

Nurse Starke was not actively unkind to us. Indeed, I believe she had cheated herself into a belief that she was rather weak-minded and indulgent than otherwise; but in this she was in error. I believe she was fond of us in a hard unyielding way, but she was sudden and impulsive in her movements, and never handled us without hurting us. There was a housemaid—Jane

Cotter—who occasionally helped to put us to bed, and sometimes Nurse Starke undressed us while Jane put our hair into curl papers, and sometimes Nurse Starke did the curling while Jane undressed us. And the manner in which these duties were to be divided became a matter of no light speculation to us as evening approached, for it was Nurse Starke's custom to pull the locks of hair out to their full length, and then roll them round a piece of paper, twisting the ends together when the curl had been rolled well home, whereas Jane Cotter first made the curl up flat with her fingers, and then encased it gently in a triangular paper, which she pinched with the tongs. Jane Cotter's flat curls were pleasant to sleep upon, but Nurse Starke's corkscrews placed a comfortable night's rest out of the question. It is impossible to sleep in peace with a double row of balls, each as big as a large chestnut, round your head. You can't move without giving four or five of them a wrench.

I think we must have been sufficiently happy as a rule, or Sunday would not have stood out in such gaunt and desolate contrast to the other days of the week. There reigned in our nursery an unaccountable fiction that Sunday was a holiday ; and in deference to this tradition we endeavoured to cheat ourselves into a belief that we were glad when that day arrived. Sunday began at a very early hour in Bloomsbury. It began to ring itself in at half-past seven when we got up, and continued to ring itself through the day at short intervals until it finally rang itself out, and us into bed, at half-past eight in the evening. There were drawbacks, however, to our enjoyment of the day. I think we were required to tackle more Collect than is good for a child of six or seven, and perhaps we did not quite understand the bearing of that Shorter Catechism which a bench of thoughtful Bishops has prepared for the express use of very young children. Even Nurse Starke, a high authority on all points of Church controversy, never succeeded in placing its meaning quite beyond all question. But Nurse Starke had a special Sunday frame of mind which discouraged close questioning, and on that day of the week, she was exceptionally short and sharp in her replies. She baffled our interrogatories by pointing out to us that there was nothing so unbecoming as a tendency to ask questions ; which seemed to us a little unreasonable, when we considered the inquisitive character of *her* share in the Catechism.

I believe I liked going to Church, though I am sure Joe Paulby did not. That rugged boy never looked so hot or so rumpled as he did during Divine Service. As I look back upon Joe in church, I am always reminded of the appearance of restless decorum presented by a Christy Minstrel "Bones" during the singing of a plaintive ballad. Joe occupied himself during the service in laying the foundations of a series of pains and penalties which usually lasted well into Thursday, for Nurse Starke had a quick eye for misdemeanours, and every crime had its apportioned punishment. Poor little Mim was too delicate to go to church, and used to sit at home in theological conference with Jane Cotter, whose picturesque and highly dramatic ideas of future rewards and punishments had a special interest for the poor little lady.

For Mim had been told that even children die sometimes, and both Nurse Starke and Jane had a long catalogue of stories in which good little people were cut off in their earliest years, and bad little people lived on to an evil old age. Mim was often weak and ailing, and at such times the recollection of these stories came upon her. Nurse Starke's grim, hard manner relaxed when she was speaking to the little sick child, and her kindness to Mim, gaunt and grudging as it was, seemed to increase with the trouble the child gave her—a never-ceasing source of wonderment to Joe and myself, who were only in favour when we ceased to occupy Nurse Starke's attention. Nurse Starke had a brother, a boy of twelve or thereabouts (though we believed him to be eight-and-twenty at least), who was a page at a doctor's in Charlotte Street ; and Nurse Starke, as a great treat, used to allow this young gentleman to spend the afternoon with us, and entertain us with his varied social powers. Gaspar—for that was his unfortunate name—was a talented boy with a taste for acrobatics, conjuring, killing flies, and putting lob-worms down Mim's back ; but notwithstanding these powerful recommendations we looked coldly upon him, and, on the whole, discouraged his visits. He had a way of challenging Joe and me to fight him with one of his hands tied behind his back, by way of a handicap, which was not what you look for in a visitor, and moreover compromised our reputation for valour in Mim's eyes. On the whole he was not popular with us, and eventually he was proscribed by Nurse Starke herself on a charge of filling the nursery candle with gunpowder,

which exploded and burnt poor little Mim's eyebrows
and eye-lashes. Gaspar eventually got into trouble
about some original draughts of his own composition,
which he supplied to his master's patients as healing
waters made up in accordance with that gentleman's
prescriptions, and spent several years in a reformatory.

I have a dismal impression of the wretched afternoons
that Mim and Joe and I used to spend together in our
great bare play-room. We were locked in by Nurse
Starke at about five every afternoon, and not released
until seven, when we had supper, and as the shadows
deepened and the fire got lower and lower, we crowded
together in a corner for warmth, and told each other
strange stories of princes and noblemen who were tor-
tured by cruel and vindictive page-boys; with an occasional touch from Joe Paulby upon caverns, demons,
vampires, and other ghostly matters until poor little
Mim screamed aloud with terror.

She was a pretty, fragile, sweet-tempered, clinging
little soul, far too delicate for the coarse inconsiderate
treatment to which she was subjected in common with
ourselves. So at last she became seriously ill, and we
noticed that the poor little child grew paler and thinner
in her cot, day after day, day after day. She was very
cheerful, although so weak, and when the tall, grave,
kind doctor came—once a day at first, and then toward
the last (for she died) two or three times a day—she
would say in reply to his question, " And how is our
Little Mim? " that she was much better, and hoped in a
day or two to be quite well again. After a time she was
removed to another room which was always darkened,

and to which we were seldom admitted, and only one at a time. An odd change seemed to come over us all. Nurse Starke was quite kind now, and used to read to her (but now about good children who lived and were very happy), and tell stories, and make beef-tea for her, and turn the cold side of the pillow to her poor little fevered head. And the oddest part of the thing was that Nurse Starke was kind to us too, and used to come of her own accord to tell us how Mim was (she was always a little better), and what messages she had sent to us, and how she seemed to take a new pleasure in the toys she had once discarded. And then she would take us, one at a time, to the sick room, and we were allowed at first to speak to her, but afterwards only to sit on the edge of the bed, (it was such a big bed now!), and hold her little dry hand. Joe Paulby would come back crying (it was a strange thing to see *him* cry, and it touched me as it touches me now to see a strong man in tears), and he would spend his half-pence—they were rare enough, poor fellow—in picture-books for our poor little dying wife. But a time came when even the picture-books were forbidden, and then the whole house was enjoined to silence, and the grave doctor—graver now than ever—came and went on tip-toe. And if we stole to the little girl's bedroom, as we often did, we were pretty sure to find great hard Nurse Starke in tears, or with traces of tears upon her face; and once when Joe and I crept down to the room, and looked in at the half-opened door, we saw the shadow of Nurse Starke on her knees, thrown by the flickering firelight on the wall. Then we knew that the end was near.

One day Captain Paulby came home earlier than

usual, looking very grave, and with him came the kind doctor, and with them another doctor, an older man, but also very kind. They went up into little Mim's room, and they stayed so long that Joe and I stole down from our old dark play-room to hear, if we could, the reason of his father's unexpected return. And Joe and I cried as if our hearts would break, for our dear little wife was dying.

Captain Paulby came out of the room, and seeing us in the passage, told us quite kindly to go back to the play-room. Joe Paulby went, but I begged Captain Paulby to let me see my dear little playmate once more, and alarmed by my excited manner and my choking sobs, he admitted me.

I had not seen her for two days, and she was greatly changed. She looked so little in that big bed that the two doctors and Captain Paulby and Nurse Starke seemed absolutely gigantic as they all bent, silently and without motion, over the little child. I think we must have remained so for nearly two hours, the silence undisturbed except by an occasional whisper from one of the doctors, and a sob from Nurse Starke. When I first went into the dark room Mim was asleep, but eventually she recognized me, and begged to be allowed to kiss me as she was nearly quite well. They laid me on the bed by her side, and her little thin arms were placed round my neck, and there we lay motionless, both of us in deep silence. At length I became conscious of a movement among the doctors, and then a loud ringing wail from Nurse Starke told me that my little wife was quite, quite well again.

THE TRIUMPH OF VICE.

A FAIRY TALE.

THE wealthiest in the matter of charms, and the poorest in the matter of money of all the well-born maidens of Tackleschlosstein, was the Lady Bertha von Klauffenbach. Her papa, the Baron, was indeed the fortunate possessor of a big castle on the top of a perpendicular rock, but his estate was deeply mortgaged, and there was not the smallest probability of its ever being free from the influence of the local money-lender. Indeed, if it comes to that, I may be permitted to say that even in the event of that wildly improbable state of things having come to pass, the amount realised by the sale of the castle and perpendicular rock would not have exceeded one hundred and eighty pounds sterling, all told. So the Baron von Klauffenbach did not even wear the outward show of being a wealthy man.

The perpendicular rock being singularly arid and unproductive even for a rock, and the Baron being remarkably penniless even for a Baron, it became necessary that he should adopt some decided course by which a sufficiency of bread, milk, and sauerkrout might be provided to satisfy the natural cravings of the Baron von Klauffenbach, and that fine growing girl Bertha, his daughter. So the poor old gentleman was only too glad to let down his drawbridge every morning, and sally forth from his stronghold, to occupy a scrivener's stool in the office of the local money-lender to whom I have already alluded. In short, the Baron von Klauffenbach was a usurer's clerk.

But it is not so much with the Baron von Klauffenbach as with his beautiful daughter Bertha that I have to do. I must describe her. She was a magnificent animal. She was six feet in height, and splendidly proportioned. She had a queenly face, set in masses of wonderful yellow hair; big blue eyes, and curly little mouth (but with thick firm lips), and a nose which, in the mercantile phraseology of the period, defied competition. Her figure was grandly, heroically outlined, firm as marble to the look, but elastically yielding to the touch. Bertha had but one fault—she was astonishingly vain of her magnificent proportions, and held in the utmost contempt anybody, man or woman, who fell short of her in that respect. She was the toast of all the young clerks of Tackleschlosstein; but the young clerks of Tackleschlosstein were to the Lady Bertha as so many midges to a giantess. They annoyed her, but they were not worth the trouble of deliberate annihilation. So they went on toasting her, and she went on scorning them.

Indeed, the Lady Bertha had but one lover whose chance of success was worth the ghost of a halfpenny—and he was the Count von Krappentrapp. The Count von Krappentrapp had these pulls over the gay young clerks of Tackleschlosstein—that he was constantly in her society, and was of noble birth. That he was constantly in her society came to pass in this wise. The Baron von Klauffenbach, casting about him for a means of increasing—or rather of laying the first stone towards the erection of — his income, published this manifesto on the walls of Tackleschlosstein :

" A nobleman and his daughter, having larger premises than they require, will be happy to receive into their circle a young gentleman engaged in the village during the day. Society musical. Terms insignificant. Apply to the Baron von K., Post Office, Tackleschlosstein."

The only reply to this intimation came from the Count von Krappentrapp; and the only objection to the Count von Krappentrapp was, that he was not engaged in the village during the day. But this objection was eventually overruled by the Count's giving the Baron in the handsomest manner in the world, his note of hand for ten pounds at six months date, which was immediately discounted by the Baron's employer. I am afraid that the Baron and the Count got dreadfully tipsy that evening. I know that they amused themselves all night by shying ink-bottles from the battlements at the heads of the people in the village below.

It will easily be foreseen that the Count von Krappentrapp soon fell hopelessly in love with Bertha; and those of my readers who are accustomed to the unravelling of German legendary lore will long ere this have made up their minds that Bertha fell equally hopelessly in love with the Count von Krappentrapp. But in this last particular they will be entirely in error. Far from encouraging the gay young Count, she regarded him with feelings of the most profound contempt. Indeed, truth compels me to admit that the Count was repulsive. His head was enormous, and his legs insignificant. He was short in stature, squat in figure, and utterly detestable in every respect, except in this, that he was always ready to put his hand to a bill for the advantage of the worthy old Baron. And whenever he obliged the Baron in this respect, he and the old gentleman used to get dreadfully tipsy, and always spent the night on the battlements throwing ink-bottles on the people in the village below. And whenever the Baron's tradespeople in the village found themselves visited by a shower of ink-bottles, they knew that there was temporary corn in Egypt, and they lost no time in climbing up the perpendicular rock with their little red books with the gilt letters in their hands, ready for immediate settlement.

It was not long after the Count von Krappentrapp came to lodge with the Baron von Klauffenbach, that the Count proposed to the Baron's daughter, and in about a quarter of a minute after he had proposed to her, he was by her most unequivocally rejected. Then he slunk off to his chamber, muttering and mouthing in a manner which occasioned the utmost consternation in the mind of Gretchen, the castle maid-of-all-work, who met him on his way. So she offered him a bottle of cheap scent, and some peppermint-drops, but he danced at her in such a reckless manner when she suggested these humble refreshments, that she went to the Baron, and gave him a month's warning on the spot.

Everything went wrong with the Count that day. The window-blinds wouldn't pull up, the door wouldn't close, the chairs broke when he sat on them, and before half his annoyances had ceased, he had expended all the bad language he knew.

The Count was conscientious in one matter only, and that was in the matter of bad language. He made it a point of honour not to use the same expletive twice in the same day. So when he found that he had exhausted his stock of swearing, and that, at the moment of exhaustion, the chimney began to smoke, he simply sat down and cried feebly.

But he soon sprang to his feet, for in the midst of an unusually large puff of smoke, he saw the most extraordinary individual he had ever beheld. He was about two feet high, and his head was as long as his body and legs put together. He had an antiquated appearance about him ; but excepting that he wore a long stiff tail, with a spear-point at the end of it, there was nothing absolutely unearthly about him. His hair, which resembled the crest or comb of a cock in its arrangement, terminated in a curious little queue, which turned up at the end and was fastened with a bow of blue ribbon. He wore mutton-chop whiskers and a big flat collar, and his body and misshapen legs were covered with a horny incrustation, which suggested black beetles. On his crest he wore a three-cornered hat—anticipating the invention of that article of costume by about three hundred years.

" I beg your pardon," said this phenomenon, " but can I speak to you ? "

"Evidently you can," replied the Count, whose confidence had returned to him.

"I know: but what I mean is, will you listen to me for ten minutes?"

"That depends very much upon what you talk about. Who are you?" asked the Count.

"I'm a sort of gnome."

"A gnome?"

"A sort of gnome; I won't enter into particulars, because they won't interest you."

The apparition hesitated, evidently hoping the Count would assure him that any particulars of the gnome's private life would interest him deeply; but he only said—

"Not the least bit in the world."

"You are poor," said the gnome.

"Very," replied the Count.

"Ha!" said he, "some people are. Now I am rich."

"*Are* you?" asked the Count, beginning to take an interest in the matter.

"I am, and would make you rich too; only you must help me to a wife."

"What! Repay good for evil? Never!"

He didn't mean this, only he thought it was a smart thing to say.

"Not exactly," said the gnome; "I shan't give you the gold until you have found me the wife; so that I shall be repaying evil with good."

"Yes," said the count musingly: "I didn't look at it in that light at all. I see it quite from your point of view. But why don't you find a wife for yourself?"

"Well," said the gnome diffidently, "I'm not exactly
—you know—I'm—that is—I want a word!"

"Extremely ugly?" suggested the Count.

"Ye-e-es," said the gnome (rather taken aback);
"something of that sort. *You* know."

"Yes, I know," said the Count; "but how am I to
help you? I can't make you pretty."

"No; but I have the power of transforming myself
three times during my gnome existence into a magnificent young man."

"O-h-h-h!" said the count slyly.

"Exactly. Well, I've done that twice, but without
success as far as regards getting a wife. This is my
last chance."

"But how can I help you? You say you can change
yourself into a magnificent young man; then why not
plead your own cause? I, for my part, am rather—
a——"

"Repulsive?" suggested the gnome thinking he had
him there.

"Plain," said the count.

"Well," replied the gnome, "there's an unfortunate
fact connected with my human existence."

"Out with it. Don't stand on ceremony."

"Well, then, it's this. I begin as a magnificent
young man, six feet high, but I diminish imperceptibly
day by day, whenever I wash myself, until I shrink into
the—a—the——"

"Contemptible abortion?"

"A—yes—thank you—you behold. Well, I've tried
it twice, and found on each occasion a lovely girl who

was willing and ready to marry me; but during the month or so that elapsed between each engagement and the day appointed for the wedding, I shrunk so perceptibly (one is obliged, you know, to wash one's face during courtship), that my bride-elect became frightened and cried off. Now, I have seen the Lady Bertha, and I am determined to marry her."

"You? Ha, ha! Excuse me, but——Ha, ha!"

"Yes, I. But you will see that it is essential that as little time as possible should elapse between my introduction to her and our marriage."

"Of course; and you want me to prepare her to receive you, and marry you there and then without delay."

"Exactly; and if you consent, I will give you several gold mines, and as many diamonds as you can carry."

"You will? My dear sir, say no more! 'Revenge! Revenge! Revenge! Timotheus cried,' quoting a popular comic song of the day. But how do you effect the necessary transformation?"

"Here is a ring which gives me the power of assuming human form once more during my existence. I have only to put it on my middle finger, and the transformation is complete."

"I see—but—couldn't you oblige me with a few thalers on account?"

"Um," said the gnome; "it's irregular: but here are two."

"Right," said the Count, biting them; "I'll do it. Come the day after to-morrow."

"At this time?" said the gnome.

" At this time."

" Good-night."

" Good night."

And the gnome disappeared up the chimney.

The Count von Krappentrapp hurried off without loss of time to communicate to the lovely Bertha the splendid fate in store for her.

" Lady Bertha," said he, " I come to you with a magnificent proposal."

" Now, Krappentrapp," said Bertha, " don't be a donkey. Once for all, I *will* NOT have you."

" I am not alluding to myself; I am speaking on behalf of a friend."

" O, any friend of yours, I'm sure," began Bertha politely.

" Thanks, very much."

" Would be open to the same objection as yourself. He would be repulsive."

" But he is magnificent !"

" He would be vicious."

" But he is virtuous ! "

" He would be insignificant in rank and stature."

" He is a prince of unexampled proportions ! "

" He would be absurdedly poor."

" He is fabulously wealthy ! "

" Indeed ? " said Bertha; " your story interests me.' (She was intimately acquainted with German melodrama.) " Proceed."

" This prince," said Krappentrapp, " has heard of you, has seen you, and consequently has fallen in love with you."

"O, g'long," said Bertha giggling, and nudging him with her extraordinarily moulded elbow.

"Fact. He proposes to settle on you Africa, the Crystal Palace, several solar systems, the Rhine, and Rosherville. The place," added he, musingly, "to spend a happy, happy day."

"Are you in earnest, or" (baring her right arm to the shoulder) "is this some of your nonsense?"

"Upon my honour, I am in earnest. He will be here the day after to-morrow at this time to claim you, if you consent to have him. He will carry you away with him alone to his own province, and there will marry you."

"Go away alone with him? I wouldn't think of such a thing!" said Bertha, who was a model of propriety.

"H'm!" said the Count, "that is awkward certainly. Ha! a thought! You shall marry him first, and start afterwards, only as he has to leave this in two days, the wedding must take place without a moment's delay."

You see, if he had suggested this in the first instance, she would have indignantly rejected the notion, on principle. As it was she jumped at it, and, as a token of peace, let down her sleeve.

"I can provide my trousseau in two days. I will marry him the day he arrives, if he turns out to be all you have represented him. But if he does not——" And she again bared her arm, significantly, to the shoulder.

That night, the Baron von Klauffenbach and the Count von Krappentrapp kept it up right merrily on the two thalers which the Count had procured from the gnome. The Baron was overjoyed at the prospect of a princely son-in-law; and the shower of ink-bottles from the battlements was heavier than ever.

The second day after this the gnome appeared to Count Krappentrapp.

"How do you do?" said the Count.

"Thank you," said the gnome; "I'm pretty well. It's an awful thing being married."

"Oh, no. Don't be dispirited."

"Ah, it's all very well for you to say that, but—Is the lady ready?" said he, changing the subject abruptly.

"Ready, I should think so. She's sitting in the banqueting hall in full bridal array, panting for your arrival."

"O! do I look nervous?"

"Well, candidly, you do," said the Count.

"I'm afraid I do. Is everything prepared?"

"The preparations," said the Count, "are on the most magnificent scale. Half buns and cut oranges are scattered over the place in luxurious profusion, and there is enough gingerbierheimer and currantweinmilch on tap to float the Rob Roy canoe. Gretchen is engaged, as I speak, in cutting ham-sandwiches recklessly in the kitchen; and the Baron has taken down the 'Apartments furnished,' which has hung for ages in the stained glass windows of the banqueting hall."

"I see," said the gnome, "to give a tone to the thing."

"Just so. Altogether it will be the completest thing you ever saw."

"Well," said the gnome, "then I think I'll dress."

For he had not yet taken his human form.

So he slipped a big carbuncle ring on to the middle finger of his right hand. Immediately the room was filled with a puff of smoke from the chimney, and when it had cleared away, the Count saw, to his astonishment, a magnificent young man in the place where the gnome had stood.

"There is no deception," said the gnome.

"Bravo! very good indeed! very neat!" said the Count, applauding.

"Clever thing, isn't it?" said the gnome.

"Capital; most ingenious. But now—what's your name?"

"It's an odd name. Prince Pooh."

"Prince Pooh? Pooh! pooh! you're joking."

"Now, take my advice, and never try to pun upon a fellow's name; you may be sure that, however ingenious the joke may be, it's certain to have been done before over and over again to his face. Your own particular joke is precisely the joke every fool makes when he first hears my name."

"I beg your pardon—it *was* weak. Now, if you'll come with me to the Baron, you and he can settle preliminaries."

So they went to the Baron, who was charmed with his son-in-law elect. Prince Pooh settled on Bertha the whole of Africa, the Crystal Palace, several solar systems, the Rhine, and Rosherville, and made the Baron a present of Siberia and Vesuvius; after that they all went down to the banqueting hall, where Bertha and the priest were awaiting their arrival.

"Allow me," said the Baron. "Bertha, my dear,

Prince Pooh—who has behaved *most handsomely*" (this in a whisper). "Prince Pooh—my daughter Bertha. Pardon a father if he is for a moment unmanned."

And the Baron wept over Bertha, while Prince Pooh mingled his tears with those of Count Krappentrapp, and the priest with those of Gretchen, who had finished cutting the sandwiches. The ceremony was then gone into with much zeal on all sides, and on its conclusion the party sat down to the elegant collation already referred to. The Prince declared that the Baron was the best fellow he had ever met, and the Baron assured the Prince that words failed him when he endeavoured to express the joy he felt at an alliance with so unexceptionable a Serene Highness.

The Prince and his bride started in a carriage and twenty-seven for his country seat, which was only fifty miles from Tackleschlosstein, and that night the Baron and the Count kept it up harder than ever. They went down to the local silversmith to buy up all the presentation inkstands in his stock; and the shower of inkstands from the castle battlements on the heads of the villagers below that night is probably without precedent or imitation in the chronicles of revelry.

*　　*　　*　　*　　*　　*

Bertha and Prince Pooh spent a happy honeymoon : Bertha had one, and only one cause of complaint against Prince Pooh, and that was an insignificant one—do all she could, she couldn't persuade him to wash his face more than once a week. Bertha was a clean girl for a German, and had acquired a habit of performing ablutions three or even four times a week; consequently her husband's annoying peculiarity irritated her more than it would have irritated most of the young damsels of Tackleschlosstein. So she would contrive, when he was asleep, to go over his features with a damp towel; and whenever he went out for a walk she hid his umbrella, in order that, if it chanced to rain, he might get a providential and sanitary wetting.

This sort of thing went on for about two months, and at the end of that period Bertha began to observe an extraordinary change not only in her husband's appearance, but also in her own. To her horror she found that both she and her husband were shrinking rapidly! On the day of their marriage each of them was six feet high, and now her husband was only five feet nine, while she had diminished to five feet six—owing to her more frequent use of water. Her dresses were too long and too wide for her. Tucks had to be run in everything to which tucks were applicable, and breadths and gores taken out of all garments which were susceptible of these modifications. She spent a small fortune in heels, and even then had to walk about on tiptoe in order to escape remark. Nor was Prince Pooh a whit more easy in his mind than was his wife. He wore the tallest hats with the biggest feathers, and the most preposterous heels to his boots that ever were seen. Each seemed afraid to allude to these extraordinary modifications to each other, and a gentle melancholy took the place of the hilarious jollity which had characterised their proceedings hitherto.

At length matters came to a crisis. The Prince

went out hunting one day, and fell into the Rhine from the top of a high rock. He was an excellent swimmer, and he had to remain about two hours, swimming against a powerful tide, before assistance arrived. The consequence was that when he was taken out he had shrunk so considerably that his attendants hardly knew him. He was reduced, in fact, to four feet nine.

On his return to his castle he dressed himself in his tallest hat and highest heels, and, warming his chilly body at the fire, he nervously awaited the arrival of his wife from a shopping expedition in the neighbourhood.

"Charles," said she, "further disguise were worse than useless. It is impossible for me to conceal from myself the extremely unpleasant fact that we are both of us rapidly shrinking. Two months since you were a fine man, and I was one of the most magnificent women of this or any other time. Now *I* am only middle-sized, and you have suddenly become contemptibly small. What does this mean?"

"A husband is often made to look small in the eyes of his wife," said Prince Charles Pooh, attempting to turn it off with a feeble joke.

"Yes, but a wife don't mean to stand being made to look small in the eyes of her husband."

"It's only fancy, my dear. You are as fine a woman as ever."

"Nonsense, Charles. Gores, Gussets, and Tucks are Solemn Things," said Bertha, speaking in capitals; "they are Stubborn Facts which there is No Denying, and I Insist on an Explanation."

"I'm very sorry," said Prince Pooh, "but I can't account for it;" and suddenly remembering that his horse was still in the Rhine, he ran off as hard as he could to get it out.

Bertha was evidently vexed. She began to suspect that she had married the Fiend, and the consideration annoyed her much. So she determined to write to her father, and ask him what she had better do.

Now, Prince Pooh had behaved most shabbily to his friend Count Krappentrapp. Instead of giving him the gold-mines and diamonds which he had promised him he sent him nothing at all but a bill for twenty pounds at six months, a few old masters, a dozen or so of cheap hock, and a few hundred paving stones, which were wholly inadequate to the satisfaction of the Count and the Baron's new-born craving for silver inkstands. So Count von Krappentrapp determined to avenge himself on the Prince at the very earliest opportunity; and in Bertha's letter the opportunity presented itself.

He saddled the castle donkey, and started for Pooh-berg, the Prince's seat. In two days he arrived there, and sent up his card to Bertha. Bertha admitted him; and he then told her the Prince's real character, and the horrible fate that was in store for her if she continued to be his wife.

"But what am I to do?" said she.

"If you were single again, whom would you marry?" said he with much sly emphasis.

"O," said the Princess, "you, of course."

"You would."

"Undoubtedly. Here it is in writing."

And she gave him a written promise to marry him if anything ever happened to the Prince her husband.

"But," said the Count, "can you reconcile yourself to the fact that my proportions are insignificant?"

"Compared with me, as I now am, you are gigantic," said Bertha. "I am cured of my pride in my own splendid stature."

"Good," said the Count. "You have noticed the carbuncle that your husband (husband! ha! ha! but no matter) wears on his middle finger?"

"I have."

"In that rests his charm. Remove it while he sleeps; he will vanish, and you will be a free woman."

* * * * * *

That night as the clock struck twelve, the Princess removed the ring from the right-hand middle finger of Prince Pooh. He gave a fearful shriek; the room was filled with smoke; and on its clearing off, the body of the gnome in its original form lay dead upon the bed, charred to ashes!

* * * * * *

The castle of Poohberg, however, remained, and all that was in it. The ashes of the monster were buried in the back garden, and a horrible leafless shrub, encrusted with a black, shiny, horny bark, that suggested black beetles, grew out the grave with astounding rapidity. It grew, and grew, and grew, but never put forth a leaf; and as often as it was cut down it grew again. So when Bertha (who never recovered her original proportions) married Count Krappentrapp, it became necessary to shut up the back garden altogether, and to put ground-glass panes into the windows which commanded it. And they took the dear old Baron to live with them, and the Count and he spent a jolly time of it. The Count laid in a stock of inkstands which would last out the old man's life, and many a merry hour they spent on the hoary battlements of Poohberg. Bertha and her husband lived to a good old age, and died full of years and of honours.

MY MAIDEN BRIEF.

LATE on a certain May morning, as I was sitting at a modest breakfast in my " residence chambers," Pump Court, Temple, my attention was claimed by a single knock at an outer door, common to the chambers of Felix Polter, and of myself, Horace Penditton, both barristers-at-law of the Inner Temple.

The outer door was not the only article common to Polter and myself. We also shared what Polter (who wrote farces) was pleased to term a " property " clerk, who did nothing at all, and a " practicable " laundress, who did everything. There existed also a communion of interest in tea-cups, razors, gridirons, candlesticks, &c.; for although neither of us was particularly well supplied with the necessaries of domestic life, each happened to possess the very articles in which the other was deficient. So we got on uncommonly well together, each regarding his friend in the light of an indispensable other self. We had both embraced the " higher walk " of the legal profession, and were patiently waiting for the legal profession to return the compliment.

The single knock raised some well-founded apprehensions in both our minds.

" Walker ! " said I to the property clerk.

"Sir!"

"If that knock is for me, I'm out you know."

"Of course, sir!"

"And Walker!" cried Polter.

"Sir!"

"If it's for me, I'm not at home!"

Polter always rejoiced if he could manage to make the conversation partake of a Maddisonian Mortonic character.

Mr. Walker opened the door. "Mr. Penditton's a-breakfasting with the Master of the Rolls, if it's him you want; and if it isn't, Mr. Polter's with the Attorney-General."

"You don't say so!" remarked the visitor; "then you'll give this to Mr. Penditton, as soon as the Master can make up his mind to part with him."

And so saying, he handed to Walker a lovely parcel of brief paper, tied up neatly with a piece of red tape, and minuted—

"Central Criminal Court, May Sessions, 1860.—The Queen on the prosecution of Ann Black *v.* Elizabeth Briggs. Brief for the prisoner. Mr. Penditton, one guinea.—Poddle and Shaddery, Brompton Square."

So it had come at last! Only an Old Bailey brief, it is true; but still a brief. We scarcely knew what to make of it. Polter looked at me, and I looked at Polter, and then we both looked at the brief.

It turned out to be a charge against Elizabeth Briggs, widow, of picking pockets in an omnibus. It appeared from my "instructions," that my client was an elderly lady, and religious. On the 2nd April then last she entered an Islington omnibus, with the view of attending a tea and prayer meeting in Bell Court, Islington. A woman in the omnibus missed her purse, and accused Mrs. Briggs, who sat on her right, of having stolen it. The poor soul, speechless with horror at the charge, was dragged out of the omnibus, and as the purse was found in a pocket in the left hand side of her dress, she was given into custody. As it was stated by the police that she had been "in trouble" before, the infatuated magistrate who examined her committed her for trial.

"There, my boy, your fortune's made," said Polter.

"But I don't see the use of my taking it," said I; there's nothing to be said for her."

"Not take it? Won't you though? I'll see about that. You *shall* take it, and you shall get her off, too! Highly respectable old lady—attentive member of well-known congregation—parson to speak to her character, no doubt. As honest as you are!"

"But the purse was found upon her."

"Well, sir, and what of that? Poor woman left-handed, and pocket in left of dress. Robbed woman right-handed, and pocket in right of dress. Poor woman sat on right of robbed woman. Robbed woman, replacing her purse, slipped it accidentally into poor woman's pocket. Ample folds of dress, you know—crinolines overlapping, and all that.—Splendid defence for you!"

"Well, but she's an old hand, it seems. The police know her."

"Police always do; 'always know everybody;' police maxim. Swear anything, they will."

Polter really seemed so sanguine about it that I began

to look at the case hopefully, and to think that something might be done with it. He talked to me with such effect that he not only convinced me that there was a good deal to be said in Mrs. Briggs's favour, but I actually began to look upon her as an innocent victim of circumstantial evidence, and determined that no effort should be wanting on my part to procure her release from a degrading but unmerited confinement.

Of the firm of Poddle & Shaddery I knew nothing whatever, and how they came to entrust Mrs. Briggs's case to me I can form no conception. As we (for Polter took so deep a personal interest in the success of Mrs. Briggs's case that he completely identified himself, in my mind, with her fallen fortunes,) resolved to go to work in a thoroughly business-like manner, we determined to commence operations by searching for the firm of Poddle & Shaddery in the *Law List*. To our dismay the *Law List* of that year had no record of Poddle, neither did Shaddery find a place in its pages. This was serious, and Polter did not improve matters by suddenly recollecting that he once heard an old Q.C. say that, as a rule, the farther west of Temple Bar the shadier the attorney; so that assuming Polter's friend to have come to a correct conclusion on this point, a firm dating officially from Brompton Square, and whose name did not appear in Mr. Dalbiac's *Law List*, was a legitimate object of suspicion. But Polter, who took a hopeful view of anything which he thought might lead to good farce " situations," and who probably imagined that my first appearance on any stage as counsel for the defence was likely to be rich in suggestions, remarked that they might possibly have been certificated since the publishing of the last *Law List*; and as for the *dictum* about Temple Bar, why, the case of Poddle and Shaddery might be one of those very exceptions whose existence is necessary to the proof of every general rule. So Polter and I determined to treat the firm in a spirit of charity, and accept their brief.

As the May sessions of oyer and terminer did not commence until the 8th, I had four clear days in which to study my brief and prepare my defence. Besides, there was a murder case, and a desperate burglary or two, which would probably be taken first, so that it was unlikely that the case of the poor soul whose cause I had espoused would be tried before the 12th. So I had plenty of time to master what Polter and I agreed was one of the most painful cases of circumstantial evidence ever submitted to a British jury; and I really believe that, by the first day of the May sessions, I was intimately acquainted with the details of every case of pocket-picking reported in *Cox's Criminal Cases* and *Buckler's Shorthand Reports*.

On the night of the 11th I asked Bodger of Brasenose, Norton of Gray's Inn, Cadbury of the Lancers, and three or four other men, college chums principally, to drop in at Pump Court, and hear a rehearsal of my speech for the defence, in the forthcoming *cause célèbre* of the Queen on the prosecution of Ann Black *v.* Elizabeth Briggs. At nine o'clock they began to appear, and by ten all were assembled. Pipes and strong waters were produced, and Norton of Gray's was forthwith raised to the Bench by the style and dignity of Sir

Joseph Norton, one of the Barons of Her Majesty's Court of Exchequer; Cadbury, Bodger, and another represented the jury; Wilkinson of Lincoln's Inn was counsel for the prosecution, Polter was clerk of arraigns, and Walker, my clerk, was the prosecutrix.

Everything went satisfactorily; Wilkinson broke down in his speech for the prosecution; his witness prevaricated and contradicted himself in a preposterous manner; and my speech for the defence was voted to be one of the most masterly specimens of forensic ingenuity that had ever come before the notice of the Court; and the consequence was that the prisoner (inadequately represented by a statuette of the Greek slave) was discharged, and Norton, who would have looked more like a Baron of the Exchequer if he had looked less like a tipsy churchwarden, remarked that she left the Court without a stain on her character.

The Court then adjourned for refreshment, and the conversation took a general turn, after canvassing the respective merits of " May it please your ludship," and " May it please you, my lud," as an introduction to a counsel's speech—a discussion which ended in favour of the latter form, as being a trifle more independent in its character, I remember proposing that the health of Elizabeth Briggs should be drunk in a solemn and respectful bumper; and as the evening wore on, I am afraid I became exceedingly indignant with Cadbury, because he had taken the liberty of holding up to public ridicule an imaginary (and highly undignified) *carte-de-visite* of my unfortunate client.

The 12th May, big with the fate of Penditton and of

Briggs, dawned in the usual manner. At ten o'clock Polter and I drove up in wigs and gowns to the Old Bailey; as well because we kept those imposing garments at our chambers, not having any use for them elsewhere, as to impress passers-by and the loungers below the Court with a conviction that we were not only Old Bailey counsel, but had come down from our usual sphere of action at Westminster, to conduct a case of more than ordinary complication. Impressed with a sense of the propriety of presenting an accurate professional appearance, I had taken remarkable pains with my toilet. I had the previous morning shaved off a flourishing moustache, and sent Walker out for half-a-dozen serious collars, as substitutes for the unprofessional "lay-downs" I usually wore. I was dressed in a correct evening suit, and wore a pair of thin gold spectacles; and Polter remarked, that I looked the sucking Bencher to the life. Polter, whose interest in the accuracy of my "get-up" was almost fatherly, had totally neglected his own; and he made his appearance in the raggedest of beards and moustaches under his wig, and the sloppiest of cheap drab lounging-coats under his gown.

I modestly took my place in the back row of the seats allotted to the Bar; Polter took his in the very front, in order to have an opportunity, at the close of the case, of telling the leading counsel, in the hearing of the attorneys, the name and address of the young and rising barrister who had just electrified the Court. In various parts of the building I detected Cadbury, Wilkinson, and others, who had represented judge, jury, and counsel, on the previous evening. They had been instructed by Polter (who had had some experience in "packing" a house) to distribute themselves about the Court, and, at the termination of the speech for the defence, to give vent to their feelings in that applause which is always so quickly suppressed by the officers of a court of justice. I was rather annoyed at this, as I did not consider it altogether legitimate; and my annoyance was immensely increased when I found that my three elderly maiden aunts, to whom I had been foolish enough to confide the fact of my having to appear on the 12th, were seated in state in that portion of the room allotted to friends of the Bench and Bar, and busied themselves by informing everybody within whisper-shot, that I was to defend Elizabeth Briggs, and that this was my first brief. It was some little consolation, however, to find the unceremonious manner in which the facts of the cases that preceded mine were explained and commented on by judge, jury, and counsel, caused those ladies great uneasiness, and, indeed, compelled them, on one or two occasions, to beat an unceremonious retreat.

At length the clerk of arraigns called the case of Briggs, and with my heart in my mouth I began to try to recollect the opening words of my speech for the defence, but I was interrupted in that hopeless task by the appearance of Elizabeth in the dock.

She was a pale, elderly widow, rather buxom, and remarkably neatly dressed in slightly rusty mourning. Her hair was arranged in two sausage curls, one on each side of her head, and looped in two festoons over the forehead. She appeared to feel her position acutely, and although she did not weep, her red eyes showed evident traces of recent tears. She grasped the edge of the dock, and rocked backwards and forwards, accompanying the motion with a low moaning sound, that was extremely touching. Polter looked back at me with an expression which plainly said, "If ever an innocent woman appeared in that dock, that woman is Elizabeth Briggs!"

The clerk of arraigns now proceeded to charge the jury. "Gentlemen of the jury, the prisoner at the bar, Elizabeth Briggs, is indicted for that she did, on the 2nd April last, steal from the person of Ann Black a purse containing ten shillings and fourpence, the moneys of the said Ann Black. There is another count to the indictment, charging her with having received the same, knowing it to have been stolen. To both of these counts the prisoner has pleaded 'Not Guilty,' and it is your charge to try whether she is guilty or not guilty." Then to the Bar, "Who appears in this case?"

Nobody replying on behalf of the Crown, I rose and remarked that I appeared for the defence.

A counsel here said that he believed that the brief for the prosecution was entrusted to Mr. Porter, but that that gentleman was engaged at the Middlesex Sessions in a case which was likely to occupy several hours, and that he (Mr. Porter) did not expect that Briggs's case would come on that day.

A consultation then took place between the judge and

the clerk of arraigns. At its termination, the latter functionary said, " Who is the junior counsel present ? "

To my horror, up jumped Polter, and said, " I think it's very likely that I am the junior counsel in court. My name is Polter, and I was only called last term ! "

A titter ran through the crowd, but Polter, whose least fault was bashfulness, only smiled benignly at those around him.

Another whispering between judge and clerk. At its conclusion the clerk handed a bundle of papers to Polter, saying, at the same time :

" Mr. Polter, his lordship wishes you to conduct the prosecution."

" Certainly," said Polter ; and he opened the papers, glanced at them, and rose to address the court.

He began by requesting that the jury would take into consideration the fact that he had only that moment been placed in possession of the brief for the prosecution of the prisoner at the bar, who appeared from what he had gathered from a glance at his instructions, to have been guilty of as heartless a robbery as ever disgraced humanity. He would endeavour to do his duty, but he feared that, at so short a notice, he should scarcely be able to do justice to the brief with which he had been most unexpectedly entrusted. He then went on to state the case in a masterly manner, appearing to gather the facts. with which, of course, he was perfectly intimate, from the papers in his hand. He commented on the growing frequency of omnibus robberies, and then went on to say :—

" Gentlemen, I am at no loss to anticipate the defence on which my learned friend will base his hope of inducing you to acquit that wretched woman. I don't know whether it has ever been your misfortune to try criminal cases before, but if it has, you will be able to anticipate his defence as certainly as I can. He will probably tell you, because the purse was found in the left-hand pocket of that miserable woman's dress, that she is left-handed, and on that account wears her pocket on the left side, and he will then, if I am not very much mistaken, ask the prosecutrix if she is not right-handed, and, lastly, he will ask you to believe that the prosecutrix sitting on the prisoner's left, slipped the purse accidentally into the prisoner's pocket. But, gentlemen, I need not remind you that the facts of these omnibus robberies are always identical. The prisoner always *is* left-handed, the prosecutrix always *is* right-handed, and the prosecutrix always *does* slip the purse accidentally into the prisoner's pocket instead of her own. My lord will tell you that this is so, and you will know how much faith to place upon such a defence, should my friend think proper to set it up." He ended by entreating the jury to give the case their attentive consideration, and stated that he relied confidently on an immediate verdict of " Guilty." He then sat down, saying to the usher, " Call Ann Black."

Ann Black, who was in court, shuffled up into the witness-box, and was duly sworn. Polter then drew out her evidence, bit by bit, helping her with leading questions of the most flagrant description. I knew that I ought not to allow this, but I was too horrified at the

turn matters had taken to interfere.   At the conclusion of the examination in chief Polter sat down triumphantly, and I rose to cross-examine.

" You are right-handed, Mrs. Black ? " (*Laughter.*)

" Oh, yes, sir ! "

" Very good.   I've nothing else to ask you."

So Mrs. Black stood down, and the omnibus conductor
took her place.   His evidence was not material, and I
declined to cross-examine.   The policeman who had
charge of the case followed the conductor, and his
evidence was to the effect that the purse was found in
her pocket.

I felt that this witness ought to be cross-examined,
but not having anything ready, I allowed him to stand
down.   A question, I am sorry to say, then occurred to
me, and I requested his lordship to allow the witness to
be recalled.

" You say you found the purse in her pocket, my
man ? "

" Yes, sir."

" Did you find anything else ? "

" Yes, sir."

" What ? "

" Two other purses, a watch with the bow broken, three
handkerchiefs, two silver pencil-cases, and a hymn-book.
(*Roars of laughter.*)

" You may stand down."

" That is the case, my lord," said Polter.

It was now my turn to address the court.   What
could I say ?   I believe I observed, that, undeterred by
my learned friend's opening speech, I did intend to set

up the defence he had anticipated. I set it up, but I don't think it did much good. The jury, who were perfectly well aware that this was Polter's first case, had no idea but that I was an old hand at it; and no doubt thought me an uncommonly clumsy one. They had made every allowance for Polter, who needed nothing of the kind, and they made none at all for me, who needed all they had at their disposal. I soon relinquished my original line of defence, and endeavoured to influence the jury by vehement assertions of my personal conviction of the prisoner's innocence. I warmed with my subject, (for Polter had not anticipated me here), and I believe I grew really eloquent. I think I staked my professional reputation on her innocence, and I sat down expressing my confidence in a verdict that would restore the unfortunate lady to a circle of private friends, several of whom were waiting in the court below to testify to her excellent character.

"Call witnesses to Mrs. Briggs's character," said I.

"Witnesses to the character of Briggs!" shouted the crier.

The cry was repeated three or four times outside the court; but there was no response.

"No witnesses to Briggs's character here, my lord!" said the crier.

Of course I knew this very well; but it sounded respectable to expect them.

"Dear, dear," said I, "this is really most unfortunate. They must have mistaken the day."

"Shouldn't wonder," observed Polter, rather drily.

I was not altogether sorry that I had no witnesses to

adduce, as I am afraid that they would scarcely have borne the test of Polter's cross-examination. Besides, if I had examined witnesses for the defence, Polter would have been entitled to a reply, of which privilege he would, I was sure, avail himself.

Mr. Baron Bounderby proceeded to sum up, grossly against the prisoner, as I then thought, but, as I have since had reason to believe, most impartially. He went carefully over the evidence, and told the jury that if they believed the witnesses for the prosecution, they should find the prisoner guilty, and if they did not— why, they should acquit her. The jury were then directed by the crier to " consider their verdict," which they couldn't possibly have done, for they immediately returned a verdict of " Guilty." The prisoner not having anything to say in arrest of judgment, the learned judge proceeded to pronounce sentence—inquiring, first of all, whether anything was known about her ?

A policeman stepped forward, and stated that she had twice been convicted at this court of felony, and once at the Middlesex Sessions.

Mr. Baron Bounderby, addressing the prisoner, told her that she had been most properly convicted, on the clearest possible evidence : that she was an accomplished thief, and a most dangerous one ; and that the sentence of the court was that she be imprisoned and kept to hard labour for the space of eighteen calendar months.

No sooner had the learned judge pronounced this sentence than the poor soul stooped down, and taking off a heavy boot, flung it at my head, as a reward for

my eloquence on her behalf; accompanying the assault
with a torrent of invective against my abilities as a
counsel, and my line of defence. The language in
which her oration was couched was perfectly shocking.
The boot missed me, but hit a reporter on the head, and
to this fact I am disposed to attribute the unfavourable
light in which my speech for the defence was placed in
two or three of the leading daily papers next morning.
I hurried out of court as quickly as I could, and hailing
a Hansom, I dashed back to chambers, pitched my wig
at a bust of Lord Brougham, bowled over Mrs. Briggs's
prototype with my gown, packed up, and started that
evening for the West coast of Cornwall. Polter, on the
other hand, remained in town, and got plenty of business
in that and the ensuing session, and afterwards on
circuit. He is now a flourishing Old Bailey counsel,
while I am as briefless as ever.

CREATURES OF IMPULSE.

Mistress Dorothy Trabbs was the buxom landlady of the "Three Pigeons," a pretty country inn on the road from London to Norwich, and Mistress Dorothy was held by competent judges to be the pleasantest landlady on that road, for she was very pretty, and very round, and very plump—too plump, some people said, but that was envy. She had a pretty daughter, Jenny, and a clumsy, cowardly, ill-conditioned, gawky nephew, named Peter; and these two, with a chamber-maid and a nondescript "odd-man," constituted her staff of assistants.

Jenny was a very pretty little girl, but so absurdly shy that her prettiness went for nothing. I suppose it was this very shyness of hers that emboldened Peter to fall in love with her; for he was such a timid donkey that an ordinarily self-possessed woman frightened him into fits. At all events he *did* fall in love with her, and he told her so. And when he told her so, Jenny forgot, for the moment, her shyness and boxed his ears soundly. He felt this blow so much that he never opened the subject again. In fact, Jenny had a proper contempt for cowards, and like all women, shy or otherwise, adored manly courage. And Sergeant Brice, of Her Majesty Queen Anne's Foot Guards, who had just returned from Malplaquet with a bullet in his right leg, but otherwise well and hearty, and who had received a billet on the " Three Pigeons," was as brave as a man need be. So Jenny fell in love with him, but nobody knew anything about it.

At the time when my story opens, Mistress Dorothy was in a terrible state of perplexity. A strange Old Lady, who declined to give any name or any reference as to her respectability, and who had no luggage whatever, had taken up her abode at the " Three Pigeons," and steadily refused to pay any rent at all. This state of things had continued for three months, and seemed likely to continue for three more months, or three years for that matter, for the Old Lady was a fairy of a malignant description, and had it in her power to inflict all sorts of punishment on anybody who displeased her. At first Mistress Dorothy declined to supply her with food, but the Old Lady explained that she could live quite comfortably without any food at all, and indeed would much prefer not to have any refreshment of any kind set before her. So, as I said before, Mistress Dorothy was in a terrible state of perplexity, and a council of war was held in the bar-parlour, in which council Sergeant Brice, Jenny, and the abject Peter assisted, together with a wealthy, but very disreputable, old miser named Verditter, who was collecting rents in the neighbourhood, and who had made the " Three Pigeons " his head-quarters because it was the cheapest as well as the best inn in the village.

Peter, abject coward as he was, had one redeeming virtue—he was not superstitious. He declined to believe in fairies at all, and especially in the particular fairy under discussion. He had, on one occasion, seen the Old Lady cleaning her teeth with a tooth-brush, and he argued, with some show of reason, that this proved she was not a fairy, as fairies did everything with a wand. So, as the Old Lady was a very weak and tottering old lady, he thought that he might venture to tackle her without incurring any serious risk. Moreover, as all the others most firmly believed in her supernatural character, he would no doubt acquire a cheap reputation for courage if he offered to undertake to get her out of the house. So he walked boldly into her room with the firm intention of bullying her out of it.

"Now, Old Lady," said Peter, " we've put up with you long enough. Pack up your tooth-brush, and be off, for your room is wanted, and your company is not."

" Take care, Peter," said the Old Lady.

"Take care ! What have I to take care of ? Why, I could manage two old women like you any day in the week ! " and he stalked about like a swashbuckler.

" Take care, Peter," answered she, " or I shall give you a sound thrashing,"

But Peter didn't care any longer, indeed he was so rude as to put out his tongue at her, and by his general demeanour he expressed the most marked contempt for her physical strength.

"Now, Old Lady, enough of this," said he; " you talk of thrashing me. ME? Come on ! " And Peter took off his coat, and squared-up to her with great bravery.

“Peter,” said she, “you have thought fit to square-up to me. You will continue to square-up at everybody you meet, until further notice.”

The Old Lady hobbled away into her bed-room, and Peter, to his extreme dismay, found himself compelled to be continually squaring-up, in an undaunted manner, at a roomful of invisible enemies. He retired in great confusion to his loft, shouting down to his friends in the bar-parlour, that he had altogether failed in his mission.

It was now Jenny’s turn to try her luck with the Old Lady. The poor little timid girl set about her work with great reluctance.

“Well, my dear,” said the Old Lady, “what do you want?”

Jenny, finding the Old Lady in an amiable mood, thought that she could not do better than endeavour to coax her out of the place.

“Dear Old Lady,” said she, “you are so kind, and so good, and so amiable, that I am sure it is only necessary to tell you that we want your room or your rent, and you will immediately humour our little wishes in this respect. Now do, there’s a dear, kind, pretty Old Lady.”

And Jenny began to kiss and coax the Old Lady, as no Old Lady was ever kissed and coaxed before.

“My dear,” said the Old Lady, “this show of affection for one you don’t care twopence about, is very disgusting, and, as a punishment, you will be so good as to kiss and coax everybody you meet until further notice.”

And Jenny retired in great confusion to her room,

calling downstairs to her friends in the bar-parlour, that she had altogether failed in her mission.

The brave Sergeant Brice's turn came next.

" Well, Old Lady," said he.

" Go away, soldier," said she. " I hate soldiers ! "

" But——"

" Go away; you're a bold, bad man ! "

And she struck so hard at the brave Sergeant with her crutched stick, that he was obliged to dodge and duck all over the room in order to ward off her blows.

" As a punishment for your impertinence in entering my room without permission," said the Old Lady, " you will be so obliging to dodge and duck, as you are dodging and ducking now, before everybody you meet."

And the bold Sergeant retreated in great amazement to his room, dodging and ducking at an imaginary foe all the way, and shouting downstairs to his friends in the bar-parlour, that he had altogether failed in his mission.

Old Verditter, the miser, had, in the meantime, been getting on very well with plump Mistress Dorothy, and having looked round the comfortable bar-parlour, and noticed the silver spoons and the silver tea-pot, and the large silver salver on the sideboard, he had settled in his own mind that Dorothy would make him a very comfortable and remunerative wife. Indeed he had got so far as to make two or three very broad hints on the subject, when Mistress Dorothy cut him short by begging him to be so good as to try what he could do to get the tiresome Old Lady out of the house. Verditter had a firm faith in the power of gold to work out any social problem, and readily undertook to get rid of Mistress Dorothy's unremunerative lodger.

So taking the big bag of gold, which he had collected from his tenants during the day, he walked fearlessly into the Old Lady's room.

" Now, ma'am," said he, " Mistress Dorothy wishes you to go, and I presume that you do not comply with her request, because you have no money with which to pay your travelling expenses to another town.   Allow me to present you with this guinea, which I have no doubt will enable you to reach your destination."

" You are an impertinent old scamp to dare to offer me money," said the Old Lady ; " and, as a punishment, you will be good enough to offer guineas out of that bag to everyone you meet, until further notice."

And the wretched miser retreated in great amazement to the smoking-room (which he knew was empty), offering guineas right and left to imaginary applicants, and screaming downstairs to Mistress Dorothy in the bar-parlour, that he had altogether failed in his mission.

Peter was getting hungry in his cock-loft, so he ventured to descend, squaring at nobody, with a great show of valour.   His only hope was that he should not meet the Sergeant, and this hope was gratified, for the only person he met was Jenny, who had ventured downstairs in order to consult her mother as to the best means of breaking the very compromising spell that the Old Lady had thrown over her.   But the mother had gone out to consult the village schoolmaster, who was a celebrated witch-finder, and a great authority on all matters connected with the Powers of Darkness.

The shy and prudish Jenny, as soon as she saw the abhorred Peter, ran up to him, and, to her extreme consternation, endeavoured to throw her arms round his neck and kiss him. Peter, who was delighted at this proof of affection from a girl who had hitherto detested him, would have offered her every encouragement if he had not felt himself unfortunately compelled to hit out right and left at her in unyielding compliance with the request of the mischievous Old Lady upstairs.

"Peter," said the retiring girl, "I hate and detest you." And so saying she once more threw her arms round his neck, and he, delighted at her change of manner towards him, and attributing her angry words to the disappointment she felt at his rebuffing her, hit out from his shoulder so violently that she had the greatest difficulty in escaping the blow.

"Peter, you brute," said she, "I don't want to kiss you, but somehow I can't help it."

And again she tried to embrace him, and again he struck out at her.

"Peter," said she, "I tell you I am doing this because I can't help it. Please don't hit me, because I am only obeying an irresistible impulse."

And as she made a third attempt to get at him, the Sergeant walked into the room, dodging and ducking, as he dodged and ducked when the Old Lady ran after him with her stick. Peter, hearing the Sergeant coming, ran out of the room as fast as his legs could carry him.

"What!" said the Sergeant, "do I see my shy and timid Jenny endeavouring to embrace that gawky nincompoop, and do I hear her excusing herself by attributing her behaviour to an irresistible impulse?"

And he dodged and ducked about the room in a wholly irrational and unaccountable manner.

"Sergeant, do not hastily condemn me," said Jenny, rushing at the Sergeant, and endeavouring to embrace him as she before endeavoured to embrace Peter.

"Jenny, I'm ashamed of you—shocked,—disgusted!" said he, dodging and ducking, as she tried to throw her arms round his neck. "I loved you for your remarkable and unexampled modesty: but really—"

"Don't, don't be hard on me, Sergeant," said she; "indeed, I am as timid and modest as ever, but an irrepressible impulse compels me to kiss every man I meet."

And she once more threw her arms around him and embraced him. The Sergeant (who had been very carefully brought up) was horrified, and rushed from the room into the street in utter disgust, dodging and ducking all the way, Jenny following him with a most demonstrative show of affection.

In the street the Sergeant met Peter. Peter was in a terrible state of mind, and encountering the Sergeant, would willingly have run away: but the spell the Old Lady had thrown over him compelled him to square up at the Sergeant in the most reckless manner imaginable.

The Sergeant, who was furious at having discovered Jenny's apparent love for Peter, desired nothing better than to give Peter a sound thrashing, but to his own intense annoyance, and to Peter's unspeakable surprise and relief, the fairy's spell compelled the Sergeant to duck and dodge as Peter struck at him as if he (the Sergeant) were in a state of the most abject fear.

" Sergeant," said Peter, " please don't be angry ; but indeed I can't help it."

And he hit the Sergeant straight between the eyes.

" I sincerely trust that this will not hurt you much ! "

And he struck the Sergeant full upon his military nose.

" I earnestly hope that you will derive no inconvenience from this round-hander."

And he planted a round-hander just on the Sergeant's left ear, as that officer ducked and dodged about, apparently in a great state of terror, but really boiling with indignation and thirsting for his adversary's blood.

" Well," said Jenny, hugging the odd-man (who was the only other person within sight, and who did not resist as the Sergeant and Peter had resisted, but who, on the contrary, patiently allowed her to do what she pleased)—" Well," said she, " I did think the Sergeant was a brave man ; and see how Peter is giving it to him—Peter, who is such a coward ! "

And she ran into the house, determined to have nothing to do with either of them.

In the house she met Verditter the miser, whom she heartily detested, the more so because there was every prospect that he would some day be her step-father ; but nevertheless she ran up to him, and explaining that he was not to misinterpret the compliment as she was acting under an irresistible impulse, threw her arms round his neck and began to kiss him as she had kissed the others. Verditter was delighted (for he was a dreadful old Turk), but it was not on that account that he presented her with a succession of guineas from his long bag; he did that in compliance with the whim of the strange Old Lady.

Jenny was very much annoyed indeed, not only at having behaved in such a forward manner to old Verditter, but also because she considered his presenting her with guineas an act of extremely bad taste. However, she did not wish to offend him by refusing his guineas, for he was a vicious old man who always resented an insult, so she pocketed them with a very bad grace, and spent them the next day with extreme reluctance on a handsome brooch and earrings, which she wore ever afterwards as a kind of punishment upon herself for having taken the old man's money at all.

As old Verditter was handing over his guineas, with a most piteous expression of countenance, to Jenny, who could scarcely conceal her annoyance at having to take them, who should come in but Mistress Dorothy. Mistress Dorothy had been trying her hand to get rid of the Old Lady, and having fairly lost her temper, endeavoured to push the Old Lady by main force out of the house. So the Old Lady compelled her to go on pushing everybody away from her until further notice.

As soon as Mistress Dorothy entered, Jenny ran away in great confusion, so old Verditter turned his attention to the buxom landlady and began, to his intense dismay and to her intense delight and astonishment, to offer her guineas from his long bag. But to *her* intense dismay, and to *his* intense delight and astonishment, she felt herself compelled to push him and his guineas away, although she would have liked to have pocketed the whole bagful.

" Ma'am," said he, handing her a guinea, " do not misunderstand me. I give you this money under an irresistible impulse."

" Sir," said she, " you are extremely good, but an irresistible impulse compels me to reject it."

Here the Sergeant entered, dodging and ducking as before.

" Sir," said old Verditter, " do not be alarmed. I am not going to hurt you. I feel myself compelled to offer you a guinea."

" Sir," said the Sergeant, pocketing the money, " I never yet was alarmed in my life. I dodge and duck like this because I am acting under an irresistible impulse."

At this point Peter entered, squaring-up in the fiercest manner at everybody.

" Sir," said old Verditter, " I hope you will not be offended, but an irresistible impulse compels me to offer you a guinea."

" Sir," said Peter, pocketing the money, " I am far from being offended, and I sincerely trust you will take this in good part."

And he knocked old Verditter down to the great astonishment of everybody. Jenny, hearing Mistress Dorothy scream, ran in to see what was the matter. By this time the state of affairs was as follows :

The miserly old Verditter, with tears in his eyes and the worst of language on his lips, was handing guineas to everyone as fast as he could get them out of his bag.

The hospitable Mistress Dorothy was trying to turn him and everybody else out of her inn.

The cowardly Peter was squaring-up at everybody, and particularly at the Sergeant, in an utterly reckless manner.

The valiant Sergeant was ducking and dodging from Peter and everybody else who came near him, as if he had been the most timid soul on the face of the earth.

And Jenny — the shy, modest, prudish, bashful, blushing Jenny—was kissing everybody right and left, as if her life depended on it. In short, there never was a more extraordinary scene in a bar-parlour since bar-parlours first became an institution in Great Britain and Ireland.

In the midst of this scene the Old Lady entered, for she was curious to see how the spell that she had thrown over the inmates of the " Three Pigeons " was working.

Directly she entered, the attention of everyone was directed to her.

The Miser gave her gold.

The Landlady tried to push her out.

The Sergeant ducked and dodged at her.

The bashful Jenny kissed her.

And the cowardly Peter squared-up to her in such a determined manner, if she had not been surrounded by the others, he would have done her a serious injury.

In short, the Old Lady, who was much more than a match for each of them taken singly, was overpowered by numbers. She never thought of this when she entered the room, which was stupid in the Old Lady.

So she at once withdrew the spell she had over them, and they all resumed their natural attributes. Then the Old Lady, who felt very foolish at the error she had committed, hobbled out of the inn for good and all.

The really curious part of this story is that, after everything had been explained, and all had been restored to their normal courses of action, none of the personages in it married each other. They were all so annoyed at having made such fools of themselves that they walked out of the inn in different directions, and were never seen or heard of again.

Except Peter, who, seeing nothing to be ashamed of in having shown such undaunted courage, remained and kept the "Three Pigeons," and prospered remarkably to the end of his days.

MAXWELL AND I.

It was a dull Christmas night that Ted Maxwell and I were spending, boxed up in our chambers on a top-floor of Garden Court, Temple. Not but that we had plenty of friends in London who were keeping it up merrily that night—friends whose merriment was tempered by the fact that circumstances beyond our control required that we should spend the afternoon and evening in chamber solitude. But that Grand Fairy Christmas Extravaganza, the One-Eyed Calendars, Sons of Kings; or, Zobeide and the Three Great Black Dogs, was due on the boards of a minor metropolitan theatre by ten o'clock on the following night, and there were two scenes still unfinished, and three or four songs still unwritten.

For we were dramatic authors, Maxwell and I. Of course we were a great many other things besides, for dramatic authorship in England is but an unremunerative calling at the best of times; and Maxwell and I were mere beginners. We wrote for magazines, we were dramatic critics, we were the life and soul (such as they were) of London and provincial comic papers, we supplied " London Letters," crammed with exclusive political secrets, and high-class aristocratic gossip, for credulous country journals; we wrote ballads for music publishers, and we did leaders and reviews for the weeklies. I had almost forgotten to add that we were barristers-at-law of the Inner Temple, esquires, because that fact was only brought under our notice twice a year; once when the treasurer of the Inn applied to us for our term fees, and once when the Directories and Court Guides made ironical application to us for information concerning our titles and country seats.

There had been an aggravating rehearsal of our extravaganza that morning. It was then discovered that a " carpenter's scene " must, absolutely, be introduced in order to allow time for the elaborate " set " with which the piece was to conclude. The last scene was, as a matter of course, unfinished; the chorus that opened the piece had not yet been written; and several " cuts " had to be made in our favourite scene. Moreover, the leading lady, Miss Patty de Montmorenci, had expressed her intention of ruining everything if she were not permitted to introduce the " *Miserere* " from the " *Trovatore*," after the comic duet between Mesrour and Zobeide; and Mr. Sam Travers, the leading low comedian, had insisted on our finding occasion for him to get over a brick wall with glass on the top of it for him to stick in.

Three or four hours' incessant work enabled us to overcome these difficulties with greater or less success. The " carpenter's scene " was written (goodness only knows what it had to with the plot !); the opening and final choruses were determined on, the necessary cuts were made, and the excised good things carefully

stowed away for our next production. Miss de Montmorenci had her "*Miserere*," Mr. Sam Travers his
broken glass.

"Now," said Maxwell, "let's see how that bit goes,
after Travers' scene—the bit between Scherazade and
Zobeide, I mean."

> Scher. One morning early when I sought my bower
> Without spec-*tator* just to *cull-a-flower*,
> I found my cavalier astride the wall,
> And in the glass entangled, cloak and all.
> And then I heard the wretched youth, alas !
> Casting some strong reflections on the glass ;
> And, after having to perdition hooked it,
> He first *un*hooked his cloak, and then—he hooked it !
>   Zo. You did not see his face !
>   Scher.   Alas ! he fled
> Ere I could make remarks upon that head ;
> But as I scanned the footsteps in the mould
> With eager curiosity, behold
> I found—

"Open the door ! For God's sake, open the door ! "

Maxwell and I started to our feet. We had "sported
our oak," as we did not want to be disturbed, and the
voice (a woman's) was accompanied by a violent knocking, as if the applicant were beating at the door with
her open palm.

We ran to the door, and as soon as we had opened it
a couple of women rushed violently past us into our
sitting-room.

"Shut the door—don't stop to ask any questions—
shut the door, I say ! "

We closed it in mute astonishment. One of the
women, the younger, had fallen on the hearthrug in a
swoon ; the elder was leaning against the mantelpiece,

her head resting in her right hand, and her left hand pressed to her side. Both were soaked with rain and splashed with slushy mud, but they appeared to be dressed in clothes of good quality, and made with some taste. The elder woman, as she stood against the mantelpiece, appeared to be about forty years of age, tall, thin, and notwithstanding her pitiable condition, ladylike. The younger woman was evidently her daughter, and appeared, as well as we could judge as she lay crouched upon the hearthrug, to be about sixteen or eighteen years old.

"I beg your pardon for entering your rooms so unceremoniously," said the elder woman, as soon as she had recovered her breath. "If you will allow me to sit down for a few moments, I will explain all."

Maxwell placed her in a comfortable armchair near the fire, and then busied himself in getting out the brandy. I prepared, in a confused sort of way, to pick up the young girl who had fainted, and who, by this time, gave some evidence of returning consciousness. After two or three attempts, I contrived, rather clumsily I am afraid, to get her on to the sofa ; and by that time she had so far revived as to be able to express her thanks for the attention. I then saw that the estimate I had formed of her age was rather over than under the mark, for she was not more than fifteen or sixteen at the utmost. She was very pale, and apparently in delicate health ; her features were pretty, without being strictly handsome ; and she had a quantity of light yellow hair, which fell in masses over her shoulders as I loosened the strings of her bonnet.

"Now," said Maxwell, as he placed a steaming tumbler of brandy and water before each of the women, "put that away, and then tell us all about it."

"I thank you very much," said the elder woman. "We ——"

"I'll not hear a word while there's a drop of brandy left in that tumbler. Drink it off directly."

But that was clearly impossible, for he had mixed it on the Jack-tar principle of "half-and-half." So on my representing this to him, he was pleased to pass a more lenient sentence, and to reduce the punishment, in each case, by one half.

"I am very grateful to you for your kindness," said the elder woman. "My daughter and I have fled from the violence of my infuriated husband, who, but for your kindness would certainly have killed us."

"May I inquire the particulars?" said he.

"My husband is a master mariner, and we occupy a house in Essex Street, Strand, where I let apartments. He is a dreadfully violent man, and this evening he was brought home, after an absence of three days, by two policemen, quite drunk. He insisted upon having more drink as soon as they had left, and he gradually worked himself into a frenzy of excitement. It unfortunately happened that one of our lodgers left yesterday without paying his rent, and as soon as this fact came to his knowledge he flew into a violent rage, and struck me here," laying her hand upon her side. "He then seized a life-preserver, and, in an agony of terror, Emmie and I rushed into the street, with the intention of seeking shelter from his violence in my nephew's

chambers, which are nearly opposite this house. In my
excitement, I could not find them for some time, and
we wandered about the Temple for, I should think, a
quarter of an hour, before we found Garden Court; and
when at length we did find it, we discovered to our
great sorrow, that his chambers were closed, and a
notice posted on his door to the effect that he had
gone out of town for a week. I heard my husband's
voice in the immediate neighbourhood, and seeing only
one window with a light in it (owing, I suppose, to its
being Christmas-day), my daughter and I made our way
to it as quickly as we could, and effected the unceremonious entrance for which we have to offer you our
humblest apologies."

"If your story is true," said Maxwell, "(and I see
no reason to doubt it), you shall have an asylum here
until we can place you beyond the reach of your husband's violence. But you are wet through. How in
the world are we to remedy that?"

"I have it," said I. "I'll run round to Mrs. Deeks,
and get a change of some kind for these ladies,"

Mrs. Deeks was one of that remarkable and much-
abused class of women, the Temple laundresses. She
was a pleasant, cheery little old woman, with a quiet
chirruping voice, and so big a heart, that you wondered
how she could find room for it in her particularly little
body. She had "done for" us during the three years
we had lived in the Temple, and had nursed me through
two severe illnesses. She was our adviser in all circumstances of social difficulty, and the present embarrassment appeared to be, pre-eminently, a case for her

interference. So Maxwell agreed that we could not do better than take counsel with her immediately; and I started off to lay the delicate circumstances of our case before her without a moment's delay.

I hurried through the half-melted slush, and driving rain, to Gate's Court, Clement's Inn, where the old lady lived. She was entertaining a select company of launresses and their "good gentlemen," and seemed to be enjoying the gentility of her position as hostess so completely, that I felt I was doing a brutal thing in interrupting her proceedings. It was a case of urgency, however, which could not wait, so I did not hesitate to lay the particulars before her, and claim her assistance.

The old lady had herself had some experience of conjugal existence under difficulties, for the late Mr. Deeks, of no occupation worth mentioning, was much given to knocking her down and dancing upon her, during the twenty years of their married life. His chief cause of complaint was that she was " much too good for him," but a merciful Providence, pitying his conscientious difficulties, had eventually removed him to a sphere in which he probably had no difficulty in meeting with congenial companionship. By virtue of her personal experiences with Mr. Deeks, and the fact that she had lived for many years in a neighbourhood where gentlemen of his stamp are common, she set herself up as a judge of bad husbands, and in that capacity entered with considerable zeal into the study of the case I placed before her.

The old lady made up a bundle of dry clothes with all expedition, and, after apologizing to her guests, started off with me to the chambers.

Our visitors were still drying themselves by the fire, and overwhelmed me with their thanks when I entered with Mrs. Deeks. Maxwell and I then made a hollow feint of having important business in a man's chambers in the immediate neighbourhood, which would detain us half-an-hour or so, and left the two ladies and Mrs. Deeks to their devices.

It was still pouring with rain, so Maxwell and I sat on the bottom step of the staircase, and took counsel together.

"Now, Ted, my boy, what are we to do?"

"This," said Maxwell, who had a turn for stating cases, "is a case of peculiar delicacy. Here we have two bachelors in chambers, to whom, in the dead of night, enter two sopping females—one middle-aged and not otherwise remarkable; the other very young, and I think I may add interesting."

"Decidedly interesting," said I.

"And decidedly interesting. They come round with an account of themselves, which on the one hand, may be as true as gospel, and, on the other, may be a story of a cock and a bull."

"That's not likely," said I.

"I did not say it was likely. I am not dealing with probabilities, I am dealing with facts. Whether it is true or not, the fact remains that two sopping females have quartered themselves on two dry bachelors."

"One dry bachelor and one wet one," was my rather captious amendment.

"Now, don't interrupt me unnecessarily; they were both quite dry when the women entered. The fact that one of them has since been out in the rain cannot be taken to act retrospectively. The two sopping females quartered themselves upon two dry bachelors."

" Be it so."

" The question then arises," said Maxwell, dropping the argumentative form in which he had opened the case, " what the devil are we to do ? "

" Precisely.   And what do you suggest ? "

" There are three courses open to us : firstly, to allow these ladies to occupy our chambers until we can dispose of them satisfactorily, and get rooms at Sams' Hotel for ourselves : secondly, to allow them to occupy our chambers and *not* get rooms at Sams' Hotel for ourselves—to occupy them conjointly in short ; and thirdly, to wash our hands of the whole affair, and, by placing the sopping ladies on the landing and once more sporting our oak, reduce the present complicated state of things to its normal simplicity."

I am bound, in justice to Maxwell, to admit that I believe that he placed his last course before me, simply that the beauty of his argument might not be impaired by the omission of any of its features. As he himself expressed it in reply to my expostulations, he did not suggest it as a prudent course—he simply threw it out for my consideration.

It did not take us long to determine that the first and second propositions alone demanded our serious attention.

" You see," said Maxwell, " you get two ladies and two gentlemen on the one hand, and a sitting-room and a double-bedded bed-room on the other. There is an utter want of proportion between the two groups, to say nothing of the fact that a cold and critical society is looking quietly on, eager to pounce upon and make the most of any step which is not characterized by the nicest discrimination."

"The upshot of all this would seem to be, that we had better let them occupy our rooms until to-morrow, and that the best thing we can do is to go and secure a couple of beds at Sams'."

"That is the conclusion to which I should have come in time, if you had allowed me to argue it out my own way," said Maxwell, rather pettishly; "but I suppose we had better let our guests know what we propose to do, before we take any further steps in the matter."

So we went upstairs again, and finding from Mrs. Deeks that the ladies were in as presentable a condition as circumstances would permit, we walked in with the intention of obtaining their agreement to our suggestion.

They were sitting by a blazing fire, comfortably wrapped up in shawls and flannel petticoats, while the dresses they had taken off were steaming away on the backs of two chairs. There was a quiet, cosy look about the old chambers, which was partly due to the fact that Mrs. Deeks had laid a substantial supper, partly to the presence of the ladies themselves under circumstances which generated mutual communicativeness, and partly to the contrast that the room afforded to the miserable splashing pavement which we had been contemplating for the last half hour. I daresay that the appearance presented by our visitors, muffled up as they were in

Mrs. Deeks's underclothing, would have been sufficiently ridiculous, if it were not that their pale appealing faces, thinned as they were by hard usage and insufficient food, their utter helplessness in our hands, and an exaggerated sense of the intrusion of which they had been guilty, brought the pathetic side of their case so forcibly before us that even Mrs. Deeks's flannel petticoats were glorified by their association with it.

We sat down to supper; Maxwell doing the host in a pleasant, cheery, country gentleman sort of way, intended to convey the impression that we were not at all taken aback by the events of the evening, and that, in point of fact, this sort of thing happened to us three times a week, or so.

"I beg your pardon," said Maxwell, "may I venture to ask whom I am addressing?"

"Talboys, sir—Mrs. Talboys; and this is my daughter Emmie Talboys. I should have told you our names before, but in the excitement of the events that brought us into your chambers, I forgot to do so."

"Pray don't mention it. I am Maxwell, my friend here is Bailey—Bob Bailey; and now that we all know one another, I'll tell you, Mrs. Talboys, what we—that is, Bailey and I—propose to do. We propose to give up our chambers to you for the night—Mrs. Deeks will see to the necessary alterations—and to take up a temporary abode in an adjoining hostelry—at Sams', in fact. Now, Mrs. Talboys, have you, or has Miss Talboys, any objection to urge to this arrangement.

Mrs. Talboys was, of course, exceedingly and unnecessarily grateful to us for our hospitality, and as the only objection she could urge was the sorrow she should feel at putting us to so much trouble, the matter was soon decided, and Mrs. Deeks received instructions to make our room as suitable to the necessities of two ladies as circumstances would allow, while we finished supper.

We soon became very pleasant and chatty together, a state of things for which, I believe, we were in no small measure indebted to the fact that tea formed one of the items in our repast, and that Mrs. Talboys presided at the tea-pot. There are no circumstances better calculated to make an Englishwoman look and feel thoroughly at home, under difficulties, then the sitting at the head of a table pouring out tea. It is a position that comes naturally to her, and she fits into it as a ball fits into a socket. She handles your tea-pot, and your milk-jug, and your sugar-basin, and your cups and saucers with an air of understanding their various relations, properties, and proportions, to which no bachelor — or married man, for matter of that—was ever known to attain. It puts her on good terms with herself and her surroundings, and Maxwell and I agreed that tea in chambers, presided over by a lady, although in Mrs. Deeks's underclothing, was as different a thing altogether to tea under bachelor circumstances as rum-punch to curds and whey.

Maxwell and I took our leave of Mrs. and Miss Talboys with as much ceremony as if they had been our hostesses and we their guests, and started off for Sams', which then stood opposite King's College. After passing an unsatisfactory night at that dingy establishment, we returned to our chambers to breakfast. Mrs. Talboys and her daughter had, it appeared, passed as comfortable a night as circumstances would permit, and after a pleasant breakfast, we took further counsel with our *protegées* as to what was to be done.

It appeared from Mrs. Talboys' statement, that her impulsive husband was expected to leave London for Melbourne the next day ; so Maxwell and I determined that our course, as far as Mrs. Talbot and her daughter were concerned, was to afford them the protection of our chambers for another night ; after which they would be enabled to return to their house without dread of further molestation. This arrangement appeared to set the mind of Mrs. Talboys completely at rest, and she overwhelmed us with expressions of gratitude. She expressed herself, however, with so much anxiety as to the condition of her husband, the lodgers, and the furniture, after the *fracas*, that Maxwell and I determined to call at the house in Essex Street on our way to rehearsal, and, in the assumed character of intending lodgers, ascertain whether any harm had resulted to the establishment or its inmates in consequence of the previous night's disturbance.

CHAPTER II.

The rehearsal was called for eleven o'clock, and as we had upwards of an hour to spare, Maxwell and I made our way at once into the heart of Captain Talboys' social privacy.   The house in Essex Street had all the appearance of a carelessly conducted lodging-house.   The windows were dirty, the blinds were awry, one of the area railings was broken, and the place generally conveyed an impression of insolvency, which the presence of a canary in the parlour window did little to remove. The street-door was open, for a drabby girl of fourteen, in ragged brown stockings, was cleaning the steps, and a rusty cat sat by her side, looking up and down the street wistfully with an expression of countenance that seemed to say, "This is a very hopeless concern of ours; I wonder if there's an opening for me at No. 15." That there was at least one inmate, however, whose spirits were not damped by this state of things, was testified by a huge voice that came rolling out at the open door, bearing upon it the *refrain* of some old-fashioned nautical song, and which ran, I think, as follows :—

> "Oh, Jenny, she cock'd her eye at me,
>   A long time ago !
> A long time ago, you lubber !
> A long time ago, you lubber !
>   A long time ago !"

Maxwell and I listened a few minutes, and eventually the singer stopped, and applause, as from a solitary tumbler, appeared to reward his efforts.   We then asked the wretched servant-girl, as a matter of form, if Mrs. Talboys was at home ?

"No, sir, missis is just gone out, sir.   Is it about the lodgings ?"

"Yes, it's about the lodgings."

" Master's in sir," said she, " I'll tell him, and p'raps he'll show 'em."

The unhappy girl, who appeared to be suffering from a chronic cold, which she relieved from time to time on the back of the hearth-stone, gathered herself together, and limped into the dining-room, whence the sounds of revelry proceeded. She came out almost immediately, with a ducking, dodging action, as if something had been thrown at her, and told us to step in.

We obeyed her instructions, not without much mis-giving, and, passing two corded chests, labelled " Captain Talboys, ship *Heart's Content*, Limehouse Reach," which stood in the hall, we found ourselves in the presence of the carousers whose voices we had heard in the street. One, evidently Captain Talboys, was a big, muscular, hairy sailor, with a low square brow, a bull neck, great brown hands, and shoulders of enormous breadth. His coat was off, and was lying on a chair hard by. He wore square-cut black trousers, a black satin waistcoat, and thick square-toed Wellington boots. His companion was a small, unwholesome-looking, fat, Jew, with a pasty complexion, black moustache and whiskers, a massive gold chain, and several thick rings on his dirty squabby fingers.

" Come in shipmet," said Captain Talboys, in a thick husky voice, " come in ; and what'll yer take ? Here's brandy, rum, whiskey, gin, anything. Help yourself shipmet ! Yo ho ! help yourself ! "

" Thank you, I don't think we'll drink anything," said I, as I stumbled over the coal-scoop, which appeared to have been the missile with which the announcement of our appearance by the drabby servant girl was greeted. "We have come about some apartments which you advertise in your window."

"Here, you gal!" shouted Captain Talboys.

The drabby girl made her appearance at the door.

"'Partments. Take 'em up," was the brief form of words in which he explained the object of our visit to the servant.

The fat Jew had been staring at Maxwell and at me rather anxiously for a minute or two, and just as we turned to leave the room he said, "Beg pardon, gents, but I think I'm speaking to Messrs. Maxwell and Bailey, ain't I?"

We had determined on two imaginary names, which we had arranged to give if any names had been demanded of us; but as the small Jew appeared to know us, we were fain to admit the truth of his assertion.

"I thort so. Here, Captain, these gents is Maxwell and Bailey, the dramatic horthers. You've 'eard on 'em, Captain; don't say yer ain't 'eard on 'em! Saw that farce o' yourn, 'Up in the World,' gents. Best thing eversornalmilife! best thing eversornalmilife! *You* know, Captain; chap up the chimney—*you* know!"

"Oh, ah!" said the Captain, "*I* know fast enough."

"Very 'appy to make your acquaintance, gents. I'm Mister Abraham Levy, of the Parnassus Music Hall; p'raps you may have 'eard on me. Any night you like to look in upon me, your card's quite sufficient, gents; either on you, or any friends o' yourn."

I said some matter-of-course words, to the effect I should be delighted, I was sure.

"By the way, p'raps we can do some business together; who knows? Yer 'avent got anything in the comic duologue line on yer hands, 'ave yer? Somethin' that would suit my Bob Saunders and little Clara Mandeville, yer know. *You* know the sort of thing I mean."

Maxwell and I regretted that we had nothing on hand that would suit him. An impatient growl from Captain Talboys warned us that he considered that the audience had lasted quite long enough; so we beat a rapid retreat, and proceeded, in company with the servant, to go through the hollow form of inspecting the apartments.

I am sorry to say, that the rooms to which our attention was principally directed were at that moment in process of being vacated by a gentleman, who had given notice of his intention to quit on the preceding evening, immediately after, and in consequence of, the disturbance between Captain Talboys and his unhappy wife. There was only one other lodger, an undesirable Irish tenant, whom Mrs. Talboys had made repeated but fruitless efforts to get rid of.

We mumbled out something to the servant about returning to-morrow, and giving a definite answer, and then made the best of our way to the theatre. The rehearsal was unsatisfactory; no one was perfect, or anything like it; properties had to be made, music to be scored and learnt, and comic dances to be decided on. At two o'clock we were all cleared off in order that the rest of the afternoon might be devoted to the last scene—a complicated absurdity, that took ten minutes to develope, and looked, eventually, more like a gorgeous valentine than anything I ever saw. The stereotyped assurance that everybody gave us, that "it would be all right at night," afforded us but little consolation, for we had often heard it before, in cases where it was very far indeed from being all right at night. So we returned to the Temple in evil spirits.

We gave Mrs. Talboys and her daughter an account of Captain Talboys' then condition, and we told her of the first floor's indignant departure. I am afraid that the result of our mission did little in the way of raising her spirits. The fact, however, that the captain's luggage was prepared for sea revived her a little; and it was settled that, if, on our calling the next day, we found that he had joined his ship, Mrs. Talboys and her daughter were to return home. As the day wore on our respective spirits revived; and, after a pleasant make-shift dinner, which we ordered in from the "Cock," we began to look upon our respective prospects with more hopeful eyes. We had a piano in the chambers, and Emmie Talboys sang some simple old English ballads, with a delightful untutored pathos which was inexpressibly charming. Maxwell, who had a fine baritone voice, also employed it to the best advantage; and so with songs and quiet chat we passed the afternoon and evening, until it was time for us to go to the theatre. We left the two ladies in possession of our chambers, and betook ourselves to the first representation of the Grand Fairy Extravaganza of "The One-Eyed Calendars, Sons of Kings; or, Zobeide and the Three Great Black Dogs."

My private impression of the One-Eyed Calendars " is that it was irreclaimable nonsense; but, as everyone had the necessary number of verbal contortions to deliver, and as every song was followed up by a nigger "breakdown," and as the management had the combined *maximum* of (stage) beauty with the *minimum* of petticoat, it was practically a great success. The authors were honoured with the customary "call," and the papers on the ensuing day endorsed (as they usually do) the opinions expressed by the audience. It is true that our satisfaction at the favourable character of the notices was somewhat damped by finding ourselves invariably alluded to as "those twin sons of Momus;" but, on the whole, we had no reason to complain of the manner in which we were treated.

The next day on my inquiring in Essex Street, I found that Captain Talboys, his Jew friend, and the two big boxes had taken themselves off. The drabby servant was in a terrible state of mind at the non-appearance of her mistress, who (she now told me) had been absent with Miss Emmie ever since Christmas night. "She was a good missis to her," she said, "and so was Miss Emmie, right good; and she'd go right off to the pleece and have them looked for, if she'd only someone to mind the house for a quarter of an hour." But the woman who usually came to cook had been drunk ever since Christmas Day, and she was at her wits' end to know what to do. And the poor little drab, who had made many gulpy attempts to keep the tears down (for she was a brave little drab), fairly gave way, as her responsibilities stood forth in all their naked magnitude before her, and cried away as if her heart would break.

Maxwell and I made the best of our way back to the Temple, and placed the facts of the little servant's anxiety and helplessness before Mrs. Talboys and Emmie who lost no time in putting on their bonnets and returning to Essex Street, after thanking us most emphatically for our kindness and hospitality. She sincerely hoped that we would kindly call on her from time to time; Emmie and she were always at home in the evening, and they would be most happy if, when we had an evening to spare, we would spend it with them.

*   *   *   *   *   *

By degrees Maxwell and I became very intimate with Mrs. Talboys, and we took an interest in assisting her with our counsel, whenever she found herself entangled in a social difficulty with which she was unable to grapple single-handed. For I am afraid that no course of training under the sun could possibly have made a good manager of Mrs. Talboys. She was a mild, weak, good-hearted, unsystematic woman, who was as unfit to manage a London lodging-house as Maxwell and I were to command a man-of-war. A very short experience of the nature of the difficulties with which the poor lady was surrounded, convinced us that she was more or less the dupe of everyone with whom she had dealings. We contrived, in course of time, to establish a system of check upon her lodgers and her tradespeople, we lent her a little money to make a few indispensable additions to her stock of furniture, and we procured her a tenant for her drawing-room floor. In a couple of months after Captain Talboys' departure, matters had so far improved that Mrs. Talboys was in a position to substitute a permanent cook for the intermittent functionary who had hitherto been in the habit of looking in from time to time to ascertain whether her services were required.

We passed a great many pleasant evenings with the Talboys, to the enjoyment of which little Emmie's unpretending musical powers contributed in no slight degree. I have not dwelt at any length on Emmie Talboys' appearance and characteristics, for, when I first knew her, she did not make any very decided impression on me. She had a quiet, retiring, unassuming way with her, that appeared rather to shun observation than to court it; and, at first, her extreme nervousness made us feel that the ordinary matter-of-course attentions which we should have paid to any other young lady, would have frightened the poor little woman out of her senses. But as she came to know us more intimately, her extreme shyness wore off, and we found beneath it a sweetness of disposition, combined with a simple unaffected pleasure in our society, which to me was irresistibly charming. She was not absolutely pretty, but her big blue eyes, her thick yellow hair, and the bright smile with which she welcomed us when she came to know us well, stood her in good stead of the advantages which mere regularity of feature would have conferred upon her. I am afraid that I must own that before I had known the little woman many weeks, I fell desperately in love with her. As I have already implied, it took some little time to bring this about; for her beauties of disposition broke upon us so gradually that to have fallen in love with her, at first sight, would have implied the possession of a discrimination of character to which I lay no claim.

They were very pleasant evenings, those that Maxwell and I spent with the Talboys. Maxwell, I think, enjoyed them almost as much as I did. He was not a man who was given to falling easily in love, and, although he was about my own age—that is to say eight-and-twenty, or thereabouts—he had a fatherly protecting way of treating little Emmie Talboys that was really very amusing. He looked upon her as a mere child, and bought playthings and sweetmeats without number for her. He had no hesitation in calling her by her Christian name, as soon as he knew what it was; and his elderly didactic manner caused her to look upon his doing so as a matter of course. We used to sit by the fire-light on the long winter evenings, and Mrs. Talboys would take counsel with Maxwell on such points of domestic economy as had turned up to perplex her during the day, while I sat by the battered old piano, and listened to Emmie's pure and gentle voice, as she sang " On the Banks of Allan Water," " The Bailiff's Daughter of Islington," or some other simple plaintive ballad which lay within the compass of her unpretending powers. Maxwell and I used often to take them to the theatre, to which we had no difficulty in obtaining free admission; and it was refreshing to a couple of battered theatrical hacks like ourselves, who had seen every piece that had been produced in London during the last ten years or so, to witness the childlike interest that the little woman took even in the common-place hackneyed incidents of the wretched farce that played the audience out. At other times, Mrs. Talboys and Emmie would spend the evening with us at our chambers; on which occasions we would ask Cranley of the Home Circuit, O'Byrne of the *Advertiser*, and one or two other fellow-Templars, to drop in; and then we always wound up the proceedings with an oyster or lobster banquet from Prosser's. We always gave out that Mrs. Talboys was the wife of Captain Talboys (impliedly of the Royal Navy), now at sea; concerning whose health and prosperity, by-the-bye, O'Byrne invariably made well-meant but most awkward inquiries of Mrs. Talboys whenever he met her.

This sort of thing went on for about twelve months. The more I saw of little Emmie Talboys, the more desperately I loved her. I don't think I ever hinted to the little woman in the most remote manner at the existence of this attachment, but I cannot suppose she was ignorant of it. In point of fact I am sure it was marked by Mrs. Talboys, and I am equally sure that she placed no impediment in the way of our being together. I had almost made up my mind to speak openly to Emmie, when an event occurred which upset all my plans.

One morning (it was in the January twelve-month after our first meeting with the Talboys) Maxwell and I returned to London after a fortnight's absence in Liverpool, where we had been to superintend the production of a Christmas piece. Among the letters that awaited us was one addressed to Maxwell from Mrs. Talboys, with a date a week old. He opened it, read it, and handed it to me. It was to the following effect:—

ESSEX STREET, *30th Dec.*, 1859.

" MY DEAR MR. MAXWELL,—I have grievous news to

tell you of myself. My husband contracted a great many debts before he left England, and as he has not been heard of for twelve months, his creditors have become most impatient. You will be distressed to hear that all my furniture has been seized under a bill of sale, that my tenants have been obliged to leave the house in consequence, and that Emmie and I are absolutely ruined. We start for Chester to-day—we used to have friends there, who may still remember us, and place us in the way of earning a respectable living; God only knows what is to become of us should they fail. Forgive me, dear Mr. Maxwell, for taking this course without consulting you or Mr. Bailey. After your exceeding kindness to me and mine, I am afraid that you will think I am acting most ungratefully in thus leaving London without speaking to you on the subject. But, when I tell you that I do so because I know that your generous nature would have prompted you to offer further assistance if I had placed our case before you, I am sure you will see that I could not, with propriety, have acted otherwise than I have done. If my husband should return soon, my present difficulties may be got over, for he will receive a large sum of money on his arrival; but, in the meantime, Emmie and I must do our best to earn a living by ourselves. Trusting that a very short time will elapse before we meet again, and with the deepest gratitude to both of you for your extreme and, to me, unaccountable kindness, believe me to be, my dear Mr. Maxwell, ever yours, most thankfully,

" EMILY TALBOYS."

We were thunder-struck at the contents of the letter: in point of fact, I had to read it two or three times before I could grasp its contents. Some minutes elapsed before either of us spoke. I sank on my arm-chair, completely overwhelmed at the misfortune that had happened to them and to me. At length Maxwell broke the silence.

" We must take steps to find them instantly ! "

" But what, in Heaven's name, can we do," said I.

" Advertise ; we will also write to the post-office at Chester—it is not improbable that they will think it likely that we have written there, and will make inquiries accordingly."

" But they don't want to hear from us."

" Yes, they do. Besides, if a woman knows, or believes, that a letter is waiting for her at a post-office, she will go and apply for it, whether she wishes to hear from the writer or not."

Maxwell had an intellectual pinnacle of his own, from which he looked down upon woman and her ways. From some cause or other (perhaps owing to its giddy height) it appeared to be unfavourable for minute examination ; at all events, woman at large was one of those topics of discussion upon which Maxwell and I seldom agreed. However, I was only too glad to catch at the small crumb of comfort that he offered me, and I agreed that there might be something in that, too.

We hurried off to the house in Essex Street. It was empty, and a torn advertisement pasted near the door, together with the litter and straw on the steps and in the road, spoke of the recent sale. A notice, to the effect that the eligible premises (adapted for a lodging-house) were to let, and that application might be made to the housekeeper within, or to Messrs. Puddick and Crowby, auctioneers and estate agents, in Catherine Street, Strand, adorned the parlour window.

We made application to the housekeeper, as advised, believing that she would be more likely to give us information about Mrs. Talboys' movements, than Messrs. Puddick and Crowby. However, she turned out to be a sodden old lady, who knew nothing more of Mrs. Talboys, except that she was a precious bad lot, as ought to be rope-ended if all on us had their jew. No, she didn't know nothing about no addresses—Mrs. T. took precious good care as nobody should—and for a good reason, too.

We left this impracticable old female in depressed spirits, and turned our attention to Chester generally. We sent carefully-worded advertisements to the *Times* and to the Chester papers; and Maxwell wrote a long letter to Mrs. Talboys, Post-Office, Chester, begging her to afford us some information as to her proposed movements, if she objected to telling us her address.

Day after day elapsed, but no letter came to us from Mrs. Talboys. I will not attempt to paint my intense grief at losing my little Emmie. Suffice it to say, that, after six weeks' interval of mental depression, which seriously affected my powers as a writer of light literature, I began to recover my usual spirits, and, excepting that I could never make up my mind to leave the Temple at the Essex Gate, or to look down Essex

Street as I passed it in the Strand, matters went on pretty well as they did before the events of which these chapters have told.

CHAPTER III.

Two years had elapsed since the disappearance of Mrs. Talboys and little Emmie. During that time neither Maxwell nor I heard anything of either of them, and I am afraid I must own that they had both completely faded from our thoughts. With the exception of an occasional "Wonder what's become of the Talboys?" they were hardly ever alluded to by either of us.

Time had not treated us particularly well. We had long ago attained that well-known five pounds a week that so many writers of light literature attain, and so few go beyond, and at an average of five pounds a week, apiece, our income steadily remained. Not so, however, our expenditure. I am bound in honour to state, that Maxwell and I were both inconveniently in debt. We were not men of decidedly extravagant habits, but each of us had his hobbies, and a hobby-horse is the most expensive riding that a beggar can indulge in. In our cases, our respective hobbies carried us considerably beyond the constable, and we were obliged to accept all sorts of work to enable us to keep our enemies at bay.

One morning, as Maxwell and I set to work, in extreme ill-humour, to complete a series of " Drawing-Room Comic Songs," which we were doing for a cheap music publisher at a guinea per song, we were interrupted by a single knock, which Maxwell rose, impatiently, to answer. He opened the door and found a flabby, shabby-genteel man in rusty black, waiting on the landing——

" Mr. Bailey, sir ? "

" No—Maxwell."

" That will do, sir. I have come—— "

" I know. It's steel pens ; I don't want any."

" No, sir, it's not steel pens—— "

" Then it's ketchup. Be off ! "

" No, and it isn't ketchup neither," said our visitor, with an impatient air of injury. " A letter, wait for answer."

And, so saying, he put a dirty, thumby envelope into Maxwell's hands. He opened it, and read as follows :—

" PARNASSUS, OXFORD STREET, *April 4th*, 1863.

" DEAR SIR,—I am in want of a short dualog for two people—self and wife—with songs. Something short and smart, to play twenty minutes or thereabouts, with practical fun, such as suits my audience. My terms for such is a ten-pound note, and if either of you got anything to suit, shall be glad. Must have it by the 6th, as we open with it on the 7th. Please send answer by bearer, and beg to remain, yours, etc.,

" ABRAHAM LEVY."

Owing to the fact that the demands for light farce had

not kept pace with our literary fecundity in that respect we had a good deal more theatrical capital lying idle on our hands than we had at the time when we first made Mr. Levy's acquaintance at Captain Talboys'. So we sent an answer by the seedy messenger, to the effect that we had something that would doubtless suit the requirements of a Parnassus audience, and would look in upon Mr. Levy that evening, and talk the matter over with him.

That afternoon, however, we were favoured with a visit from Mr. Levy, who, having occasion to call at his solicitor's in Clement's Inn, to instruct him to defend an action by the Dramatic Authors' Society for an infraction of copyright, availed himself of the fact of his being in our neighbourhood, to look in upon us, and to arrange preliminaries.

We submitted our plot to Mr. Levy. A lady and gentleman, of high rank, who have been betrothed in early infancy (as is customary in the best English families), but who had taken the deepest dislike to each other, owing to the fact that the gentleman was said to possess an inordinate and unnatural passion for baked sheep's head—a dish which the lady held in aristocratic abhorrence—and that the lady was never happy unless she was devouring peppermint—a confection for which the gentleman entertained the profoundest disgust—meet unexpectedly in the centre of the maze at Hampton Court. The mutual embarrassment and annoyance caused by this most awkward *rencontre* is enhanced by the fact that, owing to the ingenious disposition of the labyrinth, neither of them is able to find a way out of it. Thus thrown together by a fate with which it is impossible to contend, they determine to put up with each other's society as best they may. The limited area at their disposal is divided into two equal parts by an imaginary line, and each undertakes to keep to his or her own territory until such time as somebody shall appear who can give them a clue out of the perplexing labyrinth. The lady thinks she cannot do better than employ her enforced leisure by singing some of the favourite ballads of her early infancy, and the gentleman (whose tastes are more material) proceeds to devote himself to the lunch which he has brought with him in a basket. The lady's attention is arrested by his movements, and in an agony of dread at the anticipated appearance of the detested dish, implores him (in a parody on " Robert, toi que j'aime ") to postpone his meal until she can escape from the maze. In a comic duet (a community of proceeding not forbidden by the terms of their treaty), he declines to entertain her suggestion, and proceeds to lunch off—not a sheep's head, but a magnificent *pâté de foie gras*. The whole truth flashed upon her in a moment. A wicked marquis, who seeks her hand, has spread the detestable calumny which has caused her detestation for her betrothed lover! She rushes to his arms and embraces him, and the gentleman, as soon as he has recovered from the astonishment with which this proceeding not unnaturally strikes him, is amazed and delighted to discover that the lady is absolutely free from all suggestion of peppermint. He at once perceives that a wealthy (but hideous) duchess, who adores him, is the author of the abominable rumour

that has estranged him' from his beloved—an explanation ensues, and matters end as happily as a comic duet
can make them.

Mr. Levy was delighted with the plot, and after sug-
gesting that the gentleman must accidentally sit upon
the pie, and put a fork or two into his pocket, and by
otherwise misconducting himself contribute to the actual
fun of the piece ; and impressing upon us that we must
on no account go in for " comedy dialogue," he took his
departure. The dualogue was duly finished, christened
" Love in a Maze," and sent in. By the next post we
received a cheque for ten guineas on the Union Bank.

The ensuing morning, as we sat at breakfast, Maxwell, who had been amusing himself with the *Times*
supplement, suddenly sprang to his feet exclaiming,

"By Jove! here's something about the Talboys!"
and he handed me the paper, pointing to an advertisement that ran as follows :—

"TALBOYS OR TALBOT.—If this advertisement should
meet the eye of Mrs. Emily Talboys or Talbot, widow of
the late Esau Talboys or Talbot, master mariner, who
died in Australia on the 14th or 18th of November last,
and late of Essex Street, Strand, she is requested to
send her address to Tenby and Campbell, solicitors,
Brabant Court, London. Any person who can furnish
such a clue to the present residence of Mrs. Talboys or
Talbot, as shall lead to her discovery, shall receive a
reward of Ten Pounds."

We bolted our breakfast and hurried, as fast as a

Hansom could carry us, to Brabant Court. Of course
we could give no information as to her whereabouts, but
giving our cards, and informing Messrs. Tenby and
Campbell that we were intimate friends of the Talboys,
they were good enough to tell us that Captain Talboys
reached Melbourne in safety, and that he had shortly
afterwards made his way to the diggings, where, after
several weeks' labour, he had made a find of surpassing
magnificence ; that he had returned to Melbourne, that
he fell overboard as he went up the ship's side in a state
of intoxication, that he was drowned, and that his widow
was entitled to a sum of seventeen thousand five hundred and sixty-four pounds—the net proceeds of his
labour in the gold fields. They further told us that
the news only reached them two days since, and that
no clue had as yet been afforded as to their present
address.

We left the office in good spirits, for the hope that we
should eventually hear something of Mrs. Talboys and
Emmie revived within us. As we were in the City we
made our way to Mr. Levy's bankers, with the view
of getting his cheque cashed, for that gentleman's
reputation as a pay-master was not so unimpeachable
as to warrant our looking upon his cheque as a nego-
tiable security of a wholly unquestionable character.
Accordingly, we were not altogether surprised to find it
returned to us dishonoured, with the announcement that
Mr. Levy had considerably overdrawn his account, and
that no further advance would be made to him. So, as
we were particularly insolvent at that moment, Maxwell
and I repaired the same evening to the Parnassus Music

Hall, with the view of inducing him to substitute a cash payment for his worthless cheque.

Mr. Levy was all apology. He had paid a large sum of money in yesterday, and found himself unexpectedly compelled to draw it that morning. But if we would take a seat in his private room, he would see if a sufficient sum of money had been taken at the doors to enable him to settle our claim.

On inquiring he found that up to that time (nine o'clock) only five pounds and some odd shillings had been received, but if we would sit down and make ourselves comfortable, he had no doubt but that he should be able to square it up in half an hour or so. We were fain to agree to this, and placing a bottle of whiskey and some cigars in a tumbler before us, he left us to attend to his duties.

Mr. Levy's private room was situated at the extreme end of the Parnassus, and as the glass door commanded the stage, we amused ourselves by watching the performance until such time as ten pounds should have been taken at the doors.

The principal element of entertainment at the Parnassus Music Hall was comic singing. A stout man, who looked like a churchwarden out of work, occupied the platform as we entered, and sang a series of dismal comic songs, "all of his own composition, sir!" as a waiter informed me.

"I'm told, sir," added my informant, "that that gent is always a-writin' songs in his 'ed. To look at him as he walks through the 'all, talkin' affable to a gent here and a gent there, and a-smokin' with this one and a-drinkin'

with that, you'd little think that all the time he was
a-composing the verses as he sings five minutes after on
the platform.   But he is, sir—rhymes and all ! "

We listened with increased interest to the singer after
this description of his peculiarities.   He was extremely
political, and was very hard upon Lord Derby, and very
patronizing indeed, when he had occasion to allude to
the Royal Family—every member of which appeared to
enjoy *ex officio* the advantage of his protection and his
encouragement—which was the more remarkable as he
was for upsetting every other constituted authority.   He
touched upon the American differences, and having de-
molished the North at a blow, proceeded to slap General
Garibaldi on the back, annihilate the police system, and
to tell us that we had a great many more bishops than
was good for us.   He was vociferously encored (my
friend, the waiter, going into ecstasies over him), and he
obligingly favoured us with another of his composition,
in which he advised Britons generally to go in for their
rights, which he described as,

> " A pipe, my brother ; a bowl, my brother ;
> A maiden fair of a beauty rare,
> To comfort your jolly old soul, my brother ;
>   Sing cheerily ho ! sing ho ! "

Then a terrible woman with big bones, a raw brazen
voice, and her hair parted at the side, came on to the
stage and screamed and roared, and slapped her
hands, and danced, and then sang again, and then
danced and sang and banged herself once more, which
was her energetic way of advising you, under all

circumstances of life, to "speak up like a ma-a-n!"
And then we had a fiddler who could play under a
chair, and over a chair, and through a chair, and on his
head, and with his head between his legs, and under all
circumstances of contortion under which a man could
reasonably be expected to play a fiddle. The fiddler was
followed by two Bounding Brothers, who, at first, were
so mutually polite (as they bounded about the stage)
that you would think they had only been introduced to
each other; but when (in the course of the performance)
they came to know one another better, you found that
the elder brother was haughty, for he repelled the
ingenious advances of the younger brother by turning
him head over heels in the air. But the younger
brother's fraternal love was too strong to be at all affected
by these repulses, although as often as he ran up to
embrace the elder brother, he was turned about by his
unnatural relative in a most distressing manner.
Eventually the elder brother began to lose his temper,
and seizing the younger brother by the middle, twirled
him violently round and round, and eventually threw him
over his head, standing over him (as he came down)
in a threatening attitude which there was no mistaking. The younger brother, who began to feel that
matters were getting desperate, fell on his knees and
prayed. The elder brother was softened, relented,
clasped the younger brother in his arms, and the two
went off, over each other's heads, in a burst of fraternal
ecstasy.

A depressed and faded middle-aged lady, dressed in
a scanty black silk dress, with a small arrangement of

artificial flowers in her bosom, and wearing black
mittens on her hands, then stepped nervously on the
platform, and began to sing, in a weak faltering voice,
a few verses of an Italian song, the purport of which
did not reach us at our end of the room. She was
suffering from extreme nervousness, and broke down
twice or three times in the song she was endeavouring
to sing.

I don't think I ever witnessed a more melancholy
spectacle. The poor lady was received with an ironical
cheer, which, in her innocence, she accepted as a compliment, and every verse was hailed with derisive
shouts, which even she was unable to mistake; so
uttering an apology to the conductor who appeared to
be remonstrating with her in no measured terms, she
left the stage amid a whirl of hooting and cat-calls,
which did not cease until a Favourite Delineator of
Negro Peculiarities appeared, when it changed to a
shout of applause.

"Maxwell," said I, "don't you know that poor
woman's face?"

"No; I didn't notice her, poor creature."

"It's Mrs. Talboys," said I.

"Impossible!"

"But it is. I'm nearly sure of it. Here, waiter,
who was the last singer?"

"What, her as made a mess on it?"

"Yes."

"Bernardini—Madame Bernardini. It's her first
night—she's on trial for an engagement. And," he
added, "I expect it's her last."

There was little else to be got out of the waiter, so we were compelled to wait until we saw Levy. More comic singers, more acrobats, more niggers, and eventually poor little Emmie Talboys!

She was announced under a different pseudonym to that which her mother had adopted; but I had little difficulty in recognizing her. If anything else were wanted to place it beyond a doubt that Mrs. Talboys and Emmie, mother and daughter, had appeared before me that evening, it would have been found in the fact that the wretched bit of faded finery which Madame Bernardini had worn in her bosom, had been transferred to that of the poor trembling little woman who stood before me.

My heart seemed to rise to my throat as I looked upon the old love I had so long lost. The same gentle timid voice bore the accents of the same old pathetic air to my ears—she was singing the "Banks of Allan Water"—and the same mild appealing face, sadly changed by privation, looked timidly on the audience as she concluded her song. She was received with insolent cheers, such as had greeted her poor mother half an hour before, and as she left the stage she stumbled, in her nervousness, over a nail in the floor, and fell heavily against the wing.

Maxwell and I started up to seek Levy, and we met him at the door, with our ten guineas in shillings and sixpences in his hand.

"Levy," said Maxwell, "who is that young girl who has just gone off?"

"Ah, Mister Maxwell, what a chap you are!"

"Tell me her name, for God's sake, man!" said Maxwell, stamping with impatience.

"No, no, Mister Maxwell; she's a good girl, she is—I don't like that sort of thing—she's a good girl, and you must leave her alone."

"Confound it, Levy, stop your infernal—no, no, I beg your pardon—there, you're a good fellow, and mean well—I respect you for it, but you mistake my meaning."

"Oh, it's all right, is it, Mister Maxwell? Well, you're a gentleman, and I don't believe you'd do a dirty thing. Her name is Tolboysh—Tolboysh."

"Then she and her mother are old and intimate friends of ours, and they are advertised for in to-day's *Times*. For God's sake let us go to them!"

"You don't say so! Vell now, only to think! Come along with me—come along with me!"

And the good-natured little Jew led the way to the wretched apartment dignified by the title of "Artistes' Room."

It was a square whitewashed room, furnished with a deal table, a small cracked looking-glass, and half-a-dozen Windsor chairs; a pot of coarse *rouge* with a hare's foot stood upon the mantelpiece, and a well-filled subscription list for an injured acrobat hung upon the wall. The room was strewn with comic hats, banjoes, wigs, and other properties in immediate use by the performers. Poor little Emmie lay on two chairs, nearly insensible, while the vulgar big-voiced woman (who had a big heart too) was bathing a wound in her forehead with a motherly tenderness which would have atoned for her vulgarity twice told. Mrs. Talboys was hovering about her daughter in a helpless anxious way, invoking blessings on the comic lady who had taken the affair into her own hands, and who announced her intention of sending them home in her brougham after it had taken her to do her "turn" at the Polyhymnian.

We were not long in making ourselves known to Mrs. Talboys, and eventually to Emmie. She was at first distressed at our having discovered her under such circumstances, but very delighted to see us notwithstanding. We all went home to her poverty-stricken lodgings in the Camberwell Road together, and when there, we gradually told Mrs. Talboys of the good fortune that awaited her.

It would be affectation to pretend that she felt any sorrow for her husband's death, and we spent a couple of hours that night in mapping out the future which was to be invested with such golden surroundings. They had had a hard time of it since they left London; their friends at Chester had procured her a little employment as a teacher in a National School, but poor little Emmie fell ill of scarlet fever, and Mrs. Talboys lost her situation in consequence. She then advertised as a morning governess, and obtained a little work in that capacity; but she was totally unfitted for the charge of children, and that source of income eventually failed her. Then she obtained a little employment as dresser and wardrobe-woman at a provincial theatre, and eventually little Emmie made her appearance on the stage, but the poor timid little girl failed absolutely. For some months they obtained a precarious living by hanging about theatres and provincial concert-rooms, getting a little employment here, and a little employment there, until at length Mr. Levy, who happened to hear her sing at a provincial music-hall, offered her an engagement in London at one pound ten a week, if, after a week's probation, she should be found up to the requirements of his audience.

That all went merrily with us after this, it is, I suppose, unnecessary to say. We took a pleasant cottage at Twickenham for Mrs. Talboys, with a pretty garden and a lawn sloping down to the Thames, and Maxwell and I used to pull up the river on fine summer evenings after our work was done and take tea with them in the open garden. I leave you to imagine the happiness these evenings afforded me. I leave you to imagine also, that it was not very long before I found out that they afforded equal happiness to little Emmie. And I leave you to imagine how it all ended.

ACTORS, AUTHORS, AND AUDIENCES.

A TRIAL BY JURY.

*An original (but tedious) play has just been damned.
The audience is furious. The manager comes
forward and implores them to listen to him. They
agree to do so. He suggests that the Author be
tried then and there, by a Jury of the audience,
for having had his play damned. They agree. A
Jury is empanneled and a Judge is appointed. A
Gentleman offers to act as Counsel for the Prosecution. The Prisoner conducts his own case.*

The Counsel for the Prosecution immediately proceeded to open the case against the Prisoner. The
Prisoner was charged with one of the greatest offences
that a man with any pretension to a literary position
could commit—that of having written, and caused to be
produced, an original stage-play, which had not come up
to the expectations of the audience. For that offence

he stood at the bar of Public Opinion in order that, after having said whatever he might have to say in defence or extenuation of his conduct, he might undergo whatever punishment, if any, the Court might be pleased to inflict.

John Jerningham, who was much agitated, deposed as follows—I am a theatrical manager. Six months ago the Prisoner submitted an original play for my approval. I accepted it because I had nothing else ready. I did not read it. That is the play that has just been damned. It is called *Lead*. I think it a very good title. I expect that by its failure I shall be four or five thousand pounds out of pocket. (*Murmurs of sympathy from the crowded court.*)

Cross-examined by the Author.—I did not read your play before accepting it, because I do not profess to be a judge of a play in manuscript. I accepted it because a French play on which I had counted proved a failure. I had nothing ready to put up in its place. I was at my wit's end. I have been there before. I soon get there. I have had no special training for the position of manager. I am not aware that any special training is requisite. It is a very easy profession to master. If you make a success you pocket the profits ; if you fail you close your theatre abruptly, and a benefit performance is organized in your behalf. Then you begin again. I am aware that some alterations were made in your play without your sanction. I did not make them myself, as I do not understand these things. I always leave the alterations in an author's dialogue to the stage-manager and company. I certainly consider myself an object of sympathy when a piece fails. I am not of opinion that I ought to be held responsible for the character of the entertainment I provide for the audience. What have I to do with it? I am only the manager.

JOHN JONES.—I was a member of the audience this evening. I have seen the defendant's play. I think it an extremely bad play. It is full of very long and (to me) very tedious speeches. I was pleased with the scene between the rival tradesmen in the grocer's back-parlour because I thought it true to nature; but I consider the scene between the Duke and the Duchess highly improbable. I hissed it on that account. No Duchess would be likely to speak as that Duchess spoke. The scene between the wicked Member of Parliament and the Home Secretary is open to the same objection. I consider myself a judge of a play. I have written a play myself. It has not been acted—not yet.

Cross-examined by the Author.—I am a journeyman plumber. I consider myself a judge of what Dukes and Duchesses would be likely to say—at least, as good a judge as any author. I have plumbed in the very best families. I have supplied a ball-cock to a Royal cistern. Dukes and Duchesses talk quite unlike ordinary people. They have a conversation of their own, which can only be mastered by means of a long familiarity with their mode of life. I consider that nothing on earth is more improbable than that a Duke would say "By Jove!"

I have never heard of a Duchess riding in a four-wheeled cab. I consider such a state of things impossible. I do not profess to be a judge of metaphysics, because I do not know what metaphysics are. I consider very likely that I am a judge of metaphysics without knowing it. I am in the habit of hissing a play as soon as I am bored. I consider it quite likely that I might be bored by scenes with which other people might be pleased. There is no accounting for tastes. I do not know whether hissing a dull scene at the commencement of a play would or would not be likely to disconcert the actors and render them unfit to do justice to their parts. I consider that that is their look out.

Lord Reginald Fitz-Urse.—I was a member of the audience to-night. I was heartily bored by the Prisoner's play. I saw nothing to complain of in the scenes dealing with High Life, but I consider the scene in the grocer's back parlour, ridiculously impossible.

Cross-examined.—I am an officer in the Grenadier Guards. I have had some experience of stage-plays. I believe that nothing is easier than to write a good stage-play. I have written one myself. I found it extremely easy. Mounting guard was an intellectual exercise not to be mentioned in the same breath with it. My play has not been produced—not yet. I have shown it to several managers—they hesitate to produce it, on the ground that it is too intellectual. I had no objection to bring it down to the comprehension of the

audience; but I did not see any way of making it less
intellectual than it was—I have no objection to state
its name—it is a burlesque called *Tom Tiddler*.

THOMAS WILKINSON.—I am a medical student. I
hissed the Prisoner's play because I thought it one of
the worst I ever saw. I objected, among other things,
to the fact that Miss de Vere had to die in Act I. I
did not know at the time that she was not really dead,
but would reappear in Act III., or I should not have
hissed. I thought it bad art. I thought it monstrous
to interest an audience in a singularly beautiful and
talented young lady, and then dispose of her finally at
an early stage in the play. If the author allows the
audience to suppose that a person is dead who is only
insensible, he must take the consequences of the im-
position he has practised upon them.

Cross-examined.—No doubt I am engaged to Miss
De Vere; but that fact does not affect my opinion. I
certainly consider myself a judge of a play. I have
written several plays; they have not been produced—
not yet.

JACOB SHUTTLEWORTH.—I am a clerk in the Home
Office. I have seen the Prisoner's play. I think it
distinctly a dull play. I did not hiss simply because I
do not see the necessary connection between a bad play
and a hiss. We do not hiss bad speeches in the House
of Commons. Perhaps it would be better if we did;
but we don't. I would hiss indecency and profanity,
and even outrageously bad taste, with all the energy at

my command; but not mere dulness. I would do this in the interest of public morals. I regard a dull author who has to depend upon his pen for his livelihood as an object of pity, not of execration. If I want to be revenged upon him, I take care to caution my friends that the house at which his piece is being played is to be avoided.

Cross-examined.—I do not in the least like your play. I entirely coincide with the general opinions which the other witnesses have expressed, though I do not agree with them in detail. For example, I think the scene between the Home Secretary and the wicked Member is very characteristic, and contains many capital hits at the maladministration of our home affairs; but I regard the scenes between the duke and duchess, and that between the two tradespeople as ridiculously untrue to nature. Personally, I regard you as a dull and tedious author. I did not hiss you, simply because I did not think that the offence of mere incompetency deserved so severe a punishment, and because hissing unnerves the actors, and prevents them from doing their best with the play under consideration. I seldom hiss, but when I do it is at the end of an Act. I am not aware that, owing to nervousness caused by sounds of disapprobation, much of the dialogue was accidentally omitted, and still more of it paraphrased. I am not aware that owing to imperfect rehearsals many of the " situations " missed fire. I am not aware that certain characters and scenes were omitted, and others re-written in opposition to your earnest entreaty. The piece is advertised as having been written by you, and I, of course, hold you responsible for every word that is spoken on the stage. I like some plays; I like a play called the *Wedding March;* I think it is an admirable piece of fooling. I think the construction of that play is inimitable, and the situations singularly amusing. I consequently entertain a respect for the ability of the author. I am not aware that it a literal translation from the French. I am not aware that characters, scenery, plot, costumes, incidents, dialogue, and construction were supplied by a French play. If I knew it, it might induce me to modify my opinion of the author's genius for stage construction as exhibited in that work. In bestowing applause upon an author I am not in the habit of distinguishing between an original play and a translation. Now that you mention it, perhaps I should do so. Now that you remind me of it, I certainly see a wide distinction between the two. Now that you direct my attention to the circumstance, I am astonished that I should ever have bracketed them together. The more I think of it the more remarkable it appears to me that I should have placed an author of original plays on the same footing with a translator. Probably I shall henceforth bear the distinction in mind. Still, I consider your play a very bad one. I consider myself a judge of plays. I have written many plays—everybody has. They have not been acted—not yet.

EMILY FITZGIBBON.—I am an actress. I played the part of Constantia in the comedy *Lead.* I have a poor opinion of it as a play. I disliked it from the first

The dialogue is most carefully written, but it is not dramatic. Having studied the play, I have found it full of literary beauties, but it is wholly lacking in well-balanced story and effective action. A series of leading articles, even though they are written in blank verse, do not constitute a play. I think the play suffers materially from being written in blank verse. Very few people on the stage can speak blank verse effectively. I speak it effectively, but I don't know anyone else who does. As a play *Lead* is as heavy as *Manfred*.

Cross-examined.—I regard your play as highly creditable to you in a literary sense, but it is wholly undramatic. It is undoubtedly a thoughtful composition. In point of fact, it is too thoughtful. It is a fact that the stage-manager suppressed several small characters. It is true that two minor parts were fused with mine to make it worthy of my reputation. I did not charge extra for rolling the three parts into one. I did it entirely in the author's interest. I do not remember your objecting to the mutilation of your play. It is not a circumstance that would be likely to dwell on my mind. I have never been hissed in my life. The parts I have played have frequently been hissed. No one has ever hissed me.

The learned Judge.—I am quite sure of that, Miss Fitzgibbon.

James Johnson.—I am a low comedian. (*Laughter.*) I played the part of Joseph Wool in *Lead*. (*Laughter.*) It is not a good part. (*Laughter.*) The humour is too subtle and refined for a theatrical audience. (*Laughter.*) In point of fact, the part labours under the fatal disadvantage of not being low comedy at all. (*Roars of laughter, in which the learned Judge joined.*) I am sorry to have to say this, as I have a personal regard for the Prisoner. (*Laughter.*) I did my best with the part. I bought a remarkably clever mechanical wig—(*laughter*) —for it—(*laughter*)—but it was useless. (*Roars of laughter.*) In my zeal in behalf of the Prisoner I introduced much practical "business" into the part that was not set down for me. (*Laughter.*) I did not charge extra for introducing practical business ; I introduced it solely in the Prisoner's interest. No doubt the Prisoner remonstrated, but I knew what an audience likes much better than he does. (*Laughter.*) The part was soundly hissed—even the introduced scene with the guinea-pig and the hair-oil. (*Roars of laughter.*)

Cross-examined—This is a scene in which I ignorantly attempted to convert a guinea-pig into a rabbit by rubbing it with Mrs. Allen's Hair Restorer. (*Roars of laughter.*) I have never known this scene to fail before ; its truth to nature ensures its success. (*Laughter.*) It would not have failed on this occasion, but that the audience was already thoroughly out of humour. (*Laughter.*) The part I played was that of a London butler. (*Laughter.*) I do not think it unlikely that a London butler would suppose that a guinea-pig could be converted into a rabbit. In a London cook such a mistake would be highly improbable, but not in a butler. (*Laughter.*) These nice distinctions are the outcome of very careful studies on my part. I am aware that you protested against the introduction of this scene. (*Laughter.*) I am accustomed to author's protests. (*Laughter.*) I consider that authors should feel much indebted to me for the valuable interpolations suggested by my humour, experience and good taste. (*Applause, in which the learned Judge joined.*) I cannot say they usually do. (*Laughter.*) Authors are a singularly vain, captious, egotistical and thankless race. I have a strong personal regard for you, but I cannot regard you as an exception. Most certainly I never have been hissed in my life. The parts I have played have frequently been hissed. No one has ever hissed me. (*Loud applause.*)

The learned Judge.—I can quite believe that, Mr. Johnson.

Miss Jessie Jessamine.—I am a singing chamber-maid. I have heard the evidence of the last witness. I agree with the general tenor of it. I have no personal feeling against the Prisoner; on the contrary, I have a strong regard for him. I devoted myself to making his play a success, as far as it was in my power to do so. I introduced a song and dance in order to give briskness to the part. I do not charge extra when I introduce a song and a dance. I introduced them entirely from motives of regard for the Prisoner.

Cross-examined.—I am aware that you protested most strongly against their introduction. I did not regard you as my enemy on that account. The part I played was that of a simple-minded young governess in a country rectory, who is secretly in love with the

Home Secretary. I did not see why such a character should not sing and dance in the intervals between her pathetic scenes. She might be supposed to do so in order to cheer her spirits. I do not consider " Father's pants will soon fit brother " an inappropriate song for such a character. There is nothing immoral in it. I see no reason why a broken-hearted governess should not endeavour to raise her spirts by dancing an occasional "breakdown." I would not dance one in every scene, because that would not be true to nature. I see no objection to her dancing one now and then. A governess would probably have to teach her pupils to dance, and she would naturally practice occasionally to keep her hand in. No, I do *not* mean her foot—I mean what I say, her hand. I wore short petticoats because the audience expected it of me. I see no reason why a governess in a country vicarage should not wear short petticoats if she has good legs. I did not charge extra for wearing short petticoats. I wore them entirely in the author's interests. Besides that, I expect to have at least one song and dance in every part I play. I expect this because I possess both accomplishments, and it is essential that I should display them to the public as often as possible. If I could dance on a tight-rope, I would not insist on displaying that accomplishment in a country vicarage, unless, perhaps, on some very exceptional occasion, such as Rejoicing on the vicar's eldest son Coming of Age. Except on such an occasion no governess in a vicar's family would be likely to dance on the tight-rope. In point of fact, I *can* dance on a tight-rope, and I did *not* insist upon being allowed to do so on the present occasion, as it would not be true to nature—so there ! I consider that truth to nature is the dramatic artist's lode-star. I do not know what a lode-star is, but I am quite sure that *Lead* is a very dull play. No, I have never been hissed. My parts have often been hissed, but no one has ever hissed me.

The learned JUDGE.—It is hardly necessary to give us that assurance, Miss Jessamine.

The evidence of this witness concluded the case for the prosecution.

The Prisoner, in addressing the jury for his defence, began by begging that they would dismiss from their minds any natural feelings of irritation which the unfortunate events of the evening might have roused. He was a dramatic author, who supported himself, his wife, and a large family entirely by writing original plays. When a piece of his failed, it meant not only so many hundred pounds out of his pocket, it also meant loss of reputation, and a reduced chance of ever being allowed to practise the only calling with which he was familiar. He was in the habit of doing his very best to please his audience, according to his humble means, and if he failed it was through no lack of careful thought and honest hard work on his part, but either through an error of judgment—to which all men, even the very greatest, are liable—or owing to circumstances which he was positively unable to control, and to which he would presently allude at some length. The unhappy play that had failed that evening, and perhaps deservedly failed—for he could not close his eyes to the fact that it was sadly lacking in those qualities which appealed at once to a mixed audience—had at least the negative merit of not being an adaptation from the French. Such as it was it was an original play. It had cost him many months of devoted labour, and the labour of those months had evaporated in one evening. He could not say that he was absolutely a ruined man, for he could no doubt, make a much larger and more certain income by translating French plays; but he had hitherto resisted the strong temptation to resort to this very easy means of earning a handsome livelihood—partly from a not unworthy zeal on behalf of English Dramatic Literature, but mainly because he considered the Dramatic Literature of Modern France to be a foul and pestilential cento of moral corruption, degrading alike to the authors who wrote the pieces, to the managers who produced them, and to the polite audiences of both sexes and of all ranks and ages who rejoiced in them. As a clean-minded gentleman he would no more think of drawing inspiration from M. Zola or M. Alexandre Dumas than he would think of drawing drinking water from a grave yard. He hoped that he should not be misunderstood. He did not ask that they should approve his play because it was original. He merely submitted for their consideration the question whether the enormous difficulties with which a dramatic author has to contend in endeavouring to write a play that shall deserve to rank as original should be placed wholly out of the question in estimating the punishment to be awarded to him who fails in such an attempt. The author of a translated play found all his materials ready at hand. There was the plot, there were the characters, there was the dialogue, there was the sequence of events (technically known as the construction), there were the situations, there were even the costumes and "make-up" all ready to his hand, all fire-new from the furnace, all duly assayed and stamped with the approving hall-mark of the wittiest and most theatrically disposed people in Europe. He had had the inestimable advantage of seeing the play "in the flesh." He could tell to a dead certainty where the play would drag if it were produced in London in its then form, and he could cut and modify accordingly. The *Wedding March* had been referred to by one of the witnesses in the highest terms, and it was a fact that the author thereof had received considerably more than two thousand pounds in return for the two days' labour he had spent upon it. But the *Wedding March* was little more than a bald translation. Every element that went to constitute it a success was deliberately copied from its French original. The dialogue was, in itself, contemptible. It derived its humour entirely from the "situations" in connection with which it was spoken. The dullest copying-clerk in Chancery Lane could have done the work as well as its so-called "author." At the same time, he was bound in fairness to admit that there were translations and translations, and that in some exceptional cases—he would instance *Duty*, by Mr. Albery—the translated play was distinctly in advance of its original, as it might very easily be in the hands of such a master of epigrammatic dialogue. *Diplomacy*, by Messrs. Rowe had far more original merit in it than is to be found in most adaptations ; but these cases stood almost alone. But he contended that the author of a translated or adapted work, however, free the adaptation, should not be classed with the author of an original play, whose only stock-in-trade was a ream of paper, a bundle of quills, and such inventive faculty as God had endowed him with. As regards the unfortunate play which had succeeded in arousing only the bitterest feelings of animosity on the part of the audience, what was there to be said against it, except that the dialogue was dull? Was it blasphemous? Was it indecent? Was it coarse? Was there one word in it which a girl of fifteen might not listen to with moral safety? If such a word could be pointed out to him his defence was at an end, and he deserved all and much more than he had received at the hands of the audience. He was anxious that he should not be supposed to maintain that a dull play should be allowed to pass muster because it was original. By no means. But he did maintain that the extreme difficulty of writing an original play, which shall not only succeed, but which shall *deserve to succeed*, should be taken into account in estimating an author's punishment. It is easy to write an original play that will succeed. Every play which contains a house on fire, a sinking steamer, a railway accident, and a dance in a casino will (if it is liberally placed on the stage) succeed in spite of itself. In point of fact, nothing could wreck such a piece but carefully written dialogue, and a strict attention to probability. Avoid these two stumbling blocks (and nothing is easier than to avoid them), and your piece will succeed triumphantly. But it is not easy to write a stage-play which, on account of its literary merit, shall deserve to succeed. The difficulty of the task may be gauged by the rarity of its accomplishment. *All for Her* was a play in which success had been most deservedly attained. Mr. Wills' exquisite drama *Olivia* was another. The fact that one play was suggested by " A Tale of Two Cities," and the other by " The Vicar of Wakefield," did not militate against their claim to originality. The authors had gathered no more from those works than they could have gathered from an anecdote told over a dinner-table. But in these cases the authors had the advantage of admirable interpretation. Without adequate interpretation the better the play, in an intellectual sense, the more likely it is to fail. He had nothing to say in defence of his own unhappy play, but he would put it to the jury whether, after the evidence of the actors and actresses engaged in the piece, they believed that the play, as they saw it, was a reflex of his intention ? He ventured to believe, on these actors' and actresses' own showing, that he had been exceptionally unfortunate. Happily for the welfare of the drama, it very rarely happened that actors took such monstrous liberties with an author's play as they had taken with his. But it is an undoubted fact that such liberties *can* be taken in ill-disciplined theatres when the actors are self-willed and opinionated, and the author a man of no influence. In any case, the audience could never be sure whether

the author was or was not responsible for the ill-timed
jest or the misplaced buffoonery that had aroused their
indignation ? He might be responsible or he might
not. Those who had had an opportunity of reading his
play had admitted that it was not deficient in thoughtful
dialogue and in a certain subtle humour ; but they contended that the dialogue was not such as would be
likely to appeal, at a single hearing, to a mixed audience,
and herein he confessed that he was in error. As a
dramatist, writing for a mixed audience, he should have
so fashioned it as to make its merits, such as they were,
instantly manifest. He had no right to call upon an
audience to buy a copy of his play and study it carefully
before committing themselves to an opinion upon it ; but
was not that error sufficiently punished by the fact that
thereby nine months of ceaseless toil had been utterly
wasted ? He could assure the audience who hissed
him and howled at him, and chaffed his dialogue, and
sneered at his sentiment that there was a pathetic side
even to failure. He trusted that this appeal would not
be regarded as the whine of a dog who had been
whipped—it was simply a protest that the dog did not
deserve so severe a whipping as he had received. He
had written a play which had failed to interest his
audience, and he had no desire to shirk the reasonable
consequences of such an act; but did it altogether
merit the public execration that had been launched at
it ? The evidence showed conclusively that the original
manuscript had been materially tampered with in face
of his earnest protest that, as the play was put before
the public in his name, the play should be his play,

and not a modified version thereof, trimmed, altered, written up and cut down to suit the views of individual actors and actresses engaged in representing it. If he was incompetent to the task of writing a good practical play—and the events of the evening pointed to that conclusion—the manager's obvious course was to apply to a more skilful author, not to take upon himself, or to entrust to a deputy, the privilege of making alterations which, in the author's opinion, placed his work before the audience in a distorted light.

There was but one other point on which he would address the jury, and he would then conclude. Immemorial custom had conferred upon individual members of a theatrical audience the privilege of expressing their disapproval of the entertainment by hissing. He had no desire whatever to abolish this privilege : judiciously and impartially used it was a valuable privilege, and undoubtedly had the effect of making authors and actors particularly careful not to abuse the toleration which an English audience was accustomed to extend towards those who attempted to entertain them. But he submitted that, except in the case of an outrage on decency, this privilege should be exercised at the end of the performance, and not in the course of it. In the first place, it was only reasonable to ask that a jury—and an audience was in every practical sense a jury—should hear a case to the end before deciding on it. It might easily happen that a tedious scene in a first Act might be justified by particularly ingenious and interesting situations arising out of it in the third; in point of fact, one of the witnesses had admitted that he hissed a certain incident under a misapprehension as to the author's intention. In the second place, a hiss always disconcerts, and often utterly unnerves, the actors who are upon the stage when it is delivered, and renders them unfit to do justice to the scenes that follow. In the case of the unhappy play which had been so heartily condemned that night, those witnesses for the prosecution who took part in the play, speak unreservedly as to the paralysing effect of the sounds of disapprobation with which certain scenes in the first Act were received. No author with any respect for himself and for his profession would endeavour to shield himself from the consequence of failure by attempting to deprive an audience of the right to express their disapproval of his play; but he respectfully submitted that it would be fairer to all concerned if those expressions of disapproval were reserved for the final fall of the act drop. The Prisoner concluded by thanking the jury for the exemplary patience with which they had listened to his defence: while he had no desire to make out that his play was anything but a dull, ineffective production, he submitted that the punishment that inevitably accompanied absolute failure was as severe as the offence of which he had been guilty.

The learned JUDGE briefly summed up the facts of the case, and

The Jury returned an immediate verdict of *Guilty*, accompanied by a strong recommendation to mercy.

The learned JUDGE—On what ground do you base your recommendation, gentlemen ?

The FOREMAN—We think that he is not solely responsible for the result. Many persons contribute to a stage performance, and the author's contribution is only a part of a whole. We think that he should not be held absolutely responsible for either failure or success. In this case manager, actor, actresses, and author were all more or less to blame. The author is one of many contributors to an unsatisfactory result.

The learned JUDGE—At the same time you consider that he has committed the offence of writing an impracticable and ineffective stage-play ?

The FOREMAN—Undoubtedly. We were never so bored in our lives. (*Murmurs of assent from the Jury.*)

The learned JUDGE, addressing the Prisoner, said— You have been found guilty by a most fair and impartial jury of the very serious offence of having written an exceedingly poor play. Several of the witnesses have testified to certain literary merits which are to be found in your work, but sitting here as your judge, it is my duty to tell you that literary merit is only one of many elements—and by no means an indispensable one—that go to make a successful stage-play. It is but one of the constituents of the dramatic pudding. Stage-craft is the water that binds these constituents into an attractive mass; without it the fabric will not hold together.

Although I cannot close my eyes to the terrible consequences that would ensue were your offence to pass absolutely unpunished, I am anxious to give the fullest effect to the very strong recommendation to mercy which the jury have appended to their verdict. On the whole, I concur with that recommendation, for I think you have received but scant justice at the hands of your opponents· The piece that has been played is not your own, and although your own play may be a bad play, you are entitled to expect that it will be played in its integrity and without additions. It is true that the plays of Shakespeare are frequently mutilated without apparent detriment to their attractive powers, but your light is not the light of Shakespeare. If I may so express myself, your night-light has been seen through a fog, and its natural glimmer is not calculated to show to advantage through such a medium. I am glad, for the credit of the dramatic profession, to believe that you are an exceptional instance of an ill-treated author. My own experience as a play-goer teaches me that at well-conducted theatres, such as the Haymarket, the Lyceum, the St. James's and the Court, pieces are placed upon the stage with excellent taste, and that the companies of those and other theatres habitually contribute a most valuable element towards such success as the author's plays may achieve. But you have not been so fortunate as to have your play produced at one of these well-regulated establishments. You have had the misfortune to fall into the hands of a manager who is no manager, and of a company who, whatever their histrionic skill may be, are wholly disentitled, by lack of taste and discretion, to such latitude as the most experienced author would gladly concede to an actor who has reasonable claims to rank as an artist. Under the exceptional circumstances of your case, and having the jury's recommendation strongly before my eyes, I think I am justified in permitting you to go at large on your own recognizances, on the understanding that you hold yourself prepared to come up for judgment when called upon to do so. I trust that this leniency will have its effect, and that you will, for the future, exercise a direct and efficient control over all plays that may be put before the public in your name.

The Prisoner entered into the necessary undertaking, and was forthwith discharged.

ANGELA.

AN INVERTED LOVE STORY.

I AM a poor paralysed fellow who, for many years past, has been confined to a bed or a sofa. For the last six years I have occupied a small room, giving on to one of the side canals of Venice, and having no one about me but a deaf old woman, who makes my bed and attends to my food ; and there I eke out a poor income of about thirty pounds a year by making water-colour drawings of flowers and fruit (they are the cheapest models in Venice), and these I send to a friend in London, who sells them to a dealer for small sums. But, on the whole, I am happy and content.

It is necessary that I should describe the position of my room rather minutely. Its only window is about five feet above the water of the canal, and above it the house projects some six feet, and overhangs the water, the projecting portion being supported by stout piles driven into the bed of the canal. This arrangement has the disadvantage (among others) of so limiting my up- ward view that I am unable to see more than about ten feet of the height of the house immediately opposite to

me, although, by reaching as far out of the window as
my infirmity will permit, I can see for a considerable
distance up and down the canal, which does not ex-
ceed fifteen feet in width. But, although I can see
but little of the material house opposite, I can see
its reflection upside down in the canal, and I take a
good deal of inverted interest in such of its inhabitants
as show themselves from time to time (always upside
down) on its balconies and at its windows.

When I first occupied my room, about six years ago,
my attention was directed to the reflection of a little
girl of thirteen or so (as nearly as I could judge), who
passed every day on a balcony just above the upward
range of my limited field of view. She had a glass of
flowers and a crucifix on a little table by her side ; and
as she sat there, in fine weather, from early morning
until dark, working assiduously all the time, I concluded
that she earned her living by needle-work. She was certainly an industrious little girl, and, as far as I could
judge by her upside-down reflection, neat in her dress
and pretty. She had an old mother, an invalid, who, on
warm days, would sit on the balcony with her, and it interested me to see the little maid wrap the old lady in
shawls, and bring pillows for her chair, and a stool for
her feet, and every now and again lay down her work
and kiss and fondle the old lady for half a minute,
and then take up her work again.

Time went by, and as the little maid grew up, her
reflection grew down, and at last she was quite a little
woman of, I suppose, sixteen or seventeen. I can only
work for a couple of hours or so in the brightest part of

the day, so I had plenty of time on my hands in which to watch her movements, and sufficient imagination to weave a little romance about her, and to endow her with a beauty which, to a great extent, I had to take for granted. I saw—or fancied that I could see—that she began to take an interest in *my* reflection (which, of course, she could see as I could see hers) ; and one day, when it appeared to me that she was looking right at it —that is to say when her reflection appeared to be looking right at me—I tried the desperate experiment of nodding to her, and to my intense delight her reflection nodded in reply. And so our two reflections became known to one another.

It did not take me very long to fall in love with her, but a long time passed before I could make up my mind to do more than nod to her every morning, when the old woman moved me from my bed to the sofa at the window, and again in the evening, when the little maid left the balcony for that day. One day, however, when I saw her reflection looking at mine, I nodded to her, and threw a flower into the canal. She nodded several times in return, and I saw her direct her mother's attention to the incident. Then every morning I threw a flower into the water for " good morning," and another in the evening for " good night," and I soon discovered that I had not altogether thrown them in vain, for one day she threw a flower to join mine, and she laughed and clapped her hands when she saw the two flowers join forces and float away together. And then every morning and every evening she threw her flower when I threw mine, and when the two flowers met she clapped her hands, and so did I ; but when they were separated, as they sometimes were, owing to one of them having met an obstruction which did not catch the other, she threw up her hands in a pretty affectation of despair, which I tried to imitate but in an English and unsuccessful fashion. And when they were rudely run down by a passing gondola (which happened not unfrequently) she pretended to cry, and I did the same. Then, in pretty pantomime, she would point downwards to the sky to tell me that it was Destiny that had caused the shipwreck of our flowers, and I, in pantomime, not nearly so pretty, would try to convey to her that Destiny would be kinder next time, and that perhaps to-morrow our flowers would be more fortunate—and so the innocent courtship went on. One day she showed me her crucifix and kissed it, and thereupon I took a little silver crucifix that always stood by me, and kissed that, and so she knew that we were one in religion.

One day the little maid did not appear on her balcony, and for several days I saw nothing of her ; and although I threw my flowers as usual, no flower came to keep it company. However, after a time, she reappeared, dressed in black, and crying often, and then I knew that the poor child's mother was dead, and, as far as I knew, she was alone in the world. The flowers came no more for many days, nor did she show any sign of recognition, but kept her eyes on her work, except when she placed her handkerchief to them. And opposite to her was the old lady's chair, and I could see that, from time to time, she would lay down her work and gaze at it, and then a flood of tears would come to her relief. But at last one

day she roused herself to nod to me, and then her flower
came, day, day, day, and my flower went forth to join
it, and with varying fortunes the two flowers sailed away
as of yore.

But the darkest day of all to me was when a good-
looking young gondolier, standing right end uppermost
in his gondola (for I could see *him* in the flesh), worked
his craft alongside the house, and stood talking to her
as she sat on the balcony. They seemed to speak as old
friends—indeed, as well as I could make out, he held
her by the hand during the whole of their interview
which lasted quite half an hour. Eventually he pushed
off, and left my heart heavy within me. But I soon
took heart of grace, for as soon as he was out of sight,
the little maid threw two flowers growing on the same
stem—an allegory of which I could make nothing, until
it broke upon me that she meant to convey to me that
he and she were brother and sister, and that I had no
cause to be sad. And thereupon I nodded to her
cheerily, and she nodded to me, and laughed aloud, and
I laughed in return, and all went on again as before.

Then came a dark and dreary time, for it became
necessary that I should undergo treatment that confined
me absolutely to my bed for many days, and I worried
and fretted to think that the little maid and I should see
each other no longer, and worse still, that she would
think that I had gone away without even hinting to her
that I was going. And I lay awake at night wondering
how I could let her know the truth, and fifty plans
flitted through my brain, all appearing to be feasible
enough at night, but absolutely wild and impracticable

in the morning. One day—and it was a bright day indeed for me—the old woman who tended me told me that a gondolier had inquired whether the English signor had gone away or had died; and so I learnt that the little maid had been anxious about me, and that she had sent her brother to inquire, and the brother had no doubt taken to her the reason of my protracted absence from the window.

From that day, and ever after during my three weeks of bed-keeping, a flower was found every morning on the ledge of my window, which was within easy reach of anyone in a boat; and when at last a day came when I could be moved, I took my accustomed place on my sofa at the window, and the little maid saw me, and stood on her head (so to speak) and clapped her hands upside down with a delight that was as eloquent as my right-end-up delight could be. And so the first time the gondolier passed my window I beckoned to him, and he pushed up alongside, and told me, with many bright smiles, that he was glad indeed to see me well again. Then I thanked him and his sister for their many kind thoughts about me during my retreat, and I then learnt from him that her name was Angela, and that she was the best and purest maiden in all Venice, and that anyone might think himself happy indeed who could call her sister, but that he was happier even than her brother, for he was to be married to her, and indeed they were to be married the next day.

Thereupon my heart seemed to swell to bursting, and the blood rushed through my veins so that I could hear it and nothing else for a while. I managed at last to

stammer forth some words of awkward congratulation,
and he left me, singing merrily, after asking permission
to bring his bride to see me on the morrow as they returned from church.

"For," said he, " my Angela has known you very
long—ever since she was a child, and she has often
spoken to me of the poor Englishman who was a good
Catholic, and who lay all day long for years and years
on a sofa at a window, and she had said over and over
again how dearly she wished she could speak to him and
comfort him ; and one day, when you threw a flower
into the canal, she asked me whether she might throw
another, and I told her yes, for he would understand
that it meant sympathy for one sorely afflicted."

And so I learned that it was pity, and not love, except
indeed such love as is akin to pity, that prompted her
to interest herself in my welfare, and there was an end
of it all.

For the two flowers that I thought were on one stem
were two flowers tied together (but I could not tell that),
and they were meant to indicate that she and the gondolier were affianced lovers, and my expressed pleasure
at this symbol delighted her, for she took it to mean
that I rejoiced in her happiness.

And the next day the gondolier came with a train of
other gondoliers, all decked in their holiday garb, and
on his gondola sat Angela, happy, and blushing at her
happiness. Then he and she entered the house in which
I dwelt, and came into my room (and it was strange
indeed, after so many years of inversion, to see her with
her head above her feet !), and then she wished me hap-

piness and a speedy restoration to good health (which could never be) ; and I in broken words and with tears in my eyes, gave her the little silver crucifix that had stood by my bed or my table for so many years. And Angela took it reverently, and crossed herself, and kissed it, and so departed with her delighted husband.

And as I heard the song of the gondoliers as they went their way—the song dying away in the distance as the shadows of the sundown closed around me—I felt that they were singing the requiem of the only love that had ever entered my heart.

WIDE AWAKE.

I am a remarkably good-looking middle-aged bachelor. Twenty years ago I sunk all my property in an annuity, and on that annuity I live very comfortably.

Ten years ago it occurred to me that I would very likely marry, so I ensured my life for ten thousand pounds.

I am a man of a particularly affectionate disposition. This amiable tendency has led me into many difficulties in my time—not the least of which was an engagement to marry my cousin Georgina Sparrow.

I supposed I loved Georgina when I proposed to her. Looking calmly back at Georgina, it seems improbable I admit—but still I *did* propose to her, and as I had no underhand motive in doing so (for I am rich and extremely handsome, whereas she is poor and singularly plain), I suppose I must have loved her more or less.

However that may be, there is no doubt at all that before I had been engaged to her for a week, I found myself wondering what on earth I had ever seen in her to admire. She was bony, angular, acid, and forty.

My uncle, old Sparrow (Georgina's father), and my aunt Julia, his wife, and Georgina's two horsey brothers, James and John, took the greatest interest in our engagement. They seemed to think it likely that I should try to get out of it, and they determined that I should not have a chance of doing so. I should have stated that I lodged at their house. I should have liked to lodge elsewhere, where I could have had more liberty and less fluff, but my natural amiability was more than a match for my sense of convenience, and I remained.

On one occasion I *did* hint at the possibility of my removing to a less dear, and less dirty sphere of action, but the indignation of Mr. and Mrs. Sparrow, the violent attitudes of John and James, and the appalling hysterics of Georgina, induced me weakly to confess that it was only my fun.

My natural amiability is such that I *must* love some one—and as it was out of the question to go on loving Georgina, it became necessary to love somebody else. I found an appropriate object of homage in Bridget Comfit, a very plump and rosy widow lady of small independent property, who lived in Great Coram Street.

To make a long story short, I will at once confess that, being engaged to Georgina Sparrow, I nevertheless secretly made love to Mrs. Comfit. I even went so far as to make arrangements to marry Mrs. Comfit at St. Pancras Church, Euston Square. I did not tell Bridget about Georgina because I knew that it would distress her, and I did not tell Georgina about Bridget, because I knew that it would distress *her*. It would also have distressed her furious father, her fluent mother, and her two very violent and impulsive brothers, John and James. I acted for the best.

The day before the day appointed for my marriage with Mrs. Comfit arrived. I did not feel quite happy that evening. I did not enjoy my dinner. Uncle Sparrow seemed to have a reproachful something in his eye which I could not account for. Aunt Sparrow was surprisingly silent. The two brothers, John and James, looked moody, and Georgina was uncomfortably affectionate. I felt rather conscience smitten.

I began to think that in marrying Bridget secretly, I was perhaps acting an underhand part towards Georgina. I had never looked at it in that light before; it had always seemed to me to be the most natural thing in the world that a man who had engaged himself to Georgina should take the earliest opportunity of getting out of the engagement.

But there is a right and a wrong way of doing everything, and I saw, when it was too late, that it would have been better to have broken her heart in a more manly and straightforward way. Still I acted for the best.

The next morning—the morning of my marriage day —I breakfasted in bed. I couldn't face the family. I am a tender-hearted old fool, and I could not feel at my ease in the presence of the woman whose heart I was deliberately breaking. So I pleaded a bad bilious headache, and remained in bed until Uncle Sparrow had started for the City (he was something—not much —in the City), and his two headstrong sons had betaken themselves to Aldridge's.

I knew that this would happen at a quarter to ten, and that at ten o'clock Mrs. Sparrow and Georgina would go down to the kitchen to have their daily row over the cook's accounts—so at ten I determined to make my escape.

I dressed—reached the ground-floor in safety—kissed a last farewell to Georgina's very long goloshes in the umbrella-stand, and eventually stood free and undetected in the street. I had yet an hour to spare before Bridget would arrive at the church, and I spent this in walking round Euston Square—which can be done in two thousand one hundred paces—and at a quarter to eleven I entered the church. There was no one there but the beadle.

I went up to him and said, "Oh, I beg your pardon, but I've come to be married." At that moment I was clapped on the back by Georgina's two headstrong brothers. My cousins and their father had been paying a visit to a money-lender in Euston Square. They saw me walking round, their curiosity was excited, and they followed me to the church. And so came about one of the most tremendously dramatic situations in Modern History.

"So, sir," said Uncle Sparrow, "you've come to be married?"

"Fire and fury!" said John.

"Zounds and the devil!" said James.

I was equal to the emergency. My natural kindness of heart prevented my admitting the truth to my uncle and my cousins, for I never distress a fellow-creature intentionally (unless she is ugly, and I am engaged to her), so I resorted to one of the most ingenious methods of getting out of a dilemma that I ever heard of. I gave a sudden start, gasped, rolled my eyes wildly, and exclaimed :—

"Where am I?"

They explained to me in language quite unsuited to the sacred edifice in which they were standing, that I was in St. Pancras Church.

"How did I come here? I don't remember anything about it! The last thing I can remember is being in bed with a bilious headache, and trying to go to sleep! And here I am, dressed and wide-awake, in St. Pancras Church. What is the inference?"

They admitted in disgracefully strong language, that they were at a loss to draw any satisfactory inference from this statement.

"My dear uncle, my good (but violent) cousins," said I, "this is very distressing to me, for I thought I had quite shaken it off. I haven't done such a thing as walk in my sleep for years."

They replied, sardonically, that they felt sure of it.

"I once remained for nearly a week in a state of somnambulism. It is most providential that you happened to be here."

They quite agreed with me.

"Another time," said I, "don't wake me suddenly. It is very dangerous to wake a somnambulist with a violent shock. Better let him have his sleep out."

This I said to keep up the illusion.

They promised that, now that they were aware of my infirmity, they would not wake me too suddenly on the next occasion.

"The best thing I can do," said I, "is to go home and go to bed again."

They heartily concurred wtih this suggestion. John took one of my arms, James took the other, and Uncle Sparrow walked behind us, keeping the ferule of his walking-stick in the small of my back.

There was nothing for it but to give up all hope of being married that day. I was sorry for Bridget; but I felt that an explanation made at the earliest opportunity would set that right. After all, it would only delay our happiness for a few days. I could not help chuckling over my presence of mind, and the ready wit I had shown in escaping from a difficulty which would have overwhelmed ninety-nine men out of a hundred. It is true I was rather surprised to find how readily my explanation was accepted by my uncle and my cousins; but that only showed how skilfully I had played my part.

I remained in bed all that day, for I really did not feel equal to facing the family in my disappointed frame of mind. But one can't remain in bed for ever, and the next morning I put a bold face on it, and came down, as usual, to breakfast.

"Good morning, uncle," said I, in my most cheerful tones. "How are you, dear aunt? Ha, John! Ha, James! Georgina, my love, good morning."

They looked at one another significantly, but made no response to my greeting.

"Lovely morning," said I.

"It's just as I thought," said Uncle Sparrow to Aunt Julia. "He's at it again."

"Hush," said Aunt Julia, "don't speak so loud. You'll wake him."

"Poor boy," said Georgina, in a half-whisper. "His eyes are wide open, though he's evidently fast asleep."

"That is always the case with somnambulists," said Uncle Sparrow. "The sleeping brain receives its impressions through the eyes, nose, and ears."

"His nose and ears are wide open also," said John.

"So they were yesterday," said James.

"A very curious instance of somnambulism came under my notice in Italy a few years ago," said Uncle Sparrow. "A very respectable young girl was found under suspicious circumstances in the chamber of an Italian noble, and the most unfavourable inferences were drawn as to her moral character in consequence. Her forthcoming marriage with a handsome young peasant was broken off, and all her old companions repudiated her. Eventually she was seen crossing a most dangerous plank over a watermill, in her petticoat body, and it became clear to all that the girl was a confirmed somnambulist. She was at once re-instated in the good opinion of her friends, and her marriage with the young peasant was celebrated with unusual rejoicings. I knew the family very well."

I looked from one to another in blank astonishment.

"Am I to suppose," said I, "that you are under the impression that I am asleep?"

"Except that his utterance is thick," said Georgina, "there is very little difference between his sleeping and waking voice."

I began to get annoyed.

“ Is this a joke ? ” I inquired, as I sat down to breakfast.

“ Take his knife away, Georgina,” said Aunt Julia; “ cut up his bacon and let him eat it with a tea-spoon.”

You can’t eat fried bacon with a tea-spoon so as to enjoy it. I therefore protested against this interference with my convenience.

“ I insist,” said Uncle Sparrow, “ on his knife being removed. John and James, sit one on each side of him and watch his movements very carefully. But be very careful not to wake him as that would be most dangerous. These trances usually last a week. John, feed him with a spoon. James, hold his tea-cup and give him a sip occasionally.”

“ Uncle,” said I, “ I beg—I *beg* that you will allow me to have my breakfast in peace. I had nothing to eat yesterday (having had a bilious headache), and I am literally starving.”

“ Now give him a bit of muffin,” said Uncle Sparrow. “ Now a spoonful of egg.”

“ Indeed, indeed, I am quite awake. I can feed myself. I want no assistance from anyone.”

“ Now a mouthful of tea—take care—its running down his waistcoat.”

There was nothing for it but to submit to be fed by the hulking brothers.

I made several appeals to their intelligence, to their sense of humour, and to their feelings as human beings, but in vain. The only notice they took of my remarks was to direct each other’s attention to the fact that I expressed myself quite coherently.

The farce was carried on through the whole day, and the next, and the next after that. Nothing would convince them that I was awake. I did all I could to persuade them to treat me like a rational being, but in vain. The two detestable brothers devoted themselves to taking care of me with extraordinary assiduity. They never left me. They took me out for a walk every day, fed me carefully at meal times, undressed me and put me to bed at night, and dressed me again the next morning.

My unfortunate condition was explained to all visitors, who took a deep interest in watching my movements, and everyone was enjoined to speak with bated breath for fear of waking me. No attention was paid by anyone to my remarks; but everyone made observations of the most unpleasantly personal description about me. And, curiously enough, no one entered the house who did not notice something unusual in my appearance and demeanour which was only reconcilable with the theory that I was walking and talking in my sleep.

Uncle Sparrow opened all my letters (including a very emphatic one from the disappointed Mrs. Comfit), and kindly volunteered to take care of them until I was in a condition to take care of them myself.

I am a man of easy temper, but there are limits to my powers of endurance. It was quite evident to me that they were simply "paying me out" for the deception I had practised on them at the church. It was, perhaps, right that I should suffer some little mortification, but I felt that matters had now been carried far enough. I spoke out with furious indignation, and told them that unless they at once gave me an assurance in writing, and signed by the whole family that I was wide awake, I would appeal for protection to the laws of my country. I did not feel quite sure under which Act of Parliament my grievance would come, but I knew that a remedy was provided for every wrong, and that to insist upon it that a man is asleep when he is really wide awake, is a wrong of a most distinct and aggravating description. But my threats had no effect upon my relations, nor was I more successful with one eminent psychologist who came three times a day for a hour and a half each time to study my case for a work on dreams upon which he was then engaged.

As I sat fuming with impatience in an arm-chair in Uncle Sparrow's study surrounded by the whole family, a letter (addressed to me) was placed in Uncle Sparrow's hand. In spite of my emphatic protest, he took the liberty of opening and reading it.

It was from the office in which I had insured my life for the benefit of my widow (whoever that might be) for £10,000. It informed me that the annual premium on my policy was still unpaid, that the fourteen days of grace had expired, and that unless the secretary received a cheque for the amount (£320) in the course of the afternoon, the policy would, *ipso facto*, become null and void.

"You had better attend to this at once," said he, handing the letter to me. "*At once*," he added, with marked emphasis. "I am surprised that you have neglected so important, so vital a matter."

I saw my advantage at a glance.

"I will attend to it, Uncle, to-morrow, if I am in a condition to do so. These trances, however, usually last a week."

"But to-morrow won't do. The secretary says expressly that the money must be paid this afternoon."

"My dear," said Georgina, "pray do not risk a delay. The matter is of the highest moment. Please be good enough to write a cheque at once."

"I will write a cheque for the amount," said I, "as soon as I am awake. But these trances usually last a week."

"Come, come," said Uncle Sparrow, "the joke has been carried far enough. We were only chaffing you. You never were wider awake in your life. Come—write the cheque at once."

"Uncle Sparrow," said I, "Aunt Julia, Georgina, John and James—you have done your best to persuade me that I have been in a somnambulistic trance for three days. At first I doubted it, but it became impossible to reject the evidence of so many dis-interested witnesses, and I am quite convinced that you were right and I was wrong. I am, no doubt, fast asleep. I admit it cheerfully, and I am very much obliged to you for the great care and attention you have bestowed on me in this unfortunate and abnormal condition. It is not likely to last above three or four days longer, and as soon as I am thoroughly awake and capable of attending to business, I will certainly send a cheque for my premium. But not till then."

"I tell you, sir," replied Uncle Sparrow, "that the whole thing was a joke. I freely admit it. But it is time that this fooling came to an end. Write the cheque, like a good fellow, or Georgina will be left penniless."

"My own, my love," said Georgina, "don't be ridiculous. You are much older than I"—that wasn't true—"and in the natural course of events I shall survive you. If the cheque is not written at once, I shall be a penniless widow!"

"I will write it," said I, "when I awake."

"Papa — Mamma — John — James," exclaimed Georgina, in a frenzy, "explain to him that he is labouring under a delusion! Oh, somebody, pray do something, or I shall be ruined."

I was firm; I insisted upon it that a cheque written in a state of somnambulism would be invalid, and that it would be a useless waste of a stamp if I were to write one in my then condition. The whole family went on their knees to me, but in vain. I stuck to my colours.

The hours crept on—it was three o'clock, and the office closed at four. Eventually, finding that nothing could shake my resolution, Uncle Sparrow rushed out to his bankers with the family plate, Aunt Julia's jewels, and a bundle of American stock, borrowed the three hundred and twenty pounds on the security, and paid my premium five minutes before the office closed.

*　　*　　*　　*　　*

The next day I came down to breakfast, wide awake. I felt that I was awake, and besides that, the whole family admitted it quite cheerfully. Uncle Sparrow begged me to favour him at once with a cheque for the amount of my premium. At first I did not understand what he meant, but a few words of explanation made his meaning clear. I expressed my natural surprise that he should take upon himself to pay the premium on a policy which I had no intention of keeping up, and I declined altogether to hold myself responsible for his act. An angry scene ensued, which resulted in a final rupture of my engagement with Georgina.

To-morrow I marry Mrs. Comfit.

A STAGE PLAY.

Most men, whatever their occupation may be, are accustomed to study man exclusively from their own point of view. A man who passes his life behind a tavern bar is apt to divide the human race into those who habitually refresh themselves in public-houses, and those who do not. A policeman classes society under two great heads—prosecutors and prisoners. In a footman's eyes, his fellow-men are either visitors or servants; in an author's, they are publishers or reviewers. Now, it is conceivable that a man may be at once a prosecutor, a visitor, and a publisher; but a policeman will take no heed of him in the two latter capacities; a footman will care nothing that he is a prosecutor and a publisher; and an author will in no way be concerned that he is a prosecutor (unless, indeed, he is prosecuting the author), or that he is a visitor, unless the visit be paid in his capacity of publisher. Each man allows his immediate surroundings to interfere between himself and the world at large. He sees mankind, not through a distorted medium, but through a medium so circumscribed, that it permits only one feature of the object looked at to be seen at one time. In short, he examines mankind, not through a field-glass, but through a microscope.

A theatre, examined through the powerful medium employed by a person whose occupation is intimately associated with theatres, is as unlike a theatre, as it appears in the eyes of the outside public, as a drop of magnified Thames' water is unlike the apparently inorganic liquid that enters into the composition of almost everything we drink. Not one person in a thousand who sit in the auditorium of a theatre has any definite idea of the complicated process by which the untidy, badly-scrawled, interleaved, and interlineated manuscript of the author is translated into the close, crisp, bright, interesting entertainment that, in the eyes of the spectator, represents the value of the money he has paid for admittance. Still less does he know of the complicated mental process by which that manuscript (supposing it to have a genuine claim to the title "original") has been put together. Let us trace the progress of a modern three-act comedy from the blank-paper stage to completion, and from completion to production.

We will assume that the author, Mr. Horace Facile, has such a recognised position in his profession as to justify a manager in saying to him, "Facile, I want a three-act comedy-drama from you with parts for Jones and Brown and Robinson. Name your own terms, and get it ready, if you can, by this day two months."

Facile's engagements allow of him accepting the commission, and he sets to work on it as soon as may be.

In the first place, a "general idea" must be fixed upon, and in selecting it, Facile is guided, to a considerable extent, by the resources of the company he is to write for. Jones is an excellent light comedian, with a recognised talent for eccentric parts ; Brown is the leading " old man " of the establishment ; Robinson is the handsome lover or "*jeune premier;*" and Miss Smith plays the interesting young ladies whose fortunes or misfortunes constitute the sentimental interest of every piece in which she plays. Probably one or more of these talented artists must be " *exploited*," and the nature of the " general idea " will depend upon the powers or peculiarities of the actor or actress who is principally entitled to consideration. The *motif* of the comedy having been determined upon (we will suppose that it is to arise from the unnecessary antagonism existing between the Theatre and the Church), Facile casts about for a story in which this *motif* can be effectually displayed. In selecting a story Facile will probably be guided by the peculiarities of the company he is writing for. Brown (the " old man ") has never played an Archbishop of Canterbury, and Facile believes that such a part would afford that comedian a chance of distinguishing himself in a new line of character; so the story must be put together in such a manner as to admit of an Archbishop of Canterbury taking a prominent part in it. It has often occurred to Facile that Robinson the *jeune premier*, could make a great deal of the part of a professional Harlequin, who, under the influence of love or some other equally potent agency, has " taken orders " notwithstanding that, at the time of his doing so, he is under an engagement to play Harlequin in a forthcoming pantomime. So the story must admit, not only of an Archbishop, but also of a serious Harlequin ; and,

moreover, the interests of the Archbishop and the
Harlequin must be interwoven in an interesting and
sufficiently probable manner. However, the fact that
there is a clerical side to the Harlequin's character,
renders this exceedingly easy. The Harlequin loves the
Archbishop's daughter ; but the Archbishop (a very
haughty ecclesiastic of the Thomas à Becket type)
objects to Harlequins on principle, and determines that
his daughter shall marry into the Church. Here is at
once the necessary association of the Archbishop and
the Harlequin, and here, moreover, is an excellent reason
for the Harlequin's taking holy orders. The Archbishop
admits him, in ignorance of his other profession, and
places no obstacle in the way of his courting his
daughter. But a good deal of the interest of the lover's
part should obviously depend on the contrast of his
duties as a clergyman and his duties as a Harlequin
(for an obdurate manager declines to release him from
his engagement in the latter capacity), and Facile sets
to work to see how the two professions can be contrasted
to the best advantage. This requires some consideration, but he sees his way to it at last. The Archbishop
(a bitter enemy to the stage, which he denounces whenever an opportunity of doing so presents itself) happens
to be the freeholder of the very theatre in which the
Harlequin is engaged ; and happening to call at the
theatre one evening, with the double object of collecting his quarter's rent and endeavouring to wean the
manager from a godless profession, he meets his
daughter's lover in Harlequin costume. Here is an
opportunity for a scene of haughty recrimination—the

Archbishop reproaching the curate for combining the pulpit with the stage (by the bye, here is the title for the piece—The Pulpit and the Stage), and the curate reproaching the Archbishop with his hypocritical denunciation of an institution from which he derives, in the shape of rent, an income of say four thousand a year. At this juncture the Archbishop's daughter must be introduced. It will be difficult to account, with anything like probability, for her presence behind the scenes, during the performance of a pantomime; but with a little ingenuity even this may be accomplished. For instance, she may have come with a view of proselytizing the ballet, who can't get away from her, because they are all hanging on irons, ready for the transformation scene. This may precede the arrival of the Archbishop. The act (the second) must end with the struggle (on the daughter's part) between filial respect for her venerable father, and her love for the Harlequin, resulting, of course, in her declaring for the Harlequin, and the Archbishop's renunciation of her " for ever."

This will fill two acts. The third act must show the Harlequin (now a curate) married to the Archbishop's daughter, and living in the humblest circumstances somewhere in Lambeth. They are happy, although they are extremely poor. They have many friends— some clerical, some theatrical—but all on the best of terms with each other, through the benevolent agency of the ex-Harlequin. Deans drop in from Convocation at Westminster—actors and actresses from rehearsal at Astley's; and it is shown, beyond the possibility of doubt, that the two professions have many points in common (here is an opportunity of introducing hits at High Church mummeries, with imitations of popular preachers, by Wilkinson, the low comedian). Now to introduce the Archbishop. Since his renunciation of his daughter he has become a changed man. Too haughty to admit his error frankly, and take her and her husband to his heart and palace, he is nevertheless painfully conscious that he has acted harshly; and, in a spirit of secret self-humiliation, he disguises himself as one of the undignified clergy, and in that capacity goes through a house-to-house visitation. The natural course of his duty brings him to the humble abode of his daughter and son-in-law. He enters unperceived (of course in ignorance of the fact that it *is* their abode) during Wilkinson's imitations, and overhears a touching scene, in which his daughter indignantly rebukes Wilkinson for giving an imitation of her Most Reverend father's pulpit peculiarities. The old man, utterly softened by this unexpected touch of filial affection, comes forward, and, in broken accents, admits both the correctness of the imitation, and the filial respect that induced his daughter to check it, folds her and her husband to his heart, and gives him the next presentation to a valuable living—the present incumbent (who is present) being an aged man who cannot, in the course of nature, expect to survive many months. On this touching scene the curtain descends.

Here is an outline of a plot which Facile believes will answer every purpose. The Archbishop, the daughter, and the Harlequin will afford three excellent acting parts. The manager will be a bit of " character " for

Jones, the eccentric comedian; the actor who gives imitations of popular preachers will fit Wilkinson's powers of mimicry to a T; the tottering old incumbent, to whose living the ex-Harlequin is to succeed, will afford Tompkins an opportunity of introducing one of his celebrated " cabinet pictures " of pathetic old men; and for the other members of the company small effective parts, arising naturally from the exigencies of the story, will readily be found.

The next thing Facile does is to arrange striking situations for the end of each act. The first act must end with an announcement from the Harlequin that he has just taken holy orders; the happiness of the Archbishop's daughter at the information, and the entrance of the manager, who tells the Harlequin that he shall nevertheless hold him to his engagement for the forth-coming pantomime. The second act must end with the renunciation of his daughter by the Archbishop, and the last with the general reconciliation. Facile then sets to work to write the dialogue. He first tries his hand upon bits of dialogue that arise from suggestive situations—perhaps the first interview between the Archbishop's daughter and the Harlequin at Lambeth Palace. Then perhaps he will write the proselytizing scene in the second act, then the dialogue that leads to the situation at the end of Act I.; and so on. After he has settled half-a-dozen little scenes of this description, he feels that it is time to arrange how the piece is to begin. The first act takes place in the Archbishop's library in Lambeth Palace. Shall the Archbishop and his daughter be " discovered " at breakfast? No: both the

Archbishop and his daughter (that is to say, the actor and actress who are to play those parts) object to be "discovered." They want an "entrance," that they may receive special and individual "receptions," and they don't like to begin a piece, as in that case they are liable to constant interruption from the arrival of such of the audience as are not in their places when the curtain rises. Perhaps Jones, the manager, won't mind beginning, as his part is likely to be a particularly good one; he might call on the Archbishop about the rent of the Theatre. But in this case there must be a servant to receive him. Well, Facile tries this: Servant discovered (dusting, of course); soliloquy (this gives the manager an entrance); knock; servant don't answer it on principle, until several times repeated; eventually admits manager; treats manager contemptuously (or, better still, as he is an Archbishop's servant, with a grave and pitying air, as who would say, "Poor worldly sheep! we—that is to say, the Archbishop and I—despise you, but we don't hate you"); servant leaves to inform Archbishop; sarcastic soliloquy by manager; enter Archbishop; thunders of applause at Archbishop's "make-up"; and so on. Probably Facile writes and rewrites this scene half-a-dozen times—it gives him more trouble than all the rest of the act put together; for there are so many ways of beginning a piece, and it is so difficult to find sufficient reason for selecting one and rejecting all the rest. However, Facile is eventually satisfied; the scenes that he has already written are tacked together with dialogue of a more commonplace order, and Act I. is completed.

At this point Facile is apt to pause and to take breath. Perhaps he will run over to Paris, or go to the seaside for a month, "to collect his thoughts." His thoughts collected, he will make a tremendous effort to begin the second act; but here all the difficulties that he experienced in beginning Act I. crops up again tenfold. We protest, from practical experience, that there is nothing in the dramatist's profession that presents so many distasteful difficulties as the commencing the second act of a three-act comedy. His first act is short, sharp, crisp, and to the point — "*totus teres atque rotundus*"—perfectly satisfactory in itself—artistically put together, and telling the audience all they require to know in order to understand what follows, and no more. The thread of interest is broken at an exciting point, and it has now to be taken up again, in such a way as not to anticipate secrets and "situations" that require time to develop. If, in commencing the first act, Facile was bothered by the choice of five hundred "openings," he is ten times as much bothered now from the fact that he has only two or three, and none of them likely to be effective when reduced to dialogue. However, a letter from the management probably wakes him up at this point. With a desperate effort he sets to work, writing detached scenes as before, and writing the opening dialogue last as before; and in process of time Act II. is completed. His work is now practically at an end. Act III. is a simple matter enough. He has laid the train in Acts I. and II., and all that remains is to bring about the catastrophe in the quickest possible manner consistent with the story he has to tell. By the time he has finished Act II., he has cleared away all his difficulties. The different peculiarities of his principal characters have not only been irrevocably determined on, but he has, by this time, become thoroughly saturated with their spirit; and he has no difficulty whatever in bringing the last act shortly and sharply to an effective conclusion. Facile, who knows his work pretty well, has a theory that no piece has ever yet been written which deserves to arrest the attention of an audience for more than two hours at a time, and he has not the vanity to believe that any piece of his is likely to prove an exception to the rule.

The piece, duly completed, is sent to the manager who is to produce it. That gentleman has sufficient faith in Facile to justify him in handing it over at once to his prompter, who proceeds to make a fair copy for his own use, and another for the Lord Chamberlain's inspection. He also copies the "parts" from which the actors and actresses are to study, and which contain simply the words that the actor for whom it is intended has to speak, the stage directions that concern him, and the last three or four words of every speech that immediately precedes his own. As soon as the parts are fairly copied, a "reading" is called—that is to say, the members of the company are summoned to hear the piece read by the author in the green-room. This is an ordeal that Facile particularly dreads. He reads abominably—all authors do—and he knows it. He begins well; he reads slowly and emphatically, with all the proper pauses duly marked; and he indicates the

stage directions with just the right modulation of voice.
All is quite satisfactory until—say on page 9—he comes
to a "point" on which he relies for a hearty laugh.
He makes his point, and dwells for a moment upon it.
Nobody notices it except the stage-manager, who thinks
he has paused because he is hoarse, and kindly pours
him out a glass of water. Much abashed at this, Facile
pounds through the rest of the manuscript at an
astounding pace—hurrying intentionally over all the
"good things" as if he were ashamed of them—which,
for the moment, he is—and slurring over stirring
passages as if they were merely incidental to the general
purpose of the scene—as though, in fact, the scene had
not been originally constructed in order to introduce
them. As he approaches the end of the second act, he
becomes quite unconscious of the fact he is reading at
all until recalled by an enforced pause occasioned by the
accident of a misplaced leaf, or the opening or shutting
of the green-room door. As he commences the third
act, he finds himself wandering into *falsetto* every now
and then; he becomes husky and out of tune; he takes
a copious drink of water, and the words immediately
begin to babble into each other in a manner altogether
incomprehensible. He falls into his old habit of slurring
over important passages, but endeavours to compensate
for this by laying such exceptional stress upon sentences
of no ultimate importance, that his audience begin to
wish they had paid more attention to the earlier
passages of the play, that they might understand more
clearly the force of the old clergyman's remark about
the weather, or the subtlety of the ex-harlequin's invi-

tation to the low comedian to sit down and make himself comfortable. Facile finds the " imitations " in the third act seem to make no impression, which is not to be wondered at, considering that he reads them " off the reel," without any modification of voice at all. At length, very much to his own surprise, he finds himself at the last page—which is always a tremendously long page to read, you never seem to get to the bottom of it, —and, with his heart thumping away in his mouth, he pronounces the word " curtain," and closes the manuscript with, " There, that's over ! " and proceeds at once to talk, with great volubility, about the sort of day that it is—the bad business they've been doing at the " Folly," or the horrible report that Mrs. Miggleton, the wife of Miggleton, the first surgeon of the day, never " shows " in society, because her husband has, at different times and in the interest of science, cut away so much of her, by way of experiment, that only the vital portions are left—about anything, in short, except the piece he has just been reading. The stage-manager distributes the " parts," and the author hurries away— in order to avoid *that row* with Miss Smith—after appointing a day and hour for " comparing parts."

In the course of this process—a very dismal one indeed—the members of the company who are engaged in the piece endeavour to decipher the parts and to ascertain the context. The copyist's errors are corrected, and everyone begins to have some idea of his or her position with reference to the other persons engaged. It is usually a long and tedious process, and eminently calculated to reduce Facile's self-esteem to vanishing point. After this preliminary canter is over, Facile thinks he may as well look up Mr. Flatting, the scene-painter, who has been at work for the last fortnight on the Archbishop's library, and who is about to begin the "behind the scenes" scene in the second act. Facile climbs into the tall, narrow, dingy shed called by courtesy a painting-room, and finds Flatting describing the "model" to the carpenter and machinist, who will have a good deal to do with it, as it is a set of a rather complicated description. Facile settles matters with Flatting, and goes home to dine, sleep, wake at eleven o'clock, and set to work till three in the morning, altering this scene, polishing up that dialogue, making it crisper here, and filling it out with business there, as the experience of the morning may have suggested. The next day is the first rehearsal proper. A table and three chairs are set in the middle of the stage against the footlights. One of these is for the stage-manager, one for the prompter, and one for the author. Very often the stage-manager and prompter are one and the same individual, but the three chairs (one on the "prompt" side of the table and two on the "opposite prompt") are always there. Facile knows something of stage management, and invariably stage-manages his own pieces—an exceptional thing in England, but the common custom in France. He is nothing of an actor, and when he endeavours to show what he wants his actors to do, he makes himself rather ridiculous, and there is a good deal of tittering at the wings; but he contrives, nevertheless, to make himself understood, and takes particular good care that whatever his wishes are,

they shall be carried out to the letter, unless good cause
is shown to the contrary. He has his own way : and if
the piece is a success, he feels that he has contributed
more than the mere words that are spoken. At the
same time, if Facile is not a self-sufficient donkey, he
is only too glad to avail himself of valuable suggestions
offered by persons who have ten times his experience in
the details of stage management. And so the piece
flounders through rehearsal, the dingy theatre lighted
by a T-piece in front of the stage which has no per-
ceptible effect at the back; the performers usually (at
all events during the first two or three rehearsals)
standing in a row with their backs to the auditorium,
that the light may fall on the crabbed manuscripts they
are reading from ; the author endeavouring, but in vain,
to arrange effective exits and entrances, because nobody
can leave the T-piece; the stage-manager or prompter
(who follows the performers) calling a halt from time to
time that he may correct an overlooked error in his
manuscript or insert a stage direction. The actors
themselves pause from time to time for the same
reason. Every one has (or should have) a pencil in
hand; all errors are corrected and insertions made on
the spot; every important change of position is carefully
marked ; every " cross " indicated as the piece proceeds ;
and as alterations in dialogue and business are made up
to the last moment—all of which have to be hurriedly
recorded at the time—it will be understood that the
" parts " are in rather a dilapidated condition before the
rehearsals are concluded.

Eventually the piece is ready for representation—

three weeks' preparation is supposed to be a liberal allowance—and with one imperfect scene rehearsal, and no dress rehearsal at all, the piece is presented to the public. It probably passes muster on the first night, whatever its merits may be; in a week or ten days the actors begin to " do something " with their parts; and in a fortnight the piece is probably at its best.

There is much, very much, fault to be found (so Facile says) with the system—or rather the want of system—that prevails at rehearsals in this country. In the first place every actor and every person engaged in the piece should have a perfect copy of the piece, and that copy should be *printed*, not written. It costs from five to six pounds to print a three-act comedy, and in return for this trifling outlay, much valuable time and an infinity of trouble would be saved, not only to the prompter, but to the actors and the author. It is absolutely necessary that every actor should have the *context* of his scenes before his eyes as he studies them. He also says (does Facile) that it is a monstrous shame and an unheard-of injustice to place three-act pieces on the stage with fewer than thirty rehearsals, in ten of which the scenes should be set as they will be set at night, and in five of which every soul engaged should be dressed and made up as they will be dressed and made up at night.

As it is now, Jones, who is always fearfully nervous on " first nights," is embarrassed to find himself called upon to repeat his scarcely learnt lines in a spacious and handsomely furnished apartment, blazing with gas and gold-foil, instead of the cold, dark, empty stage on which he has been rehearsing them. This is of itself enough to drive the words out of the head of Jones. Then Jones, who has practised several scenes with Brown (on the stage an "old man," but in private life an airy, dressy gentleman of thirty summers), finds himself called upon to speak his words, not to the dressy Brown, but to a white-headed and generally venerable ecclesiastic, in gold spectacles and knee-breeches—that is to say, Brown, the Archbishop. These surprises (for to a nervous man they *are* surprises) are enough to unhinge Jones altogether. He makes a mess of his part for a night or two, picks up again after that, and in a fortnight is the talk of the town. Now, if Jones had had an opportunity of rehearsing with Brown the Archbishop, instead of with Brown the Swell, and if he had rehearsed his scenes in the Archbishop's library and not on the empty stage, Jones might have become the talk of the town from the first. In first class French theatres this system is adopted. Parts are distributed, learnt perfectly, and then rehearsed for six weeks or two months, sometimes for three or four months. Scene rehearsals and dress rehearsals occupy the last week of preparations. Actors and actresses *act* at rehearsal: they have been taught and required to do so from the first, and the consequence is that a bad actor becomes a reasonably good actor, and a reasonably good actor becomes an admirable actor by sheer dint of the microscopic investigation that his acting receives from the stage-manager and from the author. And until this system is in force in England; until the necessity for longer periods of preparation for rehearsals that are rehearsals in fact and not merely in name—

rehearsals with scenery, dresses, and " make-up," as they are to be at night; every expression given as it is to be given at night; every gesture marked as it is to be marked at night; until the necessity for such preparation as this is recognized in England, the English stage will never take the position to which the intelligence of its actors and actresses, the enterprise of its managers, and the talent of its authors would otherwise entitle it. At least, so says Facile.

THE WICKED WORLD.

AN ALLEGORY.

CHAPTER I.

HERE is a blank sheet of paper—several blank sheets of paper. What shall I put upon them? I declare I don't know. Shall it be a fashionable story of modern life? I know nothing of fashionable life. A mediæval romance? It would take too much cramming. A sea story? I know nothing about the sea, except that it makes me sick. A fairy tale then? Well, a fairy tale be it.

"But," says the acute reader, "if you decline to write a story about fashionable life because you know little of Fashion, how is it that you propose to write about fairies, of whom you must know still less?" Exactly. I know nothing at all about fairies—but then neither do you. If I attempt to depict fashionable life, and make his Lordship the Duke dance a double horn-pipe in September, at a Buckingham Palace ball, with the Right Honourable Lady Annabel Hicks, daughter of Sir Wickham Hicks, Puisne Judge, and Member for Birmingham-super-Mare, you may be down upon me for a group of solecisms ; for no doubt you move in the distinguished circles I attempt to describe, and therefore know more about them than I do. But in Fairyland we meet on other terms, and there I am your lordship's equal. *Habes.* Let us get on.

The scene, then, is in Fairyland. Not the Fairyland of the pantomimes, but the Fairyland of My Own Vivid Imagination. A pleasant, dreamy land, with no bright colours in it—a land where it is always bright moon-light—a land with plenty of impalpable trees, through which you can walk, if you like, as easily as my pen can cleave the smoke that is curling from my cigar as I write—a land where there is nothing whatever to do but to sit and chat with good pleasant-looking people, who like a joke, and can make one, too—a land where there is no such thing as hunger, or sleep, or fatigue, or illness, or old age—a land where no collars or boots are worn—a land where there is no love-making, but plenty of innocent love ready made.

There are no men in this Fairyland. I can't have a man in my Paradise—at least, not at first. I know so much about men, being myself a man, that I would rather not think of them in connection with a place where all is calm, and gentle, and tranquil, and happy. I know so little about women, that I propose to people this happy, dreamy, peaceful place with none but women. There must be no envy, hatred, malice, or uncharitable-ness of any kind in my Fairyland. There must be nothing sordid, nothing worldly, nothing commonplace. Universal charity must reign in my Fairyland, and that, you see, is why I people it with women.

Well, they are all women, and all the women are supremely lovely. They wear long robes, high in the throat, falling loosely and gracefully to the very feet, and each fairy has a necklace of the very purest diamonds. They have wings—large soft downy wings—six feet high, like the wings of angels. And by some spiritual contrivance, which I will not detain you by enlarging upon here, these wings won't crumple and crackle under the fairies when they sit down. So you see, you theatrical managers, my Fairyland is not yours. When I conceive a Fairyland with creaky phenomena and indelicate inhabitants who take a pride in their baggy, bony knees, I will come to you for suggestions on the subject. But I have not yet conceived such a Paradise. Faugh!

My tale opens upon a group of fairies—beautiful, simple girls, with beautiful simple names. There were Mary, and Annie, and Janet, and Mattie, and Bessie, and Kate, and fifty others whose names you can select for yourselves. They were chatting pleasantly together—not talking all at once, as boisterous men will do—but listening cheerfully and patiently to one another; for all had something to say that was worth hearing, and each was ready to listen to the other. Mary was the Queen of the Fairies. I make Mary the Queen, because I like the name "Mary" better than any other name I know. People are made kings and queens on earth for no better reasons, and many of them turn out fairly well. The conversation turned on the wickedness of the world. Kate had once been a mortal, but she died, and on account of her surpassing purity was translated to Fairyland. She was the only mortal who had ever been so distinguished. Among the fairies she was an authority on the subject of the wickedness of the world (though in truth she knew very little indeed about it), and all questions that related to the world were referred to her for her decision, which was final. For I should have told you that although my fairies exercised an influence over the destinies of mortals, they did not mix with them. They kept themselves to themselves: they were not obliged to do so, but they hated wickedness, and the world was very wicked.

Well, the Fairy Kate was relating some of her experiences, and the other fairies were affected almost to tears at the revelations she made. Not that the Fairy Kate's revelations would have shocked you and me very desperately, but the other fairies had no idea of the wickedness of which the world is capable, and listened aghast to matters which we gross mortals look upon with little or no disfavour. Indeed, the Fairy Kate did not enter very deeply into the subject of her remarks, for she had only an amiable, half-instructed good girl's knowledge of them, and she spoke according to her twilight.

She said, for instance, that whole nations devoted themselves to each other's annihilation for reasons which would not operate to produce a coolness between two private individuals. But then she forgot that a nation consists, perhaps, of fifty million private individuals, and that an affront offered to such a nation is fifty million times as great as the same affront would be if directed against an individual member of it. She also said that when people gave alms they required that the fact should be advertised in the public prints through the length and breadth of the land. But she forgot that as example is better than precept (which is also very good in its way), it follows that, although it is good to exhort people to acts of charity, it is still better to let them see that you are actively charitable yourself; and if an example is good it cannot be too widely diffused. I mention the statements of the Fairy Kate to show that her knowledge of the world was, after all, very superficial, and not at all to be relied upon.

The effect of the Fairy Kate's remarks was that the other fairies were so dreadfully shocked at her picture of the wickedness of the world, that they came to consider whether some steps might not be taken to improve its condition, and bring its inhabitants generally to a proper sense of their duties to one another.

It was proposed that, with a view to ascertaining the present state of the world, a Woman should be summoned to Fairyland, and interrogated on the subject. For, after all, the Fairy Kate's information was of no recent date, and matters might have improved since she left the earth. So the Fairy Bessie suggested that a Mortal Woman should be summoned forthwith. The suggestion was received with high favour by all the fairies, and Fairy Janet suggested, as an amendment, that the word "Man" should be substituted for "Woman." A man, she argued, is naturally in a position to see much more of the world than a woman, and his information would, therefore, be more valuable. (Amendment carried unanimously.)

So a cloud was sent down to earth with instructions to envelop and carry up into Fairyland the first mortal it happened to see. These instructions had to be repeated several times, for the cloud was rather foggy, but eventually it was made to understand them, and it started on its mission.

The time that elapsed between the departure of the cloud and the arrival of a real live man appeared interminable to the fairies, but, at length, after many hours' absence, it did return with a magnificent young Prince. The stupid cloud, instead of bringing up the first man it saw (a very ragged drunken old beggar, who would have answered the fairies' purpose as well as anybody else), looked out for a young and handsome man, in the absurd belief that the presence of such an one in Fairyland would give greater pleasure to his beautiful employers. The idea was ridiculous, but the cloud meant well, and the fairies did not scold it.

CHAPTER II.

Prince Paragon was a very brave and handsome youth, the son of a powerful King, whose dominions were situated in what, many thousand years afterwards, proved to be the (*soi-disant*) United States of America. He had many weaknesses, and a few vices, but they were not such vices as the world has ever dealt very hardly with. He was a generous young man, and had a profound respect for womankind.

His cousin, Prince Snob, was a handsome, boastful, courageous, reckless, unscrupulous young scamp. He was in the habit of boasting of his successful love affairs, which were, in truth, very numerous. One day, in the presence of Prince Paragon, Prince Snob told a long story how for a wager he had undertaken to break the heart of a young, beautiful, and innocent girl, and how he had succeeded in doing so—for she died of her love for him. Prince Paragon, who made love quite as successfully as Prince Snob, but who never broke hearts intentionally, was very indignant with Prince Snob, and challenged him to fight. The challenge was accepted; and it was as Prince Paragon was on his way to the meeting that the cloud enveloped him, and took him up into the skies. It will be easily understood that Prince Paragon was furious at this occurrence, for he felt sure that his disappearance would be attributed by his enemy to rank cowardice. When he arrived in Fairyland he was extremely sulky.

"Oh, what an ugly pout!" said Queen Mary. "I hope our society does not displease you?"

"I don't know who you are, ma'am," said the Prince, "or how I came here; but I have an important engagement which I am now quite unable to keep."

"Business?" said Fairy Kate—sober, thoughtful Kate.

"Um—m—m!" said the Prince considering.

"Pleasure?" said Fairy Bessie—light-hearted little Bessie.

"Um—m—m!" said the Prince. "Both."

"Well," said Queen Mary, "we are fairies." The

Prince bowed.   " We want to know all about the wickedness of the world, and we have sent for you that you may give us some information on the subject."

" Ah," said the Prince.   " Exactly.   Do you want to know everything ? "

" Everything ! " they all exclaimed.

" Do you *insist* on my telling you everything ? "

" Most decidedly."

" What shall I begin with ?   Love ? "

" Sir ! " exclaimed the Queen of the Fairies, " you forget that you are addressing ladies."

" Pardon me," said the Prince, " but if the bare mention of love shocks you, I think I would rather leave the selection of the matters on which you wish to be instructed in your hands."

" What was the nature of the business on which you were proceeding when we interrupted you ? " said Queen Mary.

" I was going to fight a duel.   I was going to kill a man if I could, and he was going to kill me if *he* could."

" A duel ! " exclaimed the Queen.   " Horrible ! And why were you going to fight this duel ? "

" Well," said the Prince, " there was a lady in the case."

" Stop ! " said the Queen, much shocked.   " Go on to something else.   Are you in debt ?   You don't mind my speaking openly ? "

" Not at all—Oh, yes ; I'm in debt."

" You owe more than you can pay ? "

" I'm afraid I do."

" Well ! " said the Queen.   " Upon my word !   And how did *that* come to pass ? "

" Why, there was a lady in *that* case, too "—

" Stop ! " said the Queen.

" I was in love with her, and gave her some handsome presents."

" Will you stop when I tell you ? " said the Queen. " Your conversation is shocking."

" Shall I go ? " said the Prince.

" No—let me see.   Do you ever tell stories ? "

" I'm afraid I do, sometimes.   I did yesterday."

" Tell us all about it," said the fairies eagerly, for they were dreadfully shocked.

" Well," said the Prince, " there was a lady in *that* case."

" There seems to be a lady in every case," said the Queen.

" There generally is," said the Prince.   " There is no complication of human events in which a woman is not implicated.   Such, at least, is my experience."

" How old are you ? " said the Queen.

" Twenty-two.   How old are *you* ? "

" Never mind," said the Queen.   " Where were you born ? "

" I was born in Bulgaria.   There was a lady in *that* case, too."

" Of course, you absurd creature !   Do you love your fellow-creatures as you are taught to do ? "

" About half of them."

" Which half ?—Stop, I know.   I'm ashamed of you."

And the fairies were so horrified that they could not take their eyes off his wicked handsome face.

" I think you are hard on me, and hard on the world,"

said the Prince. " I am not an anchorite, but I am not
a scamp. I would not knowingly do an unhandsome
thing. I never fight except in defence of my honour, or
of the honour of some one who is dear to me. I only
run into debt because I am liberally disposed. I only
tell stories to prevent innocent people from getting into undeserved trouble. I only love women in an
honourable—"

" *Will* you hold your tongue ? " said the Queen. " Go
on," she added, rather unreasonably,

" Really," said the Prince, " the world isn't such a
bad world after all. I wish one of you would come down
to earth with me, and judge for herself."

" Yes," said the Queen, considering ; " that's not a
bad idea. But who would go ? "

"I would go with him, dear Queen," said all the
fairies in a breath. They feared not the Wicked World,
for they were strong in their own excellence.

" No," said the Queen. " The perils of the journey
are great. It is fitting that I, your Queen, should set
an example of intrepidity and unselfishness when such
an example is necessary. At all risks I will go to
earth : I will go for one year, and at the expiration of
the year I will return and tell you all about it."

And Queen Mary and the Prince got into a cloud, and
descended to the Wicked World.

CHAPTER III.

The Queen of the Fairies and Prince Paragon arrived safely on earth, and proceeded by train to his father's Court. But before getting into the train she unhooked her wings and left them at the cloak-room of the station "to be called for," so as not to attract attention. The Prince introduced her to his father as a lady of high rank. The old King received her very graciously, but his mother the Queen and his sisters thought she looked a great deal too demure and quiet.

The Queen of the Fairies was regularly installed in Court quarters, and—solely with a view of ascertaining what the wickedness of the world really was—entered into all the Court festivities. Her extraordinary beauty, her modesty, her simple grace, and her unaffected disposition enchanted everybody except the old Queen and her daughters, who saw through all this, and called it slyness.

Prince Paragon fell in love with the beautiful Queen Mary, and so did Prince Snob. But Queen Mary had been so horrified at Prince Paragon's reckless confessions in Fairyland that she could not bring herself to like him at all. Prince Snob, however, gave her to understand, in so many words, that he, Prince Snob, was a good man, who had only committed one fault in his whole life (when he was only six years old, he had made use of the bad word " D—v—l " on strong provocation). As he was a very good-looking man, she allowed herself to think leniently of his early error, and on the strength of his sincere repentance she eventually bestowed her heart upon him. For the Fairy Mary, when she came down to the world, invested herself with human attributes and instincts, and so fell in love, as other good girls have done, and will do, until the whole system of things undergoes a radical change.

For the present I must dismiss Prince Paragon (who, at first, appeared likely to become the hero of my fairy tale), for I have to occupy myself with the Fairy Queen's love for Prince Snob.

The poor lady became quite infatuated with the hypocritical scamp. In course of time she saw through his hypocrisy, but her love for him had taken so fixed a possession of her that she could not shake it off. She also learnt that Prince Paragon was really a very good young fellow—with certain human weaknesses, no doubt —but still a very good young fellow, as young fellows go. But she had a simple old-fashioned notion that a woman should only love one man in the course of her life-time, and she had made her choice and intended to keep to it. Still, although she loved Prince Snob devotedly, she resolved not to marry him until he reformed ; for she had another old-fashioned idea. which was—that one ought not to marry a man one can't respect. So she went on loving him in her innocent way without respecting him a bit, hoping by her devotion to him, and by her good example and precept, to make a respectable man of him.

Prince Snob's affection for the Fairy Queen was born partly of his admiration for her beauty, but mainly of his admiration for her magnificent diamonds. He was dreadfully in debt, and he was mean enough to ask her, time after time, for jewels, which he sold, and so these jewels disappeared one by one, until at last there was none left. Prince Snob was very indignant when he found that the Fairy Queen had no more diamonds, and plainly told her that unless she could borrow some jewels or some money (he wasn't particular which), and by so doing prove that she did possess some mortal weaknesses, a sense of what was due to a Fairy Queen would compel him to feel wholly unworthy to possess her.

Terrified at this dreadful threat (for she had had to part with all her fairy attributes on descending to earth), she called upon Prince Paragon, who still loved her devotedly, and begged him to advance her some money. He gave her at once all that she required, and she returned with her pockets and her two hands full of gold, to Prince Snob, and poured the money into that disgraceful fellow's hat. Prince Snob embraced her, telling her that he was quite reassured now that he found she was not absolutely perfect—that she really was open to the influence of some mortal weakness (as if he had not already had proof of that!)—and he assured her that he began to think himself once more really worthy of her.

Well, this money was soon squandered, and again the Prince urged her to borrow more, and again she resorted to Prince Paragon, who again supplied her. This occurred so often that at length Prince Paragon asked her what she did with her money, and I am sorry to say that

her regard for Prince Snob led her to tell Prince Paragon
a story.   So she told him that she had lost the money
at play.   Prince Paragon spoke to her very kindly and
very sorrowfully, and represented to her how unladylike
it was to gamble for such high stakes.   The good Prince
still loved her, and was dreadfully distressed to see her
going, not step by step, but staircase by staircase (if I
may so express myself), to her ruin.   At length,
actuated by his sincere regard for her, he refused to
advance her any more money, and the miserable Fairy
Queen was in utter despair.

A scene ensued with Prince Snob which is almost too
terrible for description.   However, here it is.

"Ma'am," said the Prince, when he heard that she
could supply him with no more money, "I am terribly
disappointed in you."

"Dear Snob," said the Fairy Queen, "don't be hard
on me.   I've done my best—indeed I have."

"Ma'am," said the Prince, "you have done nothing
of the kind."

"Indeed, I have borrowed money for you, until I can't
induce anyone to lend me any more."

"Yes, you have borrowed money—*but you have not
yet stolen money.   Steal!*"

"Oh, Snob, you are joking."

"Do I look as if I were joking?"   And indeed he
did not.   "Steal immediately, or I have done with
you."

The Fairy Queen was at last aroused to a sense of her
position.

"Prince Snob, you require of me that which is not

ordinarily required of ladies by their lovers, and I decline to obey you."

" Very good, ma'am ; then you will understand that our association is at an end. I thought that, Fairy Queen as you are, you had, nevertheless, some mortal failings—some pardonable blemishes, which would serve to bring you down to the level of a human being. You are much too good for me : you are a Fairy Queen ; I am an erring mortal,—for I know I have my faults——"

" No, no ! " said the Queen, in an agony.

" Yes, indeed I have," rejoined the Prince. " I am an erring mortal, and I am wholly unworthy of you. Good morning, ma'am."

And he left her abruptly.

The Fairy Queen was utterly miserable. She went to good Prince Paragon, and told him all about Prince Snob's treatment of her. Prince Paragon was furious. He sought out Prince Snob, and immediately challenged him to mortal combat.

" All right ! " said Prince Snob, who had plenty of pluck. " But no clouds this time."

Prince Paragon was stung by the taunt. " Come on ! " said he.

And Prince Snob came on. They fought valiantly, but Prince Snob was eventually overpowered. He fell, and as Prince Paragon was about to pass his sword through the calf of Prince Snob's left leg (for Prince Paragon did not want to kill his adversary outright), the Fairy Queen rushed in and implored Prince Paragon to spare his rival.

" I won't hurt him seriously, ma'am," said the Prince.

I am only going to pass my sword through a fleshy part."

He said this sarcastically, for Prince Snob's calves were notoriously insignificant.

"Spare him even that," said the Queen. "My year has just expired, and I must return to Fairyland. Let me take him with me. If I cannot bring myself down to his level, I can at all events raise him to mine."

"Oh!" said Prince Paragon. "Then I wish you good morning."

"Stay," said the Queen. "Won't you come, too?"

"But I should be in the way."

"You goose! I'm not going to marry him. I want to make a fairy of him; and I'll do the same for you, too."

And a cloud descended and took them all up into Fairyland as soon as the Queen had redeemed her wings from the custody of the woman at the railway cloak-room.

CHAPTER IV.

(I THINK this will be a very short chapter.)

The Fairy Queen arrived in due time at Fairyland with Prince Paragon and Prince Snob. They had not had a comfortable journey in the cloud, for they were crowded (it was only a cloud for one), and Prince Snob kept trying to push Prince Paragon out of it.

" Well," said the Fairy Queen to the other fairies, " here I am, safe and sound. Why, how cross you all look ! "

" If we had known that we were to have had the pleasure of the society of these two gentlemen we would have prepared a larger cloud," said Fairy Bessie, rather spitefully.

" Fairy Bessie," said the Fairy Queen, " I don't like innuendoes. Speak openly, I command you."

" You—I beg pardon—you do what ? " said Bessie, as if she had not understood the Queen.

" I *command* you ! " said the Fairy Queen, with great dignity.

" Only the Queen commands *me*," said Bessie.

" I *am* the Queen, miss ! "

" Oh, dear, no ! You are deposed. You *would* go to earth, you know, alone with that gentleman, and we all thought it bold, so we deposed you. Fairy Mattie is our Queen now."

" Is this so ? " said Mary to Fairy Lizzie.

" Certainly," said Lizzie. " We don't think your conduct respectable."

" Will you tell your Queen that I am here, and would like to speak to her ? "

" I can't. The Queen and I are not on speaking terms."

" Will you tell some one else to tell the Queen ? " said the poor ex-monarch.

" I can't even do that. In fact, we are none of us on speaking terms with one another."

The poor ex-Queen went about from fairy to fairy, but

from all she received the same answer : "We are not on speaking terms with each other."

At length the Fairy Kate came up. (I think it was the Fairy Kate who I said had once been on earth? Let me look back. Yes, the Fairy Kate.) Well, the Fairy Kate came up, and she alone of all the fairies seemed glad to see the ex-Queen.

"What in the world is the reason of this extraordinary demoralization among my late subjects?" said poor Mary.

"I think I can explain," said Kate. "The presence of the mortal whom we summoned into Fairyland a year ago has contaminated us. We were all good and happy till he came, but since that unfortunate event we have fallen into all kinds of uncharitable ways of thinking. We quarrelled dreadfully, talked at one another, and said the most unkind things about each other's hair. We can't get on at all. He brought a worldly atmosphere with him (I recognized it directly), and this has worked its evil effect upon us. We are as so many women!" And the Fairy Kate burst into tears.

All the other fairies exclaimed, "Yes that's the secret of it!" and they burst into tears.

"But," said Fairy Bessie, "independently of this, we have really heard such things of you! We hear that you fell in love with a man, and that you ran into debt, and that you borrowed money, and that you told stories, and that you actually were the cause of a duel between two of your admirers. All this is very, very dreadful!"

How they knew all this I cannot for the life of me

imagine, as they had held no communication whatever with the world during the ex-Queen's absence.

"It is all true," said the Queen, "and, as you say, it is very dreadful. But make some allowance for me. See what evil effect the presence among you of one mortal, and that one a very good one, has worked! The mere fact of your having breathed an atmosphere in common with him has robbed you of those social excellences for which you were all so remarkable; you have become vain, tetchy, jealous, and morose. If this is the legitimate and necessary effect of the presence of one good mortal among you for half an hour, think what I have had to undergo, who have been compelled to associate for a whole twelvemonth with men and women of all descriptions! Believe me, fairies, we are too vainglorious, too proud of our excellence, too unmindful of the fact that we were good because we had no temptation to do wrong. We despised the world because it was wicked, forgetting that the wickedness of the world is born of the temptations to which only the inhabitants of the world are exposed. Let us forgive one another, and endeavour to think more charitably of the errors of those who are subjected to temptations from which we are happily removed."

The fairies were much affected by the ex-Queen's remarks, and Queen Mattie resigned on the spot. The Fairy Kate approached Prince Paragon and Prince Snob (who were standing rather awkwardly apart during the scene I have just described), and welcomed them. She shook hands with Prince Paragon, but when she looked at Prince Snob she gave a shriek, and fell fainting into his arms. Prince Snob was the villain who had broken her heart when she was a mortal on earth.

Prince Snob was so much moved that he retired into a corner and reformed upon the spot. He offered to marry the Fairy Kate, then and there, but that, of course, could not be. So the Fairy Kate was sent down to earth as a mortal, with instructions to allow Prince Snob to marry her, and to return to Fairyland immediately upon his first act of unkindness; and Queen Mary received the same permission with respect to Prince Paragon. Neither the Queen nor the Fairy Kate returned until they were widows, when they resumed their fairy attributes for good and all. Their weeds were so much admired that widows' caps became the fashion in Fairyland, and are universally worn to this day.

This chapter is not so very short, after all.

THE FINGER OF FATE.

I AM going to give you an instance of the desperately strong measures Fate will take in order to bring about an event she has set her mind on.

I am a middle-aged bachelor, of staid and careful habits. I am pretty comfortably " off," having an independent income of £400 a-year, and a Civil Service pension of £700 a-year. I was for many years Secretary of the Warrant Officers' Shirt-frill and Shaving-Soap Department, a branch office under the Admiralty, Somerset House.

I have led a quiet and retired life—shunning society in its gayest sense, and associating intimately with three or four other heads of subordinate departments, and with no one else. I am naturally nervous, and, I am afraid, irritable. I hate bright colours, unnecessary conversation, useless noises—such as vocal and instrumental music, and the neighing of horses—and I can't bear to see people in quick motion. If I had my way, no one should speak to me except on matters of pure business, and only then when the communication could not be conveniently reduced into the form of a memorandum. Above all other things, I detest forward people—and above all other forward people, I detest strangers, who address me on immaterial topics in public conveyances.

I had occasion, a few weeks after my retirement from official life, to travel to Liverpool by the limited mail on my way to Jamaica. A railway journey to Liverpool is detestable, but posting is worse, and walking out of the question.

It was a cold night in April. There were very few passengers by the limited mail. There were only four first-class carriages to Liverpool: of these, three were occupied by ladies—one in each carriage; the fourth was a smoking carriage and empty. I don't smoke, but the train was on the point of starting, and the guard assured me that it was unlikely that we should take up any first-class passengers on our way. It was a new carriage, and had never been used. At all events I should be safe from female intrusion; so I jumped in. The train started, and I had my carriage all to myself. The train did not stop till we reached Rugby. At Rugby a lady opened the carriage door. She was a stout plain middle-aged woman—five-and-forty, I should say. She was extravagantly dressed in showy colours. Her complexion was very dark—she was, in fact, a Mulatto —and she wore a respectable moustache.

This wouldn't do; I could settle *her* at all events.

"I beg your pardon, ma'am, but this is a smoking carriage."

"Exactly," replied the lady, with a strong foreign accent, "but I smokes."

This was a contingency that I had never contemplated.

"You give me light, sar?" said the foreign lady.

Here was a chance of escape.

"I have no lights, madam."

"Ah, dash!" she said. "But, no consequence——Guard!"

The guard came up.

"You give me light?"

And he gave her a light, and then he disappeared.

I was nearly choking with the fumes of her detestable Havannah. At last I could stand it no longer.

"I beg your pardon, but I object to smoking."

"Ah," replied the lady, "you object to smoke—you travel in smoking carriage. Donkey — jackass donkey!"

She said these last three words with the air of one who had done a short addition sum, and was stating the total.

I had never travelled abroad, but I knew that foreigners are remarkable for their politeness.

"I entered this carriage to avoid the society of ladies."

"Me, too," said the foreign lady. "Dash! I hate lady. I like gentleman." Then she added as an after-thought, "You are haughty old customer, but I like *you*—you rummy old passenger!"

I was exceedingly annoyed at this. I plume myself upon my good taste in dress—that is to say, I study to dress myself in such a manner as to call for no remark of any kind, which I hold to be the perfection of good taste. My personal appearance is simply gentlemanly, without anything remarkable about it. It has been my constant study to be gentlemanly but usual; and to be called a " rummy old passenger " was under the circumstances an irritating thing. However, I maintained a dignified silence.

It was a very cold night, and having regard to the strong dash of negro blood in my fellow-passenger's veins, thought it would irritate her if I let down the window.

Accordingly, I did so.

" Thank you, old passenger," she said : " I like fresh airs. I let this one down too ! " And she lowered the other window.

I couldn't stand the draught so I put up my window —and she put up hers. Something like this occurs in " Box and Cox."

I was sulkily furious by this time. In half-an-hour we should reach Stafford, and I determined to change my carriage at that station. In the meantime I tried to sleep, but the foreign lady kept up such an incessant clatter that sleep was out of the question.

" Where you going, old passenger ? You not tell ? Secret, eh ? Ah, sly old dog ! You old cashier, perhaps, bolting with bank moneys, eh ? Confidential clerk with employer's cash-box in portmanteau, eh ? Old boy going up north to marry old girl on the sly, eh ? Bagman and ashamed of it, perhaps, eh, you old passenger ? Bah ! Bagman good as anybody else ! Never be ashamed—look at me ! Me not blush at myself. What you say I am ?—eh ? You not guess.

Duchess? No! Countess? No! Lady of large property—wife of Liverpool merchant? Devil a bit! Missionary woman? No! Tight-rope dancer? No! Stewardess on West Indiaman spending pay? Yes—Hullo! What's that?"

I did not know what it was, but there was a sudden snap and our carriage suddenly slackened speed, and eventually stopped. I put my head out of the window. The coupling had broken, and our carriage and the guard's van had been separated from the rest of the train. The driver knew nothing about it; and there we were, half-way between Rugby and Stafford at 12 p.m. on a very cold April night!

"Good Heavens!" said I, in the very greatest alarm, "the coupling has broken and we are left behind by the train! We shall be smashed by the next down train!"

"Not a bit, you old strange one!" replied she, without even looking out of the window. "Guard at end of train. If we broke off, he broke off too."

The guard had, in point of fact, rushed forward, moving his lantern in the faint hope of being able to attract the attention of the driver, but in vain. So he returned, very excited, but very sulky.

"What in the world are we to do?" asked I.

"Get out of this, you and your old woman, while I run back to Tamworth to telegraph. Come, out you go——"

"But where are we to go? It is raining hard, and we shall be soaked through and through."

"There's a light yonder across the common. You'd better trot over there, you and your old woman, and knock 'em up. I don't know the country just here." And off he went like lightning.

"His advice very good, my old man," said my companion. "I take your arm, and we trot. Come, rum chap."

There was no help for it. I succumbed, and we had a squashy walk over a pathless and furzy common, half a mile in diameter. My companion had a knack of tumbling down in a sitting attitude at the faintest provocation; and if I lifted her up once I lifted her up twenty times. Twenty times sixteen stone is exactly two tons—which represents the weight I lifted off Copley Common that night. (I have since had reason to believe that her actual weight was fifteen stone three, but I say sixteen stone because I take into consideration the moisture with which her clothes were saturated.)

At length, after twenty minutes' difficult walking, we reached the light that had attracted our attention. It proceeded from the window of a very small cottage. We knocked, and eventually the door was opened to us. In the meantime, my companion, who had informed me that her name was Dolly Fortescue, sang negro songs in a deep contralto.

"Wot is it?" said the cottager.

"There has been an accident on the line, and we want shelter."

"Wot'll you give?"

"A guinea," said Miss Fortescue. "This rum old card give a guinea."

"Well, you can lie in the stable. My cottage is chock-full."

He took a lantern and showed me the way to the " stable," which was a hut with one stall and a loose box in which was a very untidy donkey. I at once declined to share this stable with Miss Fortescue, preferring to risk a night in the rain. I stated my intention.

"Old boy is quite right. He's a rummy old passenger, but he's quite right. Come along, queer little old man —we walk somewheres else."

"Now, lookee here," said the man. "Wot's your game, you two? Wot are yer up to? Is this here a lark? Where's my guinea! Come!—be a gentleman afore ye goes! None of this with ME you know! Give us 'old of my guinea! Come!"

" Old man," said Dolly to me, "pull out employer's cash-box and give guinea like bird."

"Wot's this here about cash-boxes?" said the man. " Come, out with that guinea! We hears a good deal about it, but we don't see none of it. Come, let's see some of it. Be a man!"

"I shall give you nothing," said I. " You are an insolent scoundrel!"

"Wot!" said the man. "Wot's this here about cash-boxes? Come along o' me!" and he laid his hand upon my collar.

" You scoundrel!" said I, "If I were a stronger man than you are I'd——"

“Wot, assault the perlice? My eye, here's a go! Come along o' me! I'm the constable. *I'll* give you a lodging. So it's cash-boxes, is it? Come along o' me—both on yer!”

And he led us to a square building at the back of his house, and, unlocking the door, pushed us in.

“Now,” he said, “I'm a-going to search you.”

And he did; but he found nothing except a few sovereigns—for my money was in my dispatch box which had been placed in the luggage van.

“Now,” said he, “how about searching your good woman? *I* ain't a-goin' to do it—and I ain't got a missus. Lookee here, suppose *you* do?”

“Sir, this lady is a total stranger to me.”

“Ah! separate responsibilities, eh? The hold story. Now, lookee here, ma'am, I ain't a-goin' to search you, because I've been properly brought up: but I'm a-goin' to shake you to see if you rattle.”

Miss Fortescue made no verbal reply, but pulled out a gigantic clasp knife.

“All rights,” said she. “Come on policeman!”

He hesitated.

“Look, policeman, I tell you what I do. I walk out of this. Good nights!” And she did.

The policeman turned pale and civil.

“Ain't you goin' along with her, sir?” said he.

“I am not. I pass the night here.”

He retired, swearing fluently, and locked the door on me.

I could not sleep—but, at all events, I was free at last from my persecutrix. I was so pleased that I sang a

merry song, and carved my name on the wall with a
rusty nail, as other prisoners have done before me. The
next day I was taken before a magistrate, who dismissed
the case at once, and I resumed my journey.

When I reached Liverpool I found that my ship was
on the point of sailing. My luggage had been placed on
board, and my half-cabin was ready for me.

We had dreadful weather at sea; we were driven
many hundred miles out of our course, and for three
weeks after leaving Liverpool I was terribly ill, and
did not leave my cabin. I believe I should not have
left my cabin at all if I had not been thrown bodily
out of it by a tremendous concussion one stormy
night.

I rushed on deck, and found everything in the wildest
confusion. A fearful storm was raging, and the ship
had shifted her cargo. There was absolutely no hope
for her, and it was impossible to launch a boat, even
if it could have lived in such a sea.

I don't want to harrow anybody, so I will content
myself with explaining that, amid the shrieks of three
hundred people, the vessel foundered.

I always take the precaution, when at sea, of wearing
a little india-rubber apparatus round my neck, which I
inflate, and in that condition it prevents my head from
going under. I inflated it hastily, and I found that it
answered admirably. I was tossed about violently for
some hours, and when the gale at length subsided, I
looked around me. No land was visible; and as I rose
and fell in the sulky lopping sea, I felt that my hour was
at hand. I looked eagerly towards the horizon on all sides,

in the vain hope of seeing a distant sail, but I saw none. There was, however, one thing in view—a dark round thing floating on the waves a mile or so from me. I struck out for it, and I was horrified to find that it was alive! Still I approached it, reflecting that death from a sea-monster was preferable to death from starvation, and to my amazement I found that it was making straight in my direction. On approaching it, I was appalled to find that it resembled nothing so much as a human head in a floating plate; and on coming within three or four yards, I discovered that it was the head of Miss Fortescue, supported above water by a contrivance similar in character to that which I myself wore. I should add that her great fat bunchy body and (I had no doubt) her legs were still connected with it.

" Not Miss Fortescue ? " said I.

" Rummy old passenger, by Gar ! " said she. " What are you doing here, sar ? "

" I am not here by choice. I was wrecked in the *Aurora Borealis.*"

" Me, too ! " said she.

" You ! " said I, " Were you on board the *Aurora ?* "

"—*Borealis,*" added she. "Yes, me stewardess. How are you ? "

" I am very cold, and this confounded thing has given me a crick in the neck."

" Situation damp," said she. " Try this, you queer one ! "

It was a flask of brandy. She held it to my lips until I had taken a comfortable draught,

" Two shillings," said she, holding the bottle to the light to see how much I had taken.

" Here it is," said I.

" Stewardess a shilling—make three."

I determined to resist this extortion, for on that line of packets the steward's fee is included in the fare. I told her so.

"You mean old chap," said Miss Fortescue. " I give you nothing more."

I tried to look dignified and indifferent, but it was of no use. You can't look dignified when you are perpetually bobbing up and down on a lopping sea supported entirely by an India-rubber bag round the neck. Besides, I was very hungry, and she had a large waterproof basket on her arm, so I gave her the shilling, which she bit and pocketed.

" Now then," said she, " what's to do next ? "

" What have you got there ? " said I.

" German sausage—cucumber—carrot—bottle barley-water—two tomatoes—a bloater—two eggs—one pound macaroni—head of endive—stick Spanish liquorice—three pounds snuff."

" What are your terms for the carrot ? "

" Carrot very dear out here, you peculiar old one. Carrot a guinea."

" Hand it over."

I gave her a guinea, and ate the carrot.

" Now," said she, " I go straight on in that direction for shore. Come along, old one ! "

" Never ! " said I ; " I will take the opposite point of the compass, and run my chance. Good bye."

And I struck out vigorously in the opposite direction.

After a day and a half's vigorous swimming, I reached the point of a low sandy shore, which seemed to stretch for miles in a direction due south, as I judged from the position of the sun. I was well satisfied to feel dry ground under my legs again, and I landed with much gratitude.

I was extremely hungry, and I walked for miles along the shore picking up mussels and periwinkles, and eating them raw. I saw no trace of a human being of any kind, and as the sun went down I began to wish myself in the sea again. Night came on and I was hungry and alone. However, I still wandered on in a listless purposeless way until I fell over something that fell across my path. To my intense joy I found, on investigation, that it was a sleeping, breathing human being. I could not tell whether it was a man or a woman, as there was no moon, and the clothes he or she wore would have suited either sex equally well. I endeavoured to awaken the figure, but in vain, so I determined to sit by his or her side until morning. Accordingly I dropped myself into a sitting posture, when, to my extreme amazement, an explosion of fire took place immediately under me! The fearful idea flashed across me that the island was a mass of slumbering fire, only waiting for accidental contact with an exciting cause to blow itself and everything for miles around into the air! On closer examination, however, I found that I had sat down upon a box of vesuvians, and one of them had exploded.

It suddenly occurred to me to use these vesuvians as a means of identifying my companion. I ignited one, but it was not a flaming vesuvian; it smouldered, and fizzed, and smelt, but afforded no assistance. I lit another and held it close to the person's nose, but it only illuminated a small circle as big as half-a-crown. I lit a third, and this time the red-hot end tumbled on to the sleeper's cheek. The sleeper started up. It was Dolly Fortescue!

I was not a bit surprised. I had brought myself to look upon Dolly as my Fate. Dolly was not a bit surprised. She looked at me—grinned—and spoke.

" That hot, you odd one ! "

When morning broke we looked about us. The island we found was about twenty-five miles long, and seven broad, principally rock—no vegetation—no fresh water. The island was crescent-shaped, the two horns being twenty miles asunder. I had landed on one horn, she on the other, and we had met in the middle. The only native inhabitants were periwinkles and mussels. So we set to work to make ourselves comfortable.

The object of this narrative is not to give a detailed account of the highly ingenious manner in which we continued to live comfortably, and even luxuriously, on our island, but rather to exhibit the caprices of a determined destiny.

I detested Dolly with all my heart, and avoided her whenever it was practicable ; but she paid me every attention, and, notwithstanding her unpleasant appearance, she was really valuable to me. She christened the island " Fortescue," and crowned me its monarch. My first act as king was to try her for drawing her knife on the policeman in Bembridge lock-up, and by that means breaking out of custody. She was found guilty by an impartial jury of ME, and sentenced to transportation for life to the other side of the island. She went meekly and uncomplainingly, but, as she took all our cooking implements with her, I was obliged to follow.

This inconvenient life went on for thirteen years. At the expiration of that period my kingdom was visited by a missionary ship, which had driven out of her course. I signalled, and my signals were answered. A boat full of Baptist missionaries put off to us, bearing many bales of tracts for our conversion. They were very much disappointed and disgusted when they heard we were Christians, and when we added we were Protestants, they moodily returned to their boat and mechanically put to sea.

I screamed aloud in my terror at their contemplated departure without us.

Their chief explained that their mission was to convert, and that we needed no conversion.

"You are Christian," said he—"Protestant, and, no doubt, Baptist. What can we do?"

"No," said I, as a ray of hope broke through the clouds that were gathering around us, "not Baptist—Church of England!"

"Ha!" said their leader; "will you let me make a Baptist of you, if we take you with us?"

"I am open to conviction," said I.

"And your wife?" said he.

"This is NOT my wife!" said I, in a passion.

"Shocking, indeed!" said he. "Will you marry her if I take you off?"

"Yes," said Dolly, "he will marry me; you melancholy old Presbyterian!"

So he took us into the boat, and we left the island. We were married as soon as we reached England.

In a week my wife had had enough of me. The arrears of my pension amounted to something considerable, and she ran off with them. I ran after her, but I could never find her. I suppose, now that I want her, I never shall.

A TALE OF A DRY PLATE.

I AM a junior partner in a large mercantile house. Certain irregularities had occurred in our Colombo branch, and I was dispatched by the firm to investigate them, and to place matters on a more satisfactory footing. I need not go into details on this point, as they are irrelevant to my story.

I sailed by the *Kaiser-i-Hind* from Tilbury, accompanied by my valet. At the Liverpool Street terminus an elderly lady in widow's mourning asked me some questions as to the conveyance of luggage from the Tilbury station to the ship; she should have sent her luggage to the docks, but had omitted to do so. As I replied to her questions, I saw that she was accompanied by a very beautiful girl of eighteen. There is no need to beat about the bush—I fell in love with her, there and then. It is a commonplace way of putting it, but I don't know that I could make matters clearer by a more elaborate method of expression. As they and I travelled to Tilbury in the same compartment, we entered into conversation, as people will readily do who know that they are to travel many thousand miles together. I learnt that the lady was a Mrs. Selby, widow of a Colonel Selby, who had died about six months since. Broken in health, and weakened by long weeping, she had been advised to take a sea voyage, in the belief that change of scene and beneficent sea air would do much to restore her to health, if not to happiness. As I happened to have met Colonel Selby on two occasions—once in London and once in a country house—my acquaintance with his widow and daughter rapidly ripened into friendship. We sailed on a fine October afternoon, and by the time we were off the " Start " I had almost established myself on the footing of an old friend.

Pass over the voyage. It lasted five weeks, but it seemed like five days. I lived but in Clara's presence. I scarcely spoke to anyone on board except to Clara and her mother. People see more of each other, if they care to do so, in a few weeks' voyage than in a lifetime on shore, and before we reached Colombo I had declared my love to Clara, and she had accepted it. If there is unalloyed happiness on earth, it was given to us as we neared Ceylon.

Unalloyed, save by the thought that we were about to part for a time ; for Clara was to go on to Calcutta, where her late father's brother was quartered, whereas I was to remain in Ceylon for three months. We were to return to England at about the same date, and it was arranged that as soon as possible after our arrival we were to be married.

I have some little skill in photography, and I had brought with me a camera and some dry plates, intending to photograph any striking scenes that I might come across during my journey. By the aid of dry plates, photography, and especially travelling photography, is much simplified. The traveller can take a photograph, shut the plate in a light-tight box, and develop it twelve months afterwards if he pleases. There is no need to encumber oneself with chemicals; all the messy portion of the process can be done at home, in the seclusion of one's own dark room. I had not intended to take any photographs on the voyage, for dry plates are extraordinarily sensitive to the action of the faintest ray of light, and it was practically impossible to make my cabin dark enough to allow of my transferring plates from the dark box to the slides without absolutely spoiling them. But I happened to have left two plates in one of the slides, and before we reached our destination I devoted one of these to Clara and one to Mrs. Selby.

We parted tearfully, but not unhappily. We were to meet in three months' time, and our lives were then to be passed together. I believe we were too full of happiness in this prospect to grieve very much over our parting. As the *Kaiser* steamed away for Calcutta, I kept the happiness of our next meeting steadily before me, and it served to keep me in good spirits.

The time passed slowly; but it passed. I had received two letters from Clara, written from Calcutta, full of life, and hope, and joy at the prospect before us. She was going to spend a month at Allahabad, and a fortnight at Bombay, and she was then to return to Marseilles by a Messageries ship, the captain of which was an intimate friend of the uncle with whom she had been staying at Calcutta. By this arrangement she would arrive in England about a month before me.

At length my sailing orders came, and on one of the happiest days of my life I set foot on board the good ship *Mirzapore*, which was to convey me to Port Said, on my way home, *viâ* Brindisi. I had written to Mrs. Selby, begging her to bring Clara to meet me in Paris. Her doing so would but shorten our period of separation by some ten or twelve hours, but I knew that these hours were golden to her as well as to me, and I was selfish for both of us. After a stormy voyage, I reached Brindisi in due course; I hurried to the Poste Restante, for I had asked her to reply to me there, but there was nothing for me. It was evident that my letter had not reached her; perhaps she had delayed a few days in Paris on her way home. She had a *trousseau* to prepare, and it is a strange article of faith among women that this can be done more effectually in Paris than elsewhere; consequently, nothing was more probable than that she was there at that moment; my letter would probably be forwarded to her, and if so, she would surely be at the station on the arrival of the train from Italy.

As I rushed across Europe I had but one thought in my mind—would Clara be at the Paris terminus to meet me? The towns flew by me when I thought of her, and yet at times the intervals between them seemed interminable. Every stoppage irritated me; yet the two days were not tedious. I could always lose all count of time by allowing my mind to dwell upon the incidents of our voyage together, and especially on the crowning incident that was yet to come. But when the doubting question arose whether or not we should meet in Paris, the train

seemed to dawdle as it never dawdled before. At length
we reached the terminus. I eagerly scanned the few
people on the platform as we entered the station, and
my heart sank when I saw she was not there. Then I
remembered that on French railways friends of passengers
are not, as a rule, allowed on the platform, and my hopes
rose again. They were soon dashed, for there was no
Clara for me in the waiting-rooms or at the entrance.

A dim sense of calamity—unknown, and the more
terrible for being unknown—took possession of me. I
hurried across Paris to the " Nord," reached Calais in
due course, crossed to Dover and made my way to
London, which I reached late at night. The next day,
at nine in the morning, I hurried to Mrs. Selby's house
in Oxford Square. I rang the bell, and it was answered
by a maid-servant in deep black. I asked for Mrs. Selby,
but so inarticulately that the girl did not understand
me. I pulled myself together, and repeated the question.
The girl stammered awkwardly. Had I not heard?
No! I had heard nothing ; was anything wrong ? The
French ship in which Mrs. Selby and Clara had sailed
from Bombay had been lost—as it was supposed—in a
hurricane between Bombay and Aden, and all souls
drowned.

I staggered as from a strong man's blow. I remember
nothing until I found myself lying on the sofa in the
dining-room, tended by an elderly gentleman, Mrs.
Selby's brother and administrator. He, of course, did
not know me ; still less did he know of my relation
towards his dead niece. I told him all, and he treated
me with the greatest kindness. He could give me no

hope ; the ship was then six weeks overdue, and the insurances on her had been duly paid.

Desolate and heart-broken I left him, and went to my mother's house in Devonshire. After three weeks of fever I began to recover strength, but the light of my life was extinct, and an undefinable sense of night was all that remained to me. As soon as I was strong enough to stand, I thought of the photographs I had taken at Singapore. They were all that was left to me of my dead love, and with a feeling of unspeakable awe, I proceeded to raise her presentment as it were from the grave. In the closely darkened room, illuminated only by the dim red light of my developing lamp, I prepared the necessary chemicals with a trembling and uncertain hand. I took the plate from the slide in which it had been enclosed for so many months, and as I looked upon its plain creamy surface, so soon to be sanctified by her image, I almost felt that I was engaged on some un-hallowed deed of necromancy. Breathless with excitement, I poured the developer upon it, and as I awaited the result, I could hear my heart thumping against my chest. I had not long to wait. Slowly, but surely and distinctly, the features of my darling came to me from the grave. Notwithstanding the inversion of its tones, it stood plainly before me—herself in every detail. As I watched the gradual perfection of the portrait, I cried like a child. At length the development was complete, and, shaking like a leaf, I took it from its bath to examine it more closely. As I did so the door of the room was suddenly opened, a flood of light was admitted, and the photograph was ruined beyond reparation.

With an inarticulate cry, I seized the intruder in my weakened grasp—it was my valet, who had accompanied me on my voyage out and home. I know not what I said to him, in my furious despair—the words, whatever they were, passed into forgetfulness as they were spoken.

" Sir, sir," said he, " I bring you great news. Miss Selby—Mrs. Selby. Their boat was picked up by a sailing ship. She encountered adverse winds, and only reached Plymouth yesterday—and—and—Miss Clara is here—and I have come to tell you so ! "

THE BURGLAR'S STORY.

When I became eighteen years of age, my father, a distinguished begging-letter impostor, said to me, "Reginald, I think it is time that you began to think about choosing a profession."

These were ominous words. Since I left Eton, nearly a year before, I had spent my time very pleasantly, and very idly, and I was sorry to see my long holiday drawing to a close. My father had hoped to have sent me to Cambridge (Cambridge was a tradition in our family), but business had been very depressed of late, and a sentence of six months' hard labour had considerably straitened my poor father's resources.

It was necessary—highly necessary—that I should choose a calling. With a sigh of resignation, I admitted as much.

"If you like," said my father, "I will take you in hand, and teach you my profession, and, in a few years perhaps, I may take you into partnership; but, to be candid with you, I doubt whether it is a satisfactory calling for an athletic young fellow like you."

"I don't seem to care about it, particularly," said I.

"I'm glad to hear it," said my father; "it's a poor calling for a young man of spirit. Besides, you have to

grow grey in the service before people will listen to you.
It's all very well as a refuge in old age; but a young
fellow is likely to make but a poor hand at it.   Now, I
should like to consult your own tastes on so important
a matter as the choice of a profession.   What do you
say ?   The Army ? "

No, I didn't care for the army.

" Forgery ?   The Bar ?   Cornish Wrecking ? "

" Father," said I, " I should like to be a forger, but
I write such an infernal hand."

" A regular Eton hand," said he.   " Not plastic
enough for forgery ; but you could have a writing-
master."

" It's as much as I can do to forge my own name.   I
don't believe I should ever be able to forge anybody
else's."

" Anybody's else, you should say, not 'anybody
else's.'   It's a dreadful barbarism.   Eton English."

" No," said I, " I should never make a fortune at it.
As to wrecking—why you know how sea-sick I am."

" You might get over that.   Besides, you would deal
with wrecks ashore, not wrecks at sea."

" Most of it done in small boats, I'm told.   A deal of
small boat work.   No, I won't be a wrecker.   I think I
should like to be a burglar."

" Yes," said my father, considering the subject
" Yes, it's a fine manly profession; but it's dangerous
it's highly dangerous."

" Just dangerous enough to be exciting, no more."

" Well," said my father, " if you've a distinct tast
for burglary I'll see what can be done."

My dear father was always prompt with pen and ink. That evening he wrote to his old friend Ferdinand Stoneleigh, a burglar of the very highest professional standing, and in a week I was duly and formally articled to him, with a view to ultimate partnership.

I had to work hard under Mr. Stoneleigh.

"Burglary is a jealous mistress," said he. "She will tolerate no rivals. She exacts the undivided devotion of her worshippers."

And so I found it. Every morning at ten o'clock I had to present myself at Stoneleigh's chambers in New Square, Lincoln's Inn, and until twelve I assisted his clerk with the correspondence. At twelve I had to go out prospecting with Stoneleigh, and from two to four I had to devote to finding out all particulars necessary to a scientific burglar in any given house. At first I did this merely for practice, and with no view to an actual attempt. He would tell me off to a house of which he knew all the particulars, and order me to ascertain all about the house and its inmates—their coming and going, the number of their servants, whether any of them were men, and, if so, whether they slept on the basement or not, and other details necessary to be known before a burglary could be safely attempted. Then he would compare my information with his own facts, and compliment or blame me, as I might deserve. He was a strict master, but always kind, just, and courteous, as became a highly polished gentleman of the old school. He was one of the last men who habitually wore hessians.

After a year's probation, I accompanied him on several

expeditions, and had the happiness to believe that I was of some little use to him. I shot him eventually in the stomach, mistaking him for the master of a house into which we were breaking (I had mislaid my dark lantern), and he died on the grand piano. His dying wish was that his compliments might be conveyed to me. I now set up on my own account, and engaged his poor old clerk, who nearly broke his heart at his late master's funeral. Stoneleigh left no family. His money—about £12,000, invested for the most part in American railways—he left to the Society for Providing More Bishops; and his ledgers, daybooks, memoranda, and papers generally he bequeathed to me.

As the chambers required furnishing, I lost no time in commencing my professional duties. I looked through his books for a suitable house to begin upon, and found the following attractive entry :—

Thurloe Square.—No. 102.
House.—Medium.
Occupant.—John Davis, bachelor.
Occupation.—Designer of Dados.
Age.—86.
Physical Peculiarities. — Very feeble ; eccentric ; drinks ; Evangelical ; snores.
Servants.—Two housemaids, one cook.
Sex.—All female.
Particulars of Servants.—Pretty housemaid called Rachel ; Jewess ; open to attentions. Goes out for beer at 9 p.m. ; snores. Ugly housemaid, called Bella ; Presbyterian. Open to attentions ; snores. Elderly

cook; Primitive Methodist. Open to attentions; snores.

Fastenings.—Chubb's lock on street door, chain, and bolts. Bars to all basement windows. Practicable approach from third room, ground floor, which is shuttered and barred, but bar has no catch, and can be raised with table knife.

Valuable Contents of House.—Presentation plate from grateful æsthetes. Gold repeater. Mulready envelope. Two diamond rings. Complete edition of "Bradshaw," from 1834 to present time, 588 volumes, bound in limp calf.

General.—Mr. Davis sleeps second floor front; servants on third floor. Davis goes to bed at ten. No one on basement. Swarms with beetles; otherwise excellent house for purpose.

This seemed to me to be a capital house to try single-handed. At twelve o'clock that very night I pocketed two crowbars, a bunch of skeleton keys, a centre-bit, a dark lantern, a box of silent matches, some putty, a life-preserver, and a knife; and I set off at once for Thurloe Square. I remember that it snowed heavily. There was at least a foot of snow on the ground, and there was more to come. Poor Stoneleigh's particulars were exact in every detail. I got into the third room on the ground floor without any difficulty, and made my way into the dining-room. There was the presentation plate, sure enough—about 800 ounces, as I reckoned. I collected this, and tied it up so that I could carry it without attracting attention.

Just as I had finished, I heard a slight cough behind me. I turned and saw a dear old silver-haired gentleman in a dressing-gown standing in the doorway. The venerable gentleman covered me with a revolver.

My first impulse was to rush at and brain him with my life-preserver.

" Don't move," said he, " or you're a dead man."

A rather silly remark occurred to me to the effect that if I *did* move it would rather prove that I was a live man, but I dismissed it at once as unsuited to the business character of the interview.

" You're a burglar ? " said he.

" I have that honour," said I, making for my pistol-pocket.

" Don't move," said he ; " I have often wished to have the pleasure of encountering a burglar, in order to be able to test a favourite theory of mine as to how persons of that class should be dealt with. But you mustn't move."

I replied that I should be happy to assist him, if I could do so consistently with a due regard to my own safety.

" Promise me," said I, " that you will allow me to leave the house unmolested when your experiment is at an end ? "

" If you will obey me promptly, you shall be at perfect liberty to leave the house."

" You will neither give me into custody, nor take any steps to pursue me."

" On my honour as a Designer of Dados," said he.

" Good," said I ; " go on."

"Stand up," said he, "and stretch out your arms at right angles to your body."

"Suppose I don't?" said I.

"I send a bullet through your left ear," said he.

"But permit me to observe——" said I.

Bang! A ball cut off the lobe of my left ear.

The ear smarted, and I should have liked to attend to it, but under the circumstances I thought it better to comply with the whimsical old gentleman's wishes.

"Very good," said he. "Now do as I tell you, promptly and without a moment's hesitation, or I cut off the lobe of your right ear. Throw me that life-preserver."

"But——"

"Ah, would you?" said he, cocking the revolver.

The "click" decided me. Besides, the old gentleman's eccentricity amused me, and I was curious to see how far it would carry him. So I tossed my life-preserver to him. He caught it neatly.

"Now take off your coat and throw it to me."

I took off my coat, and threw it diagonally across the room.

"Now the waistcoat."

I threw the waistcoat to him.

"Boots," said he.

"They are shoes," said I, in some trepidation lest he should take offence when no offence was really intended.

"Shoes then," said he.

I threw my shoes to him.

"Trousers," said he.

" Come, come ; I say," exclaimed I.

Bang ! The lobe of the other ear came off. With all his eccentricity the old gentleman was a man of his word. He had the trousers, and with them my revolver, which happened to be in the right-hand pocket.

" Now the rest of your drapery."

I threw him the rest of my drapery. He tied up my clothes in the table-cloth ; and, telling me that he wouldn't detain me any longer, made for the door with the bundle under his arm.

" Stop," said I. " What is to become of me ? "

" Really, I hardly know," said he.

" You promised me my liberty," said I.

" Certainly," said he. " Don't let me trespass any further on your time. You will find the street door open ; or, if from force of habit you prefer the window, you will have no difficulty in clearing the area railings."

" But I can't go like this ! Won't you give me something to put on ? "

" No," said he, " nothing at all. Good night."

The quaint old man left the room with my bundle. I went after him, but I found that he had locked an inner door that led up stairs. The position was really a difficult one to deal with. I couldn't possibly go into the street as I was, and if I remained I should certainly be given into custody in the morning. For some time I looked in vain for something to cover myself with. The hats and great coats were no doubt in the inner hall, at all events they were not accessible under the circumstances. There was a carpet on the floor, but it was fitted to the recesses of the room, and, moreover, a heavy sideboard stood upon it.

" However, there were twelve chairs in the room, and it was with no little pleasure I found on the back of each an antimacassar. Twelve antimacassars would go a long way towards covering me, and that was something.

I did my best with the antimacassars, but on reflection I came to the conclusion that they would not help me very much. They certainly covered me, but a gentleman walking through South Kensington at 3 a.m. dressed in nothing whatever but antimacassars, with the snow two feet deep on the ground, would be sure to attract attention. I might pretend that I was doing it for a wager, but who would believe me ?

I grew very cold.

I looked out of window, and presently saw the bull's-eye of a policeman who was wearily plodding through the snow. I felt that my only course was to surrender to him.

" Policeman," said I, from the window, " one word."

" Anything wrong, sir ? " said he.

" I have been committing a burglary in this house, and shall feel deeply obliged to you if you will kindly take me into custody."

" Nonsense, sir," said he ; " you'd better go to bed."

" There is nothing I should like better, but I live in Lincoln's Inn, and I have nothing on but antimacassars ; I am almost frozen. Pray take me into custody."

" The street door's open," said he.

" Yes," said I. " Come in."

He came in. I explained the circumstances to him, and with great difficulty I convinced him that I was in earnest. The good fellow put his own great coat over me, and lent me his own handcuffs. In ten minutes I was thawing myself in Walton Street police station. In ten days I was convicted at the Old Bailey. In ten years I returned from penal servitude.

I found that poor Mr. Davis had gone to his long home in Brompton Cemetery.

For many years I never passed his house without a shudder at the terrible hours I spent in it as his guest. I have often tried to forget the incident I have been relating, and for a long time I tried in vain. Perseverance, however, met with its reward. I continued to try. Gradually one detail after another slipped from memory, and one lovely evening last May I found, to my intense delight, that I had absolutely forgotten all about it.

UNAPPRECIATED SHAKESPEARE.

THE theory that I am about to propound is so audacious that, at the request of the Publisher of this work, I begin by stating that he has no sympathy whatever with it. He is a family man, and his life is a valuable life, and he is quite right to be cautious. For myself, I have the courage of my opinions. I have no doubt but that the Publisher has the courage of *his* opinions, but he has not the courage of *my* opinions, and, indeed, it would be unreasonable to expect it of him.

My theory is that the people of England have no real appreciation of the merits of their most distinguished poet. I do not refer to a thoughtful few, of whom I am one, and the reader is another, but to the mass of English-speaking men and women, educated and otherwise. I am prepared for the storm of indignant rejoinder with which this expression of opinion will be met. I am prepared to hear that the people of these islands hail Shakespeare as the greatest poet, the most profound thinker, and the most accomplished dramatist the world has ever produced. That the only theatre in which his plays are adequately presented is crowded with enthusiastic audiences. That they have mosaiced a hundred of his pithy apophthegms into our daily conversation.   That a popular speaker, however un-popular and insignificant, has only to wind up his speech with half-a-dozen lines of Shakespeare (and to make it clearly understood that they *are* Shakespeare's) and he will sit down amid thunders of applause.   That to mention any other author in the same page with Shakespeare is to insult that other author, however distinguished he may be in the abstract, by reminding society of his relative insignificance.   All this is quite true.   My argument is, not that Shakespeare does not deserve all that is said and done in his honour, but that he deserves so much more.

He deserves to be read, but who reads him ?   I read him, and *you* read him, and probably Mr. Irving reads him, but how many more read him ?   A few, no doubt, but how many ?   I do not mean "how many dip into him ?"   I mean how many read him right through as they read Dickens, Thackeray, Tennyson, and Carlyle—or as they used to read Byron and Walter Scott, and Cooper and Marryat ?   Not to have read every novel of Thackeray is to be at a serious social disadvantage. No man with any pretence to a cultivated mind will publicly admit that he is not acquainted with every important poem of Tennyson.   But how many Englishmen can lay their hands upon their hearts and say that they have read *The Two Gentlemen of Verona* from beginning to end ? or *All's Well that Ends Well* ? or *Richard the Second* ? or " The First, Second, and Third Parts" of *Henry the Sixth* ? or *Julius Cæsar* ? or *Coriolanus* ? or *Troilus and Cressida* ? or *Cymbeline* ? or *Love's Labour Lost* ? or *Timon of Athens* ?   A few,

no doubt, but how many? I do not mean that these
books are never "looked into," but how many have
read them as they have read "The Newcomes," or
"David Copperfield," or "Adam Bede," or "Ivanhoe,"
or "Childe Harold," or the "Idylls of the King?" A
few, no doubt, but how many? How many of those
who bubble over about Shakespeare could give a brief
abstract of the plots of the plays above mentioned—or
quote half-a-dozen lines from any of them? A few, no
doubt, but how many?

Of *Hamlet, Macbeth, Romeo and Juliet, Othello, The
Merchant of Venice, As You Like It, Henry V., The
Merry Wives of Windsor*, most people know something,
for most people *have seen those plays acted*. But how
many know anything about those plays of Shakespeare which are never acted? The gentleman who is
reading these lines knows all about them, but how
many of his friends are as well informed as he? Let
him invite the first acquaintance he meets (who has no
professional connection with the stage) to favour him
with a sketch of the plot of *Cymbeline*, and note the
result. The chances are ten to one that that acquaintance, if he ventures on an answer at all, will describe
Cymbeline as a Queen of Britain. Of *Troilus and
Cressida* he will be equally ignorant.

The truth is that Shakespeare is not light reading.
But an absolute ignorance of the works of Shakespeare
is most properly held to be disgraceful, and so when it
comes to pass that a play of Shakespeare is adequately
presented people rush to see it in order to familiarize
themselves, in the readiest and easiest and most agree-

able way, with works with which it is considered—and most rightly—that all Englishmen should be familiar.

But of those who go to a theatre at which a Shakespearian play is presented, how many are aware that the play is not Shakespeare's, but a trimmed and docked and interpolated and mutilated and generally desecrated version of his play? How many are aware that the tragedy of *Hamlet*, as Shakespeare wrote it, contains about four thousand five hundred lines, *of which only about two thousand two hundred are usually delivered on the stage?* I shall be told that that is quite enough, and perhaps it is, but how is this sentiment to be reconciled with the enthusiastic veneration in which all people profess to hold the works of Shakespeare? What author can be fairly judged by a play of which one half is deliberately suppressed? Shakespeare's *Taming of the Shrew* contains about three thousand two hundred lines, the "Acting Edition" of this comedy contains only about a thousand! Then, again, how many are aware that in very many cases—I believe I may say in all cases—the actual order of the scenes is changed, merely to provide time and stage-room for elaborate scenic display? If such an outrage were attempted on a play by, say, Mr. Tom Taylor, would it not be regarded as an insult to his memory? When *Henry VIII.* is presented, it is customary to omit the last two acts— not because they were not written by Shakespeare, but because the star-part, Wolsey, finishes in the last act but two! But who cares? So with the *Merchant of Venice.* The last act is rarely presented because Shylock is not in it; though, in justice to Mr. Irving, I should state that upon the occasion of his recent revival of this play it was allowed to proceed to its legitimate conclusion.

The *Taming of the Shrew*, a five-act play, is usually reduced to three acts, sometimes to two, occasionally to one! The *Comedy of Errors*, a five-act play, loses nearly three thousand lines in representation!

But who cares? Who resents these atrocious liberties? *I* do and the reader does, but who else? A few, perhaps, but how many? Who calls out from the pit to the "star" who deliberately cuts out the last two acts of *Henry VIII.* because he has no part in it—"You insufferably vain and sacrilegious impostor, how dare you lay your mutilating hand upon the immortal work of a genius whom we revere as we revere our religion? Restore the fourth and fifth acts of this great play! Perform them at once, or up go your benches!" *I* am in the habit of publicly addressing the star-tragedian in these words, and so is the reader; but who else does so? No one else—probably because it is not generally known that two acts have been suppressed. As for the "star," in all probability he has never read those acts. Why should he? There is no Wolsey in them.

In truth—and it is a lamentable truth—the *popular* knowledge of Shakespeare is almost entirely derived from performances of mutilated versions of his plays. Of those plays in their entirety, and of the plays that are seldom or never performed, the mass of Englishmen know little or nothing.

I will point the moral of this paper with a quotation from the "Players' Preface to the Folio Edition of Shakespeare's plays."

"It is not our province who only gather his workes and give them to you, to praise him. It is yours that reade him. And there we hope, to your divers capacities, you will finde enough both to draw and hold you; for his wit can no more lie hid than it could be lost. Reade him, therefore, and againe, and againe, and if then you do not like him, surely you are in some manifest danger, not to understand him."

COMEDY AND TRAGEDY.

In 1745, Mdlle. Céline was "leading lady" at the
Théâtre Français. She was a very beautiful woman,
twenty-five years old, and of irreproachable character.
Mddle. Céline was only her stage name, inasmuch as
she was the wife of Philippe de Quillac, late a lieutenant
in the Royal Bodyguard, and now an actor of small
parts in the theatre of which his wife was a distinguished ornament. De Quillac was a young man of
good family, and of some small fortune. He honestly
fell in love with Céline while he was still a lieutenant
in the army, and honestly married her, and as a consequence of this social down-step (for actors and actresses
were held as little better than outcasts in those days),
he had to resign his commission. Having nothing
better to do, he took to the stage, for which, it must be
admitted, he had no special talent. Nevertheless, his
own industry, backed by his wife's influence, obtained
for him an engagement at the Français—a consummation
which he had earnestly desired to bring about, in order
that he might be constantly at his wife's side. In
truth, she stood greatly in need of a protector, for the
Duc de Richelieu had condescended to make two

z

distinct attempts to carry her away, as she left the stage door.

Her personal beauty, which was considerable, would probably have been insufficient of itself to incite that distinguished blackguard to take such determined steps; but her reputation as a spotless woman was a standing insult to him, and he made up his mind to avenge it. He laid siege to her in the orthodox fashion of those clumsy times. He sent her flowers, with notes in them. He composed immetrical quatrains in her honour. He obtained access to her at rehearsals, and delivered monstrous compliments, puffed out with complicated allegory. He was so obliging as to invite her to supper on many occasions, and on one occasion he carried his condescension so far as to offer to sup with her. These delicate overtures were a source of incessant irritation, both to Céline and to her husband. De Quillac sent many challenges to the Duc de Richelieu, but they were treated with contempt. De Quillac was an actor, and it was impossible for a nobleman of Richelieu's rank to cross swords with him. Eventually Richelieu's attentions became more definite, and they finally culminated in two attempts to carry her off, as she was leaving the theatre after performance. These experiments were made, not by Richelieu himself, but by his servants, who, having no great interest at stake, allowed themselves to be readily defeated by De Quillac and other actors of the theatre.

These renewed insults, and the impossibility of bringing their instigator to account, rendered De Quillac's life intolerable, and at length he and his wife determined to lay such a snare for their distinguished enemy as would bring him fairly into De Quillac's power. To achieve this end, Céline gave out that as she found it impossible to get on with her husband, they had resolved to separate. She further explained that a life of respectability was rather a Quixotic end to aim at, and that she had resolved, thenceforward, to see a little more of the world, and to taste a little more freely of its pleasures; and to this sensible determination she was encouraged by the approval of many distinguished persons of both sexes, whose careers were so strictly in accordance with their proffered advice, that their good faith in giving it was placed beyond suspicion. The news quickly reached Richelieu's ears, and he, also, was pleased to compliment her, in an atrocious ode, on her extreme good sense. This was the more disinterested on his part, as his appetite for the chase was in direct ratio to the difficulty of the country, as he was candid enough to explain to her in the last verse but one. That she might not, however, be unduly cast down by this information, he assured her, in the last verse, that he intended, despite the facilities that this new order of things seemed to promise, to renew his solicitations at an early opportunity. Céline intimated her determination to signalize her new method of life by a pleasant supper party, to which Richelieu, and many other eminent debauchees of the Court of Louis XV., were invited.

The night of the supper arrived, and Céline received her guests in a *salon* on the ground floor of her hotel. She was, to all appearances, in admirable spirits, and

received them with infinite good humour. Richelieu
arrived last, and the frankness of her welcome, tempered
as it was by a touch of profound respect for his exalted
rank, seemed to him to be the very essence of good
breeding.   Supper was eventually announced, but at
this stage Céline pleaded a headache, and on this plea
contrived to remain behind.   Richelieu, infinitely pained
at the news, was so good as to offer to remain with her
until she should feel well enough to rejoin her friends—
an offer which Céline gratefully accepted.

Left alone with her, he, as a matter of course, con-
doled with her on her affliction, and suggested many
remedies, which she pettishly rejected.

"Bah!   Monsieur le Duc, are you so young a hand
as not to understand that there are headaches for which
a congenial *tête-à-tête* is the best remedy?   These
friends of yours—they worry me.   They talk so much,
and they do not talk well.   I can listen to you, but not
to them."

"I am infinitely flattered, Madame, at the compliment you are so good as to to pay me.   I cannot
doubt its good faith, for it is a conclusion that you have
arrived at after some deliberation."

"You allude to the silence with which I have
hitherto received your attention.   You must remember
that I was not a free agent.   The acts of a woman who
is embarrassed by the incessant presence of a jealous
husband must not be judged too strictly.   But there,
he is gone, and I am to all intents a widow."

"You would have been a widow in very truth, long
since, if I had found it possible to comply with his

pressing invitations. But what could I do? Personally, I have the profoundest respect for his calling, but in my position I was helpless. Am I forgiven?"

And so saying, he took her hand affectionately in his.

"I did not desire his death, Monsieur, nor do I now. He has done for me all that was necessary; he has gone to Marseilles, and he has pledged his word that he will not return. Nay, Monsieur le Duc, be reasonable."

The Duke had placed his arm round her waist.

"You must make some allowance. I am hungry—here is a feast. Have I not said grace enough?"

"Nay, Monsieur, I cannot allow this. Remove your arm, I pray; your friends will be returning. If they should see us thus——"

"My friends will not return yet awhile, and when they do they will give us fair notice of their approach. Céline, I love you. Céline, I have waited long and patiently. Céline, I——"

At this point he looked over her shoulder, and saw, standing behind her De Quillac, white and stern, with a drawn sword in his hand. The truth flashed upon Richelieu in a moment.

"This is a trap," said he.

"It is a trap," replied Céline.

"It is a trap," repeated De Quillac. "For many months you have grossly insulted my wife, and, through my wife, myself. I have sent you challenge after challenge, but my messages were ignored by you. Inflamed beyond endurance at the many outrages you

have dared to inflict upon us, we have devised this plan
to get you into our power."

"And this is with your consent, Madame ?"

"Entirely."

"What do you wish me to do ?"

"Those doors lead to the garden. You must fight
me there, to-night."

"And if I refuse ?"

"I will kill you where you stand."

"But you are an actor, and, by your profession, proscribed. I cannot fight an actor."

"Monsieur, I have laboured long and wearily to
attain the position which I have just achieved—that of
a member of the Théatre Français. It has been the
aim of my ambition, and that long-coveted reward has,
within the last few days, been conferred on me. Here
is my engagement, signed and sealed. By this act "—
and here he tore the paper into two pieces—"I annul
my engagement, and I pledge you my honour that
under no circumstances will I ever appear on the stage
again. Now, M. le Duc, I am no longer an actor, and
you cannot refuse to meet me."

"Madame," said Richelieu, turning to Céline, " I
have no desire to injure you or your husband. I have
wronged you sufficiently, and I would willingly make
amends. I implore you not to expose your husband to
the danger he is courting."

Céline's lip quivered for a moment ; it was for a
moment only.

"Monsieur le Duc, you must fight my husband."

"Let me remind you," said the Duke, " that I am

one of the most skilful swordsmen in France. Let me place distinctly before your eyes the fact that in going out with me your husband runs no risk, for he encounters a certainty. I implore you to use your influence to check him, if you have any regard for him, for if I cross swords with him, I assure you, on my honour, that I will kill him."

Céline was deadly pale, but her resolution did not desert her.

"Monsieur le Duc, you must fight my husband."

"Good. It shall be as you will. I make but one stipulation—that the fact that I have consented to meet an actor shall never be known to any but ourselves."

"You have my promise," said De Quillac.

"And mine," said Céline.

"Then, sir," said the Duke, "if you will be so good as to lead the way, I will do myself the honour to follow you."

De Quillac turned to his wife, and, taking her in his arms, kissed her fondly.

"I am ready, Monsieur," said he,

And the Duke and the actor went through the double doors into the garden.

At this point the full significance of the Duke's warning seemed to dawn upon her. The loss that she was, almost to a certainty, about to sustain—the knowledge that this great risk was undertaken on her behalf, with her consent, and almost at her instigation, destroyed the stern stuff of which the woman was made. She rushed to the door that had just closed.

"Philippe!—come back! for the love of Heaven, come back!"

It was too late, for, through another door came her guests, warmed with wine. With a supreme effort she assumed a thoughtless gaiety of carriage, and entered, almost recklessly into the tone of *persiflage* which prevailed among those who had supped. She felt that it was impossible to be silent—she must say something, or do something incessantly, or her fortitude would assuredly break down.

"Come, what shall we do? Have you nothing to propose? Shall we sing—dance—what shall we do? But be quick! I cannot bear delay. Suggest something, for Heaven's sake——."

Several suggestions were made. Each in turn was eagerly acquiesced in by Céline. At length some one recollected that Céline had a singular faculty for improvisation. Give her a suitable subject, and she would extemporise a poem upon it, in excellent rhymed Alexandrines. It was suggested that she should favour the company with an example of her remarkable facility in this respect.

"With pleasure—anything you please—give me a subject—quick! quick!—I cannot wait."

It was debated among the company whether the subject to be proposed should belong to the domain of Comedy or of Tragedy. Some were for one—some for the other. To Céline, it was a matter of indifference, so that the question was quickly settled. At length a gentleman present solved the difficulty by proposing that she should extemporize in Comedy first, and in tragedy afterwards. Céline was ready—all that she waited for was a subject.

A comedy-subject was proposed. An unsuccessful lover had surreptitiously obtained access to his mistress's chamber in a woman's disguise.

It was enough. Céline, in the character of the lady, commenced her improvisation. She detected the imposture, and proceeded, in withering terms, to ridicule the contemptible device to which her suitor had resorted.

At this point, one of the guests—a Monsieur L'Estrange—exclaimed:

"Hush! I pray your pardon for this interruption; but I am certain I heard a sound of swords clashing in the garden."

"It is nothing, sir," said Céline. "My servants are amusing themselves. We are enjoying ourselves here—let them have their enjoyment also. It is nothing, I assure you."

She proceeded with the improvisation. She pointed out to her disguised lover how well a woman's garb befitted such a woman's soul as his, and recommended him to adhere to a costume which he carried with such address. Her manner was buoyant and defiant—perhaps a little too much so; still everyone was delighted with the exhibition. At a critical point in the verse, L'Estrange, who had been listening at the garden-door, again interrupted her:

"Madame, I am bound to interrupt you again. The clashing of swords is distinctly audible. I am certain you cannot be aware of what is going on. You must permit me to examine the garden."

Céline rushed to the door, locked it, and withdrew the key.

"It is nothing, Monsieur, I assure you. You must not enter the garden. The fact is, that I am preparing a little surprise for you all, and if you go into the garden at this moment, you will destroy everything. Pray permit me to continue."

So saying, she gave the key of the door to the physician to the theatre, who happened to be among the guests, enjoining him, at the same time, not to part with it on any consideration.

She attempted to resume her improvisation, but she found it difficult to take up the thread at the point at which it had been broken. It was, in truth, a struggle between Comedy and Tragedy, and Tragedy had the best of it, for a loud exclamation, as from a man in acute pain, broke upon her ear, and her resolution gave way at once.

"Gentlemen, I cannot go on. It is useless to attempt to disguise my agitation from you. You must see that I am terribly overwrought. Gentlemen, for the love of Heaven, interfere to save my husband. He is in that garden, engaged in a duel with the Duc de Richelieu! The shriek that we all heard was his—he is dying—perhaps dead! For God's sake interfere to save him, if it be not too late!"

And so saying, she endeavoured, but vainly, to break open the door which she had so recently locked.

At first the guests were alarmed, till they recollected that the exhibition of Comedy was to be succeeded by one of Tragedy, and they concluded that this was but the fulfilment of the second half of her promise.

" Admirable! What passion—what earnestness ! " and a round of applause rang round the room.

" Gentlemen, pray do not mock me. I am not acting ; I am in earnest. My husband is dying, perhaps dead. For Heaven's love, help him while there is yet time ! "

A murmur of admiration was the only reply that this appeal elicited. The spectators were as men spellbound.

" Doctor, you have the key ; I gave it to you. I love him. He is in deadly peril. Give me the key, I say, give me the key, or I shall die ! "

It was agreed by all present that Céline had surpassed herself—that is to say, by all but one.

" Gentlemen," said the Doctor, " this lady is not acting ; she is in earnest. See her colour comes and goes."

" Nonsense, Doctor! Madame is acting, and acting admirably. Strange that so old a hand as you should be deceived."

" It would be strange indeed if I were deceived, but I am not. I take upon myself to believe that she is in mortal earnest, and in that belief I shall comply with her wish."

Undeterred by the ridicule with which his resolve was received, he went to the door and unlocked it Celine rushed eagerly towards it, when she saw, standing in the open doorway, her husband, pale, stern, and unwounded.

A few hurried whispers passed between them.

" You are safe ? "

" I am."

" And the Duke ? "

" Wounded to the death."

With a great effort she recovered her presence of mind, and taking her husband's hand, led him forward.

" This ladies and gentlemen," said she, " is the little surprise of which I spoke. I am delighted to think that my attempt at improvised Tragedy has met with your cordial approval."

A prolonged round of applause followed this announcement. It was admitted on all hands that, admirably as she had shone in Comedy, it was in Tragedy that she carried off the palm.

ROSENCRANTZ AND GUILDENSTERN.

AN ORIGINAL TRAGEDY IN THREE ACTS, FOUNDED ON AN OLD DANISH LEGEND.

ARGUMENT.

KING CLAUDIUS, *when a young man, wrote a five-act tragedy which was damned, and all reference to it forbidden under penalty of death. The King has a son—* HAMLET—*whose tendency to soliloquy has so alarmed his mother,* Queen GERTRUDE, *that she has sent for* ROSENCRANTZ *and* GUILDENSTERN, *to devise some Court revels for his entertainment.* ROSENCRANTZ *is a former lover of* OPHELIA, *to whom* HAMLET *is betrothed, and they lay their heads together to devise a plan by which* HAMLET *may be put out of the way. Some Court theatricals are in preparation.* OPHELIA *and* ROSENCRANTZ *persuade* HAMLET *to play his father's tragedy before the* King *and* Court. HAMLET, *who is unaware of the proscription, does so, and he is banished, and* ROSENCRANTZ *happily united to* OPHELIA.

ACT I.

Interior of King CLAUDIUS's *Palace.* CLAUDIUS *discovered seated in gloomy attitude.* Queen GERTRUDE *at his feet, consoling him.*

Q. Nay, be not sad, my lord!

CL.   Sad, loved Queen?
If by an effort of the will I could
Revoke the ever-present Past—disperse
The gaunt and gloomy ghosts of bygone deeds,
Or bind them with unperishable chains
In caverns of the past incarcerate,
Then could I smile again—but not till then!

Q. Oh, my dear lord!
If aught there be that gives thy soul unrest,
Tell it to me!

CL.   Well-loved and faithful wife,
Tender companion of my faltering life,
Yes; I can trust thee! Listen then to me:
Fifty years since—when but a headstrong lad—
I wrote a five-act tragedy!

Q. (*interested*).   Indeed?

CL. A play, writ by a king—

Q.   And *such* a King!—

CL. Finds ready market. It was read at once,
But ere 'twas read, accepted. Then the Press
Teemed with portentous import. Elsinore
Was duly placarded by willing hands;

We know that walls have ears—I gave them tongues—
And they were eloquent with promises !

    Q. Even the *dead* walls ?

    Cl. (*solemnly*).   Aye, the deader they,
The louder they proclaimed !

    Q. (*appalled*).   Oh, marvellous !

    Cl. The day approached—all Denmark stood agape.
Arrangements were devised at once by which
Seats might be booked a twelvemonth in advance.
The first night came !

    Q.   And did the play succeed ?

    Cl. In one sense, yes.

    Q.   Oh, I was sure of it !

    Cl. A farce was given to play the people in—
My tragedy succeeded that.   That's all !

    Q. And how long did it run ?

    Cl.   About ten minutes !
Ere the first act had traced one-half its course
The curtain fell—never to rise again !

    Q. And did the people hiss ?

    Cl.   No—worse than that—
They laughed ! Sick with the shame that covered me,
I knelt down palsied in my private box,
And prayed the hearsed and catacombed dead
Might quit their vaults, and claim me for their own !
But it was not to be !

    Q.   Oh, my good lord,
The house was surely packed !

    Cl.   It was —by me.
My favourite courtiers crowded every place—
From floor to floor the house was peopled by

The sycophantic crew.   My tragedy
Was more than even sycophants could stand !
   Q. Was it, my lord, so very very bad ?
   CL. Not to deceive my trusting queen, it was !
   Q. And when the play failed, did'st thou take no
       steps
To set thyself right with the world ?
   CL.   I did.
The acts were five—though by five acts too long,
I wrote an Act by way of epilogue—
An Act by which the penalty of death
Was meted out to all who sneered at it.
The play was not good—but the punishment
Of those that laughed at it was Capital.
   Q. Think on't no more, my lord.   Now, mark me
       well !
To cheer our son, whose solitary tastes
And tendency to long soliloquy
Have much alarmed us, I, unknown to thee,
Have sent for Rosencrantz and Guildenstern—
Two merry knaves, kin to Polonius,
Who will devise such revels in our Court—
Such antic schemes of harmless merriment—
As shall abstract his meditative mind
From sad employment.   Claudius, who can tell
But that they may divert my lord as well ?
Ah, they are here !

Enter GUILDENSTERN, *who kneels.*

  GUILD.   My homage to the queen !

Enter ROSENCRANTZ.

Ros. In hot obedience to the Royal 'hest
We have arrived, prepared to do our best.
    Q. We welcome you to Court.   Our chamberlain
Shall see that you are suitably disposed.
Here is his daughter.   She will hear your will
And see that it receives fair countenance.

[Exit King and Queen.

Enter OPHELIA.

Ros. Ophelia !   [*Both embrace her.*
    Oph. (*delighted and surprised*).   Rosencrantz and
        Guildenstern !
This meeting likes me much.   We have not met
Since we were babes.
    Ros.   The queen has summoned us,
And I have come in a half-hearted hope
That I may claim once more my baby-love !
    Oph. Alas, I am betrothed !
    Ros.   Betrothed ? To whom ?
    Oph. To Hamlet !
    Ros.   Oh, incomprehensible.
Thou lovest Hamlet !
    Oph.   Nay, I said not so—
I said we were betrothed.
    Guild.   And what's he like ?
    Oph. Alike for no two seasons at a time.
Sometimes he's tall — sometimes he's very short-
Now with black hair—now with a flaxen wig—

A A

Sometimes an English accent—then a French—
Then English with a strong provincial " burr."
Once an American and once a Jew—
But Danish never, take him how you will !
And strange to say, whate'er his tongue may be,
Whether he's dark or flaxen—English—French—
Though we're in Denmark, A. D., ten—six—two—
He always dresses as King James the First!

    GUILD. Oh, he is surely mad !
    OPH.   Well, there again
Opinion is divided.   Some men hold
That he's the sanest far of all sane men—
Some that he's really sane, but shamming mad—
Some that he's really mad, but shamming sane—
Some that he will be mad, some that he *was*—
Some that he couldn't be.   But on the whole
(As far as I can make out what they mean)
The favourite theory 's somewhat like this :
Hamlet is idiotically sane
With lucid intervals of lunacy.

    ROS. We must devise some plan to stop this match !
    GUILD. Stay ! Many years ago, King Claudius
Was guilty of a five-act tragedy.
The play was damned, and none may mention it
Under the pain of death. We might contrive
To make him play this piece before the king,
And take the consequence.

    ROS.   Impossible !
For every copy was destroyed.

    OPH.   But one !
My father's !

Ros.   Eh ?

Oph.   In his capacity
As Chamberlain he has *one* copy.   I
This night, when all the Court is drowned in sleep,
Will creep with stealthy foot into his den
And there abstract the precious manuscript.
    Guild. That's well-bethought, in truth ! but take
        good heed.
Your father may detect you.
    Oph.   Oh, dear, no.
My father spends his long official days
In reading all the rubbishing new plays.
From ten to four at work he may be found :
And then—my father sleeps exceeding sound !

ACT II.

Apartment in the Castle.   Chair R.

Enter Queen, Rosencrantz and Guildenstern.

    Q. Have you as yet planned aught that may relieve
Our poor afflicted son's despondency ?
    Ros. Madam, we've lost no time.   Already we
Are getting up some Court theatricals
In which the Prince will play a leading part.
    Q. That's well-bethought—it will divert his mind.
See—here he comes.

Ros.   How gloomily he stalks!
As one o'erwhelmed with weight of bitter care.
He thrusts his hand into his bosom—thus—
Starts—looks around—then, as if reassured,
Rumples his hair and rolls his glassy eyes!
   Q. (*appalled*). That means—he's going to solilo-
      quize.
Prevent this, gentlemen, by any means!
   Guild. We will, but how?
   Q.   Anticipate his points,
And follow out his argument for him;
Thus will you cut the ground from 'neath his feet
And leave him nought to say.
   Ros. *and* Guild.   We will!—we will!
   Q. A mother's blessing be upon you, sirs!   [*Exit.*
   Ros. Now, Guildenstern, apply thee to this task.

   Enter Hamlet; *he stalks to chair, throws himself
                  into it.*

   Ham. To be—or not to be!
   Ros. (*R. of Chair*).   Yes—that's the point!
Whether he's bravest who will cut his throat
Rather than suffer all—
   Guild. (*L. of Chair*).   Or suffer all
Rather than cut his throat?
   Ham. (*annoyed at interruption, resumes*).   To die—
      to sleep——
   Ros. It's nothing more—Death is but sleep spun
      out—
Why hesitate?   [*Offers him a dagger.*

Guild.   The only question is
Between the choice of deaths which death to choose.
                              [*Offers another.*
    Ham. (*in great terror*). Do take those dreadful things
        away.   They make
My blood run cold. (*Resumes.*) To sleep, perchance
        to—
    Ros.   Dream.
That's very true.   I never dream myself,
But Guildenstern dreams all night long out loud.
    Guild. With blushes, sir, I do confess it true !
    Ham. This question, gentlemen concerns me not.
(*Resumes.*) For who would bear the whips and scorns
        of time———
    Ros. (*as guessing a riddle*). Who'd bear the whips
        and scorns ? Now let me see.
Who'd *bear* them, eh ?
    Guild. (*same business*).   Who'd bear the *scorns* of
        time ?
    Ros. (*correcting him*). The *whips* and scorns.
    Guild.   The whips and scorns, of course.
                              [Hamlet *about to protest.*
Don't tell us—let us guess—the *whips* of time ?
    Ham. Oh, sirs, this interruption likes us not.
I pray you give it up.
    Ros.   My lord, we do.
We cannot tell *who* bears these whips and scorns!
    Ham. (*not heeding them, resumes*). " But that the
        dread of something *after* death———"
    Ros. That's true—*post mortem* and the coroner—
Felo-de-se—cross roads at twelve P.M.—

And then the forfeited life policy—
Exceedingly unpleasant.

   Ham. (*really angry*).   Gentlemen,
It must be patent to the merest dunce
Three persons can't soliloquize at once.

      [Rosencrantz *and* Guildenstern *retire up.*

(*Aside.*) They're playing on me ! Playing upon *me*
Who am not fashioned to be played upon !
Show them a pipe—a thing of holes and stops
Made to be played on—and they'll shrink abashed
And swear they have not skill on *that !* Now mark——
(*Aloud.*) Rosencrantz ! Here !

     [*Producing a flute as* Rosencrantz *comes down.*
       Exit Guild.

        This is a well-toned flute ;
Play me an air upon it.   Do not say
You know not *how !*   [*Sneeringly.*

   Ros.   Nay, but I *do* know how.
I'm rather good upon the flute—Observe—

       [*Plays an elaborate " roulade."*

   Ham. (*snatching it from him, peevishly*). Bah—every-
     thing goes wrong!

      [*Throws himself into a chair as if buried in*
      soliloquy.

    Enter Ophelia *white with terror.*

   Oph. Rosencrantz !
   Ros.   Well ?
   Oph.   I've found the manuscript,
But never put me to such work again !
   Ros. Why, what has happened that you tremble so ?

Oph. Last night I stole down from my room alone
And sought my father's den.   I entered it!
The clock struck twelve, and then—oh, horrible!—
From chest and cabinet there issued forth
The mouldy spectres of five thousand plays,
All dead and gone—and many of them damned!
I shook with horror!   They encompassed me,
Chattering forth the scenes and parts of scenes
Which my poor father wisely had cut out—
Oh, horrible—oh 'twas most horrible!

[*Covering her face.*

   Ros. What was't they uttered?

   Oph. (*severely*).   I decline to say.
The more I heard the more convinced was I
My father acted *most judiciously!*
Let that suffice thee.

   Ros.   Give me then the play,
And I'll submit it to the Prince.

   Oph.   But stay,
Do not appear to urge him—hold him back,
Or he'll decline to play the piece—I know him.

   Ham. (*who has been soliloquizing under his breath*).
And lose the name of action!   [*Rises.*

          Why what's that?

   Ros. We have been looking through some dozen
      plays
To find one suited to our company.
This is, my lord, a five-act tragedy.
'Tis called "Gonzago"—but it will not serve—
'Tis very long.

   Ham. (*interested*). Is there a part for *me?*

Oph. There is, my lord, a most important part—
A mad Archbishop who becomes a Jew
To spite his diocese.

    Ham.   That's very good !

    Ros. (taking MS.). Here you go mad—and then,
           soliloquize :

Here you are the sane again—and then you don't :
Then, later on, you stab your aunt, because——
Well, I can't tell you *why* you stab your aunt,
But still—you stab her.

    Ham.   That is quite enough.

    Ros. Then you become the leader of a troop
Of Greek banditti—and soliloquize—
After a long and undisturbed career
Of murder (tempered by soliloquy)
You see the sin and folly of your ways
And offer to resume your diocese ;
But, just too late—for, terrible to tell,
As you're repenting (in soliloquy)
The bench of bishops seize you unawares
And blow you from a gun !

    Ham.   That's excellent.
That's very good indeed—we'll play this piece.

    Oph. But pray consider—all the other parts
Are insignificant.

    Ham.   What matters that ?
We'll play this piece.

    Ros.   The plot's impossible,
And all the dialogue bombastic stuff.

    Ham. I tell you, sir, that we will play this piece.
Bestir yourselves about it, and engage

All the most fairly famed tragedians
To play the small parts—as tragedians should.
A mad Archbishop !   Yes, that's very good !

ACT III.

Room in the Palace prepared for a Stage performance.

Enter King Claudius *and* Queen, *meeting*
Rosencrantz.

Q. A fair good morrow to you, Rosencrantz.   How
march the Royal revels ?

Ros. Lamely, madam, lamely, like a one-legged
duck.   The Prince has discovered a strange play.   He
hath called it " A Right Reckoning Long Delayed."

Cl. And of what fashion is the Prince's play ?

Ros. 'Tis an excellent poor tragedy, my Lord— a
thing of shreds and patches welded into a form that
hath mass without consistency, like an ill-built
villa.

Q. But, sir, you should have used your best endeavours to wean his phantasy from such a play.

Ros. Madam, I did, and with some success, for he
now seeth the absurdity of its tragical catastrophes, and
laughs at it as freely as we do.   So, albeit the poor
author had hoped to have drawn tears of sympathy, the

Prince has resolved to present it as a piece of pompous folly intended to excite no loftier emotion than laughter and surprise. Here comes the Royal Tragedian with his troop.　　　　　　　　　[*Enter* HAMLET *and* Players.

HAM. Good morrow, sir. This is our company of players. They have come to town to do honour and add completeness to our revels.

CL. Good sirs, we welcome you to Elsinore.
Prepare you now—we are agog to taste
The intellectual treat in store for us.

HAM. We are ready, sir. But before we begin, I would speak a word to you who are to play this piece. I have chosen this play in the face of sturdy opposition from my well-esteemed friends, who were for playing a piece with less bombastick fury and more frolick. But I have thought this a fit play to be presented by reason of that very pedantical bombast and windy obtrusive rhetoric that they do rightly despise. For I hold that there is no such antick fellow as your bombastical hero who doth so earnestly spout forth his folly as to make his hearers believe that he is unconscious of all incongruity ; whereas, he who doth so mark, label, and underscore his antick speeches as to show that he is alive to their absurdity, seemeth to utter them under protest, and to take part with his audience against himself. For which reason, I pray you, let there be no huge red noses, nor extravagant monstrous wigs, nor coarse men garbed as women in this comi-tragedy ; for such things are as much as to say, "I am a comick fellow—I pray you laugh at me, and hold what I say to be cleverly ridiculous." Such labelling of humour is an impertinence to your audience, for it seemeth to imply that they are unable to recognise a joke unless it be pointed out to them. I pray you avoid it.

First Player. Sir, we are beholden to you for your good counsels. But we would urge upon your consideration that we are accomplished players, who have spent many years in learning our profession; and we would venture to suggest that it would better befit your Lordship to confine yourself to such matters as your Lordship may be likely to understand. We, on our part, may have our own ideas as to the duties of heirs apparent; but it would ill become us to air them before your Lordship, who may be reasonably supposed to understand such matters more perfectly than your very humble servants.

[*Exeunt* Hamlet *and* Players R. *and* L.

Cl. Come let us take our places. Call the Court
That all may see this fooling. Here's a chair

[*The* Court *enter.*

In which I shall find room to roll about
When laughter takes possession of my soul.
Now we are ready.

The Curtain rises.—Enter a loving couple lovingly.

She. " Should'st thou prove faithless?
He.   If I do
Then let the world forget to woo,
The mountain tops bow down in fears,
The midday sun dissolve in tears,

And outraged nature, pale and bent,
Fall prostrate in bewilderment!"

> [*All titter through this—breaking into a laugh
> at the end, the* King *enjoying it as much
> as anyone.*

Orn. Truly, sir, I hope he will prove faithful, lest
we should all be involved in this catastrophe!

Cl. (*laughing*). Much indeed depends upon his con-
stancy. I am sure he hath all our prayers, gentlemen!
(*Aside to* Rosencrantz.)   Is this play well known?

Ros. It is not, my lord.

Cl. Ha! I seem to have met with these lines before.
Go on.

She. "Hark, dost thou hear those trumpets and
    drums?
Thy hated rival, stern Gonzago, comes!"

> [*Laughter, as before.*

Q. And wherefore cometh Gonzago?

Ros. He cometh here to woo!

Q. Cannot he woo without an orchestra at his elbow?
A fico for such a wooing, say I!

Cl. (*rather alarmed—aside to* Ros.).   Who is
Gonzago?

Ros. He's a mad Archbishop of Elsinore. 'Tis a
most ridiculous and mirthful character—and the more
so for that the poor author had hoped to have appalled
you with his tragedical end!

> [*During this the* King *has shown that he has
> recognized his tragedy. He is horrified
> at the discovery.*

Enter HAMLET *as Archbishop.*   (*All laugh except
the* KING, *who is miserable.*)

HAM. " Free from the cares of Church and State
I come to wreak my love and hate.
Love whirls me to the lofty skies—
Hate drags me where dark Pluto lies ! "

[*All laugh except* KING.

Q. Marry, but he must have a nice time of it between
them ! Oh, sir, this passeth the bounds of ridicule, and
to think that these lines were to have drawn our tears !

OPH. Truly mine eyes run with tears, but they are
begotten of laughter !

HAM. Gently, gently.   Spare your ridicule, lest you
have none left for the later scenes.   The tragedy is full
of such windy fooling. You shall hear more anon. There
are five acts of this !   [*All groan.*
(*Resumes*). " For two great ends I daily fume—
The altar and the deadly tomb.
How can I live in such a state
And hold my Arch-Episcopate ? "

ROS. (*exhausted with laughter*). Oh, my lord—I pray
you end this or I shall die with laughter !

Q. (*ditto*). Did mortal ever hear such metrical folly !
Stop it, my good lord, or I shall assuredly do myself
some injury.

OPH. (*ditto*). Oh, sir—prithee have mercy on us—
we have laughed till we can laugh no more !

HAM. The drollest scene is coming now.
Listen——

Cl. (*rises*). Stop!   [HAMLET *about to resume.*
                     Stop, I say—cast off those mum-
    meries!
Come hither, Hamlet!
    HAM. (*takes off robes and comes down*). Why what
ails you, sir?
    CL. (*with suppressed fury*). Know'st thou who wrote
this play?
    HAM.   Not I, indeed,
Nor do I care to know!
    CL.   *I* wrote this play—
To mention it is death, by Denmark's law!
    Q. Oh, spare him, for he is thine only child!
    CL. No—I have two—my son—my play—both
        worthless!
Both shall together perish!   [*Draws dagger.*
    HAM. (*on his knees*).   Hold thine hand!
I can't bear death—I'm a philosopher!
    OPH. Apollo's son, Lycaeus, built a fane
At Athens, where philosophers dispute:
'Tis known as the " Lyceum."   Send him there,
He will find such a hearty welcome, sir,
That he will stay there, goodness knows how long!
    CL. Well, be it so—and, Hamlet, get you gone!
        [*He goes to the Lyceum, where he is much
            esteemed.*

CURTAIN.

www.ingramcontent.com/pod-product-compliance
Lightning Source LLC
Chambersburg PA
CBHW051221120726
47905CB00004B/1212